"You're trying to drive me insane…"

"For the last twenty minutes, you've tormented me every way possible, clearly trying to push me past what's bearable," Ian said. "Admit it, admit that you are trying to drive me mad with desire."

"I was asleep." I peeled myself off his stomach and sat up, pulling my legs out from between his and sitting astride his thighs. "I'm sorry if I was tormenting you in my sleep, but I didn't intend anything. Hoo boy. Sitting like this did *not* help things, huh?"

I looked down to where a very obvious bulge in his pants was pressed up against the thin material of my sleeping shorts.

He made a choked noise that didn't contain any actual words.

"You're really…wow. Do you mind if I touch?"

"Why not?" he managed to get out, a touch of hysteria about the words. "It seems entirely reasonable given that you've been sleeping on me for the last hour, torturing me with your soft belly, and your breasts, and the way you breathed on me. Why not touch me, too?"

MEMOIRS *of a*
DRAGON HUNTER

KATIE MacALISTER

FOREVER

NEW YORK BOSTON

Copyright © 2018 by Katie MacAlister
Excerpt from *Dragon Fall* Copyright © 2015 by Katie MacAlister

Cover illustration by Craig White. Cover design by Elizabeth Stokes.
Cover copyright © 2018 by Hachette Book Group, Inc.

Forever
Hachette Book Group
1290 Avenue of the Americas, New York, NY 10104
forever-romance.com
twitter.com/foreverromance

First Edition: August 2018

Forever is an imprint of Grand Central Publishing. The Forever name and logo are trademarks of Hachette Book Group, Inc.

The publisher is not responsible for websites (or their content) that are not owned by the publisher.

The Hachette Speakers Bureau provides a wide range of authors for speaking events. To find out more, go to www.hachettespeakersbureau.com or call (866) 376-6591.

ISBNs: 978-1-5387-6108-3 (mass market), 978-1-5387-6107-6 (ebook)

Printed in the United States of America

OPM

10 9 8 7 6 5 4 3 2 1

MEMOIRS *of a*

DRAGON HUNTER

PROLOGUE

"Ah, Ian, there you are. I was wondering if I should tackle that demon myself, but now you're here."

Ian Iskandar studied the man seated on a tall metal stool behind a bunch of expensive medical equipment. "Do we have to have this argument again?"

"We wouldn't have to if you'd simply see reason and stop denying who you are."

Ian shook his head. "I came because you said you needed my help. I assumed it was for your research. If you need someone to tackle a demon, you'll have to ask your daughter for aid."

"You were the best dragon hunter in North America for centuries."

"I was the *only* dragon hunter in North America for

centuries," he countered, and shook his head a second time. "No. I'm not discussing this. I made my decision, and I am standing by it. If you don't need me for your research—"

"Oh, but I do." Adam bustled over to a table and picked up a battered leather notebook. "It's because of my research that I called you. My esprit is gone. I'm positive a demon has her."

Ignoring the stirring of his own demon self, Ian glanced toward the wall where a sword in a leather scabbard hung from a hook. That never failed to come alive at the most inopportune moment. "How did a demon get the esprit out of your sword?"

Adam Larson looked chagrined. "Well, as to that...she might have wanted a little time off, and since I knew I'd be working here, I told her she could go to the zoo. But a demon must have gotten her, or she'd be back by now."

"No," Ian said simply, and turned to the door, intending to walk out of the room. He'd go back to his bleak, colorless life, his soul as cold as an arctic night.

"This is important, Ian," Adam called after him. "I'm close. Very close. But I need my esprit returned. I'm vulnerable without her. Please. I need you."

Ian debated the wisdom of standing there, of considering Adam's request. Pain lashed him, but he drove the memories down, deciding quickly. He would do this one thing. He would find the esprit, and then return to the gray misery of his life. Surely no one could be harmed in the act of locating one small spirit. "Since you are my mother's favorite cousin, I will find your esprit. Do you know for certain that a demon has her?"

"No, although there's one who's been skulking around. Its name is Dorito. No, that's not right. Schwarma? Whatever its name, I want my esprit back. Now, please hurry. Helen will—"

The fine hairs on the back of Ian's neck stood on end just a fraction of a second before the air behind him swirled. He turned to confront whoever entered, but a flash of blinding light sent him flying backward, slamming him against the wall with enough force to make him see red and yellow splotches.

Sound was dulled, with only the wild beat of his heart audible until he managed to regain awareness, and with that came the roar of dragon fire from deep within him. He leaped to his feet, intending on attacking, but stopped immediately when he saw a small girl of about eight years old, her skin the color of polished ebony, her big eyes turning to him in obvious supplication.

That gaze pierced Ian like nothing had in all the long years of his life. He started to move forward, pausing when a woman sidled through the doorway, a long black sword held easily in her hand.

"The spirit says you are close to making dragon hunters stronger," the woman said, addressing Adam with a voice as rough as sandpaper on gravel. She was a demon, of that Ian had no doubt. "I can't have that. In fact, the less of you there are, the happier I'll be, and since Anzo loves finding slaves, I'll simply solve the problem of what to do with you by letting her have you."

To Ian's horror, the demon reached out and tore open the fabric of space, leaving a gaping, inky rent in the air itself.

"Come along," the demon said, gesturing toward the blackness. "It'll go easier for you if you don't make me escort you there myself. I have plans for this little spirit."

"No," Adam protested, backing away, clutching his notebook. "I have work to do. Important work. I just need a little more time."

"Time's up," the demon said with a sickly sweetness that seemed to slide across Ian's skin like acid. "I guess you want to do this the hard way."

The little girl, Adam's esprit in human form, continued to gaze at Ian with liquid brown eyes, as soft as a still pond in shadows. Those eyes pulled at him, speaking volumes without a single word being uttered.

The demon inside him struggled to gain the upper hand. Ian gritted his teeth, dreading the familiarity of the scene. It was like a nightmare come to life—his dragon side and his demon side fighting for control, a relative in peril, the helpless knowledge that he couldn't be what he needed to be.

"Do not make me repeat myself!" the demon snarled, gesturing with her sword.

Adam cast a horrified look at Ian. "I...I...can't..."

Sweat beaded on Ian's brow as he slowly, painfully wrestled control from his inner darkness. His skin crawled when the demon stepped forward, one hand reaching out toward Adam. His mind screamed a hundred warnings, mingling with the memories that he kept locked away within himself.

Ian closed his eyes for a moment, sick with the knowledge that he couldn't live with himself if he failed again. "I'll go."

The words hit the air with a finality that seemed to reverberate in his bones.

The demon paused and slid a questioning glance his way. "You? Who are you?"

He met her gaze. "I am a dragon hunter. If your master wants a sacrifice, then I will go in Adam's place."

"Ian, no! You would be putty in a demon lord's hands without your *élan vital*," Adam protested, looking as sick as Ian felt, but there was no other way. He would not fail again.

The little girl smiled, her eyes lighting with little golden sparkles. Then she was gone, a light bobbing for a moment on the hilt of Adam's sword where it flared briefly before subsiding. "What? No!" The demon spun around, trying to find the girl.

"Take it!" Adam rushed past Ian, snatching up the sword and thrusting it at him. "I bequeath my *élan vital* to you. Take it and use it to protect yourself. Ian—I will not rest until—"

"Argh!" The demon lunged, but Ian was too quick. He swung the sword, but the demon bobbed, avoiding his attack. Her movement left her at a disadvantage, however, a fact that Ian used by grabbing her free arm and throwing her forward into the rent in space.

He glanced back, his soul singing a dirge of sorrow. "Finish your work," he told an astonished Adam. "I'll keep the demon off your neck for as long as possible."

Before Adam could respond, Ian flung himself into the tear.

He hit the floor hard, flat on his face, his chin taking the brunt of it, the sword underneath him.

"—unexpected visit. What are you doing here?"

"Er...I...uh...I brought you a present, my lord. A dragon hunter."

"Oooh, I've never had one of those. And such a handsome one. Goody."

Through the pain and disorientation, Ian noted the glare the demon turned on him. He grabbed the sword, using it to get to his feet, his head spinning.

An elegant woman with a sensual voice and languid movements strolled toward him, her bright blue eyes drinking him in. "So very yummy." She stopped before him, one finger tracing the line of his jaw. Ian fought to keep from stepping back, a dark, insidious pain seeping outward from his belly, gripping him with iron claws.

"And how delightfully horrified you look. My darling, what good times we shall have, you and I." The woman...no, not woman, demon lord...smiled at him.

Ian was filled with dread at the sight of her.

What had he done? What the hell had he done?

DAY ONE

"I CAN'T BELIEVE YOU'RE TAKING THE WHOLE SUMMER off. Teachers are so lucky. You don't have to work all year long like the rest of us."

That's how it started. Or at least, according to the writing class I took, it's where the action started. And action, according to Manny Vanderbris, creative writing teacher extraordinaire, is the most important thing when writing.

So I'm starting my book with action—that of me setting up my laptop on a small writing desk, my next-door neighbor Teresita idly watching me arrange a tablet of paper, five freshly sharpened pencils, and a red pen in proper symmetrical order on the desk. "You'd be surprised how much work we do in the summer. We have classes to take, summer school to teach, side tutoring jobs, meetings and webinars and planning. It all has to be done before school starts again. Would you mind not doing that?"

"Sorry. You've been so normal lately, I forgot your OCD."

I returned the five pencils she'd taken from the small vase that was set at two o'clock on the desk, at a perfect distance from the computer to avoid spilling onto it, and yet easily reachable by my right hand. I fought against the anxiety that suddenly swelled, reminding the small panicked animal that I imagined lived in my brain that everything was in its place, exactly where it needed to be, and moving the pencils into place again would serve no useful purpose. "If you were anyone but someone I've known since I was four years old, I'd take offense to that *normal* bit. OCD people are perfectly normal. We have issues that we have to cope with, just like everyone else. Ours simply get in the way sometimes."

Teresita shifted away from the wall and wandered over to the mantelpiece. I bit my lip against the request that she not move my things around, telling the anxiety animal that it was okay if someone else touched my possessions. It was even bearable if they were moved out of place.

"Veronica James, did you just lecture me in your teacher voice? You did, didn't you? I'm sorry about the 'normal' thing... You know I think you're perfectly sane, even if you did have nutball parents. And your therapy has helped so much. I'm proud of you, girl! When I think about that year when you couldn't leave your apartment because you couldn't stop tidying and making sure everything was in its place; and then I see you now, it's like you're a whole new person. What's your book going to be about?"

"I don't know." I glanced over the writing table, allowing the rightness of everything to fill me with a glow of happiness. Embracing that happiness went a long way to dealing with the anxious animal in my head. "I haven't gotten that far. Mr. Manny says it's best to meditate before writing because that lets your inner storyteller speak without fear of failure. I have a yoga DVD I'm going to use to do that."

"Yoga in order to write?" She lifted, one by one, a series of seven small ceramic horses that galloped across my mantelpiece in a riot of white flashing manes and tiny pounding hooves. "That sounds like a load of bunkum. Shit, is that the time?" She dropped one of the horses and spun around, hurrying toward the door. "I told Dan I'd be gone for five minutes, and it's been almost half an hour. He'll think I've run off with that hot guy who moved in downstairs yesterday. Good luck with your book. See you later!"

"Bye," I called after her, wincing only a little when she slammed my door shut. "And why people can't close a door properly, let alone be in a room without touching other people's personal things…"

I couldn't stand it. I bustled over to the mantelpiece, arranging the horses the way they were meant to be, *tsk*ing over the chip on the hoof of the horse Teresita had dropped. The animal in my head shrieked that it was no longer perfect, but also, I couldn't throw it away. That would leave only six horses, and six wasn't right...

"Geez, Veronica," I lectured myself. "And just when Teresita was praising you. Deep breaths, girl. It's fine. A chip doesn't matter. The little horses are all where they should be, and that chipped one is just fine."

My phone chirped just as I forced the anxiety animal back into its cave, still thinking about the chipped hoof. I glanced at my phone but didn't recognize the number. "It's not like I can't glue it together...Hello?"

"What are you trying to glue together?" The voice on the phone was female, slightly breathless, and familiar. "I'd say the pieces of your life, but you are the smartest woman I know, and I'm sure by now you have all your kinks figured out."

There was only one person who referred to my condition as kinks. "Helen?" I asked, startled.

"Ronnie!"

I hadn't spoken with my half sister in years. Literally years. "I haven't heard from you in four years, eight months, and twenty-seven days. Where on earth have you been? Have you talked to Mom? The last time I talked to her—which, sadly, was her calling me to bail her out of a DUI charge—she said you were out in the South Pacific helping set up some sort of a school for orphans. Are you back?"

"I am, and the school I was setting up wasn't for orphans. Well, not exactly. Kind of. What are you doing?"

"I teach high school math, but you know that. Or you should know it." Carefully, I set down my chipped horse and decided to worry about repairing its hoof later. "I told you a few years ago in a Christmas card that once I got a handle on my issues, I got a job at the local high school. What are 'not exactly' orphans?"

"They're people who are in hiding. Listen, Ronnie, I'm in a bit of a hurry. Can you meet me? Now?"

"Right now?" I glanced around my sunny apartment. Everything from the two goldfish who swam lazily in a large tank to the writing desk glittered in a golden-red glow of the setting sun. An air purifier hummed away in a manner that reassured me it was sucking all sorts of dust and allergens from the air. I loved my apartment. Everything was in its place; everything was bright and clean and fresh. There was no yelling, no drunken fits of violence, no apathy-induced squalor. It was my own little haven, and now that I had conquered my mental animal, it was a place of peace. "I don't think I can. I have dusting to do under the bed, and I want to vacuum my heating vents, and then I have some yoga to get done in order to write my book."

"You're still trying to write a novel?" Amusement touched her voice. "Is it the same one you said you were going to write as soon as you left college?"

I bridled briefly at the *still*. "I've taken the summer

off to write, and these things don't just burst out of your head, you know. You have to prepare for them. You have to set up a dedicated writing area. You have to get into the mental mind-set of writing, and free your inner muse with yoga and meditation. All that takes time and effort. What did you need? Is something wrong? Oh, Lord, did Mom get out of prison early? I thought she was supposed to be in until next year?"

"I had no idea she was incarcerated again, so I'm afraid I don't know where she is. Listen, Ronnie, what I need is too complicated to tell you over the phone. Can you postpone your dusting and novel-writing and meet me at..." There was a muffled sound of her speaking and a low answering voice. "Can you meet me at the Fashion Armadillo?"

"The what?"

"It's a clothing store at the far end of the strip mall out on Sunset. Do you know it?"

"I thought that mall closed. Are you there with someone? Is it a man? You know I've broken up with Austin, right? If you had an idea of doing a couples thing, I'm solo now."

"Good, he was a sociopath."

"He was not! He was just a bit rigid about things, and had rules that he liked everyone to follow."

"That's putting it mildly. No, no, don't get your feathers ruffled; this has nothing to do with you, your quite possibly homicidal maniac of a former boyfriend, or a couples' date. Just come to the mall and I'll explain it all. As soon as possible, okay?"

I glanced at the clock that sat exactly in the center between two windows and allowed a little exasperation to tint my voice. "I have things to do, Helen."

"I know, but this is important. Life-changing sort of important. Please come. I...I need to see you again. I want to tell you something that it's time you knew."

"If I was Mr. Manny, I would tell you that you're foreshadowing, and that is a big no-no." I sighed loudly. "All right, I'll come out to the Fashion Armadillo, although what on earth you're doing there—"

"Great. See you in a few."

She hung up before I could say anything more. I stared at my phone for a few minutes, cast a regretful glance at my now-perfect writing table, and mentally apologized to my inner storytelling muse who was waiting for me to do some yoga so she could start the novel I'd been planning on writing for the last twelve years.

Exactly twenty-six minutes later I stopped my VW Bug in front of the now-darkened windows of the last shop in a somewhat seedy strip mall on the outskirts of town. There were no cars in the parking lot, and a tall sodium light meant to illuminate the path of shoppers flickered and buzzed loudly. I sat for a minute staring at the faded, garish painting of an armadillo wearing a flowered hat and psychedelic dress, dancing across the front of the obviously dirty shop windows, and wondered just what the hell Helen was playing at.

To my right, the parking lot yawned empty and

mostly dark, only five of the lights actually working. Even so, the place had a decayed, forgotten air to it that gave me the willies. Making sure my door was locked, I dialed the number Helen had used to call me, counting the rings until an automated voice mail picked up and informed me she was not available.

"Helen?" I rolled down my window and leaned out, my voice sounding hushed in the stillness of the night. Although Sunset was one of the main streets in my little Oregon town, the noise from the cars as they zipped by was muffled and distant. "Helen, goddammit, where are you? I am not going to wander around an empty mall that probably has drug users and other squatters holed up inside one of the empty stores. Helen?"

A metallic sound came from behind the building, the sort of sound you'd hear if someone knocked over a hubcap.

I sat for a moment in my car, wishing I'd never agreed to come out, wishing I was back safe in my little apartment, wishing I was at that moment performing downward dog in order to kick-start my muse.

But a sister is a sister, even when she has a different father and left home at age sixteen under somewhat mysterious circumstances.

"Familial guilt or not, she is so going to hear about this," I grumbled, pulling from my purse a bottle of pepper spray and a bottle of hand sanitizer. With one last glance around the parking lot to make sure no druggies were streaming out of the empty shops intent on beating me to death and stealing my car, I got out, locked it, and set the alarm, and holding the pepper spray in one hand and hand sanitizer in the other, I made my way around the back side of the building.

I thought at first that no one was there. Big black shapes of squarish trash bins were scattered down the back wall, as well as a few boxes, wooden crates, and two stacks of pallets.

"Helen?" I asked, my voice a lot more wavery than I had hoped it would sound.

One of the shadows next to the nearest trash can moved. "There you are. I was wondering when you'd get here."

Relief swept over me at her voice. I hustled forward, the faint glow of light from the parking lot barely showing Helen sitting on the ground, leaning back against the trash can, her legs out in front of her. "For the love of God, woman, what are you doing?"

"Waiting for you. Pull up a pallet and sit."

"Are you kidding?" I glanced around, my nose wrinkling in disgust. "Who knows what those pallets were used for. It's probably germ city. I don't wish to pick up some mystery superbug resistant to every known antibiotic."

Amusement was evident in her voice. One arm swept out toward me, offering me an indefinable black object. "Fine, but do you mind sitting down? It hurts my neck to look up at you like that. You can sit on my coat. I swear I have only normal germs that antibiotics love."

I hesitated for a moment, the animal in my mind screaming we should have brought some disinfecting spray, but told myself that was stupid; Helen was my sister and wasn't an unclean person, so I accepted her coat. I made a little pad and sat cross-legged next to her on it, ignoring the urges that drove me to leave. "You want to tell me why we're here and not at a decent place, like a Starbucks where we could have the waitstaff wipe down a table so we could sit without catching diseases?"

"I do and I will." She shifted slightly against the trash can in order to look at me, her face pale in the faint light. I studied it, noting that although she had the same honey-brown hair that we shared with our mother, her features were not at all like mine. Where my face was round, hers was delicately boned, with cheekbones that she didn't have to highlight. Her eyes were dark, whereas mine were a particularly blah shade of gray. She had the lithe, elegant body of a ballet dancer. I was shaped like a potato, with short, stubby legs, a long torso, and arms that I felt were inadequate for my body. I disliked the fact that my proportions felt so wrong when she was the perfect balance of form.

"You remember when Dad left suddenly?"

I nodded. My stepfather had always been a nice man, one who was away for more time than he was home, but since his presence brought calmness and sobriety to our disturbed mother, we always cherished the time he was with us. It was a little oasis of sanity in an otherwise insane life. "I was seventeen. Mom went downhill after he left for good. You must have been about thirteen."

"I was. That was the summer I was sent to the McManahans."

"Foster care." I made a face. "Again, I feel like I should apologize for going to Gram and Gramp's house, and not making them take you, but you know how small their house was, and they had Aunt Ruth and her kids there, too."

"Sweetie, I didn't call you here to make you feel bad about our respective horrible childhoods. And for the record, I loved the McManahans and wanted to stay with them, but you know how Mom was when she came out of rehab—everything was going to be better, she was done with addiction, et cetera. But all of that is neither here nor there. What I wanted to point out was that when I was sixteen, I left home. Did Mom ever tell you why?"

I raised my eyebrows. "No. She didn't talk about it other than to say you ran off to be with your dad, which made me feel a lot better about having my own life in college. I figured if you were with him, you'd be safe. Isn't that where you went?"

"No. Well, kind of." She shook her head. "It's all a bit complicated, but I have to tell you about it quickly. We don't have much time."

"We don't?" I glanced around. "Are the murderous car-stealing druggies coming to get us?"

She gave a little laugh that ended abruptly on a hiccup. "No, it's too late for that. Ronnie, did you ever feel like . . . like something was different with Dad?"

"Yes," I said slowly, not wanting to say anything I might regret. He was, after all, her father, and I assumed he was still alive despite not having heard anything from him in more than sixteen years. "He was always kind of . . . distant . . . with me. I thought at first it was because I was a stepkid, but he was that way with Mom, too."

"It wasn't you, or Mom. He had to do that to protect us. All of us. Just like I have to protect you now."

"Protect us from what? Oh, God, is he some sort of drug kingpin with a secret life?"

She gave a half laugh. "No, and you have a serious obsession with the idea of drug users. Look, there's no way to tell you this easily. I'm just going to have to blurt it out. Are you ready?"

"I don't know," I said somewhat wildly. "What on earth are you going to blurt out? Is it bad? Will I hate it? Good God, are you in the wrong body and you want to be a man now? Because I will totally support you transitioning—"

"Dad was a dragon!" she said loudly, interrupting me.

I stopped gibbering and stared at her. "He was what?"

"A dragon."

I blinked a couple of times. "Let's take this slowly. Dragon like the big scaly mythical creatures with wings, that breathe fire and have a virgin fetish?"

"Yes, except they don't have wings. They have a human form and look just like you and me, although Dad said he could breathe fire when he got really mad."

"You're joking, right?" I asked, my brain trying to wrap itself around the idea. It wasn't having much success.

"I wish I was."

"But dragons are...Helen, they just aren't real."

"I assure you they are. Just forget what you know from mythology, and imagine them as a different type of person."

"Even if I could imagine that, dragons aren't good news. At the risk of more censure, if they were people, they'd be the sort who sell drugs cut with antifreeze and get little kids hooked on it."

She shook her head, a sense of weariness settling around her. "You're letting literature bias your opinion. Not all dragons are bad, although sometimes they have a bad impact on the mortal world."

"Mortal world? Are you saying your father wasn't mortal?" I felt like I was being pulled out to sea by a violent undertow, one that was threatening to consume me. The anxiety monster tried to panic, but I reminded it that it held no more power over me. "Holy shit, Helen! Are you saying your dad isn't really a man?"

"He's a man. He's just also a dragon. A half-blood dragon, actually, a dragon hunter." She hunched over for a moment. "And because I'm of his bloodline, that makes me the same."

I stared at her. There was nothing more I could do. I just stared.

"When I was sixteen, I came into my powers. Dad had left a letter for me, telling me what was happening, and where I could find him. I did so, and he told me that my whole life had to be devoted to protecting mortals from the bad things in the world."

"Bad things like drug lords?"

She gave a horrible-sounding chuckle. "Sure, if you like. Mostly demons, but also any number of other malignant forces that are hidden just beyond our view. Dad said that dragon hunters exist to protect the mortal world against the threats that they don't even know are there. And if they fail to do that, they're...well, summoned."

"This is all like something out of a fantasy movie," I said, trying to assimilate all the information. I'd say Helen was hallucinating, but she appeared all too lucid. "Do I want to know where they're summoned?"

"Not really."

"Was your dad summoned? Is that why he disappeared?"

"He was, but he didn't stay that way for long." She turned away for a moment. "Someone took his place. He didn't tell me who, and there wasn't time to ask him what happened before...Dad was fine for a week and a half, and then...He's dead now."

"Oh, Helen, I'm so sorry." I put a hand on her shoulder, giving her a little squeeze. I don't know at what point my brain had processed the information she was feeding me, but it was starting to, and my heart went out for the pain my sister was feeling.

She coughed and hunched over again. "I have to do this quickly. I need your help."

"Sure," I said, wondering if I could write this all down and use it in my book, then decided it was too far-fetched even for a novel. Mr. Manny had many things to say about using improbable premises. "Whatever I can do, I will."

"Good. I'm sorry about this."

"Sorry about—aieeeee!"

While I spoke, she reached out and grabbed my arm, biting my bare wrist so hard that her teeth cut into my skin.

I tried to jerk my arm back, but she pulled me forward, then moved slightly and pressed my arm against her stomach. It was warm and wet and horrible, and I gave in to the anxiety that washed over me, struggling to get away from Helen, to get away from the germs that would infect me.

I needed to wash myself, right then, my whole body. Wash, and wash, and wash. I doubted if there was enough water to do all the washing I knew would be needed.

"What the hell?" I shrieked, trying to backpedal and pull my arm from her, my mind desperately focused on the need to wash, but her grip was like iron. I swore a red light kindled in her eyes as she looked straight into mine, her nose a few inches from me.

And at that moment, an odd thing happened—the look in her eyes scared the animal in my head back into its cave, stopping it from chanting its demands into my brain, and left me filled only with perfectly normal panic and horror.

Helen's breath ruffled my hair. "Now my blood flows through your veins. You can pick up where I am forced to leave off. Swear to me that you will do what is right, Ronnie. Swear you will be what I can't be."

MORE OF DAY ONE.
DAY ONE PART TWO?
DAY ONE, THE SEQUEL?
DAMN, THESE CHAPTER
TITLES ARE HARD

"You're bleeding on me!" My voice sounded rough and harsh, as if it were made of rock. With a massive effort, I snatched my arm from Helen's grip, scrabbling backward on the ground until I put a yard between us. "Do you have any idea how unsanitary that is? Holy shit, Helen! You could give me a disease! Not to mention what I'll pick up from this festering pool of unsanitary vileness that we're in now. I'm going to have to be tested for hepatitis or tetanus. And possibly rabies. Can people catch mad cow disease?"

She slumped back against the garbage bin, and I saw for the first time that where her midsection should be was now a blackish, bloody hole.

"Sweet bottle of Clorox, what happened to you?" I asked, forgetting for a moment the mind-numbingly horrible surroundings to crawl forward to her. "Did you call 911? Okay. We got this. Sit still. Don't move. What happened?"

She gave a weak chuckle. "I can't remember ever seeing you so flustered. Stop fussing, sister mine. My time is come. There's nothing medics or anyone but you can do for me. Dragons may be immortal, but it doesn't mean we can't be killed, and losing most of your internal organs is one way of doing it. Please swear that you'll help. I don't want to go until I know you're on top of it."

"On top of what?" I asked, panic filling me despite my attempts to keep it at bay. I knew it was a short hop from panic to a full-fledged anxiety attack, and I desperately wanted to keep that animal leashed. I couldn't take my eyes off the sluggishly gushing hole, absently noting that Helen's blood was a different shade than what was normal.

"On top of my job. Listen closely, because I really don't have much time to spend on lengthy explanations. There's a woman with two little girls who will be arriving tomorrow. She's in danger—evidently there's a man who means trouble for her. He may very well know she's coming here."

"Is she running from an abusive relationship?" I asked, remembering one of my fellow teachers who left her job because of an asshat of a husband who liked to knock her around. "There's no women's shelter in town, but I know of a retreat run by some Buddhist nuns that takes in desperate women. Assuming this friend of yours needs a safe place from a boyfriend or husband who thinks it's fine to beat women."

"Sure, we'll say she's running from a bad ex. My contact says that this woman has something that he wants. Don't ask me what because it would take too long to explain. Just know that she has something, and Alexander will do whatever it takes to get it from her."

"Alexander?" I managed to tear my eyes from the wound. Her eyes had little tiny flashes of gold, like a little fire was lighting up the inside of her irises.

"That's the name of the man. He is evidently quite ruthless, and in addition to that, he works for a demon lord."

"Excuse me? Demon *lord*?" I will say something for how the day turned out—it confused the bejeepers out of my anxieties, giving me something else to focus on.

"Trust me, it's bad news. My informant says he's responsible for…" She gave an odd sort of gasping gulp. "For Dad's death, but that doesn't matter now. You have to find this woman, Ronnie. Hide her. Find somewhere safe for her and her two girls to go. They are very special, all of them. You have to do this for me." She grabbed my wrist again, the bite a stinging reminder of what had happened just a few minutes ago. "Swear you will do it."

"I swear," I said, wanting desperately to get at the hand sanitizer I'd stuck in my pocket. One particularly cruel part of my mind pointed out that this situation was every nightmare come to fruition, and I was helpless to stop it. "Helen, please let me call an ambulance. How you can even talk with that massive hole in you—"

She slumped back again, her body resembling a discarded rag doll. "Thank you. You don't know how much this means to me."

I opened my mouth to speak, but a sudden wave of nausea hit me like an anvil to the gut.

"Ungh," I said, crawling a few feet away. "Don't feel good."

"Don't fight it. It'll be over quickly."

"What will?"

"The change. My blood is changing your blood. In effect, you are becoming a dragon hunter, too."

"What—" The words stopped abruptly as my bile flowed, and I vomited up the contents of my dinner.

Then I vomited up anything else that had been hanging around my stomach. And then for another four minutes, all I did was dry heave as my body apparently tried to expel all my innards. At least, that's what it felt like. And when it was over and I wiped my mouth on the sleeve of my hoodie (mentally noting I'd have to throw it away since there wasn't water hot enough to wash vomit out of cloth), I made my painful way over to Helen.

"Have to...call...You're bleeding too much..." My throat burned, and I had to swallow a few times before I could speak.

"I told you to stop fussing." She gave me a wan smile. "Dragon hunters can stand a whole lot more than the average mortal."

"At least let me try to stanch the flow of blood," I said, hesitating a moment before pulling off my hoodie and using the clean part of it as a compress on her wound. She leaned into me, the silence of the night closing around us for a few minutes. "Who did this to you, Helen? It was a person who punched this hole in you, wasn't it?"

She shook her head. "Who did this doesn't matter. Here, you should have this." She slipped her phone into my hand. "It has one or two contacts who might be helpful to you. Other dragon hunters. Tell them what happened, and they'll do what they can."

With an effort, she dragged a long black scabbard across her body and laid it between us, panting slightly at the exertion. I stared at it in surprise.

"What the hell, Helen?" I pushed it away from me. "A sword? You have a freakin' *sword* with you?"

"Yes. It's part of what makes a dragon hunter. A normal one would, that is. This one is empty. I don't know that it will be much use to you." She closed her eyes for a few seconds before opening them again and gesturing toward the weapon. "It's missing...no, that's too long of a story to tell now. I don't have any choice. Take it."

Feeling like I was expected to examine it, I pulled the sword from its scabbard. It was long and thin, like a katana, but slightly curved. I shuddered a little at it, imagining it covered in blood and guts and untold repulsive things. "I don't like weapons of any sort. I'm a pacifist."

She gave another one of those hoarse, horrible laughs. "I'm afraid those days are over, Ronnie. If the sword was whole, I would tell you that it's your *élan vital*, a representation of your soul in physical form. But the soul was taken from it and used to...No, I can't go into that now; it would take far too much time. Just take the sword. It was mine, but now I pass it to you. You might find another esprit for it."

I stared at it for a moment. "Helen, I can't!"

"You must. Once it's whole, this sword is a dragon hunter's most powerful weapon against evil."

"I can't take your soul sword! Not just because that thought is creepy as hell—what sort of a soul do you people have?—but because the second I step out in public with it, I'll be arrested for carrying a weapon."

"Mortals can't see it," she said, her eyes closed again. Her face was pale now, her skin taking on a waxen look that made me feel sick all over again. "It's bespelled."

"You're giving me an invisible sword? Holy scrubbing bubbles, Helen! Do you know what you're saying?"

"Yes." She tried to smile, but it didn't stick. "I know how it sounds."

"I don't think you do. An *invisible sword*? So now I'm Wonder Woman?"

"She had an invisible plane. This is a sword."

"Great, so instead of being arrested for carrying

a weapon, I'll be arrested for carrying a *concealed* weapon."

"Only if the officer is a demon." I stared at her until she added, with a wan wave of a hand, "They can cast wards to make bespelled weapons visible to them. But that's really not here nor there…what's important is that you take it, Ronnie. Say you accept it. You have to accept it for it to be yours."

"I—I—" I was about to protest that there was no way in this world that I was going to accept a weapon that was some sort of representation of my soul, but another look at her face had me biting back the words. If it gave her some comfort, then I'd say just about anything. I pushed aside all of the warnings screaming in my head, my anxiety animal strangely calm in this dire situation. "I accept it. This sword, this *élan* thing. It's mine now. Is that okay, or do I need to say something else?"

Her shoulders relaxed, a tiny smile curving one side of her mouth. "No, that's enough. Use it. Get another dragon hunter to help you with it. Tell them what happened to me, and they'll help you repair it."

"I don't know what happened other than you have a huge hole in you and are dying, but aren't panicking or doing anything you should be doing." I was suddenly frustrated that I was so helpless to prevent what was happening right in front of me.

"Trust me, this is the lesser of two evils." She was silent for a moment while I tried to will myself to do something. *Anything.* "So, you're writing a book."

My jaw dropped for a moment, but I caught a whiff of my breath and snapped it shut again. "You're joking, aren't you? You're sitting here dying after telling me you're a mythical dragon—"

"Very real dragon hunter."

"—Dragon hunter, and you're making conversational chitchat?"

One of her shoulders rose in a shrug. "Well, it's kind of interesting. What's it going to be about?"

I didn't know what to do. Should I panic for her? Should I drag her to my car and drive her to the nearest hospital? Should I yell for help?

In the end, I did none of that. Instead, I humored her, figuring if she wanted her last moments to be spent discussing something so trivial, who was I to deny that? "Mr. Manny says to write what you know, so it'll be about my life."

"Ah. What will you call it?"

"I don't know."

"You'd better pick a good title. Something snappy that will look good on the movie screen in case it goes over well." She leaned into me, closing her eyes for a moment.

And at that moment, I had a bird's-eye image of what I looked like—covered in blood that was both my own and Helen's, sitting against a filthy dumpster in an abandoned mall, surrounded by garbage and refuse, the whole place probably crawling with vermin of every ilk. I sat there cradling my sister, whom I had known for a few short years before she disappeared, only popping into my life twice since, and with every passing second her life ebbed away.

I wanted to scream at the world, to shake her and make her understand that she shouldn't just give up this way. I wanted to run away and pretend none of this had happened. I wanted to return to my lovely apartment and well-ordered life, and bathe in gallons of antiseptic.

But I couldn't leave Helen. Not here. Not this way. I held her, determined that if she was dying, she'd die in my arms. Not alone in filth and squalor. Instead, I'd surround her with love and unconditional acceptance.

I'd distract her from the horrible end that awaited her as best I could. "How about *Memoirs of a Dragon Hunter*?"

"You can't call it that."

"Why not? You guys are hunters of dragons, I presume."

"No, we're hunters who are dragons. There's a difference." The words came out more a sigh than actual speech.

"I suppose it doesn't really matter to my title." I desperately searched my brain for something to distract her from the suffering she was clearly feeling. "Do only you guys call yourselves dragon hunters? Or do other people know about your secret name?"

"Some know. Most refer to us as half-blooded dragons."

"*Diary of a Half-Blood*. That sounds kind of Harry Potterish. How about *Memoirs of a Badass Chick*?"

"I have never..." Her breath rattled loudly in her throat, her body convulsing with each word. Fingers dug deep into the flesh of my arm where I pressed my hoodie against the gaping hole in her torso. "...heard you call yourself a chick." It took a good ten seconds of gasping tiny little breaths, the maroon blood now sluggish and barely seeping around the edges of the hoodie. "The change is really taking hold of you."

I was silent for a moment, fat, hot tears rolling down my face as I leaned my cheek against the top of her head. "I don't want you to die, Helen. I know I haven't been a good sister. I haven't kept in touch like I should have, but you know how it was at home—"

"I know..." She gasped for air again, the gurgling sound making me want to scream at the world. "It wasn't you...Something about me was different..."

"All we had was each other." Gently I hugged her, guilt mingling freely with bone-deep sadness. "But I ran off to go to college, leaving you with Mom and her bottles. God, Helen, can you ever forgive me for that? I was so selfish."

She seemed to rally for a minute, giving me a rueful half smile. "I would have done the same, Ronnie. Home was toxic once Dad wasn't there to buffer us. There's nothing to forgive, so stop making yourself a martyr."

My nose desperately needed a tissue, and I managed to dig a small wad of them out of my pocket without disturbing her too much. "I've wanted to tell you how sorry I was that I left you alone for the last four years. I had a really good therapist who made me see just how shitty home was for us with an alcoholic, narcissistic mom and absent dad—no reflection on your father, by the way. Mine is just as flaky…oh crap, sorry."

"Stop apologizing." Her back arched, pulling her out of my arms for a few seconds before she collapsed back onto me, her words coming out as little gasps. "Put that emotion you worked through in therapy into your book."

"My great American novel isn't important. You are." My nose ran freely, the wetness mingling with the tears that made my eyes burn, my throat aching so hard I was amazed I could speak. My tissues were now a wadded mass of moisture that I somehow felt reflected my life. "I don't want to lose you now that I found you again."

"Dragon hunters…" She clutched my arm even tighter, her fingernails digging into my flesh, little crescents of blood forming. "Dragon hunters…"

Her head slumped back against my shoulder, her body convulsing uncontrollably.

"Dragon hunters what?" I asked, my mind wailing and screaming. How had this come to be? What had she done to deserve this end?

She stiffened, her head tilted back, her mouth open in an O and her eyes wide and staring. Her lips didn't move, but I heard the whisper as it drifted away on the wind.

"Come back."

STILL DAY ONE. REALLY HAVE TO WORK ON CHAPTER HEADERS. CONSULT MR. MANNY ABOUT WHETHER NUMBERS OR DESCRIPTIONS ARE BETTER, AND IF YOU CAN HAVE TOO MANY DAY ONES

EONS PASSED. AT LEAST, THAT'S MY IMPRESSION. Great, long eons in which entire eras of dinosaurs could have risen, ruled the Earth, and faded away until they were nothing but calcified bones buried deep in the crust of the Earth. That's how long it seemed since I had left my apartment, gotten into my cute VW Bug, and driven off to find my long-lost sister.

I stood over a dark stain on the ground next to the dumpster, all that remained of my sister's body after she died. It seemed dragon hunters didn't linger in the world once they had ceased to live, since Helen's body had crumbled into a black, sooty ash that swirled upward into the night sky, leaving nothing behind but a deep ache in my heart.

Dragon hunters come back, she'd said. I clung to those words, hoping that meant that her death was somehow a temporary thing and that I'd see her again. I said a silent prayer over the black stain, calling on whatever deity would listen to me to take care of my sister, to guide her to wherever she was going, and most of all, to let her come back if that's what she wanted.

An odd sense of comfort settled over me when I made my way back to my car, just as if Helen's being had approved of my act. Perhaps it was a form of self-protection, perhaps my mental animal had finally gone nuts itself, or perhaps it really was Helen, but my spirits lightened with every step until, by the time I reached my car, I felt like I had a handle on my life again.

"Right. First things first. Hand sanitizer for as much of me as I can reach until I can take the longest, hottest shower in the history of long, hot showers." I got into my car and pulled out the small bottle, and without thinking about one of the main ingredients of hand sanitizers—alcohol—squirted it on my bloodied wrist.

The screams of agony almost rattled my car windows, so loud and strident that it took me a minute to realize they were coming from my mouth. It didn't take nearly that long for the nerve receptors in my wrist to register the sensation of alcohol on an open wound.

"Ack! Ack! Ack!" I screamed, and first I tried to claw the hellfire inferno off my wrist, then ripped the bottom half of my cotton shirt off in order to wipe away the pain.

It didn't work. For ten agonizing minutes I searched frantically in my car for water that I could use to rinse off my wrist, and by the time I was cursing my compulsively tidy ways, the worst of it was over. I bound my wrist with a strip of torn shirt, ignoring the blood smeared down to my palm and up almost to my elbow, and tried to focus on getting myself home without having any more catastrophes strike.

I didn't need to look in the rearview mirror to see how much I'd changed in the eons that had passed since I had left my apartment to meet Helen. I pulled into my parking spot and turned off the engine, feeling alternately numb and exhausted and heartsore, with just a tinge of hysteria every now and again that made me giggle the sort of giggle that gets you locked up in a psych ward.

Averting my eyes from my reflection in the side mirror, I grabbed the bundle wrapped in my vomit hoodie, which I'd placed on the passenger seat without due regard to hygiene or the very real possibility of ruining the upholstery, and staggered out of the car toward the stairs.

That's when I remembered Helen's sword, the one she'd given to me. I'd left it behind with her ashy remains, too befuddled to take it with me when I ran from the hellish cesspit of nightmares.

"Crapballs," I said to myself, using the last clean bit of my hoodie to pull open the door to the stairwell. "I'll have to get it in the morning. Assuming no druggies get it first and hock it for more…"

I stopped when voices drifted down from the second floor.

"—have two kids, but I'm thinking about getting a nanny, so if you wanted some company at the gym, I'd be happy to introduce you around."

I frowned and paused before making my way up the landing that led to the second floor. Who was Teresita trying to talk into going to the gym? She hated the gym. She hated all sorts of structured exercise, going so far as to refuse to join me at the local yoga school.

"That's very kind of you, but I've only just moved in, so I'm not really looking for an exercise partner, or a gym—"

That was a man's voice. I leaned against the bannister, suddenly too exhausted to move. I thought of frowning even more, but it seemed like too much of an effort after having survived the eons that occurred between Helen dying in my arms, turning into a puff of black, ashy smoke and disappearing before my eyes, and me driving home. Besides, the most important thing right now was to take a two-hour shower. My skin positively crawled with the thought of all the filth on me.

Something inside me pooh-poohed the idea of germs, shocking my anxiety animal. I considered this calm new voice in my head, and wondered at it. Also, why was it urging me to pay attention to the man speaking, when we all knew I needed to sanitize everything on my body immediately, if not sooner?

It has to be mental exhaustion, I told the calm voice,

but germs, filth, vomit, and blood nonetheless, I eaves-
dropped.

I'll give him this—the stranger had a nice voice,
baritone, not deep, but deepish. It was a mahogany sort
of voice, I decided. Rich and warm and dark. It also
had the tiniest hint of an accent, but I couldn't quite
figure out what it was.

"No? How about lattes? You drink coffee, don't
you? I can fill you in on the best coffee shops around
the neighborhood. Not the chains, of course, because
they're so...well...commercial, but some really good
independent coffee shops that sell ethically sourced
coffee served by immigrant and migrant peoples seeking to better their lives."

"I prefer tea over coffee, thank you. If you don't
mind, Miss...Mrs...."

"O'Hanlon. Teresita, actually. And you are?"

"Iskandar."

"Iskandar? What sort of a name is that? I mean,
what ethnicity is it? I'm all over ethnicities. My mom
was from Guatemala, but Dad was born in Mexico
City. Whereabouts is your family from?"

"Tajikistan."

"How interesting. Does it mean something in Tajikistani? Is that your first name or last name?"

"It's my surname. If you don't mind—"

"Well, it's very unique. I like, though. Is your first
name as exotic as that?"

He hesitated a moment, then said, "No, it's Ian. I
really must—"

"Ian Iskandar." Teresita all but purred his name. I rolled my eyes to myself, making a mental note to remind her that ladies who had husbands they claimed they adored shouldn't be purring at strange men in the hallway. "That's just a lovely name."

"Thank you. And thank you for the welcome, but I really must get to my unpacking."

I wondered what a Tajikistani accent sounded like. This man had a Celtic lilt to his voice. Irish, maybe? Scottish? I roused myself at last and rounded the landing, slowly making my way up the flight of stairs, one leaden foot in front of the other. By the time I emerged at the top, I could see Teresita with a man who quite accurately fit the description of "tall, dark, and handsome." Only maybe not so handsome as more…imposing.

"If you need a hand, I'm just one floor above you in three-F. Give me a shout any time, and I'll be happy to— Sainted Mary, Veronica, what happened to you?"

By the time she finished speaking, Teresita had caught sight of me. She stared in openmouthed disbelief. The man with her cast a quick glance my way and edged behind her, clearly intending on using my arrival as the distraction he needed to get away from what was obviously an *un*welcome welcome wagon.

"Oh, you know." I lifted a wan hand, noticed it was the one with a bit of my shirt wrapped around the bite, and lowered it to lift the other one. Unfortunately, that had the vomit hoodie. "Just out and about."

Her expression of disbelief deepened into horror as

her gaze shifted over to the bundle. "What in the name of all the little scarabs in Egypt is that?"

"It's a vomit hoodie."

"A what?"

"A vomit hoodie. A hoodie that has vomit on it."

"It's . . . bloody."

"And blood. A hoodie with vomit and blood. I was . . . er . . . not feeling good. Food poisoning."

"What?" The look she gave me told me clearly she didn't believe a word.

"The kind that makes you bleed."

She cocked an eyebrow at my arm.

"From your wrist. It's a rare food poisoning, thankfully. And speaking of that, I need to use up approximately half of the town's water supply in the longest shower ever taken, so I'll talk to you later."

"What on earth— Oh, Ian! You must meet your other upstairs neighbor. She's right over your apartment, so if her yoga gets to be too noisy, you'll know who to complain to. This is Veronica James."

The man named Ian had almost made his escape, but froze in the act of hurrying down the hall and paused to give me a murmured hello and polite bob of the head.

I lifted the vomit hoodie in a friendly, if exhausted, wave. "You have to forgive Ronnie," Teresita continued, her gaze roaming over me as if she couldn't believe what she was seeing. "She's not normally covered in dirt and blood." She sniffed delicately, her nose wrinkling in reaction. "Nor does she usually smell like . . . What *is* that smell?" The ashy black smoke that

Helen's body had dissolved into was quite pungent, faint whiffs of it clinging to my disgusting hoodie. "Er…"

"Were you at a bonfire?"

"No. Another time—"

"What *is* that horrible stench?"

Ian, who had turned away in preparation for making a second stab at freedom, froze for a moment and shot me a questioning look. His nostrils flared a little, as if he was trying to catch the scent.

I backed up to the bottom of the next flight of stairs.

"Damn, girl, what *have* you been up to?"

"I'll tell you later," I said tiredly, and gave Tajikistan Ian a weak smile. "Sorry to meet and dash, but I really have to…" I lifted my vomit hoodie again, too tired to continue speaking.

"Take the longest shower ever taken, yes, I heard," he said, and with a curt nod to the still-distracted Teresita, he finally made his escape into his apartment.

I looked at Teresita, thought about how insane any explanation I could make would sound, and turned to the stairs, trudging my slow, painful way up each step. Teresita wasn't my closest friend for nothing, and she took advantage of that status by pelting me with questions all the way up the stairs, following me into my apartment, even going so far as to crowd into the bathroom when I staggered in and began to unwind the bit of shirt from my wrist. "I don't understand what happened to you. Where did you get food poisoning? Why are you so filthy? Your OCD freaks out at even the tiniest bit of dirt, and you never have so much as a hair out of place, and now you look like a bag lady who's lived out of a trash bin for the last six months."

"The term 'bag lady' is politically incorrect and demeaning to transient peoples," I said with dignity, wincing when the impromptu bandage revealed the bite on my wrist to the air.

"I will apologize to any transients I meet, but until then, what happened to you? Is that a bite mark? What bit you?"

"My sister Helen."

She gawked at me, then opened her mouth to ask me what would probably be about a hundred questions.

"No," I told her, shaking my head. "Not now. I'm too tired and my wrist hurts—here's a pro tip: do *not* put hand sanitizer on a bite unless you want to feel like your flesh is made up of molten lava—and I need to burn my hoodie, and possibly shower with a bottle of bleach, then brush my teeth and mouth with mouthwash at least six times. Go home, please. I'll talk to you later."

"But—"

"Please," I said, and willed her to just this once do as I asked.

To my amazement, she did. "All right, but bang on the wall if you need me. And put some ointment on that bite. You don't want to get rabies or whatever weird thing you get when people bite you…"

I sagged with relief when the door closed behind

her, and spent the next twenty minutes sighing over and over while I stood under the hottest water I could bear, scrubbing my hair three times, my body four times, and my wrist—painful as it was—a record twelve times.

By the time I was dry, dressed, and had applied antiseptic ointment to my wrist, I was more than ready to crawl into bed and pretend the evening had never happened, but alas, Teresita had other ideas.

"Dan said I should check on you to make sure you didn't hit your head on the toilet while vomiting up your guts," she said, letting herself into my apartment with the spare key I'd given her for emergencies. "He's so thoughtful, isn't he?"

I lifted my head to look at her from where I'd poured myself onto the couch. "Normally, yes, but I haven't vomited anymore, so my head is safe from toilet dangers. And I'm really tired."

She lifted a bottle. "I brought wine."

"All right, but don't grill me. I've been through a hell of an evening and don't want to go over it again. Is that a zinfandel? You know how I feel about them."

"Gewürztraminer," she said, fetching two glasses from my minuscule kitchen. She sat next to me on the couch, extricated the cork, and poured out two generous glasses of a fruity wine. "Now, spill, girlfriend."

I glared at her over the rim of the wineglass, took a sip, and closed my eyes for a moment while the warmth of the wine made its way down into my stomach. "I just got done telling you that I didn't want to talk about it."

"I know." She waved a dismissive hand and took a big sip of wine. "But that was just for show. Mmm, this is a good one. Let's start with your sister. I take it this is the sister you said you hadn't seen in, like, forever?"

It took me until I'd finished the first glass of wine before I decided that what the hell, I might as well tell her, because there was no way she'd accept any cover story I could manufacture. Teresita was as persistent as a terrier when it came to people. That triggered a thought, and before I could vet it for appropriateness, it was out into the open. "Why were you hitting on that poor new guy? I thought Dan was the be-all and end-all of your life."

She looked surprised. "He is, and I wasn't hitting on Ian."

"It sure looked like you were." I changed my voice to mimic her sexy purr. "Ian Iskandar. What an interesting name."

She smacked me on the foot, which was resting on her legs. "Silly! I was checking him out for you."

"Uh-huh." I drank a little more wine, relishing the heat it gave to my insides. For some reason, despite the warmth of the early summer days, and the heat of the long shower I'd just taken, I felt chilled, as if there was a nugget of ice inside me that was radiating cold to my limbs. "Sure you were."

"I was!" She sat upright and pushed my feet off her

legs. "You know I've done everything I can to find you a man."

"Yes, and I've asked you more than once to please stop matchmaking for me. I'll find a man when I find a man."

"That sentence made no sense."

"It's the wine talking. But seriously, I am fine. I don't need a man to complete my life or some such bullshit."

She looked like she wanted to have that old, familiar argument about why I should trust her judgment in matching me up since she'd found husbands for two of her sisters, but let that go for the more tempting morsel. "Why did your sister bite you?"

I sighed and held out my glass for more wine. "I'll tell you what happened, but I want your solemn promise now that you are not going to run straight to Dan and tell him I'm bonkers, because, trust me, this is going to sound like I am. But I'm not."

"Oooh," she said, settling back against the couch. "Give it all to me."

I did, and by the time I was finished, she was speechless for a good three minutes. She sat considering everything I'd told her, her hands idly rotating the now-empty bottle of wine as if she was seeking understanding in its depths. Finally, she looked up. "Okay. So how are we going to find this woman?"

I shook my head at her and managed a little laugh. "You can't possibly tell me you're going to accept the whole ridiculous story without even one protestation."

"Sure I am. You don't lie, so I know you're not pulling a fast one on me. You wouldn't bite your own wrist, and even if you did, you couldn't get your mouth at that angle," she said, nodding toward my wrist. "But most of all, you'd never willingly mess yourself up and be as filthy and disheveled as you were a half hour ago. Therefore, it must be true. Do you feel any different?"

"How so?" I asked.

"Like…" She shrugged and set the empty bottle on the coffee table. "Like a superhero."

"I'm not a superhero, despite being the possessor of an invisible sword."

"I dunno. Your sister vanished in a puff of smoke, and her last words were 'I'll be back.' That sounds awfully superhero to me."

"She was not the Terminator, and she said that dragon hunters come back." I paused and considered her words. "I just wish I knew when. And how. Will I recognize her? Will she be a new person but with the same mind? Or will she have a new mind, one that doesn't know me?"

"I don't know the answer to any of that." Teresita tipped her head to the side to consider me. "You don't look any different now that you're cleaned up. Although I think… yeah, I think there is something different."

"What?" I asked, suddenly panicking. I didn't feel like I had changed at all, other than being tired and cold. "Do I have scales? Spiky wings? No, wait, Helen said dragons don't have wings. They look like normal people, evidently. How do I look different?"

"It's your eyes. There's just more there," she said slowly, her gaze moving over my face. "There are little flecks of silver light that show every now and again."

"My eyes are gray," I said, relaxing back into the couch.

"But they didn't silver-light-sparkle at me before, so I'm calling this a new effect. Can you...you know...*do* anything?"

I stared at her in dumbfounded surprise. "Like what?"

She spread her hands in a gesture of ignorance. "I don't know! You're the expert on dragons."

"I'm hardly that."

"Well, you are one now, so you'd better figure some of it out." She looked me over nose to toes. "What are dragon people supposed to do?"

"The only thing that Helen mentioned was that her dad could breathe fire when he was mad. And before you ask, no, I don't think I can do that."

"Oh." She slumped back, clearly unimpressed at my transformation. To be honest, I was as well. I just didn't *feel* any different. Although there was the fact that my anxiety wasn't pinging nearly as much as was usual, and normally, just the idea of the vomit hoodie being in the same building as me would make my mental animal go nuts.

If it helped calm the animal, maybe being part dragon wasn't going to be so bad after all. I sighed. "There are so many questions, and I don't know the answer to any of them."

"Like who is the lady you're supposed to find? Did your sister tell you her name?"

"No, just that she was coming here and needed help, and something about her renting a house because this was a safe town." I rubbed my arms, my flesh goose bumpy. "The biggest thing I want to know is who punched that hole through Helen. She said it didn't matter, but seriously, she was dying and not in her right mind. Of course it matters who did that to her. Was it a demon? Another dragon? Something I don't know about, because evidently, there's a whole world out there that I had no idea existed?"

"I always suspected there was a lot more going on than we knew about," Teresita said darkly.

"That's just common paranoia."

"Possibly. I think we need to do some research on dragons and demons and the ghouls your late sister mentioned."

I lifted a wan hand. "I should, but I can't even summon up the energy to crawl into bed."

"That's why you have me here to help you. I can do oodles of research while the kids are at day camp," she said, patting my leg before getting to her feet. She wobbled a little, then giggled. "Shouldn't have had that last glass, maybe. Go to sleep, *chica*. I'm your trusty sidekick, and I say we'll brainstorm finding your lady in the morning, and who killed your sister, and how we can send him to kingdom come for that act."

"Maybe we shouldn't," I said, pulling a soft blanket around me. "It might be dangerous. I wouldn't want you getting hurt. Dan and the kids would never forgive me."

"Pfft," she said at the door, waving one hand in an expansive gesture. "What could be dangerous about a superhero half-blooded dragon woman and her fabulous Latina bestie saving people?"

Despite feeling she was dead wrong, I couldn't make my brain work enough to pull together an objection, and so dragged myself off to bed shivering and idly wondering if it was possible to simultaneously have a fever and be ice cold.

A buzzing woke me just as I drifted off to sleep, and it took me a few minutes before I realized that it was Helen's cell phone ringing, not mine. I propped myself up on an elbow and looked at the phone. The number showed, but there was no name attached to it. I answered it, regardless, desperate for some answers to the questions Helen had left behind her. "Hello?"

"I don't know who you are, or why the half-breed trusted you with her phone, but don't get too comfortable," a man's voice said into my ear. I shivered, almost able to feel his breath on my cheek. "Your life isn't worth a brass farthing."

"Alexander?" I asked, the word coming out a whisper filled with horror.

He laughed, his voice chilling me even more than I already was. "If you want to live, forget whatever she told you."

"She said you were dangerous," my mouth said before my addled brain could approve the words.

"And she was right. Learn from her mistakes. I may not know who you are, or where you live, or what you love, but I will find out all three, and when I do, I will destroy you just as easily as I destroyed her. Save yourself and flee before that happens."

Bile rose in my throat so swiftly, I barely had time to fling the phone away before I bolted for the bathroom. As I clung to the toilet and retched up the wine I'd drunk, the sound of Alexander's mocking laughter followed.

What on earth had I gotten into? And how was I going to fulfill my promise to Helen and not end up like her? I flushed away the rejected wine, reached for antibacterial wipes, and after making sure the seat was suitably sanitized, rested my arm on it, staring into the water.

How was I going to get out of this in one piece?

CHAPTER FOUR

"OKAY, THIS IS THE LAST OF IT: TWO GUINEA PIGS, A litter of newborn hamsters, and a massive amount of kitty litter. Where do you want the— Oh, sorry, didn't know you were on the phone."

Ian shot an annoyed look at the woman who appeared at the bathroom door, awkwardly trying to hold the towel around his waist while at the same time listening to the voice pelting him with questions.

"I have a little job for you," the voice purred into his ear.

Ian gestured with his elbow for Sasha to leave the bathroom, but she just grinned and leaned against the door looking interested. He turned his back and said, "Let me guess: you want more of your rival's demons destroyed."

"Always, darling, and don't pretend you don't enjoy it."

Ian made a face to his reflection. "I'm a dragon hunter. Killing demons is my reason for being."

"Is that the boss?" Sasha whispered loudly. He sent her a warning look over his shoulder, but she just perched herself on the counter and watched him with bright eyes.

"And that is so exactly why I was thrilled when you joined me," Anzo said with sickening sweetness. "You want to kill demons. I want Asmodeus's legions thinned . . . It's a win-win situation. But this time, I have something a little different in mind."

Ian's stomach tightened. "I assume it's something heinous."

"No, of course not, darling." The voice on the phone grew silky smooth, but with an edge that felt like a razor blade against his flesh. "I'm told by one of my minions who actually reports to me from the mortal world—unlike you—that there's a courier I might use. I want you to find her for me."

Ian swore to himself. He had a bad feeling he knew who Anzo was talking about.

"I can't be everywhere to hear everything. And evidently you don't need me to spy if you have demons running around gathering intel."

"Darling," Anzo said in a drawl that made him sick to his stomach. "You are my most trusted servant. Well, one of them. Of course I need you to be everything, so you had best step up your game, lest I summon you to my side, hmm?"

Ian swore to himself again. For the last two months he'd been trapped in Abaddon, doing Anzo's dirty work, and he very much wanted to avoid a repeat of the experience.

"Back to this courier that you failed to tell me about. According to my minion, you aren't too far away. You should be able to find her easily." Her voice sent little ripples of an unpleasant chill down his back that had nothing to do with the fact that he was wet and naked.

"Is she doing her spell thing on you?" Sasha asked. "Is she compelling you to do evil things right now? Should I hit you over the head and make you unconscious so you won't give in to her demands that you dance naked for her? Or worse?"

Ian glared even harder, but Sasha was not one to take a glare in the spirit in which it was intended.

"I was informed that the courier will have with her two little spirits. I will naturally want them, too."

"They aren't spirits as you know them," Ian said carefully, the pain in his stomach growing as he felt the conversation spiral out of control. Whatever else happened, he had to put Anzo off the subject of the esprits. "They come from the Court of Divine Blood."

Anzo made a disgusted sound. "I can't use a being of light in Abaddon. Leave them behind when you bring me the courier. Her I *can* use in my plan to overthrow Asmodeus."

He thought quickly about how to deflect Anzo from the idea of kidnapping an innocent woman. A familiar sense of failure made the pain in his gut spread outward. "I will try to find her if you feel that's wise, but I don't see how she will help you with your grand scheme to take over leadership of Hell."

The sound of two cats hissing at each other was audible from the other room. With a muttered curse, Sasha hopped down off the counter and dashed off to intervene. Ian took that moment to slip into a pair of jeans.

Anzo the demon lord—doe-eyed, golden-haired, and as sensual as the day was long—sighed, the sound sending another ripple of cold down Ian's back. "Darling," she drawled again in the voice that Ian had come to dread. "The workings of my mind are not important to you, so long as you follow my commands. And it is a command."

The pain of his inner demon struggling to gain the upper hand almost caused him to double over. He focused for a moment on his breathing, a coping mechanism that sometimes worked.

"There is one other thing."

He breathed in, holding his breath for a moment, rousing the dragon fire that always slumbered within him. When the breathing didn't work to control the darkness, the fire usually could.

"I'm told there was a man who was foolishly trying to eliminate the demon in your kind."

Ian allowed the fire to fill him, directing it at the darkness within.

"There was," he said after another moment of struggle. "He was killed while I was with you in Abaddon."

Another person he failed, another black mark on the tattered shreds of his soul. So much for his grand sacrifice to save Adam.

"I understand his daughter was also killed. Despite my direct command that she be brought to me."

Ian's fire tried to consume the darkness, but it was too great. "Why did you want Helen Larson? She was not helping her father."

"Because you are so effective at demon elimination, darling," Anzo said with a soft laugh that would have taken a few years off of Ian's life if he hadn't been immortal. "And if I had a team of dragon hunters working in concert… well, you can see how wonderful that would be."

Ian swore to himself, and he knew he would do whatever it took to keep any other dragon hunters from her grasp. "Why are you telling me this?"

"Because there is sure to be another one to take her place. There always is with your kind, isn't there?"

"Not always." He thought quickly. Sasha had told him Helen Larson was dead, but hadn't mentioned anything about her *élan vital*. If the sword was lying around where the esprit could be taken and used… he had to find Helen's remains and take her and her effects so they would not be violated.

"I want whoever takes her place," Anzo said sharply. "And you will get her for me."

"It's okay," Sasha said, popping her head into the room while Ian was trying to think of a way to answer such a horrifying request. "Paul was trying to get

Ringo's fave mousie toy, and George got caught in the middle, as usual. You want me to unpack the animals, or do you need me to save you from being forced to conduct the most heinous ritual sacrifices of innocents imaginable?"

Ian made a shooing motion that had the young woman rolling her eyes, but she turned and went out to deal with the menagerie inhabiting the rest of the apartment. With apparent nonchalance he said to Anzo, "I will do what I can. I really am busy, so if that's all—"

"My sweet one, how you disappoint me. Here I was congratulating myself for having the sensibility to order my demons to set up mobile phone reception in Abaddon, just so your dulcet tones could caress my ears, and all you want to do is end this delightful conversation. Is that any way to behave? Your destruction of so many of Asmodeus's minions has given me great pleasure, and I wished to reward you. Perhaps a gift, to show you the extent of my . . . devotion."

The pain in his gut turned to nausea. "You don't need to do that. I don't need anything, and any gift you send will simply draw my attention from the job at hand."

"Can I get a ferret?" Sasha called from the other room. "I saw a cool one being offered on Craigslist. It has three legs, and some sort of respiratory illness, but it's totally tame and needs a home."

"Modesty becomes you not," Anzo said, and Ian could just picture her tapping her reddened lips with one tapered finger. "Now, what shall I give you? A body servant? A slave? The head of your enemy on a platter?"

Ian scribbled the words "NO FERRETS!" on a scrap of paper from the box of bathroom things and marched it to the bedroom door so Sasha could see it.

She made a face at him and continued to decant the hamsters and gerbils into their appropriate homes.

"I should go. It's going to take a while to find this courier, and I know you are anxious for her." Ian was aware he should use more flattery and sweet talk, but the fact that Anzo would detect an outright lie kept him to neutral statements.

"Yes, go, sweetness." Anzo's acquiescence raised warnings in Ian's head. She sounded entirely too satisfied with herself. "Let me know what you find. I believe I shall use this new phone service to contact others. It's been so long since I had contact with the mortal world."

Ian sent up a little prayer of thanks for that small mercy.

"But remember that my patience is not endless." Anzo's voice was as smooth as velvet, but with razor-sharp edges that physically hurt Ian. "I want the courier found in the next twenty-four hours."

"Impossible," Ian declared, his mind filling with dread. "It will take me several weeks to search."

"Very well," Anzo said with a dramatic sigh. "You always do wrap me around your manly fingers. You may have until the end of the week."

The pain of his demon side lashed him, claiming upper hand against his dragon self. Sasha looked up, a little frown pulling her eyebrows together. She sat cross-legged in the middle of the floor, in a simple white summer dress, her waist-length brown hair pulled up into what Ian knew was called a messy bun.

He swore to himself again. Sasha was entirely too empathetic for his taste, and one of her greatest desires was saving him from what she referred to as dark threads running through what remained of his soul. Her attempts to do so could have dire consequences if he didn't remain focused. Fighting the pain, he said, "Two weeks would be better."

"So would having you in my bed. Would you care to barter that for some extra time?" Her voice was pure seduction, and it left his blood cold.

"The end of the week it is," he said quickly, pushing aside the thought of what being her sexual slave would mean.

"Excellent," she said with a light little laugh that pierced his skin like shards of glass. Little bits of the tattered remains of his soul were stripped away, floating off on a sea of regret and despair. "Smooches, lovey!"

Sasha watched him closely, her eyes alert, obviously sensing his agony.

The call ended, and with a sigh of relief, he set down the phone, his body feeling like he'd gone ten rounds with the current heavyweight champion.

"Your scars are bleeding," Sasha pointed out, her hands full of gerbils.

"They're brands, not scars," Ian replied, forcing down the pain and darkness before returning to the bathroom.

Both of his arms were covered in sleeves of what looked to mortal eyes like intricate tribal tattoos, the design going across the upper part of his chest. He touched a spot near his collarbone, the thickened skin beneath the tattoo hinting at its true source: brands that bound him to Anzo, leaving him powerless against a cruel master. And to think he'd gone willingly to this sacrifice, and for what? Adam was dead, just a week after Ian had tried to save him. And yesterday, Helen Larson had lost her life. So much death. So many failures…

His finger came away stained maroon. The spells carved into his flesh bled, a reminder of the power Anzo wielded even at so far a distance.

"There's some hydrogen peroxide in the bathroom box," Sasha called from the living room. "Do you want me to cast a ward on you? I've been practicing, and I think I have the good health one down. Mostly. There's a tricky bit at the end that kind of gets away from me, but I think it will be okay."

For a moment, despair swept over him, giving his inner demon free rein. He doubled over, clutching the edge of the sink while wave after wave of agony rippled outward from his belly. His dragon side struggled to regain control, to keep the demon half in check, to rule it and push it back into abeyance. For what seemed like the thousandth time, he cursed his inability to cope with his heritage.

Sasha appeared in the doorway. The girl had what in others would be classed an uncanny prescience, but he knew better. She simply could feel the darkness emanating from him when his demon side kicked up a fuss. "Wow, you are in a bad way. Burn it out, Ian."

"I don't think that's going to work," he gasped, willing himself to ignore the pain, to push it into the depths of his mind.

"Take your own advice, silly-billy," she counseled, but her hand rubbing his back was comforting. "Let it out with fire. Just don't burn down this apartment, because I don't think the insurance company is going to believe two fires in one week is anything but arson."

He let her light tone wash over him, his mind focused on the ability to conjure fire, allowing his dragon to gain strength, to leash the pain and cage the demon that wanted so desperately to rule him. Once again the fire rose within him until he spat out a ball of it into the sink, the bright flames playing merrily on the sides of the curved marble. He gathered it in his hands, spreading it across his arms and chest, effectively cauterizing the still-bleeding brands.

"Better?" Sasha asked, her eyes as bright as ever, but with a shadow behind them that momentarily startled him.

He felt as if he'd been run over by a freight train. "Yes, thank you."

"It's what you tell me to do when life gets hairy," she said, her thin shoulders moving in a shrug under a light cotton sundress. "And speaking of bad crap going down, what did the boss lady want?"

"The same as usual," he replied, pulling on a shirt. "Destruction of Asmodeus. Power. This time it's a courier you said was coming to town with two esprits. Are you sure of that?"

"I wouldn't have told you about them if I wasn't sure," she answered.

"It just seems oddly coincidental."

Sasha grinned at him. "Life is funny that way, huh?"

He eyed her suspiciously. For some reason, he had the feeling the coincidence had its roots in Sasha. "Indeed."

Sasha watched him return to the bedroom. "What are you going to do?"

"I have to go out."

"To find the little angels?" She dashed out of the room, calling over her shoulder, "Let me just stuff all the furballs into their houses, and I'll be set."

"There's no hurry—you don't need to come with me. I'm not tracking the courier right now. There's another task I need to see to."

"What?" she asked when he finished dressing and buckled the belt from which hung his *élan vital*.

"I owe it to Adam Larson to see to his daughter."

"She's dead," Sasha said blithely. "There's not a lot you can do for her, is there?"

"I can make sure her possessions are held safe," he answered. There were times when he wondered why, two weeks before when Anzo had finally allowed him to return to the mortal world, he agreed to taking on an apprentice, but then he remembered he didn't have a choice in the matter.

"What belongings? Her sword? Who would want that? No one can use it but a dragon hunter."

He leveled a long look at Sasha. "If the demon who threatened to take Adam found the esprit in Helen Larson's sword, do you think it would remain there for very long?"

"Good point. Is finding her stuff dangerous?" Sasha asked, hurriedly filling water and food bowls for the various animals.

"Not particularly."

"Risky?"

"Hardly."

"Does it have the potential to let me mingle with mortals and learn their secret ways?" she asked, her eyes hopeful.

"Not in the least," he said, gathering his phone, wallet, and car keys. He wondered absently if the woman who'd caught him the night before on the stairs would be lying in wait for him. The last thing he needed was unwanted attention from the mortals in his new home. Not with his tie to a dangerous demon lord. "I'm simply going to look at where Helen Larson died and see if she left anything behind other than her *élan vital*."

"Adventure!" Sasha shrieked, and leaped to her feet. "I'll go with you! I love adventures! Can I take my *élan*?"

"After yesterday?" Ian affixed her with a look he

hoped was stern, but feared was merely martyred. "No."

"Oh, come on, Ian. She asked for it. *Literally.*"

"So you say, but I don't think you've told me exactly what happened."

She grinned at him. "Like I'd keep anything from you?"

"A death is a death, and should be avoided at all costs."

"Yes, but—"

"Repeat the code," he said.

Sasha moaned, and waved her arms in the dramatic manner of an emotional teenager. "I know, I know, but—"

"Repeat it," he commanded.

She rolled her eyes, made a face, but at least said as quickly as possible, running the words together, "*Dragon hunters protect. Always protect. At the sacrifice of themselves, they protect.* Which is what I did. Kind of. Zizi's toenails! It's like you think I don't know what I'm doing. Now, can we go? I want to stop by that free trade coffee place the woman with the hots for you mentioned last night."

"How in the name of Abaddon did you hear that?" he asked, pausing at the door. She stood right behind him, barefoot and bare-legged, appearing to the mortal world to be an innocent young woman of about eighteen or nineteen, fresh-faced and wholesome as the day was long.

The world didn't know her as he did.

"I heard with my ears, silly."

"You weren't on the stairs—another woman was there, one covered in blood and vomit who ran away as soon as she could."

"Yeah," Sasha said slowly, her grin growing. "Kind of interesting, wasn't that?"

"In what way?"

She gave a little one-shouldered shrug. "Nothing in particular. I just thought it was interesting."

"Hmm. Where were you?"

"Boy, you have to know everything, don't you!" Like quicksilver, her mood changed from impish to petulant. "If you must know, I wasn't behind Miss Blood and Gore. I was upstairs, looking down."

"Why were you upstairs?" Ian couldn't help but ask, even though he knew well he might regret doing so.

"Just looking around. I like to see where mortals live. Come on, come on, there are adventures to be had out there! Let's go get them! And coffee. Lots of coffee. Can we get some pastries, too? Mama loves her pastries!"

Ian sighed and followed Sasha out the door. It was shaping up to be a very long day.

DAY THREE.
WAIT, IS IT DAY TWO? NOW I'VE LOST TRACK OF TIME, AND MR. MANNY IS GOING TO YELL AT ME WHEN I TURN THIS IN TO HIM. CHAPTERS ARE HARD, YO.

"Right, here I am. Let's get started on your list."

"What list?" I asked, and rubbed my face. My brain was still rummy from the disturbed sleep due to equally disturbing dreams. "What time is it, anyway? Why are you so peppy and happy? Isn't it like the crack of dawn or something?"

Teresita bustled into my apartment holding two lattes, a gym bag slung over her shoulder. "It's ten, and I'm energized because I have two kids, one husband, and an aged Saint Bernard to cope with in the morning. Also, I'm happy because the kids are off to day camp, my husband had his good morning fun while we were showering together, and Ralph is off to doggy day care with a box of his special treats. My day is yours, *chica*, so let's not waste any of this precious time. Did you make a list already?" She set down the lattes on my tiny square orange-and-yellow tiled table and looked around.

"No. I just got up." I pushed my hair out of my face and frowned at the sight of my arm. The bandage I'd wrapped around my wrist was rumpled and twisted, no doubt from my restless movements at night. "It's ten? Really? I never sleep late like that."

"Here, drink it. I got you a triple shot," she said, pushing the latte at me before heading to my kitchen, busying herself with the toaster. "You need carbs and a shower. I'll whip you up a little something while you're in the shower, okay?"

"You don't have to—"

"Pshaw," she said, waving a spatula at me while peering into my fridge. "I didn't eat breakfast because I was thinking of fasting, but you have mushrooms and peppers, and an omelet sounds divine right about now. Cheese or no cheese?"

I lifted an eyebrow, and after a moment's struggle, gave in to the inevitable. Teresita in full force was like a bulldozer, simply plowing the path she'd chosen without regard to anyone else's plan. "Definitely cheese. Thank you for the latte. Don't forget to wash everything before you use it. And your hands. And the counter could probably use another wipe again before you chop things. Oh, the cutting board was sterilized, but you could always give it a wash, too. I'll be back shortly."

"I will wash all the things because I know how you are. Take your time. Oooh, pepperoni! Oh, it's made with turkey. Blech. Veggie omelet it is."

Twenty minutes later I emerged from my bedroom on a cloud of steam, clean, properly clothed, the latte consumed, and most of my brain cells now functioning.

"This looks lovely," I told Teresita as we sat on my tiny balcony and shared an omelet, English muffins, and a bowl of green grapes. "Did you wash the grapes?"

"Yes."

"With the veggie wash?"

"You know that stuff is bad for you, right?"

"Not as bad as *E. coli* and other things you can get from unwashed fruits and vegetables." I took a bite of the omelet and sighed happily. "This is delicious. I didn't think I was hungry, but, boy, I'm downright famished."

"Of course you are. You're a badass dragon hunter now. That has to burn a whole lot more calories than just a schoolteacher. How's your arm?"

"Oddly fine. In fact, better than fine." I held out my arm to show her. "It's totally healed. Not even a mark to show where Helen chomped on me."

"Wow." Teresita gave me a hard look. "You really are a superhero now."

"I'd scoff at you, but it's rude to scoff at anyone who just made you food."

"Dead right. Okay, let's get this show under way." She pulled out a tablet of paper and pen, and started writing. "Number one: figure out who killed your sister, and why. Number two: find the woman on the run from the bad ex. Number three—"

"Wait a minute," I said, pushing back my now empty plate. "What's this about finding Helen's killer?"

Both of her perfectly sculpted eyebrows rose. "You don't mean to say you don't care who killed your sister."

"Of course not! I care very much. I want whoever did it to be punished. But it's not anyone...you know...*normal*."

"Mortal, you mean? That's the term your sister used."

"Normal," I argued. "My sister was mortal, although she wasn't quite...normal."

"I don't know," Teresita said, tapping the pen on her chin as she thought. "Wouldn't you say you were immortal if you could come back?"

"Maybe. I guess so. Oh, I don't know. The point is, no person in their right mind killed Helen. It had to be someone *different*. Someone who was weird."

"Like she was?" Teresita's eyebrows rose even higher, and I flushed with embarrassment.

"Helen wasn't weird. She just marched to the beat of her own drummer. We both did. According to my therapist, that was our coping mechanism, our way to keep structure in lives that were filled with chaos and turmoil. If we weren't a part of it, then we weren't emotional hostages to my mother's abuses."

Teresita gave a little shrug. "That's not what I was

talking about. Your sister was half-dragon, half-demon, and one hundred percent badass. She had a sword, for freakin' sake. Where is it, by the way?"

"Back where she died." I grabbed our empty plates and carried them into the kitchen. Now that I'd had caffeine and food, I felt oddly restless, filled with a strange energy and need to be doing something. Making a list wasn't a bad idea, but I wanted to be acting rather than just planning.

"Why did you leave it there?" Teresita looked oddly distressed. "Out where anyone and their brother could take it?"

"I doubt if anyone is going to be lurking behind a derelict strip mall," I said, scrubbing the dishes and sink. "Except maybe deranged heroin addicts, but I can't imagine even them wanting to hang out back there. It was seriously rancid, Teresita."

"We'll make getting it first, then. Number zero: go to Fashion Armadillo and fetch the fancy sword." Teresita made a note on her tablet.

"Maybe it's better left there," I suggested. "Where no one can find it, and I can't hurt anyone with it, I mean."

Teresita gave me a stern look. "Have you forgotten your promise to help that battered woman?"

"No, but—"

"You need the sword. Your sister said so. Plus, it might help us to examine the area where she died. How else are we going to find out who killed her?"

"I thought about hiring a private detective. One

who's used to dragon hunters, assuming there is such a thing. Regardless, going back to that wretched strip mall isn't going to help."

"You never know." She consulted her watch. "If we get going now, we can be back to hunt for the lady and her kids. Did you look at your sister's phone?"

"No." The memory of the phone call from the evening before haunted my waking thoughts as they had those in my sleep. "I had a...disturbing call last night."

"Who from?"

"I don't know. Some man who seemed to know that Helen was gone and that I had her phone."

"Was he a heavy breather? Was he one of those phone sex pervs?" Teresita hoisted her gym bag. "You know you can block their number, right?"

I retold the conversation, adding, "That man seriously messed with my head. Even his voice sounded...evil."

"Ugh." Teresita thought for a moment, then whapped me on the arm with her notebook. "Do you think *he* killed your sister?"

"I don't know." I avoided thinking too much about that. I was still caught in an emotional tangle of grieving for a lost sister and hope that she would, in fact, come back into my life. It was a strange combination, one that left me feeling as if the ground beneath my feet was uneven. "I assume either he did, or someone he knew did, because how else would he know that I wasn't Helen when I answered the phone?"

Teresita's eyes widened. "Ooh, good point. What are you going to do about it?"

I loaded the dishwasher with our dishes, grabbed a couple of disinfectant counter wipes, and wiped off the counters, stove, and assorted other surfaces. "About the phone call and threat? Nothing. I promised Helen I would help this woman, and I will. If I can. The problem is, I don't know where to start, short of going up and down every street in town asking if anyone is in trouble."

"I have it!" Teresita said suddenly, snapping her fingers and pointing at me. "John and Aspen!"

"Who?"

"John and Aspen Fuller. You remember them—my mom used them to buy her house."

"Oh, the real estate agents? What about them?"

"They handle rental properties as well as sales. Mom says Aspen told her they have fingers in all sorts of pies. And since they are the only real estate agents in town, I just bet you they would be able to tell us where this desperate woman and her kids settle."

I rubbed the back of my neck, wishing absently I'd gotten more sleep. I felt distinctly out of sorts, both wired up and exhausted at the same time. "I don't know…"

"What?" Teresita asked, her hands on her hips. "Why not?"

"For one, I don't like them. They're big in that creepy church over on Sparrow Avenue." That slipped out before I realized it. Immediately, I apologized.

"Sorry, Teresita. I didn't mean your church was creepy, per se—"

She waved away my embarrassment before it had time to really take hold. "Don't worry about it. We stopped going to the Church of the Mortified Flesh of the Anguished Witness after just a few visits. They didn't ever seem to have regular worship hours and always seemed to be kind of put out when we'd show up on a Sunday morning. Plus Dan didn't care for John Fuller, and you know me—I was a good Catholic girl until I took that comparative religions class in college that opened my eyes and had me running to atheism. Besides, their church had a seriously bad vibe about it. Aspen says it used to be a funeral home."

"Bad juju all around," I agreed.

"However," she continued, frowning when I wiped down the counters a second time, "Aspen is chatty as all get-out, and I just bet you she would know if there were any new renters in town."

"I guess we could ask her." I threw the wipes into the trash, contemplated taking it down to the bin behind the building, but decided there was nothing in it but a few eggshells, and those weren't going to contaminate anything. I washed my hands, adding, "I have no idea what sort of excuse I'm going to make for knocking at some woman's door and asking if she has left a man who beat her up, though."

"Eh," she said, waving a hand. "We'll worry about that when we get there."

"You know how I hate that," I grumbled, gathering

up my wallet and keys, and following her to the door. "It doesn't hurt to have things planned out in advance."

"You seriously need some spontaneity in your life, sister."

"Are you kidding? Spontaneity turned me into a mythical monster. I think that's enough for one day."

The drive out to the strip mall didn't take long, and Teresita chatted the entire way out about a brave new life she envisioned for us, one where we battled evil and rescued the worthy. I let her ramble, being mostly focused on just what on earth I was doing even thinking I could fulfill the promise I had made to Helen.

I wasn't a superhero, the animal in my brain yelled. No matter what Helen said, I was just me, an average person with a whole lot of anxiety, a desire to write a book, and a natural talent for mathematics. That was Veronica James to a tee, and nowhere in a description of me could the words *badass dragon woman* be found.

"—and once they finally make a movie about us, Salma Hayek can play me—or do you think I should go with Jennifer Lopez?—and we'll find some cute white girl for your part. Someone a little quirky. Maybe that woman who does all those impressions on *Saturday Night Live*—ugh. Is this the place?"

I had pulled around to the entrance of the alley that ran behind the strip mall, unable to go farther because of the massive, rusted shape of a long-abandoned dumpster. I couldn't see beyond it to where I had found Helen, but just the sight of the bulky metal shape brought a flood of emotions. I sat staring at the dump-ster, the memories of the day before all too real.

"Hey, girl, you okay?" Teresita asked.

I pulled myself back from the mental abyss and let out a long, shuddering breath. "Yeah. Just a little... It's all so fresh in my mind."

She unbuckled her seat belt and leaned over to give me an awkward hug. "I'm sorry, Ronnie. I should have thought how hard this would be for you. If you like, I'll go find your sword."

"No, it's okay. I can do this." I summoned up what I fervently hoped was a smile that imparted bravery, al-though to be honest, I'd settle for confidence. "It's just a place, and I don't believe in ghosts."

"Oooh." Her eyes opened wide. "I wonder if *they* are real, too?"

"I hope not. I'm about at the limit of impossible things to believe before breakfast."

She was silent for a moment, then gave me a pat on the arm. "How about I stay here in the car and let you have a few moments by yourself with your memories."

"You're a remarkably good friend," I told her; then before I could think about it anymore, I got out of the car and moved around the large dumpster. Ahead of me were several smaller dumpsters, and the same assorted broken crates, torn boxes, and assorted garbage strewn along the entire back side of the building. I picked my way across the rotting debris from someone's fast food meal and tried to find the exact spot where Helen had sat slumped.

A glint of metal caught my eye from under a flattened cardboard box. I started toward it, saying under my breath, "There you are," when a shadow moved from behind the overturned dumpster beyond. A man moved forward and reached for the sword.

My sword. A surprising surge of possessiveness rose in me at the sight of the man near it. Helen had said it was bound to me, and yet now this stranger was clearly going to take it. As if he had the right! Blithely, I ignored the fact that I hadn't wanted the sword to the point where I had left it discarded in a pile of trash, and rushed forward to snatch it from him. "Hey! That's mine!"

The man grabbed the sword before my fingers could close around it. "No, it's not."

I didn't think through what happened next. I see that now—my brain didn't have time to actually pause and consider a reasonable plan of action. Instead, something inside, some instinct that I didn't know I possessed, suddenly kicked into high gear, and I leaped forward onto the man, one arm around his neck, wrenching him to the side in a move that would have done a martial arts master proud.

Unfortunately, the sword stealer wasn't as impressed as I was by my newfound prowess. Before I could even wonder at my strange new braveness, an anvil hit me in the middle of my chest and sent me flying backward to the building's wall.

Only it wasn't an anvil; it was my attacker. And that's when I got a good look at him. "It's you!" I gasped, most of my breath knocked out of me by the blow. "You bastard!"

A sound similar to a roar emerged from me as I threw myself on my new neighbor while he was in the process of picking up the sword. He stumbled backward a few steps, then went down with me riding him like he was a rented mule. I grabbed his hair and slammed his head onto the filthy broken pavement.

His eyes were green, a pale, washed green like sea glass, but suddenly, the shape of his pupils changed, elongating a bit, and little flecks of green light formed on the outer edge of the irises, just like they were flames. It was weird and strangely compelling at the same time.

With an oath, he flipped me over until I was crushed beneath him, the entire length of my body pressed into the vile, disease-riddled ground. "Who the hell are you?" he snarled.

The panicked animal in my brain did something odd then. Rather than throwing me into a huge freak-out, it joined up with this strange new badass self and had me bringing my knee up under my attacker at the same time I punched him in the throat and twisted out from under him. I snatched up the sword and ripped it from the scabbard, standing panting with it in my hand, when he leaped to his feet.

That's when I noticed he had a sword, too. We stood staring at each other, both of us breathing hard, and then suddenly the pain must have worked its way through his neurons, because he doubled over, grabbing his groin. I watched him for a moment, the wildness in my mind slowly fading, the animal crawling back to its hidey-hole.

I pointed the sword at him. "What are you doing here? Why were you trying to take my sword?"

"*Your* sword?" Slowly he straightened, his face twisted with pain. "That isn't yours. It belonged to a dragon hunter."

"I know. She was my sister. Wait, did you know Helen?"

"Your sister." Slowly he straightened up, his face reflecting lingering pain and a whole lot of suspicion. "Is that why you're here? Because your sister died here?"

"Well, yeah." I made a vague gesture toward the ground. "Also, I left her sword here."

"Bollocks!" he snapped. I thought at first it was directed at me, but realized that he was just swearing to himself.

"Er..." I started to say, but was interrupted.

"Ronnie?" Teresita called out. I skirted the sword thief Ian Iskandar and moved out to where I could see her standing at the large dumpster. "Everything okay? You're not having a panic attack, are you?"

"No," I yelled, waving my sword at her. "I just stopped our neighbor from stealing this."

"What? Hang on..." She scrambled over the boxes and crates, heading for us. I turned back to face my erstwhile attacker, but before I could say anything, he snatched the sword from my hand and bolted.

For a few stunned seconds I stared after him, not believing what had happened. Then fury hit me in a wave of red heat.

"Oh, he did not!" I growled, and took off at a run down the length of the mall. "Hey! Ian! What the hell? That's mine! You can't have it! Dammit, come back here and face me like...like...whatever you are!"

He ignored me, his long legs eating up the ground. I charged after him, but he beat me to the end of the building, his long black duster flapping behind him as he rounded the corner. I ground my teeth and raced toward it, ignoring Teresita's demands to know what I was doing. I found a burst of speed I don't remember ever accomplishing in the past and skidded around the corner to see Ian disappearing into the front seat of a black four-door sedan. I had a fleeting glimpse of a woman's startled face at the window before the car started up. Clearly, the craven sword thief Ian was going to peel out of there, leaving me with a whole lot of questions, and not a lot else.

"Over my dead body!" I yelled, and just as Ian hit the gas, I wrenched open the back door and flung myself inside, hitting my head into the far door as I curled up my legs to avoid having them slammed by the other door.

I AM DEFINITELY NOT WONDER WOMAN (NOTE TO SELF: ASK MR. MANNY IF IT'S OKAY TO USE COMMENTS AS CHAPTER TITLES)

"CHRISTOS!" IAN SLAMMED ON THE BRAKES, MAKING the car fishtail wildly. My body hit the front seats, following which I tumbled to the footwell, where I flailed around trying to get onto the seat proper.

"Oooh, we caught a big fish," a woman's voice said.

I clawed my way up onto the seat, glaring at the woman, who was turned around to look at me.

"Hello," she said, sticking out a hand. "I'm Sasha."

"I am not a fish!" I told her, shoving my hair back out of my face so I could see. "And I don't care who you are, although, that said, hello. That man stole my sword!"

"Oooh," she repeated, grinning at me.

"Sit down," Ian told her, his voice gritty and filled with anger.

She turned to look at him. "Why?"

He glanced in the rearview mirror. "We're being chased."

I looked out through the back of his car. Teresita was running toward us, her arms waving wildly in the air. "That's just my friend Teresita."

An odd martyred expression flickered across his face. "Of course it's your friend. You probably have dozens of them lurking about waiting to help you at every turn. Admit it! You do, don't you!"

I was a bit taken aback by the way he snapped out the words. What a very odd, angry man he was. "Yes, I have friends. What sort of person doesn't have friends? If this is some sort of feeble attempt to make me think you're nuts, and therefore not prosecute you for stealing my sword, you can just nip it in the bud, because I'm not going to fall for it. Give me back my sword!"

Teresita had reached us by the time the last word left my lips, and without a second's hesitation, she opened the car door and got in next to me, panting heavily. "Ian! I thought that was you. I knew we would see you again—Daniston is too small a town not to see people you know—although you guys could have told me you were going jogging. I would have worn better shoes. Hi. You must be a friend of Ian. I'm Teresita." This last was addressed to the woman in the front seat.

Ian banged his forehead on his hands, still firmly gripping the steering wheel.

"I'm Sasha." The young woman turned around and smiled broadly at Teresita, pumping her hand up and down several times. "Aren't you pretty! Your skin is the color of a caramel latte, and I love your hair. You have so many shades of brown in it. Is it a glamour, or is it real?"

"Sasha," Ian said, kind of sighing when he said the name. He looked perilously close to rolling his eyes when he turned his head to look at her. She looked like she was about seventeen or eighteen, too old to be his daughter, but definitely too young to be a romantic partner. Unless he was into that. Ick. "You can't say that sort of thing."

"Really?" She wrinkled her nose in a delightful sort of way that reminded me of anime girls with big, innocent eyes, wistful expressions, and soft, breathy voices. "Why not?"

"Because it's not polite." He made an odd sort of half grimace, half apologetic smile at Teresita in the rearview mirror. "Please forgive Sasha. She meant no rudeness."

"I can see that," Teresita said, forcibly extracting her hand from where the girl was still shaking it. "And none taken. I'm quite proud of my heritage, as a matter of fact. My hair is all my own, although I will do the lemon juice in summer thing just to throw in a little natural highlights. What...uh...Are you two related?"

Bless Teresita—if there was one thing I loved about her, it was the way she wasn't afraid to ask whatever was on her mind. It usually coincided directly with something that I very much wanted to know but was too shy or awkward or anxious to ask.

And right at that moment, I was delighted she peppered the man whom I'd glimpsed the night before with nonstop questions, because I, too, wanted to know what he was doing behind a decaying strip mall with my sister's soul sword. "I'll tell you what's rude! Stealing my sword. Which, I'd like to point out again, you have, and I want back."

"Us? Related?" Sasha gave a peal of (charming and bell-like) laughter before adding, "Zizi's shiny red earlobes, no! I'm his girlfriend."

"The hell you are!" Ian said quickly, glaring at her.

"Look, you're clearly having a lover's spat—" I said, leaning forward so I could look into the front seats. Lying next to Sasha's legs, my sword poked upward, just out of my reach. Possessiveness burbled up and spread out across my chest, making me feel hot and prickly, as if I were in the process of getting a bad sunburn. "If you could just give me back my sword— I'm really getting tired of asking for it—then we'll be on our way and you guys can work out your relationship issues."

"We have no relationship issues," Ian snapped. "She's not my girlfriend."

"I'm not?" Sasha's expression changed to confusion. "Then what am I?"

"Sword!" I said loudly, and hit the back of Ian's seat with both hands. "S. W. O. R. D. It's not that hard a word to understand. Sasha, it's the one right there, leaning against your leg. If you could just slip it back to me—"

"The word you are searching for is *apprentice*," Ian said, ignoring me other than sending me a fast glare when I hit his seat. "A mandatory one."

"You love me," she said, blowing him a kiss. "Admit it!"

He did roll his eyes then.

"Sorry," Sasha said, turning back to Teresita. "I'm an apprentice, not girlfriend. I've been at the Court of Divine Blood for so long, I've forgotten what you mortals call things."

"The Court of—" Teresita started to ask, but I'd had enough.

"ARGH!" I screamed, and threw myself forward until I dangled over the arm of Sasha's seat, snatching at my sword. I'd just grabbed it when Ian's fingers closed around mine. A little tug-of-war took place at that moment, which I'm glad to say I won by dint of using my free arm to hit him on the back of his head with my elbow.

"Cheese and toast!" Teresita said, gasping when I pulled my sword into the backseat, cradling it to my chest. "Did you just hit him?"

"She's done quite a bit more than that to me," he said in a low growl, rubbing his head.

"Well, you started it! You stole my sword. Twice!"

"I had no idea who you were. You could be anyone. An *élan vital* is special. You can't just demand one and expect to receive it."

I hugged the sword even tighter. "What part of 'this was my sister's sword' do you not understand?"

He moved so fast he was just a blur. One moment I was in the car glaring at the back of his head, and the next, the door I'd been leaning against was open and I fell backward out onto the pavement. Ian grabbed the back of my shirt and literally hauled me up onto my feet, giving me a little shake just like I was an errant puppy. "I repeat: who *are* you?" he asked, his face shoved into mine. His eyes did that weird fire thing where the outer edge of his irises seemed to turn into light green flames.

Rather than being intimidated, however, I felt the same flush that hit my chest before, this time spreading outward and upward until I thought I must be steaming with anger. I shoved him backward, whipping my sword from the scabbard and holding it to his throat. "Your worst nightmare."

To my surprise, the thick cords of his neck became visible when he tipped his head back and laughed. "You have no idea just how horrible my nightmares are," he finally said, leaning into the sword just a little, enough that a thin trickle of blood started at the sword tip and ran down his neck. "You want to end them for me? Go right ahead. You'll be doing me an immense favor."

The sight of the blood, the same maroonish color that had leaked out of Helen, brought sanity to my overwrought mind. I stepped back, lowering the sword. "I'm not going to kill you, if that's what you're asking."

"Then tell me who you are. Why do you keep saying

that *élan vital* belonged to your sister? Helen Larson had no sister."

"How do you know that?" I asked, curiosity getting the better of me.

He grimaced and gestured away the question. "It's not important. I know, however, that sword is not yours. You will surrender it to me, and I will see to it that it is returned to the Court, where the esprit can be replaced and the sword given to a worthy dragon hunter."

"Like hell you will," I said, waggling the sword in what I hoped was a menacing manner. "No court in the world is going to make me give back something that is legally mine." I backed up a few more steps, prepared to bolt should he move toward me.

"Not a mortal court," he said, then hesitated, pinning me back with a piercing look that made a by-now familiar flush wash upward from my chest. "Why do you insist that Helen Larson was your sister? Her father had no other children."

"We had the same mom, but different dads, not that it's any of your business. I'm only telling you so you'll stop arguing with me."

"A half sister." For a second, Ian looked like he wanted to cry. "Adam never told me. Of course he didn't. Why did I believe this was going to be easy?"

"What's going on?" Teresita asked, trotting over to where Ian and I faced each other, Sasha on her heels. "Are you two arguing? You don't even know each other. I thought we were going for a ride?"

"It's a showdown," Sasha said succinctly, doing an odd little jig before she patted Ian on the arm. "Dragon hunter versus dragon hunter. Who will come out on top?"

"He's a dragon hunter, too?" I asked, eyeing Ian. That would explain why he knew about my soul sword.

"You are *not* a child of Adam Larson," Ian stated baldly.

"Ronnie? Why are you pointing like that? In fact, let's back it up a bit, because I am so lost in this conversation," Teresita said plaintively. "Would anyone like to clue me in to what's going on? All I can see is Ian rolling his eyes toward heaven, and Ronnie pointing a finger at him. I take it that the Wonder Woman sword is here? Who is Adam Larson?"

Distracted, I gave her a little frown. "Adam was my stepdad. And I told you, Wonder Woman has the invisible plane, not an invisible sword, and besides, I can't mention that in the book or the DC franchise will come after me."

For a moment, Ian looked as confused as Teresita. "What book?" he asked.

"The one I'm writing about my life. Or I will be just as soon as I can get my yoga started. Mr. Manny was very adamant about the yoga. Why did you run off with the sword if you thought it belonged to Helen?"

"She's dead." Ian was silent for a moment, his gaze crawling over my face. "A fact that you must know, since no dragon hunter would give up an *élan vital* unless he or she was on the verge of death."

"She died in my arms, as a matter of fact," I said,

swallowing back a painful lump in my throat. "How did *you* know she was dead?"

He turned, and without a word marched back to the car, getting in and gunning the engine in what I'm sure was meant as a hint to Sasha, who just smiled at us, her anime-large eyes sparkling with secret delight.

"What a very rude man," I couldn't stop myself from saying.

"He is, isn't he? Torture will do that to you. Strip away social niceties, that is," she said pleasantly.

"Torture?" Teresita asked, looking interested. "Literally or figuratively? Does he have a dark past? Is he all brooding and angsty? He looks like he could be brooding and angsty."

"He can be as broody as he wants so long as he leaves me alone," I said, then slipped the sword back into the scabbard. A thin black leather belt was threaded through the latter, so I buckled it around my waist, moving it until it hung down my left hip. "And can we address the fact that the day I turn into a mythical being, the guy downstairs ends up being one, too? Coincidence? I think not."

"Yeah," Teresita said, turning to cast a suspicious look over at the car. "That is kind of odd. I mean, how many dragonistas are there?"

"Twelve worldwide," Sasha said, then pointed at the sword. "You're gonna need that."

"I am? Why?"

As I spoke, a van pulled off the highway and into the parking lot at the far end of the mall. I paid it no mind, assuming it was someone who was turning around, or possibly a drug user coming to shoot up in the privacy of the filthy back alley.

Instead, the dirty white van rolled to a stop for a few seconds before it meandered slowly up and down the aisles.

"I hope you know how to use it," Sasha said with another bright smile. "Aim for the head; it's usually more effective. I'd help if I could, but Ian hid my sword from me. One little outing to help someone escape eternal torment, and boom, your *élan vital* is confiscated. That's not in the least bit fair, is it?"

"Wait, you're a dragon hunter, too?" I asked her, shaking my head in confusion.

"Is everyone here a dragon except me?" Teresita asked. "What is that guy doing? He's going to ruin his shocks."

I had lost interest in the van, but realized with a start that it was now heading straight for us at an increasing speed, bouncing over the various cement blocks intended to keep cars in tidy rows.

"Ack!" I screamed, and grabbed Teresita, shoving her toward the car.

Ian must have noticed the van, too, because he suddenly leaped out of the car and yelled for Sasha. "Protect the mortal!" he ordered.

"How am I supposed to do that?" she grumbled. "You won't let me have any weapons."

"Just protect her. You—you say that you're a dragon hunter! Come with me."

"My name is Ronnie, not 'you'!" I yelled as he did a TV-hero move of rolling over the hood of the car and racing straight toward the oncoming van. I watched for a few seconds, hesitating. Assuming the people in the van had bad intentions, should I stay where I was and protect my friend and Sasha, or should I help Ian? And just who was in that car, and why were they attacking?

The van slammed on its brakes, and before it even came to a complete halt, three men boiled out of the back, with the driver and another man joining them. Ian didn't hesitate; he just ran straight at the men, a sword like mine suddenly in his hands, the sunlight glinting off the polished metal.

"Ian does so enjoy a good battle," Sasha said, standing alongside the car, leaning against it while she shaded her eyes to watch Ian plunge into the circle of men. Two of them were armed with knives, while the third had a crossbow, and a fourth some sort of black metal object that looked like a tire iron. The fifth danced around with his fists raised, evidently a proponent of bare-knuckle fighting. "When he's not doubting himself, that is, which I have to admit is a lot of the time."

"Who are they?" I asked when Ian spun around, his sword flashing. One of the men fell to his knees.

"Ronnie!" Teresita demanded, and started shoving me forward.

"What? Stop it! You're hurting my back."

"Go help Ian!" she ordered, and continued to shove.

"Why? I don't know who those men are, and Sasha just said Ian likes a fight."

"You're a dragon superhero! It's your job to help him!"

"Says who?" I moved to the side so she'd stop pushing me forward. "Helen didn't mention anything about that."

She slapped her hands on her thighs and did a little foot stomp before pointing over at where Ian was now covered by the five men. "He's our neighbor!"

"One who stole my sword," I pointed out.

"How can you be so uncaring? He might be hurt!"

"I'm not uncaring. I'm just not huge on getting into fights with people." I glanced over at the ruckus. It was true that the free-for-all was going strong, although one man was laid out, his arms moving feebly. "Besides, Ian's down to just four."

"It doesn't matter! It's your job now."

I sighed. Despite not wanting to get involved in whatever issue Ian had with the men, I supposed I would have to do something to stop them. "I don't know. Do you really think—"

"Yes!" she shouted, and made shooing gestures at me. "Go be a badass dragon...er...dragonette!"

"All right," I said with another martyred sigh and glanced at Sasha. "Those are bad people, aren't they? I don't want to be sued later because Ian has anger management issues and picked a fight with people who did nothing wrong."

"Oh, yes. They're demons in human form," Sasha said, buffing a nail, but she gave me a curiously sharp glance from under her lashes. "We're the only ones who can destroy them. It's all in the sword, you know? The *élan*. Demons can't stand it. It makes them crumple up and turn to ash. Kind of like that one that Ian just gutted." She clapped her hands and yelled loudly, "Nice job, boss man, but you better watch your back!"

"Dammit!" I ran forward then, mentally yelling at myself for my reluctance to get involved. I thought of pulling my sword out so I could wave it and threaten the demons in the very best swashbuckling manner, but the cautious part of my mind pointed out that it was the sheerest folly to run with a sharp object in my hand, so I kept the sword sheathed until I was close enough to hear the men swearing at Ian. One remained prone on the ground, while another disappeared just as Sasha said, leaving behind a nasty black pile of ash.

I didn't know what plan of action I had in mind when I arrived at the fight, but I felt it was only fair to warn the men—demons—that I meant business. "Demons!" I yelled over the grunts and oaths and thuds of the fight. "I want you to know that you have options other than violence. If you continue to beat up Ian— oh, that was underhanded, sir! I just kicked him there a short while ago!—then I, as a dragon hunter, will have no other option but to take action."

The nearest demon, the one with the tire iron, leaped onto Ian's back, using him to springboard over to me. Before I knew what was happening, a red wave of anger spread out from my belly, and I found myself sword in hand, doing a spinning move that I had hoped would impress the demon with my prowess.

It didn't. I stumbled over my own big feet and fell, screaming as I tried to keep the sword from skewering me. The demon leaped onto my back and started pulling at my hair while screeching unintelligible things.

Panicked, I struggled to get the sword out from underneath me, managing to roll over onto my side, which, sadly, exposed me to the demon's vengeance.

"Die!" he snarled, his saliva spraying my face. I brought my knees up and tried to slash at him with the sword, but he simply knocked it out of my hand and started strangling me. I tried to scream, but only horrible clotted grunts emerged from my mouth. Just as huge black blotches began eating away at my vision, a flash of light skimmed past my face, and the demon's head was separated from his body. I sat up and stared in stark horror, both hands on my neck while gasping for air, and watched as the head bounced away. Almost instantly it turned into a nasty, oily black, ashy smoke and drifted away on the wind. The body did the same when it collapsed to the ground. Above me, looking down with an inscrutable expression, stood Ian.

There wasn't time to dwell on the fact that he had just decapitated a demon that almost killed me—the two other demons rose from the ground where Ian had knocked them back, the one with a knife coming for me, while the other kicked Ian's legs out from under him, sending the pair to the ground in a furious twisting mass of man and demon. The third demon rolled over to join the action.

I crawled over to where my sword was, holding it with hands that shook horribly.

"Dragon hunter," the demon in front of me said, spitting at my feet, his lips pulled back to reveal very sharp, pointed teeth. There was something about his face that didn't look right, not quite human. Perhaps it was the angles and contours, or perhaps it was the way he seemed to emit dread in palpable waves. "I will take your corpse to my master, and watch him flay the flesh from your body and feed it to his dogs. Prepare to die!"

"You know the problem with a chatty demon?" I asked, managing to parry a thrust he made with a wicked-looking long dagger now stained maroon.

He paused for a moment, his horrible pointed teeth snapping together. "What?"

Panting, I nodded over his shoulder to where Ian staggered forward. He thrust his sword straight through the demon's chest, covering me in a spray of black demon blood.

"You are too busy gloating to realize your buddies are gone, and now it's two against one. Oh, my goddess! OH, MY GODDESS! Is this blood? It's all over me! Goddess knows what sort of horrible disease I could pick up from it!" I did a horrified little dance at the spray of black across my shirt, then hurriedly tucked my sword under my arm in order to pull out my hand sanitizer. I wanted to douse myself with it but knew that wasn't practical. "I'm going to have to burn this shirt, too! Holy gallon of bleach, that smoke stinks."

Ian stood panting before me, blood dripping from a

nasty gash over his left eye. "Tell me, do you always announce to demons that they have options other than violence?"

"I've never attacked anyone before, and it seemed only fair to warn them that I have this badass sword, just in case they wanted to reconsider. I mean, it can't be a very good life being a demon, and perhaps they are regretting their career path." I decided to ignore the blood splattered across my front. The alternative was to rip my clothing from my body, and I wasn't prepared to do that, so instead I told myself the demon blood wasn't there and pulled from my pocket both a tissue and a latex glove. I donned the glove and used the tissue to dab at the cut that was dripping blood down Ian's face. "You should probably get a doctor to have that stitched; otherwise it's going to keep bleeding."

He grabbed my hand, giving me an odd look with mingled exasperation and curiosity. "Dragon hunters do not warn demons of impending attack. We end their existence whenever we encounter them in order to protect those whom they would destroy without prejudice. We do not try to rehabilitate them into less destructive careers. What the hell was the matter with you? Why did you let that demon get you onto the ground? Did you want to be killed? Or is this your attempt to drive me insane with guilt?"

"I didn't let him do anything," I said, pulling my hand back, confused by Ian's ranting. I had a moment's qualm about what to do with the bloody tissue, but decided that since it was his blood, he could keep it, and accordingly pushed it into the pocket on his coat, swiftly followed by the glove. "I've never used a sword before, and I was worried I was going to stab myself with it. Why would that make you feel guilty?"

He stared at me for a moment as if he couldn't believe what I'd just said, then strode past me, shaking his head and muttering under his breath.

"That was awesome!" Teresita said, running over to where I stood, frowning at my sword. I had nothing on me with which to clean it, and it was stained black in spots, presumably splattered from the demon's blood. "Did you see Ian? He was all *swoosh*, *swoosh*, and *boom*! One dead demon. Did you see the way his head went flying? It was like something out of a Quentin Tarantino movie! Holy moly, he was awesome. That demon was all over you until Ian *bang*, *zoom*ed his head right out of there."

I gave her a sour look that she evidently read accurately.

"You were…uh…" She stopped, unable to continue.

"Inefficient?" I said, arranging a martyred expression.

"Well…it was your first time fighting. I suppose everyone has to start out learning from square one. Only you went down awfully fast."

"That demon was a bastard. Also, I don't like fighting people. For one, you usually have to touch them in order to fight, and for another, I'm not a violent person. I don't suppose you have a rag on you, do you?"

I asked, examining the sword. I hated to put it away in the scabbard when it was dirty.

"What would I be doing with a rag?"

"I can see I'm going to have to add that to the items I carry in case of emergencies." I looked at Sasha when she meandered over to us. Beyond her, next to the car, Ian stood with a cell phone to his ear. "Is there some cleaning compound recommended for swords?"

"Yes. The clothing of your victims. Did your dead sister ask you to do something for her?"

"Why on earth would you ask that?" I shook my head, confused by her quicksilver conversational changes of topic. "Did you know Helen?"

"Everyone has heard of her." Sasha tipped her head and blinked her big anime eyes at me. "I hope you do what your sister asked, because I just don't see that there's anything else Ian will want to barter for. He has this thing about failing to protect innocents, you know, and he's going to balk big-time at you because of that. Toodles!"

"Huh?" I was about to ask to what she was referring, more than a little uncomfortable at the idea that she knew of the quest Helen had given me before she died, but Sasha just gave us both a cheery smile, then marched back to the car. Ian, still on the phone, got in and, without a look at us, drove off.

I stared first at the car as it pulled out onto the highway, then at the empty van, and finally, to Teresita. She had a thoughtful look on her face and was tugging absently on her ear. "What the hell was that all about?" I asked her.

"I think," she said slowly, looking at her phone to check the time, "it means we need to do some research. Or we could go meet with Aspen and John, although I suppose it is easier to look up what we can first."

"You think Sasha was talking about the woman Helen wanted me to find? How did she know about that? And why would that be a bartering point with Ian? Does that mean he wants the woman, too?"

"He's a dragon hunter like your sister," Teresita said with a little shrug. "Maybe all you guys are hunting for this chick."

"Maybe. But what am I supposed to be bartering for?" We started across the parking lot to where my car was parked.

"Lessons on how to fight without falling down and having demons throttle you?"

I glared at her. "I stumbled, and I told you, I'm not a fighter."

"Then you better learn how to be one pretty quick, because I don't see how you're going to be a superhero without fighting."

"Also, I was worried about the sword. Those things are dangerous! I could have gutted myself on it."

"My point exactly. You need training. Ian is clearly a master at fighting, and falling without impaling himself on his sword. Therefore, he can teach you, and you can be the badass you're supposed to be." She took off at a jog, calling over her shoulder to me, "Come on! Google is awaiting, and we have damsels to rescue."

"From vague and unspecified threats that could be

anything from a jealous ex to outright murder and may-hem. Sometimes I have to wonder if Helen wasn't hallucinating the whole thing." I followed after Tere-sita, my steps dragging. The anxious beast in my head asked me what I'd gotten us into.

"I wish I knew," I told it under my breath. "I really wish I knew."

CHAPTER SEVEN

A RASPY, BUZZING SOUND FILLED THE APARTMENT. Ian frowned at the door, setting down the washcloth he was using to wipe the blood off his face.

"Door!" Sasha said helpfully from where she sat cross-legged on the floor, holding a one-legged chicken and a duck who was clearly molting on her lap while she read something on a tablet computer.

"Thank you," Ian said drily. He paused at the sight of the chicken. "Do I want to know where you got those two?"

"Probably not, since it involves breaking into someone's yard and rescuing them from certain death. What's Facebook? It keeps telling me I should have one, but I don't like books that have faces. They are always rude, and you have a hard time shutting them up, not to mention they go on and on about the most boring bits of trivia, and refuse to let you leave until you've listened to at least ten of their personal anecdotes."

"Sounds about right." Ian opened the door. A woman stood before him, her blond hair pulled back tightly into a bun, her expression such as to raise the fine hairs on the back of his neck. "Iskandar," the woman said. "The master sent me."

Ian tried to slam the door shut on the demon. He knew that face, knew that rough, grating voice.

The demon blocked the door, insinuating herself into the room a few inches.

"There is nothing here for you," he snapped, trying to shield her view of the apartment. He fought the urge to strike her down, knowing Anzo would not take the death of a favorite lightly. Then there was Sasha to think about. He would protect her at all costs.

"I am to assist you," the demon announced, her lip curled. "Or so says our master. Do you defy her?"

Ian hesitated, wondering what Anzo's reaction would be to an outright refusal. A little shiver went down his arms. He had a feeling the outcome would be very bad. "For what purpose did Anzo send you?"

"She thinks you need help." The demon gestured toward a small black suitcase on wheels. "I will remain with you until such time as the courier has been taken into custody."

Ian's eyes narrowed, fear and worry crawling in his gut. He really did not want this murderous demon anywhere around. She was far too dangerous. "I don't need help. I work alone. I always have, and I always will, so you may tell Anzo that I will find the woman when I find her, and sending minions to pester me will only draw my attention from the problem at hand."

He tried to shut the door, but the demon shoved against it, attempting again to gain entrance. Ian stood firm. No one entered his domain without his permission.

The woman issued a low, guttural snarl. "You of all people must know that I am *not* a lowly minion. I am a wrath demon, exalted in the master's eyes and first in her honor. I lead seventeen legions of my own demons and possess the sword known through Abaddon as Deathsong! I have slain mortals and immortals alike for eight centuries and am feared by all who gaze upon me! I am Falafel!"

Ian choked down his inappropriate laughter at her ridiculous name. But the realization that Anzo was up to something struck him almost immediately. Why else would she send the very demon who was responsible for his bondage, and most likely Adam's death? A normal demon was bad enough, but a wrath demon was just a step away from being a demon lord, and this one was particularly vicious. He did *not* need her moving in with him.

Not while he had Sasha to protect.

"Your very presence here is a violation of the laws set down by the premiere prince of Abaddon. Thus, I do not have to abide by your demands. Goodbye."

He gave the door a hard push before she could react and locked the three locks that kept outsiders from his sanctuary.

The demon started pounding on the door almost immediately.

"Problems?" Sasha asked, looking up as he ignored the knocking and strode over to the small table where his cell phone, wallet, and keys lay.

"Nothing that I can't take care of. Here. Go see a movie."

"Huh?" Sasha moved the duck and chicken to a small, partially filled children's wading pool, one side of which contained a few cinder blocks above the water level. The chicken settled into a small roosting area created with shredded paper and grass cuttings, while the duck happily splashed in the water below it. "Are you trying to get rid of me?"

"Yes." He gave her money and his car keys before moving over to the window. Outside, an ancient fire escape clung to the side of the building. "Go out this way."

"Well, this is very interesting. I love it when you act unexpectedly. Can't I stay to watch your behavior with the demon who's trying to beat down the door?"

"Sasha," he said, warning dripping from his voice.

She giggled, took the keys, and climbed out through the window onto the metal fire escape. "Shall I bring you some food after the movie, or will you be busy entertaining your girlfriend?"

"The demon?" he asked, horrified at the thought.

She giggled again. "No, your new protégée. The one who lives upstairs. Hey, if she becomes your apprentice, does that mean I graduate to full-fledged dragon hunter?"

"She's not my girlfriend or my apprentice. Go away and stay away."

"For a few hours, or forever?"

He ignored the twinkle in her eyes and firmly closed the window before winding his way around the various animal domiciles to the door. He opened it to find exactly what he thought he'd find: a very angry wrath demon.

"You are insubordinate!" she snapped. "The master will not be pleased to know you have treated me such and will no doubt punish you. I will greatly delight in watching the punishment." She cracked her knuckles in a menacing sort of way. "I might even plead with her to conduct it."

"Go back to your realm," he said, his odd sense of humor making him want to laugh hysterically. As if dealing with Sasha's burden along with his own wasn't enough, now he was expected to take on a wrath demon? No, it was too much. He drew the line at cohabiting with a being who was able to destroy him without breaking into a sweat. "I don't need or want your help."

"Wrath demons do not help—"

He closed the door in her face. He knew he'd hear from Anzo about treating her favorite badly, but there was little the demon lord could do to him that he hadn't already survived.

A knock sounded just as he turned to go back to the bedroom. He sighed to himself, then steeled his nerves and jerked open the door.

Falafel wasn't alone. The woman from upstairs, the dragon hunter with the prettiest gray eyes he'd ever seen, stood next to her, shooting curious side-eye to the wrath demon.

"Er...hi." The woman cleared her throat nervously. "I thought I should check on your cut."

He stared at her for a moment, desperately trying to dig her name out of the recesses of his memory. Victoria? No, Veronica. That was it. Her friend, the chatty one, called her Ronnie.

"My cut," he said stupidly, before remembering that she'd been poking at it earlier, when he had destroyed the five demons.

"Yeah. It looks like you didn't see a doctor after all." She studied his face.

"Who," Falafel said in a tone that seemed to be made up of sharp edges, "is this?"

Ian had a horrible vision of the demon finding out that Veronica was the dragon slayer whom Anzo sought, and the carnage that would follow. Without thinking of the consequences of such an action, he answered, "She's my woman."

Veronica's eyes widened when he pulled her through the door and straight into his arms, pausing only to whisper, "Please don't take offense" in her ear before kissing her.

He intended the kiss to be purely functional, a

farce to sell the first story his abused brain could come up with, but the second his mouth touched Veronica's, all those intentions of pretense went flying. Her lips were warm and soft, delightfully so, enough that on their own, his body came to life and demanded an immediate introduction to all the various parts of her. But when she parted her lips in what he assumed was an outraged gasp, her heat sank deeply into his awareness, saturating his thoughts and bringing his always-burning dragon fire roaring to sudden life. She tasted spicy, as if she'd been eating cinnamon, and sweet, and the heat of her tongue when it touched his made the dragon in him demand possession of her. Of her mouth. And dear goddess, all the rest of her.

He was aware that she'd put both hands on his chest and pushed back, and reluctantly he let her go. It was a struggle, since dragons did not like to relinquish what they wanted, but decades of mastering both sides of his psyche allowed him to drop his hands with only a faint sense of disappointment.

Until he looked into her eyes, those lovely gray eyes ringed with thick black lashes, and saw the answering flames. He knew then that she was truly a dragon hunter. No one else showed their inner self in such a manner.

But why was she so very bad at what she was born to?

"What the hell?" Veronica said, glaring at him. Then her gaze dropped to his lips, and she repeated, in much less anger, "What the actual hell?"

"If you think to sicken me with displays of affection, you will fail," the wrath demon said, curling one lip when she eyed Veronica. "What you do with mortals is of no concern to me or the master, so long as you do the job you have been given. We will discuss—"

"Nothing," he interrupted, tugging Veronica farther into the room. "Now is the time I spend with my woman having sex. Go back and tell your master I will do the job as I see fit, or she can release me and find someone else to do it."

"Sex!" Veronica said, looking horrified.

"Yes, sex. You know." He gave her a look that simultaneously warned her and pleaded with her. "The sex we have every day at this time."

"We do not have sex—" she started to object, but he cut her off by pulling her tight to his chest, so her face was buried in his shoulder.

"—in front of others, no, of course we do not. The demon is taking herself off right now so we can have our afternoon sex time."

"I can wait," Falafel said, moving past him into the room. "It can't take that long."

Veronica, who had been struggling against him, mumbling something that he didn't understand, dug her heel onto his foot, causing him to loosen his hold a little.

"Can't…breathe…" she gasped, sucking in vast quantities of air.

"Ha ha, you take my breath away, too," he said, sending a worried look at the wrath demon. Clearly, a term of endearment was needed to sell the idea. He wracked his brain for one, but drew a blank until he remembered the movie Sasha had watched a few days before. "Er…hot lips."

"Hot lips!" The words came out strangled. Veronica's eyes were positively blazing when she glared up at him.

He bent down and whispered furiously, "Play along with me, and I'll do whatever you want."

She had been about to say something that was no doubt quite cutting, but at his words, she stopped and gave him a long, curious look. "Anything?" she whispered back.

"Within reason." He glanced over at the wrath demon, but she was baring her teeth at the cats who had come over to see her.

"Deal." She wriggled her way out of his hold and said loudly, "Sorry about that show of public affection. I'm just so happy to see you…uh…hugsy wugsy cuddle-boo."

The wrath demon turned her glare on Veronica. "Your attempt to make me puke has failed. Nonetheless, such acts of subordination are not to be tolerated. Dragon hunter, send your woman away. We have work to do."

To his amazement, Veronica threw herself full force into her pretend role. He had a few uncomfortable moments wondering what it was she'd demand from him as a price, but decided unless it involved the murder or torture of innocents, he'd have to do as she wished.

"Now, you just listen here," Veronica said, rounding on the demon. Her hands were on her hips, and her chin jutted out as if she was looking for a fight. He glanced quickly at her waist, but didn't see her *élan vital*. Unobtrusively, he slid his hand down, reassured by the weight of the sword at his side. He had absolutely no doubts as to what lengths Falafel would go. "I don't know who you are—"

"My name is Falafel! Bow before me, mortal being!" the demon demanded with an arrogance that would have taken away Ian's breath if he hadn't been so well acquainted with demon folk.

Veronica blinked twice. Ian kept his hand on his sword, ready to protect her should the demon strike. "Falafel? Did you say— No, you couldn't have. I must have heard wrong. Who names their kid Falafel?"

"What is the problem with my name?" Falafel slapped her hands on her legs, clearly irritated. "I see nothing funny about it! It is an old and much feared name! You will give me the respect we deserve!"

"It's also a delicious meal, but that doesn't give you the right to tell Mr. Snuggy Bumps and me when we get to have sexy times. And that's right now, so please leave."

The demon sucked in approximately half the volume of air in the apartment. "You dare to speak to me with such insolence? Pathetic mortal! If my time were not taken up with much more valuable tasks, I would lesson you as to the proper way to speak to me!"

"Eh," Veronica said, brushing a nonexistent speck

off her shoulder. "Do us all a favor and get over yourself. Oh, and leave. Ian and I wish to be alone."

Falafel turned her furious gaze to him. "Have you nothing to say?"

"On the contrary, I have quite a few things to say." He pulled the sword from its sheath and carefully ran a finger down the blade, feeling the runes come to life under his fingertip. The gesture was not wasted on the wrath demon. She did not back away in fear as a lesser demon might have done, but the look she gave to the *élan vital* was definitely wary. "But as none of them concern you, your presence is not wanted or needed. I don't care if you return to Anzo or not, but you will not remain here."

She watched with eyes that spat black sparks as he strolled to the door, still holding the sword, and opened it. "You do not have the power to make me leave."

"Perhaps not, but my woman certainly does." He arranged his expression into one of bland disinterest. "Or have you been trapped so long in Abaddon that you have lost the ability to notice the scent of the Court of Divine Blood?"

Falafel lifted her head and sniffed the air. Had Ian believed in any benevolent gods, he would have prayed then that enough of Sasha's scent remained for the wrath demon to catch, and hopefully, misinterpret as originating in Ronnie. "I don't smell anyth— Oh."

Veronica looked puzzled for a moment, but at a signal from him—unseen by the demon, who was subjecting her to a thorough visual inspection—she sat on the couch, crossing her legs and saying, "That's me, all right. I'm always over at the Court of Benign Blood."

"Divine Blood," Ian correct.

"We at the Court call it Benign," Veronica said with an airy wave of her hand. "It's an in-joke. We love those sorts of things in between cases."

Ian looked worriedly at the demon, but if she was confused by Veronica, she didn't show it. She took a step closer and sniffed again. A look of annoyance crossed her face. She hesitated, as if she was going to argue further, but in the end, made a guttural noise in her throat, did an about-face, and marched to the door.

"You have not seen the last of me," she said in a tone that implied she was spitting on him, adding, "I will remember your actions today."

"As I will remember yours," he warned, making sure to lock the door after she left. He turned around to face his guest, feeling as if a huge weight that had been crushing his chest had been suddenly rolled off of him, allowing him to draw a proper breath once again.

Veronica was watching him, her arms crossed, her expression most decidedly jaded. "Who was that? Another girlfriend? Because I don't like being your excuse to dump someone. If you don't have the balls to tell her to her face—"

"That was a demon."

Veronica's eyes widened. "*That* was a demon? Like those guys who attacked you earlier?"

"Not quite. This one is a wrath demon. A particularly nasty one, as a matter of fact. She has little regard for anyone but herself, and thinks nothing of murdering to get what she wants. Are you saying you didn't know she was a demon?" He frowned, wondering if she was feigning ignorance, or if she truly was clueless.

"Of course I didn't know she's a demon! A murderous demon! It's not like she had it stamped on her forehead." Veronica gave him a look that clearly said he was the one lacking. "Why aren't you calling the police to have her arrested? Wait, are there demons everywhere? Should I get some…I don't know… demon-away? Holy water? Crucifixes?"

He sighed and, taking her arm, steered her past the various animal cages, homes, and crates, until he reached the couch. "Sit down. I think we'd better have a talk. Something isn't right."

"You can stop touching me, for one," she said, pulling her arm from his grip and rubbing it as if he'd hurt her. "I don't like it at all."

"You most certainly could have fooled me with the way your tongue was all over mine a few minutes ago," he said drily, and moved a large tuxedo cat that had settled into the spot where Veronica had been sitting earlier.

"I was not all over your tongue," she objected, sitting nonetheless. "I was shocked and stunned into…into…well, tongue flailing, I guess you could call it."

"And the fact that you dug your fingers into my shoulders and moaned?"

She lifted her chin and looked down her nose at him with obvious scorn, not an easy feat considering he was still standing. For some bizarre reason, he thoroughly enjoyed the haughty way she attempted to treat him. He'd always had a weakness for women who resisted being cowed. "I was trying to stop the horrible and repulsive assault upon my person, obviously."

He lifted an eyebrow, absently stroking the cat in his arms, who was purring loudly and making biscuits on his forearm.

"Fine," she said, almost spitting out the word. "It wasn't horrible or repulsive, but that doesn't mean you have the right to grab me and slap your lips all over mine."

"No, I do not have that right," he agreed, clearly taking her by surprise. "And I apologize for that. I do not normally kiss women unless they have given me an indication they are willing to receive such attentions."

"Apology accepted. Is it against the dragon hunter rules to ask why a demon was offering to help you?"

He felt himself give in to a sigh. "It isn't against any rules, although most dragon hunters prefer to work on their own. It is certainly my policy to do so."

"And yet you've got Sasha with you," she pointed out, her head tipped to the side.

A wry expression slipped past his control for a few seconds. "That is entirely a different matter, I assure you."

"Really? How so?"

"That you will have to hear from Sasha," he said, unwilling to reveal information about his charge until he knew more about the woman before him. Dragon hunters had been corrupted before, and probably would be again. "In answer to your original question, the demon Falafel said she was sent to aid me in finding someone."

"You too? I've got a similar mission from my sister." Veronica sighed.

He was unable to contain his curiosity any longer. "Why can't you recognize a demon when you see one?"

She shrugged one shoulder. "Am I supposed to? If so, that'll be one more thing to add to the list."

"What list?"

"The list of things I want you to teach me. You said you'd do anything I asked, right? Well, I want you to teach me how to be a dragon hunter. How to fight like you did. And evidently, how to recognize demons. Do you normally have demons in your apartment? And why do you have so many animals? Did you used to run a pet shop, or are you simply an animal hoarder in the making?"

"They're Sasha's. I have no time for animals," he said sternly.

"Uh-huh. What's that, then, a meat loaf?" Veronica nodded toward his chest.

Ian was startled to find that somehow, without being aware, he'd set down the cat and picked up a guinea

pig and was now stroking it to the point where it was
on its back, its four little feet waving in the air, making
moans of pure guinea pig bliss. Hurriedly, he set the
beast down and, just as swiftly, changed the subject.
"What do you mean you want to know how to fight?
How in the blazes of Abaddon have you lived if you
don't know how to use your *élan vital*?"

She pursed her lips, instantly drawing his attention
to her mouth, and lips that he now realized were like
ripe berries just waiting for him to taste their
sweetness...He shook away such ridiculous thoughts,
a bit astonished at them. He was not a fanciful man,
nor particularly romantic. Lips, he told himself firmly,
were just lips. There was nothing berry-like about
them.

"Does that really matter? Helen said I should ask a
dragon hunter if I needed help, and I do, so I'm asking
nicely for it. If you are one of the good guys, aren't you
obligated to help me?"

"No," he said simply, dragging his gaze from her
fascinating mouth.

"No, you're not one of the good guys, or no, you
aren't obligated to help?"

"Both. Neither. Possibly one of the two." Her eyes
were outstanding, true gray, but with flecks of silver
and black within. He shook his head again, wondering
what was wrong with him that he was allowing an attractive woman to so disorder his thoughts. "I will help
you because that was our bargain, but only so long as
you continue the pretense of a relationship."

She pulled back a little, suspicion evident in her body language. "This wouldn't be some weird-ass way to get me to kiss you, would it? Because I'm so not into that."

"You don't like to be touched, I know. I heard you the first time."

"No, it's not that." Her cheeks pinkened a little, a fact that secretly amazed and delighted him. How long had it been since he'd made a woman blush? She made an abrupt, undefined gesture. "I mean, as kisses go, that kiss was okay. You didn't make me want to barf or anything."

"We shall be grateful for small blessings," he said gravely, amused despite himself.

"It's just…normally I don't like to be touched unless I know someone well. That goes for kissing, too. In addition to that, it strikes me that this whole plan is an awfully convenient way for you to touch me and kiss me and pretend I'm your girlfriend without going to the actual trouble of, you know, maintaining a relationship."

He set the guinea pig down in its habitat, moved a second cat to the tall cat tree that lurked in the corner, avoided stepping on a gerbil that was rolling around in a plastic habitat ball, and decanted a bowl containing a fish from a chair in order to sit. "Are you saying you want a relationship with me?"

That would not be a good idea. Not good at all. He was the last person who should ever consider having a relationship with anyone, let alone someone who didn't know how to combat demonic forces. So why was he so intrigued with the thought of forming an attachment to her?

"No, of course not!" She looked vaguely scandalized.

"Why not?" Against his better judgment, his mouth formed sentences that he knew he was going to regret. "Do you not like men in that manner? Or is it something about me, personally, that repulses you?"

"I'm not repulsed by you at all," she said, her brows drawing together. "In fact, you're...well...kind of cute. Attractive, even."

"Then why wouldn't you consider a relationship with me?" He knew he should stop talking, but that strange quirky side of his nature refused to be quieted this once. "Are you asexual? I don't wish to make you uncomfortable if you are."

"I appreciate that, and no, I'm not asexual or uncomfortable. And I didn't say I wouldn't consider a relationship with you, it's just that I'm not looking for one—wait, does this mean this *is* some weird ploy to get me into bed? Because if it is—"

"Who mentioned sex?" he asked, caught up in the conversation despite the sane part of his mind demanding that he escort her out of the apartment.

"You did. Several times. To your other girlfriend. Not that I'm a real one, but still, even a pretend girlfriend knows when sex is mentioned." Humor danced in her eyes.

"Ah. You have me there." He cleared his throat and

wondered when the last time was he'd enjoyed chatting so much with a woman. "I feel obligated to stress that the wrath demon is not my girlfriend."

Veronica glanced around the room. Although he'd told Sasha numerous times to keep her things confined to her room, the living room was strewn with various pieces of feminine apparel, magazines, electronics, miscellaneous things that she was always picking up, and assorted unguents that did things beyond his range of experience. "What about your other girlfriend? The jailbait one?"

"Sasha is hardly that," he said, amused. "She's older than I am."

"You're kidding!" Veronica stared at him in disbelief. "She doesn't look more than eighteen, if that."

"And yet, she was born sometime in the reign of Charlemagne, if I am remembering correctly."

"Is she..." Veronica glanced around, and scooted a little closer to his chair, her voice dropping to a conspiratorial whisper. "Is she a demon, too?"

He considered the woman in front of him for a few seconds. What a puzzle she was. Enticing and yet not interested in him in a physical way. A dragon hunter, and yet apparently unskilled to the point of being a danger to herself and others. And quick-witted, yet unknowledgeable about the most basic things a dragon hunter must know. He was beginning to realize that what he first thought was an act was nothing more than genuine innocence.

She had no idea of the world around her, and that

thought frightened him greatly. "You truly don't know what the Court of Divine Blood is, do you?"

"Nope." She sat back, both hands around one knee. "But you're going to tell me, right? As part of my dragon superhero training?"

"I suppose. The Court is what the mortals think of as heaven, although it is not filled with fluffy clouds and angels playing harps. It usually takes the form of a city, and is filled with endless officials who—"

Veronica, glancing over his shoulder to the window, squawked, froze for a second, then suddenly lunged at him, throwing herself into his lap and grabbing his hair with both hands. Before he could ask her what she was doing, her lips were on his, pressing fleeting (and highly erotic) kisses along his mouth.

"She's there," she whispered in between kisses.

"Who's where?" he asked, his mind muddled by the sudden wave of lust that threatened to release his dragon fire. He cupped her hips, shifting her slightly so she was no longer crushing his penis, and reveled in the heat of her body pressed against him.

"That demon lady. She's at the window, on the fire escape. She looked annoyed to see me sitting by myself."

He slid her off his lap and rose. "I would like to pick you up. Do I have your permission to touch you?"

"Yes, and you know, you don't have to ask me like I'm some sort of germaphobe. I just don't like people I don't know touching me, but since I just threw myself into your lap and kissed the life out of you, I think we can assume I know you."

He scooped her up in his arms in as dramatic a gesture as he could manage, then picked his way through the animals to the bedroom. He was more than a little amused that she thought her fleeting kisses qualified as kissing the life out of him, but his voice was neutral as he said, "Falafel can't see into my bedroom, so if you don't object, I will take you in there and leave her with the impression we are carnally engaged."

"That's fine with me." She kicked her legs a little. "I've never been picked up like this before. I have to admit, it's kind of fun. Is it hard on your back? Do you have to lift weights in order to haul women around like this?"

"Do you always ask so many questions?" he asked, setting her down in the relative darkness of the bedroom.

"Yes. My therapist says that if you don't ask questions, you'll never find the truth. Do you ever answer the questions that people ask you?"

"Sometimes," he said, making sure the blinds were fully down.

She sat on the end of the bed. "I take it now is not one of those times?"

"I suspect it will be." He sat next to her. "But before we get into a question-and-answer scenario, why don't you tell me first about your experience being a dragon hunter. Adam Larson was well known to the dragon hunters, as was his daughter, but I had never heard him speak of you. I take it your father was also a dragon hunter? What was his name?"

"I don't think my dad's name is going to help you," she answered, giving him a quizzical look.

"No? Why not?"

"Because he wasn't any more woo-woo than my mom was. She's nuts, but she wasn't..." She waggled a hand around. "Superheroish. Far from it, if I'm honest. My dad dumped us when I was about two years old so he could be with one of his students. He was an English professor. A bad one, according to my mother, but she has her own set of issues, so I try not to believe too much she says. Although when she's going through a sober stint she can be unusually prescient. Wow. That was a lot of personal info you probably didn't want to know. Sorry."

Ian frowned, one part of his mind distracted by Veronica's nearness...and heat...and that vaguely floral scent that reminded him of carnations nodding lazily in a warm summer afternoon. "That makes no sense. You're saying neither of your parents was a dragon hunter?"

"That's right." She leaned back and gave him a pleasant smile, one he felt as a warm glow deep in his belly.

He shook his head at both what she'd said and the belly-glow. "That is impossible. You can't suddenly just become a dragon hunter. I believe full-blooded dragons can be created such by having a demon cursed to them, but that is very rare, and you are not a dragon.

"Wait, what?" she interrupted, looking horrified. "You mean to say you're a demon, too?"

"Yes, but the dragon in us allows us to control it." He gave a little shrug. "All dragon hunters have a dark side. Surely you must feel it trying to use you?"

"No!" Her horror turned to speculation. "I wonder...you know, the animal in my head has been unusually quiet."

"The *what*?" It was his turn to look surprised.

"That's what I call my anxiety disorder." She bit her lower lip and looked thoughtful. "If there's a dragon and a demon in me, and the dragon is controlling the demon, maybe that's helping to control the anxiety beast, too. Still, I don't like the idea of being part of a demon. Can you take it out?"

"I don't believe so, no."

"Rats." She looked down at herself, just as if she were expecting to see a manifestation of evil. "What does the demon bit feel like?"

"Darkness," he said succinctly. "An absence of soul. An emptiness wanting to compel you."

"I don't feel that. In fact, I don't feel anything demony inside me. I feel a bit...more...but I figured that was the superhero dragon part. I don't feel empty or soulless. Maybe the demon part didn't come with the dragon part for me?"

He shook his head, more confused than ever. "It doesn't work like that. By our very nature, we are both dragon and demon. There is no other way."

"There is if your sister gets mouthy on your arm," she said, pulling up the sleeve of her shirt. "You can't see anything now, but you'll have to take my word that last night, this was super gory. Helen bit me. She said I had to take over for her helping a woman who was on the run from an abusive boyfriend or something, and I said I'd do it…"

Ian felt like he'd been struck by a grand piano. He had never heard of a dragon hunter creating another hunter in such a manner. Adam Larson had not mentioned such a thing as being possible, but he was so deep in his research on eliminating the demon influence that perhaps he simply overlooked it. Still, if demon hunters could be made without invoking a demon lord… he considered whether that fact could help him in any way.

He didn't see how it could. Every demon knew there were only three ways to escape bondage to a demon lord: death, release by the demon lord (which had never happened in the knowledge of those who resided in Abaddon), and convincing a pure soul to take his place.

Ian made a face at the last thought. He was all too familiar with it.

Perhaps he could kill Anzo… He dismissed the thought the instant it crossed his mind. It would take a lot more than just him to destroy her, and all her minions would die with her.

"… said I'd find her, but do you have any idea how difficult it is to find an abused woman who's in hiding? It's not like you can call up the nearest women's shelter and ask if there is anyone there who fits the description. I don't even know where to start, although my friend has an idea— Are you okay? You look like you're having a painful gas bubble or something."

"Sorry?" With a start, Ian realized that Veronica had been telling him about her sister while he was mulling over the idea of making a dragon hunter to take over his burden. "No gas bubbles, painful or otherwise. When your sister bit you, how long did it take you to change?"

Her nose scrunched up in an adorable manner. Once again, the nearness of her walloped him like a sledgehammer. One wrapped in lust and desire. "Maybe five minutes? It hurt like hell, and I barfed up my dinner, but after that, it seemed to be okay. Except I keep getting hot flashes, you know? One moment I'm perfectly normal, and the next I feel like I'm burning up from the inside."

If he could find a suitable mortal, find a pure soul to take his burden... but he couldn't do that. A mortal being had no power against a demon lord. But an esprit did. They were goodness personified, pure and unable to be tainted through use. If he could convince an esprit... Once again, he dismissed the line of thought. He might be desperate to be out of Anzo's control, but he had not yet sunk so low as to demand someone else save him.

He pushed away the grimness of his future, and addressed himself to the promise he'd made to Veronica. "Very well, since you did as I asked with regards to the wrath demon, we shall have a lesson in what it is to be a dragon hunter."

"I should get two lessons for today," Veronica said with raised eyebrows. "After all, I pretended to be your girlfriend twice."

He was amused, but kept his lips steady. "Two lessons, then, although we only have time for one. The first rule is that you must at all times carry your *élan vital*. I see you do not have yours now, which tells me your sister must not have informed you how important it is."

"Oh, she told me. It's my soul sword." Veronica made an awkward gesture. "I just don't...you know...it's a sword. It's not easy carrying that around."

"Mortals cannot see it," he explained.

"I know, I know. Helen said as much. But even so, it's kind of hard to get used to having it always hanging off you. It gets in the way."

"It can save your life where nothing else can. Besides, the esprit inside it gives you strength even if you aren't using the sword itself."

"Es-PREE?"

He spelled the word for her, noting, "That is the French pronunciation."

"Wait, the sword has not only a bit of my soul stuck to it, but there's also a ghost in it?" She looked like she wanted to panic, but wasn't quite ready to commit to that path.

He pulled out his *élan vital*. The runes on it glittered with a soft silver light in the dim room. "All *élan vital* have esprits who willingly bind themselves to the weapon. Without them, it would be simply a sword."

"So what's an esprit when it's at home?" she asked, reaching out to trace a finger the length of an intricate protection rune.

Ian fought to keep from snatching the sword out of her reach. "Esprits are beings of purity and light. They devote themselves to helping those who need it—and a handful of them give themselves to dragon hunters. In general, though, esprits are few in number and are highly sought by those who would use them up without a second thought."

"What use are they other than living in your sword?"

Ian gave a little shrug. "They are conduits of change. For a dragon hunter, they give us the strength to destroy demons, changing that dark power into light. For others, they convert mortal energies into those of other realms."

"That is way too metaphysical for me," Veronica said, trailing her fingers down another rune.

"I'm not too well versed in everything they do," he admitted. "I tend to focus on the dragon hunter side of their abilities. And as a note of etiquette, never do that."

"I wouldn't destroy anything, let alone pure light spirits," she protested, her fingers drawing over the sight rune that gave him clarity of mind.

"I was referring to touching another hunter's *élan vital*. It's considered an extension of the hunter, and is quite rude to touch it unless invited."

"Oh!" She snatched her hand back. "I'm so sorry. I didn't know."

"That's why I told you." After a moment's thought, he laid the sword across her thighs. "Since you are new to this, and since the esprit doesn't seem to mind, you may examine it."

"That sounds almost risqué," she said with a rusty little chuckle that delighted him. She turned the sword over, examining the runes and scrollwork etched into the blade itself. "Don't most men think of swords as being an extension of their penises?"

"I am not most men."

"No, you're not," she said, her gaze meeting his. A little spark lit in her eyes, making her blush and drop her gaze.

An uncomfortably charged silence fell between them for the count of three, which Veronica broke by clearing her throat.

"Your sword is very pretty. I like it," she said, handing the *élan vital* back to him, then evidently realized that comment could easily be misconstrued given their discussion. "Your real one, that is, not your...er..." Her gaze dropped to his crotch, which, of course, immediately reacted just as if she'd stroked him.

He heaved a mental sigh at his body's insistence on being attracted to her. There were times when his libido was a pain in the arse. So to speak. "Yes, I understood you were referring to the actual sword."

"Not that your dick isn't nice. I'm sure it is," she said hurriedly. "Not sure as in I've seen it, but the rest of you is quite nice, so I can't imagine that...uh...it would be anything but...oh, lordisa, I've really just lost control of this conversation. Mr. Manny is going to be bleeding all over this."

"Who or what is Mr. Manny, and why would he bleed on you?" Ian asked, welcoming the distraction from the conversation. He really needed to get a grip on his emotions. And needs. And desires, of which there were suddenly a whole list's worth that concerned Veronica.

"He's my writing instructor. Bleeding refers to using a red pen to edit. Mr. Manny is very big on conversations not wandering away when they should be making a point."

He stared at her in disbelief for a few seconds. "Are you planning on writing our conversations down in the novel you're writing?"

"Sure. Why wouldn't I? They're just made for a book, don't you think?"

"I don't think anything of the sort."

She gave his leg a little slap. "That's because you don't think like a writer. This whole thing with dragon hunters is perfect for me. There are bad guys, and dragon superheroes, and invisible swords, and daring missions, which I have no idea how to complete, and all sorts of really juicy bits that Mr. Manny will positively slobber over."

He was shaking his head even before she finished speaking. "You can't do that."

"Why not?"

The sound of the doorknob clicking just as the door opened killed the answer. Simultaneously, they grabbed each other, both sharing the obvious concern that the wrath demon had returned, which resulted in clunking their heads together painfully, which Ian ignored in order to flip Veronica on her back, his body covering hers while he kissed her cheeks and neck.

She gave very convincing moans of pleasure, her hands busy sliding underneath his shirt in order to stroke his back. The feel of her fingernails gently tracing patterns on his back triggered the dragon within him, his fire roaring to life, and the simple sexual interest from before now a raging need to possess. He knew it was madness to touch her, to kiss her silky flesh, but it would have taken a stronger man than he to resist the lure of her mouth when she turned her head to chase his lips. And when her tongue twined around his in an erotic dance, the molten fire that never seemed to die within him rose to the fore.

"—didn't want to watch it when it was halfway through, because you really need to see the start in order to see where the movie is going, so I decided to come home— Oh."

Dimly, Ian's mind registered the fact that someone was speaking, but for a moment, the bulk of his awareness was focused on Veronica. She was fire and desire; she was a temptress leading him joyously astray. Her body moved beneath his in a way that was meant to entice, not protest, and her hands and soft little moans urged him on when he knew he should stop.

Her tongue just about drove him mad. He was just considering how fast he could get them both out of their clothing when the bed dipped next to him, and he looked up in confusion.

"Who do you have under there— Oh, hi, Ronnie!" Sasha sat cross-legged, a cat in one hand and a guinea pig in the other. "Sorry to interrupt, but since you both still have your clothes on, I figured it was okay. Does this piggy look pregnant to you? I think she might be."

Memory of the wrath demon returned to him, and he rolled off of Veronica, one hand on his *élan vital* as he quickly scanned the room.

There was no one there but the three of them.

"Well, this is just plain awkward," Veronica said, sitting up while pulling her shirt down from where it had ridden up. "Um. Hello, Sasha. Don't you knock when you come into Ian's room?"

"Why should I?" the girl asked, tipping her head to the side.

"Because he's a grown man, and you're just a... well, you *look* like you're just a girl."

"Look like? Someone's been telling tales about my age, I see," Sasha said, casting an amused glance at Ian. He ignored it, mentally lecturing himself about what had just happened.

"He wasn't gossiping," Veronica reassured her. "I thought you were his girlfriend, and he said you weren't, and... well... that's all."

"Aw, that's sweet," Sasha said, patting Veronica's arm. "You checked before you jumped his bone."

"Bones," Ian said with yet another mental sigh. "The term is 'jumped his bones.' Bone, singular, has a quite

specific meaning, whereas the former is more general-
ized."

"Ah, sex, you mean? But Ian doesn't have sex."
Sasha eyed Veronica. "Well, he hasn't, not since I've
been with him. I assume that's going to change? It is,
isn't it? I can see by the way both of your eyes are all
flamey that it is. Okay, I'll knock from here on out. Did
you guys want to have sex now? Or can I tell you about
the two demons I saw on the way back from the movie
theater?"

"Unless there is something special about them that
I need to know, don't bother," Ian said, moving away
from the bed and the temptation that Veronica posed.
Really, what had he been doing, giving in to those
demands when anyone could have walked into his bedroom? There was no faster way to die than to forget
basic precautions. "The wrath demon and Anzo both
made it clear there are others in the area."

"We aren't having sex, so you don't have to leave on
my account," Veronica said. "I'm just pretending to be
Ian's girlfriend in exchange for him teaching me. So,
was that the end of the lesson, or is there more?"

"Oooh, are we having sex lessons?" Sasha dumped
the cat and guinea pig on the bed and pulled out of
a pocket a small notebook and pen. "Mind if I take
notes? I haven't seen mortal sex, and I want to make
sure I do it right when the time comes for me to jump
bones."

"We weren't having those sorts of lessons. Ian's
teaching me how to be a dragon hunter," Veronica told

her, adding, with obvious pride, "He let me touch his sword."

Ian sighed for what surely had to be the fifteenth time that day. He had many regrets in his life, but he was starting to feel that agreeing to Veronica's terms was going to be the biggest of them all.

WHO'LL STOP THE RAIN. WAIT, THAT'S A SONG TITLE. CAN I USE SONG TITLES FOR CHAPTER HEADERS? ASK MR. MANNY HOW HE FEELS ABOUT THAT.

I HURRIED UPSTAIRS FROM IAN'S APARTMENT, MY MIND full of things I was to remember from our impromptu lesson. "Keep your shoulders down and elbows fluid. Don't be afraid to wait for a good opportunity. Haste makes waste...wait, that's what Grandma used to say." I paused outside my door and made a few parrying motions that Ian had shown me. "If I can't kill the demon outright, at least disable him so he has to return to Hell to regenerate a new body. Except the name of Hell isn't hell, but I can't remember now what it is. Whew. I just don't know if I can actually attack someone with a sword—"

I unlocked my door as I was speaking and stepped into my apartment, flipping on the light, and automatically tossed my keys to a ceramic bowl shaped like a goldfish, then froze, horror creeping along my skin.

My apartment, my beloved, bright, cheerful apartment, looked like a bag of Skittles had thrown up all over it. The kitchen table was overturned and broken, chairs were smashed and flung willy-nilly around the room. My couch, a lovely tangerine beast with lime cushions, bore long slash marks from back to seat, bits of cushion torn from its innards and strewn about. Across the horror of my tiny living room, I could see my set of Fiestaware dishes smashed on the kitchen floor, bright blobs of red and yellow and turquoise lying forlornly among the debris from overturned trash bin.

Slowly my head turned, and I looked toward the bedroom, my feet automatically shuffling forward, my mind refusing to believe what my eyes communicated. I stopped at the door of my bedroom, feeling as if I'd been punched in the gut. My bedroom, my haven against all ills, was utterly destroyed, shreds of clothing and bedding everywhere. It was as if a tornado filled with claws had ripped through, tearing apart everything in its path.

The panicked, anxious animal in my head started shrieking, and for once, I gave in to its demands and squatted down on my heels, my arms wrapped around me, rocking silently back and forth while I tried to make sense of the invasion.

Who had done this? Why had it happened? I shuddered at the idea of someone, a stranger, in my nice, safe apartment, touching my things. The destruction I could live with, but the invasion of my privacy...I started shaking, feeling myself on the verge of hysteria.

Flee! the anxious animal inside of me screamed, *Get out of the tainted place! Go to somewhere safe and clean!*

Where? I asked the animal, still rocking on my heels while I frantically tried to think of somewhere to go. A hotel? I shuddered hard at that thought. So many people crammed into small spaces. No, that wasn't an option. Teresita? That thought lasted for a moment, hope gilding it into an attractive option, but almost immediately I had to discard it. She wouldn't have room for me, not with her kids and husband. And there was the fact that my presence might put her in danger, although how, I wasn't exactly sure. But then, I didn't understand why someone had trashed my home. That left my mother, but down that path was madness. Even if she was out of prison, I would never be able to stay with her and retain any amount of sanity.

The image rose in my mind of a man with a nice chin, nicer chest, and lips that could make my head swim with the slightest touch. *Ian*, the frightened animal said with a hopeful whimper. *Go to Ian. He will protect us.*

I stopped rocking on my heels and slowly stood up, my skin crawling with the horror of my violated apartment, but something within me balking at the phrase "he will protect us." I didn't need protecting. I was a dragon hunter, dammit. I was supposed to be the one protecting innocent people. "And I will not be a victim again! I can cope with this. It is not unclean, or tainted, or filthy because some horrible person or persons were here. It's just a mess, and I should call the police."

The bravery of my words helped push out some of the horror, and I pulled out my cell phone only to remember that it had died a few hours before. I scanned the debris of my apartment, hoping the charger I kept in the kitchen would be sitting on the counter, but the counters were covered in trash from the bin. I took a step forward, intending on pushing the garbage to the floor in order to get the charger, but my hand froze in midair, my animal screaming nonstop in my brain.

I swallowed hard, spun around on my heel, and found myself knocking on Ian's door even before I realized I'd left my apartment.

"Hi," Sasha said, opening the door to me. "I figured you couldn't stay away from Ian. You guys were practically setting fire to each other with your eyes. Ian! Your pretend girlfriend is here. You might want to give him a minute—I think he went to take a cold shower after you left."

I shivered, fighting my brain and emotions to remain in control. Before I could say anything, though, Ian strolled out of the bedroom, a frown pulling down his brows. Part of my mind was disappointed to note he was fully clothed, but the other half was too busy being relieved to chastise me for hopes of catching him in nothing but a towel. "I thought we arranged to meet tomorrow for the second lesson— What's wrong?"

I shivered again when he hurried over to me, his hands reassuring on my arms. With a little half sob that I was heartily ashamed of, I said, "Can I use your phone? Mine is dead and the charger...I can't get to the charger."

Sasha's eyes widened as Ian led me into the room, pulling out his cell phone as he did so. "Why can't you get to the charger?" he asked.

I took the phone. It was warm from the contact with his body, and for a moment I felt suffused with heat. I wanted to burn in the fire that was Ian, wanted him to heat every square inch of me. "Someone trashed my apartment. I...I can't...Someone touched everything! Had their hands all over my things. My plates and my clothes and the little ceramic horses, and everything I own."

"You were searched?" Sasha whistled. "Can I see?"

"I guess so," I said, rubbing my arms, still fighting tears. "It's a horrible sight, though."

Without another word, she bolted through the door, the sound of her footsteps pounding up the stairs drifting down to us.

Ian was watching me closely, one hand still on my upper arm. I wanted desperately to throw myself against his chest, to bury my face into him, to hide away from my fears and anxieties and the world itself, but I hadn't survived two decades of therapy to give in to such craven desires.

"I'm strong," I told him. "I can do this."

"Yes, you can," he agreed, and released my arm. "Were you robbed?"

"I don't know. Everything was—" I pushed down revulsion, having acknowledged it, as my therapist advised before taking the power from the emotion. "Everything was destroyed. Broken. Torn up."

He frowned. "That doesn't sound like a normal break-in. Did you have valuables in your apartment?"

"No, nothing. Just a few pieces of my grandmother's jewelry, and those aren't particularly expensive. My laptop is old, and my TV is nothing special."

He glanced at my waist. "Where is your *élan vital*?"

Panic flared again. "It's in my bedroom. Holy squeegee, do you think—"

He ran past me before I could finish. I hesitated a moment, the memory of the invasion into my perfect little haven still strong in my mind, but I reminded myself that I was better than my fears, and resolutely marched up the stairs to the open door of my apartment.

"Wow. It's like someone deliberately broke everything they could find," Sasha said, coming out of the kitchen. She stepped carefully around the bits and pieces, the fingers of one hand doing an intricate dance in the air. I wondered if it was some sort of physical tic, or if she was even aware she was doing it.

"It makes me wonder who could be so angry at me." I looked around and rubbed my arms again.

"Angry with you?" She tipped her head and pursed her lips. Ian emerged from the bedroom, his frown even blacker. "Oh, no, this isn't because someone is angry with you."

"The wanton invasion into, and destruction of, my home doesn't say someone is angry at me?" I asked, goose bumps rippling up my arms when I looked around at the broken remnants of my existence. "Then what does it mean?"

"At best, it's a warning," Ian said, his voice as grim as his eyes. He took his phone from my hand, quickly typing out a message. "Your *élan vital* is gone."

"Oh, no. Helen's sword—that can't be good." I chewed my lower lip and looked around the mess again, hoping to find some sign of it. "Why would someone take it? You said earlier in the lesson that each sword is unique to the dragon hunter, and that only that person can use it."

"A sword can be bequeathed to another, as mine was. And as yours was. But other than that, no, it can't be used by anyone else."

"So then why would someone take mine if it's of no earthly use to them?"

"It's of use if they can stop you from wielding it," Ian said, striding past me to the door. He reached out and hooked his hand around my arm without even slowing down. "There's also the matter of the esprit contained within it. If someone wished to steal that, they might take the entire sword."

"Hey!" I said, forgetting to be freaked out by the invasion of my apartment. "What do you think you're doing? I told you I don't like to be manhandled."

"No, you said you don't like to be touched by people you don't know well, and since your tongue was in my mouth doing things that are possibly illegal in at least three states, I believe I qualify as someone you know. I assumed you didn't wish to stay here tonight."

I shivered for the umpteenth time in the last hour. "No. Dear goddess, no. I can't touch...I mean, I can, but just the thought...I'm going to have to work up to it."

"Don't worry," Sasha called from the middle of my living room. She stood ankle-deep in debris. "I'll help clean up. You go on down with Ian and have some dinner and sex. You'll feel better afterwards, and by the time you are done, I'll have things in a better shape here."

"Are you sure?" I hesitated, part of me uncomfortable to know she would be there alone, in an area that in my mind was now tainted with the scent of danger, and the other guilty because I should be doing the cleaning, not her. Oddly, the idea of her touching my things didn't bother me at all. It must be because the violation I'd already suffered was so much greater.

"Am I sure that you'll feel better after sex, or sure I will clean up here?"

"We are not having sex," I told her, sliding Ian a quick glance before adding, "I just need a little time to steel myself to get in here and deal with it."

She waved a hand. "It's fine. I have mad skills."

"With what?" I asked over my shoulder when Ian tugged me to the stairs. "What a very strange girl she is."

"She comes from a strange place," Ian said while we

made our way down the stairs to his apartment. "Although she's not a girl. I rather doubt if she's really female."

"Is she transgendered or gender-neutral? If she'd prefer I use a different pronoun—is it ze or zhe that's right to use for gender-neutral people?—just let me know, and I'll be happy to oblige. Sasha is very sweet, no matter what her...his...gender is, and I wouldn't like to hurt her feelings."

Ian gave me an odd look. "I don't think she requires gender-neutral pronouns, although you could ask her."

I glanced around the hall when Ian pulled out his keys to unlock the door, and whispered, "You never did tell me what she was. Like...she's from a magical place, right?"

"She's from the Court of Divine Blood."

"The fake heaven?"

"There's nothing fake about it. In fact, it's older than the mortals' version of heaven."

"So she's a not-angel?" I wrinkled my nose, trying to fit that image to Sasha.

"There are no such things in the Court, just officials. Sasha is not one of them, however."

"What is she, then?"

"She's been acting as an apprentice," he said, opening the door and gesturing me in.

"Yes, I know she's your apprentice—"

"Not really. We just say that because it's easier. She was apprenticed to someone else."

I hesitated when he moved past me into the kitchen,

wanting to know more about Ian and Sasha, but not wishing to appear rude. "Is it a secret who that person is?" I asked, moving a big marmalade-colored cat from a kitchen chair before sitting down. "I don't want to be nosy, but if she's not your apprentice, what's she doing living with you? She might not be underage, but she sure looks it, and people are going to talk if they see you guys living together openly."

"It won't matter if you present yourself as the subject of my affections," he said, rubbing his chin. "Which would you like first? Me helping you clean up your apartment, or dinner?"

I blinked with astonishment, a warm, fuzzy feeling growing in the pit of my stomach. "You'd really help me clean it up?"

"Of course."

"But…why?"

He cocked an eyebrow. "You are a dragon hunter. You are upset. You are my pretend girlfriend. Pick any of the three."

I couldn't help but smile, the warmth of his gesture making me a bit light-headed. "Actually, since Sasha is upstairs now and I'm starving, I'd really rather have dinner. But I don't want to put you to any trouble."

"It's no trouble," he said, pulling various items out of the refrigerator.

"Can I borrow your phone again? I need to call the police."

"The mortal police?" He pulled out a chopping board. "There's no need."

"There sure as hell is. My whole place was trashed— What do you mean *mortal* police? Is there an immortal police?"

"They're called the Watch, and yes, people like us have our own police force."

I thought about that for a moment. "Okay, that's kind of cool. Are they, you know, psychics and stuff who can tell if you are a criminal just by looking at you?"

"No. They are simply a police force who are used to working with the Otherworld."

"Great. I'll call them."

"I've already texted the local branch. They should be here before midnight." He pulled out a knife, clearly about to start chopping up vegetables.

"Um…" I bit my lip, not wanting to sound like a lunatic, but knowing myself well enough to say something. "Would you mind if I asked you to wash your hands before you did that? And I assume you washed the veggies already? Because you have no idea how many germs those things can get in stores. People touching them, and sneezing on them, and ugh, so many other things. I once saw a woman rubbing tomatoes on her breasts before putting them back."

He stared at me for a moment. "You are aware that as a dragon hunter, you are now more or less immortal, yes? You can't die from common mortal germs or diseases."

"It's not about dying; it's about putting unclean things in your mouth." I gave a little shudder. "I know you think

I'm crazy, but honestly, the idea that I'd eat someone else's cooking is a huge step for me. I don't even eat at Teresita's place, even though I know it hurts her feelings. But she has kids, and you just never know where they've been, or what they've touched, and even if they *say* they've washed their hands, they just don't have the concept of cleanliness down pat, you know?"

He paused while in the act of washing his hands. "The same could be said of me. You don't know where I've been, yet you kissed me easily enough."

"That's because I assume you haven't been using your mouth to do things like touch doorknobs."

He said nothing more, just washed the veggies and began to chop up red and green peppers.

"Thank you." Mollified, I sat down on a wooden kitchen chair.

"How long have you been this way?" he asked, waving a knife at me.

"It started coming on during high school. My therapist said it was a coping mechanism because my mother is an alcoholic, and verbally and emotionally abusive. Are those mushrooms?"

"Yes. Do you have any allergies or specifications as to types of food you won't eat?" he asked after washing the mushrooms.

"I'm allergic to shellfish, and I loathe many vegetables. Unhealthy, I know, but true."

"Ah." He looked down at the food he'd chopped. "I was making a stir-fry, but if you'd prefer not—"

"No, that's fine." I settled back in the chair, jumping

a little when the fat marmalade cat leaped onto my lap and settled in with a deep purr. "I can always eat around anything I don't like. Are you actually going to cook?"

"Yes, and I assure you that the kitchen is clean. I don't allow the animals in here."

I looked down at the cat.

"Ringo!" he ordered, and pointed to the other room.

The cat gave a hurt look, but leaped down and wandered out of the kitchen.

"That's some pretty impressive cat-handling skills you have there," I commented. "Just the fact that your animals aren't eating each other is amazing, but I've never seen a cat listen to a command."

He gave a one-shouldered shrug. "That's Sasha's influence. She explained to them that they had to live in peace, and they do."

"Wow. Girl has some mad skills. You don't have to do that just for me. Although thank you for thinking of it." I was relieved by his precautions despite the knowledge that eating somewhere other than my own home wasn't dangerous. "What I meant by my cooking comment was...well, isn't that a little...I mean, you're a dragon hunter."

His eyebrows rose as he chopped peppers, onions, and finally, chicken breast. "Yes, I am. I also eat, and that means I must prepare food."

I was torn between the desire to talk to him about nothing in particular, just to enjoy hearing him talk (and finding out interesting things about him, like the fact that he cooked), and the need to utilize the time to the best of my ability. I had so many questions...

Helen's voice echoed in my memory, telling me to call the numbers on her phone for help. "If I asked you to help me, would you?" I asked.

"I thought I already have. Cleaning up your apartment aside, you'd be dead if I hadn't intervened with the demons at that mall."

I waved that away, more than a little embarrassed by the fact that I'd been so inept at that fight. "I meant if I asked you now to help me with a problem I have finding someone."

He froze for a few seconds, turning slowly to look at me. "Who are you searching for?"

"I told you—a woman who is leaving an abusive boyfriend. Or husband. Helen never said which. Anyway, Helen asked if I'd help her out, but didn't give me her name or contact info."

He turned back to the stove. "I doubt if I can be much help in that situation. Unless the woman was a member of the Otherworld, I have no abilities that would help find her. You'd do better to engage a private detective."

"Otherworld being...?"

"The non-mortal beings."

"Oh, man. We can't use that word around Teresita. She'll have Member of the Otherworld t-shirts made up for us so fast, your head will spin. You never did tell me what you're doing here."

"Making dinner."

"In Oregon. In this town, specifically. I assume it has something to do with that Falafel demon person."

"Not really, although she was sent to assist me in locating a valuable person."

Idly, I fished a bit of carrot out of a bowl. "Maybe we can help each other."

He cocked an eyebrow at me, and I acknowledged that although I'd told myself that our arrangement was strictly so I would get the lessons I badly needed, I wouldn't be at all sorry if that demon lady showed up again, necessitating me to enjoy Ian's attentions.

The man certainly knew how to kiss. The memory of his mouth on mine, not to mention the strength of his warm body beneath my hands, was enough to make me feel flushed and uncomfortable. I shifted in my chair, my clothes suddenly very constrictive and irritating, and distracted myself with the first thing that came to my mind. "You must have known Helen was dead if you were picking up her sword."

He paused stirring the food for the count of seven. "I knew."

"How?" I asked, suddenly feeling like a wet, clammy hand gripped my stomach.

He didn't answer. Suspicion and fear grew within me. I wanted to both vomit and shake him, demanding he answer my questions. "Whoever killed Helen wasn't a normal person. A mortal, as you insist on calling us. But you're not normal. Did you kill my sister?"

Slowly, he stirred the vegetables, then turned off the heat. "I am a dragon hunter."

"And that means what in this instance?" I don't know why I pursued the conversation as hard as I did—I was dreading every single word.

"Dragon hunters do not kill other dragon hunters." He looked up, his eyes flamey around the edges of the irises. "Not unless they are under a compulsion of someone like a demon lord, in which case they would be unable to resist."

"That wrath Falafel woman. She was a demon, and she said 'the master' sent her to help you. Are you under the compulsion of a demon lord, Ian?"

He turned away to get a couple of bowls. "I am bound to Anzo, yes."

My heart seemed to turn to lead in my chest, and I had an almost overwhelming urge to cry, to scream, to run away and hide in bed with all the blankets pulled over my head. "Did you kill my sister?"

"If I said I did not, would you believe me?" he asked, suddenly turning to me. His eyes looked different somehow, as if something about them had changed. It took me a few seconds to realize it was the pupils. They had elongated a little, making me think of cat's eyes.

Weren't cats supposed to be sly? Mysterious? *Heartless predators?*

I shook my head, then nodded, then shook my head again. "Hell, I don't know what to believe. You just admitted that you were in the perfect circumstance to kill her, and you're not denying it, but you don't seem like the murdering sort of man. And I kissed you. Could

I kiss a murderer and not know it? I'd like to think I couldn't, but if you *were* a murderer, wouldn't that mean you were good at deceiving people? In which case, why did you do it, Ian? What had Helen done to you? How could you kill an innocent woman who hadn't done anything to you?" Tears were rolling down my cheeks, and angrily, I searched my pockets for tissues, but there were none. I snatched up a bit of paper towel and blew my nose without regard to how obnoxious a gesture that was.

"There's much to be said about someone who could start off thinking I was innocent, and end up with me slaughtering innocents." He took a deep breath and set down the bowls of food on the table before me. "I can't prove a negative, Veronica. I can only tell you that I was not present when your sister was killed."

"Of course you weren't—she died in my arms. I told you that. Only I was there," I said, blowing my nose a second time, getting up to dispose of the paper towels and wash my hands. Ian couldn't be a murderer, the sane part of my mind argued. I would know if he was. Somehow, I would know. Surprisingly, the anxious mental beast didn't have anything to say other than wishing I'd pulled out a fresh bottle of hand sanitizer before I'd left my apartment that morning. I took that as a sign I was right—my anxieties were always the first to suspect the worst in people.

Or was I just trying to fool myself?

"I wasn't present when she was attacked." Ian raised his hands in a gesture of innocence that I wanted all too much to believe. "You can believe me, or not, but it is the truth that I was not there."

I eyed him, a new (and almost as distressing) thought coming to mind. "But you know who did it?"

He said nothing for a few seconds, then repeated, "I wasn't there. I didn't witness the attack."

"But you know who did," I repeated, certainty filling me. Horribly, relief mingled in with the certainty, relief that I hadn't made out with my sister's murderer, and also relief that I hadn't found attractive a man who could kill. At least, kill things that weren't demons. "Who did it? Your demon lord?"

"She can't leave Abaddon," he said with a shake of his head, and served up a bowl of rice.

"Falafel?"

"I doubt she was in the mortal world yesterday."

"Then who...Sasha! It was Sasha, wasn't it? Oh, what am I saying?" I sat down again and rubbed my forehead in a desperate attempt to massage some sense into the chaos within. "Sasha wouldn't kill anyone. She's like a living, breathing anime girl, surrounded by animals and sweetness and quirkiness. What am I going to do, Ian?"

"About what?" he asked, holding up a wineglass.

I shook my head, then made a face, nodded, and accepted the glass he poured for me. "About my sister being killed by someone. I assume a demon, since who else could punch a hole through a person? About finding the poor woman on the run from a bad boyfriend. About learning how to be a dragon hunter when I'm just a neurotic mess most of the time."

"I can't help you with anything but the last." He sat down and pushed the rice over to me.

"I know, I know, you have your own jobs."

He made an odd sort of one-shouldered shrug and quirked his lips. "One less now."

"Oh?" I gave him a moment to explain, but when he didn't, I helped myself to some food. "You could tell me about Helen. That might help."

"Tell you what?"

"Whatever you like. How you met her. Whether you were friends. How long you knew her. Who killed her."

"I've never met her," he said with an even tone, but I sensed an undernote of emotion, powerful and yet wary. A glance at his eyes confirmed my impression—for a few seconds, they were flamey again. Idly, I wondered how he did that, and if it hurt.

"You can't tell me anything about her?" I asked, trying to sort through a welter of confusing thoughts. I was exhausted and knew my thinking wasn't the best, but I had an almost desperate need to understand what had happened to a sister I barely knew. The fact that Ian hadn't once denied knowing who killed Helen hadn't escaped my notice, yet I couldn't help circling around the question of who he was protecting if not Sasha. But that was silly—she was no more a murderer than I was. And yet, it seemed very much like he was protecting someone...

"Helen Larson was a dragon hunter. She was well respected. Beyond that..." He chewed on a mouthful of stir-fry and rice. "I'm sorry. I only heard about her from her father."

"You knew Adam?" Suspicion nudged my brain again.

"Yes." He kept his eyes down, focused on the food before him.

"Did you know him well? That is, were you friends, or just...you know...working acquaintances?"

His lips tightened, which had to make it hard to eat. "I knew him well enough. Why all the questions?" He looked up then, his eyes narrowed. "I understand interest in your sister's life, but why do you care about Adam Larson? What do you know about him?"

"Other than the fact that he had the patience to deal with my mom, who was crazy at the best of times and drunk the rest, not much. He was a biochemist who traveled a lot while he was married to my mom, so we only saw him every few months, and then for just a couple of weeks at a time. Mom said he worked for an international rescue organization, and that's why he had to travel a lot—to help the needy." I gave a little laugh. "It makes sense now that if he was out dragoning with demon battles and whatever else you guys do—*we* do—then I suppose it was more or less the truth."

His eyes lit up again, and this time I couldn't stop my mouth from asking, "Does that hurt when you do that?"

He blinked a couple of times. "Do what?"

"Get flamey around the edges of your eyes." I gestured toward my eyes. "Around the colored part, the irises. It's like you have a ring of fire around them sometimes; then it fades to nothing. Also, your pupils get a bit... longish."

He lifted his eyebrows for a moment like he couldn't believe I asked the question, then gave a little shake of his head. "I keep forgetting you are new to this. Dragon hunters manifest fire differently from normal dragons. They have control over fire, but because our blood is tainted with that of demons, we can't use it as they do. It shows itself in our eyes in times of anger or pain, or other strong emotions."

"Why are you strong emotion eyeball-firing over mentions of my stepfather?" I asked, wondering if I really wanted to know the answer.

"If you are done eating, you may want to go up and check on Sasha," he answered, rising and taking the dishes to the sink. "She can sometimes get a bit enthusiastic with her... mad skills. I'll be up shortly to help you."

"Oh, you are so trying to avoid answering the question. Why, Ian? Are you hiding something from me about my stepdad? You didn't kill him, too?"

He gave a harsh bark of laughter. "Just the opposite, actually. No, do not ask any more questions. I've answered as many as I'm going to tonight. Go upstairs and wait for the Watch, if you like."

I decided he *had* answered a lot of my questions, and made me dinner to boot, so I wouldn't press him anymore that night. "But don't think I'm going to be so accommodating tomorrow morning. I want to know what you know about Hel—" I had opened the door while I was speaking, and came face-to-face with a man who had slicked-back blond hair and a mustache that made me think of seventies porn stars.

"Gah!" the man yelled, and before I could blink, he pulled out a black sword and charged me.

IN WHICH I GET STABBED. WAIT, IS THAT FORESHADOWING? CRAPBALLS!

I SHRIEKED WHEN THE MAN RAN AT ME WITH BOTH hands holding a long sword with a glinting black blade. I also leaped to the side, but not before the sword just caught me, slicing through my shirt and slashing along my rib cage.

"Ack!" I screamed, and grabbed at myself while at the same time scrambling backward and looking desperately for something to use as a weapon to defend myself. The anxious beast in my head surprised me then—rather than freaking out and demanding I curl up into a fetal ball of misery, it roared to life with a heat that had my cheeks flushed, demanding I attack.

Without thinking, I grabbed the nearest heavy object (an art glass bowl holding a goldfish), quickly scooped out the fish, and threw the bowl at my attacker's head. The man attempted to dodge it, but tripped over a gerbil cage, which left his head directly in the path of my missile. It hit him smack on the forehead, sending him tumbling over the back of the couch, a welter of splattered blood and water following.

"What is going on—" Ian appeared around the corner of the kitchen and stared at me standing in the middle of his living room, panting, with a goldfish flopping around in my cupped hand. "What are you doing with Gene Simmons?"

"He tried to attack me!" I said, grabbing with my free hand at my side. It came away bloody. "Correction, he did attack me. Oh, goddess, I'm bleeding. I'm going to die, I just know it, and then my sister will haunt me because I didn't save the abused woman. Can a ghost haunt another ghost, do you know?"

"Goldfish seldom attack anyone, let alone make them bleed," Ian said, ignoring my panicked babbling to take the goldfish from me and look around. "Where's his bowl?"

"Oh. You mean the blond guy isn't Gene Simmons? The bowl is on the floor, but I think it broke."

Ian hurried to the kitchen, where the sound of running water could be heard. I hesitated a moment, then slowly shuffled my way around the edge of the couch to see if the man was still out.

He was, the sword having skittered across the wood floor until it bumped into the wall. I resisted the urge to kick the unconscious man, noting that his blood was black.

"I think Gene is okay, although in the future, I'd appreciate you not throwing the animals' homes," Ian called from the kitchen. "We lost the other three fish a week ago in an accident with Ringo, and it took Sasha five days before she'd stop wearing a monk's cowl in mourning."

"You don't think he's dead, do you?" I asked, looking down at the blond man.

"No, but if you had him out of water for much longer, he would have been."

"Not the fish. The man."

"What man?"

"He doesn't seem to be breathing." I poked the man with the toe of a shoe. "I don't think he's a normal person, though. I mean, what sort of normal person attacks other people with swords?"

"What are you talking about?" Ian reemerged from the kitchen with a glass pitcher, now housing the goldfish Gene Simmons.

"Him." I pointed, and Ian came around the couch, stared for the count of six, then sighed.

"What is she doing behind the couch?"

"She? Are you blind? That's a guy."

"No, it's Falafel." He squatted down next to her and examined the bloody welt on the man's forehead. "Demons can take whatever form they like, and some change frequently. Evidently Falafel felt like a change."

"Is she...he...transgendered, too? Because I didn't get an answer on the Sasha question, and I don't want to offend anyone."

"It doesn't really matter." Ian shrugged and glanced up at me, his eyes narrowing on my side. "What happened to you?"

"Your demon friend there sliced me open with a sword." I pulled up my shirt to examine my side. "Holy Clorox, it's bleeding like crazy! I need drugs. And antibiotics. Should I go to a doctor? I should, shouldn't I? I hate doctors. There are so many sick people there, and germs everywhere. What if I fainted? Oh, man, I might faint. Things are getting woozy. I feel lightheaded."

I weaved a little, my panicked animal racing around my head screaming we were about to keel over. Ian rose to look at my side, made a *tch*ing noise, and without so much as a "Do you mind?" peeled my shirt off and bent down to look at my torso.

"Hey!" I covered my breasts even though they were tucked away inside my bra. "Were you raised by wolves? You ask before you take off someone's shirt! Ack! Don't touch it! I've been stabbed—it'll hurt if you touch it! Plus you'll get my blood on your hands."

"My apologies for the shirt removal, but I wanted to see if you really were about to faint. This doesn't look like it's more than a superficial scratch, but I have some antibiotic cream in the bathroom you can use if you'd like to clean it up. Also, I was a medic in the First World War, so if you are worried about a scar, I can get a needle and some thread and stitch it up." He straightened up and turned away just as if that was that, and nothing to freak out over.

"Needle…" I swallowed hard, a big lump in my throat warning me that all was not well in my stomach. Just the thought of Ian sewing me up had bile rising dangerously high. "Stitch it up…ungh…"

Blackness swamped me when I fell forward, my panic level through the roof. I remained in the abyss of nothingness for a bit before slowly coming to again, sound being the first thing that I noticed.

"What is she doing here again?" The voice that asked was male, and sounded decidedly peeved.

I opened my eyes, and found myself lying on the couch, my shirt still off, but several strands of gauze wrapped around my rib cage. Obviously Ian had patched me up after I'd swooned.

Standing in the middle of the room, the blond Falafel stood in her male porn star form, her face furious.

Ian looked tired. "What do you think she's doing here? I told you that she was my woman. And now you've harmed her, and I won't be able to leave her on her own."

"Faugh," Falafel snorted. "There's no reason to baby mortals. If she dies, she dies. That's one less of them to get in our way."

"You are seriously obnoxious, and I'm not just talking about your seventies porn mustache," I said, getting to my feet. I wobbled once, but managed to straighten up and give Falafel a mean look despite the fact that I was shirtless and wounded.

I noticed that Ian hadn't bothered to bandage *her* wound. That made me smile at him where he stood at the end of the couch. He looked startled for a moment.

"Be quiet. Speak when you are spoken to," the demon snapped. "In fact, I have had enough of you. Begone!"

I straightened my shoulders, marveling momentarily that once again the anxious beast in my head demanded I fight. "Look, you may think you're a badass carrying around a sword with which to run innocent people through, but let me tell you a thing or two. For one, you don't have the right to tell me to leave someone else's apartment. And for another, I have my own sw—mmrph."

Ian grabbed me before I could finish speaking, pulling me into a sudden and intense embrace. "Don't speak, hot lips. You don't have to tell the demon anything."

I pushed back and looked up at his face, about to tell him that pretend girlfriend or not, he did not have the right to call me by that atrocious endearment or to grab me like that, but I saw the warning in his eyes before I spoke. The edges of his irises glittered with green fire, and his pupils were long and narrow. He was in full dragon mode, which meant he was either afraid or angry.

"Uh...okay," I said, making a note to have a chat with him later about the form his warnings took.

He looked over my head to the demon. "Why are

you here again, Falafel? I told you that I don't want
you around."

"And I told you that the master sent me to ensure
you complete your duties." Falafel looked downright
mean. "I tire of repeating myself to you. Send your
woman away, and let us be about your business."

"You are so one note," I told her. "I can't use you
in my book at all, even though now I desperately want
a character I can call Porn 'Stache. But characters are
only interesting if they have depths of emotion, and all
you do is rant and rave with anger. FYI: it gets old
really fast. You might want to read up on a second
emotion so you don't bore people to death."

"Bore!" I thought her head might explode, and
backed up a step before I realized what I was doing.

The black sword lay where it must have fallen, on
top of the gerbil cages that sat on the coffee table. I
glanced at the weapon, wondering how different it was
from my stolen soul sword.

"You speak to me with such insolence?" Falafel
sputtered, and breathed heavily for a second. "It is in-
tolerable! I will not stand it! Iskandar, if you will not
lesson this...this...*thing*, then I will!"

I snatched up the sword the second she started toward me, saying, "Dude, you really need something
other than an off and on switch."

Ian had been moving around the coffee table, clearly
at the end of his patience. Just as I picked up the sword,
he spun around, his eyes wide. "Veronica, do not touch
that!"

"Why?" I tossed the sword from one hand to the other, getting a feel for its weight and balance, things that I knew from Ian's lesson were important. This one felt fine. "It's just a sword. It's not like I don't know how to use one after those two lessons. Anyway—"

"Aieee!" Falafel let out a screech so loud it felt like it tore my eardrums to shreds. "Deathsong! You dare touch it?"

She lunged forward toward me, and I quickly whipped through the mental notes I'd taken when Ian had given me a dragon hunter lesson. I made sure my weight was balanced on the balls of my feet, that my legs were spread slightly, my elbows bent, and that I was relaxed. When Falafel leaped onto the coffee table, knocking the gerbil cages everywhere, still screeching in some language that sounded like it was made up of gravel and nails, I reacted as best I could. I slashed forward with the sword, then spun it around and slammed the hilt into her head, sending her flying backward.

"Are they okay?" I asked, dropping the sword to gather up the cages of the gerbils and hamsters, their squawks and squeaks of protest telling me that at least they were still alive. "Oh, thank the stars, no one looks like they're hurt."

Ian didn't wait; he was on Falafel when she struggled to her feet, the pair of them falling over the couch onto the floor. His sword flashed in the light as he brought it to her throat. "Do not tempt me to end your life," he said in a near snarl, his chest heaving. For a moment, I could swear I saw fire on his hands, but it was gone before I was sure of what I'd seen.

Hurriedly, I stuffed the cages back onto the coffee table, feeling I should help him, but not wanting the animals to get stepped on should the fight continue.

"You don't have the balls," the demon all but spat back at him despite the fact that his sword was pressing into the flesh of her throat. "Anzo would destroy you the instant she heard about my end."

Just as I finished with the last animal cage, I saw a blackness that seemed to glow around one of Falafel's hands. It was like a miniature cloud the size of a loaf of bread had formed, and as I stared in wonder at it, I noticed that symbols like runes flashed in it before dissolving and being replaced by others.

"It would be worth it to rid the world of you," Ian said, some of the tension in his body relaxed, and he sat back, although his sword was still held to her throat.

I stared at his sword, at the runes on it that were glittering so brightly. He'd told me all dragon hunters had spells inscribed on their swords to grant them various strengths.

The runes were spells.

Falafel was drawing a spell in the air, a black spell, and I knew in an instant that she was going to cast it on Ian.

She raised her hand, the black cloud following. Time seemed to dilate at that moment, stretching each second out tenfold. Ian started turning his head to look at her hand, but I saw in a flash that he wouldn't be able to stop her from casting the spell, and that although I wasn't sure it would kill him, I knew I had to prevent it from being put into place. Without thinking, I reached out blindly, my fingers closing around the black sword. I rose, bringing it up high with both hands, and in a fluid motion, swung downward, narrowly missing Ian in the arc. Falafel's eyes widened just as the fingers in her hand spread to release her spell, but I was faster. For what seemed like an eternity, I stood above her, staring downward at the curious expressions that passed over her face: disbelief, horror, and finally, anger. A black line appeared across her throat, just above where the tip of Ian's sword touched her flesh, the line spreading and thickening as I watched.

Her hand dropped to the floor with a dull thud, and at that noise, time seemed to return to normal.

Ian stared down at her for a second before getting to his feet, his face expressing disbelief. "What did you do?"

"Uh…" I swallowed, confused by my actions. "Stopped her, I think. It's all kind of a blur, to be honest, but I could see she was going to cast a spell. At least I think it was a spell. It was little symbols on a black cloud, and that seems to be gone. Is she…okay? She's not moving."

"No," Ian said, sliding his sword back into its sheath. "She wouldn't be, not without her head attached to her body. Wrath demons aren't easy to kill, but using one of their own swords to decapitate them will do the job."

I stared down at the demon for a few seconds. She looked frozen to me, her expression locked into anger. "But... her head is still on."

"Do you really want me to pick it up to show you it's not?" he asked.

I shuddered. "Uck. No. But... if she's dead, why hasn't she disappeared into black... Oh."

As I spoke, the body did an odd little shimmer, then evaporated into a pungent black smoke that had me backing up, waving the air in front of my nose.

Ian looked down at the black stain on his carpet and sighed. "There goes the cleaning deposit."

"I just killed a demon, my very first demon—hell, the first thing I've ever killed, because I don't even squash flies or spiders—and all you can think about is your cleaning deposit?" I waved the sword around dramatically. "Get with the program, Steve!"

"My name is Ian," he said, frowning.

"That was a quote," I said, waving the sword some more. "At least I think it is. Maybe it isn't, but it should be. Oh, goddess, I killed someone. I cut off a head. Is it wrong to panic? Because I kind of want to."

Ian gently took the sword from me, grimaced, then dropped it onto the floor, looking at his hand as he did so.

"Are you okay?" I peered down at his hand. "It looks like you got burned. Did the sword do that?"

"Yes." He eyed my hands. "What's curious is that you don't seem to have an issue with it. What do you feel when you hold it?"

"Nothing." I picked it up from where it lay, examining it. It was broader and heavier than Helen's sword, and the blade was solid black, but the hilt was silver in color, and carved with odd symbols. "Are these marks spells like what's on the soul swords? They look different to me."

"They are different. They are banes, meant to give the demon access to powers that you should not be able to use." He narrowed his eyes as I gave a few experimental swishes in the air with the sword. "This makes absolutely no sense. Dragon hunters cannot wield weapons used by wrath demons."

"This one doesn't feel bad. It feels..." I thought for a moment. "Kind of familiar in an odd way."

"That makes no sense," Ian repeated, shaking his head. "Even with our demonic blood, they are beyond our abilities. They would consume rather than allow themselves be used. Unless..."

"Unless what?" I asked, concerned that something horrible might happen to me.

"Unless Adam's experimentations on your sister changed her more than I imagined, and that change was transmitted to you."

"Huh?"

Ian looked deep in thought, but since he didn't seem to be horrified, I decided to come back to that point. "Whatever the problem with normal demon swords, this one seems to be okay. Would it be all right if I used it until I can get my own back?"

"I should say no, but at this point..." He gave a

shrug. "If it doesn't hurt you, and you don't feel any surge of dark power when you touch it, then I assume your unique nature means that you have an affinity to it."

"It's okay," I said, wiping the blade on some tissues I found on a side table. "It's not as pretty as Helen's. Do you think Falafel was the one who broke into my apartment and trashed it?"

"I don't believe so, but I'll let Sasha answer that." He looked over my shoulder and asked, "Did you sense demons?"

"Not a one. There was someone there, all right, but it wasn't a straight-out demon. The man from the Watch said the same thing—it was something different, you know? Kind of demony, but not, if you know what I mean. Which I hope you do, because Zizi knows I don't." Sasha glided into the room, looking pointedly at the stain on the carpet. "It looks like you had one here. The wrath demon chick?"

"Yes." Ian's expression was impassive. "Veronica dispatched her. Is the Watch still upstairs?"

"Ooh, demon sword, very cool." She trotted past me toward the kitchen. "No, he left. Said there was nothing he could do other than file a report of malicious destruction of property. Oh, he says they got in through your door, Ronnie, probably with some sort of skeleton key. I think that's what he called it. Anyway, he said you should use some protective wards when you sleep at night so the person can't get back in. Did you leave me food? I'm so hungry I could eat grilled behemoth."

"I guess I'll go back to my apartment," I said, gesturing toward the door with my sword. I suddenly felt all shades of awkward, my movements feeling gawky and clunky, but worse, I had the feeling I was an outsider in a closed circle consisting of Ian and Sasha. "Thanks for dinner."

Ian said nothing, just looked at me, and after a moment of waiting for him to respond, I gave a feeble wave and left.

I don't quite know what I had expected to see at my apartment. I had some half-formed idea of Sasha's "mad skills" being of the magical sort, where I'd open my door and find everything restored and put back, and normal to the point of not even being able to tell that an invasion had happened.

"This is anticlimactic," I said to myself when I stood in the doorway and surveyed the interior. It didn't appear as if anything had been changed. Not one thing had been picked up, nothing had been pieced back together (magically or otherwise), and nothing had been cleaned. It was all as big a mess as it had been before, with the exception of a note stuck on the inside wall saying the Watch had been there and found no threat present, along with a command to call the attached number if I had any information helpful to solving the crime.

"Fat lot of good that did," I murmured to myself, looking around my destroyed apartment. I toyed with the idea of calling the regular police, but figured there was nothing they could do or say that would help me.

Ian had offered to help, but I didn't feel right in taking him up on it. Not when he'd been so nice as to make me dinner.

I'd just have to cope on my own.

NOTE TO SELF: DON'T LET MR. MANNY SEE THIS CHAPTER.
ALSO, COME UP WITH PITHY CHAPTER HEADER

GRITTING MY TEETH, I WADED THROUGH THE ANKLE-deep layer of detritus, my heart breaking at each little destroyed object I passed. My books, my cute little telephone table that had held a cactus, my little white ceramic horses that had galloped across my mantelpiece...all lying broken and crushed and bearing an air of being forgotten. I stopped at the doorway to the bedroom. The mattress had been shredded, bits of stuffing and foam scattered everywhere. The floor was littered with colorful shreds of fabric that I identified as my clothing. Books were torn apart, the pages shredded or crumpled underfoot.

The panicked animal in my head surveyed it all and wept.

I opened my door, intending to flee the desecration, and jumped when I found Ian there, his hand raised to knock.

His gaze searched my face. "I take it Sasha's cleansing didn't help?"

"She didn't clean anything," I said, making sure she wasn't standing in the hallway behind him before continuing. "Everything is still...broken, crushed, and spread out all over my apartment. She's a nice girl, and I'm sure she meant well, but if you offer to clean things up, the least she could have done was shoveled things into mounds for me to sort through."

"That's not the sort of cleaning she offered to do," he said cryptically. "I'm here to help. Where do you want me to start?"

I looked over my shoulder at the mess and felt as if a yoke made of lead had settled on my shoulders. "Honestly? I don't think I can cope with this tonight."

"Fair enough." He took my hand and, without a word, led me downstairs to his apartment. Sasha was nowhere to be seen as we entered. He nodded toward the door across the living room. "I'm afraid your choices for the night are the couch or my bed, and the cats usually sleep on the couch. You're not allergic, are you?"

"No, but would you misinterpret me if I said I'd prefer your bed? I don't want you thinking I'm angling for the sex, but sleeping with three cats sounds like it would make my animal go into overdrive."

He just looked at me as if I had said something untoward.

I explained. "I think of my anxiety as an animal that lives in a cave in my mind, remember?"

"I remember, but I don't think I've ever met someone who thinks of anxiety in quite that manner."

I gave a little shrug. "It helps me visualize it and control it when it wants to take over."

"I am very familiar with that need to control one's inner self," he said with a twist of his mouth. "As to the cats, I can't blame you for not wanting to sleep with them. I will be happy to extend the courtesy of my bed to you if that's what you desire."

I started for his bedroom, but paused. "With no sex, right?"

One of his eyebrows rose. "I can't say I would turn down the offer if you made it, but I have yet to force myself on a woman, and I have no intention of starting now."

"Okay, good, because although I will admit I liked kissing you for Falafel's benefit, I'm not looking for a real partner. I just want you to teach me what I need to do in order to make Helen rest easy."

A half hour later I was sitting in Ian's bed, wearing a pair of sleeping shorts and a tank top borrowed from Sasha. "I appreciate this, I really do. I know Teresita would let me stay with her, but her spare bed is a futon on her kids' bunk bed, and…"

Ian emerged from the bathroom where he was getting ready for bed. He was shirtless, and clad in a pair of flannel comfy pants.

I stared at the expanse of bare chest, trying desperately to get my tongue uncleaved from the roof of my mouth. He had tattoos up both arms and across his upper chest, some odd tribal design that did nothing to distract the eye from the thick muscles and hints of a six-pack.

"Sleeping with children is never conducive to rest, or so my mother used to say." Ian strolled over to the bed just like he hadn't been hiding the body of a Greek god under his clothing.

"You have a mother?" I realized with a start that I had spoken that inane bit of conversation and made an effort to stop mentally drooling over his bare torso. "Sorry, that came out sounding stupid. Only…you said dragon hunters are part demon. Does that mean your mom was a demon, or was she a dragon?"

"She was both. My father was a mortal." He got into bed and gave me an odd look. "Is something wrong? You look bilious."

I swallowed back a good gallon of saliva and shook my head. "I'm fine. Just…you have really interesting tats. I don't think I've ever seen ones like it. I have a hummingbird on my calf that I got when I was drunk, after my friends convinced me that I wouldn't get HIV or hepatitis from the tattoo gun, but yours are really…detailed."

"Yes," he said, and then rolled onto his side, presenting me with his back. I was interested to see the tattoos went across the upper half of it as well. "I'm going to sleep. Feel free to read if you like. I can sleep with lights on."

Well! I thought to myself, feeling somewhat let down. I must have been more tired than I thought, because I found myself saying, "It's not like I thought you'd make a move on me, because you don't seem like that kind of a man—I wouldn't be here if I thought you were—but at least you could…you know… acknowledge that we're two adults, together in bed, and we've kissed several times today."

Ian rolled over to look at me. "Are you asking for a good-night kiss, or do you simply want me to say I fancy you?"

"Neither," I said with haughty outrage, then ruined it by adding, "*Do* you fancy me?"

"Do you seriously have to ask?"

"Yes." I frowned at him. "I wouldn't ask if I didn't want to know. Wait, are you saying you think I'm fishing for compliments? Because I'm not."

"I didn't think you were." He rolled over so I had his back again.

"I notice you didn't answer my question. That's okay, though. It's not important. I just wondered if you were, you know, *interested* in me."

"Are you interested in me?" he asked without moving.

"Yes," I said, mentally writhing at the fact that my mouth was now speaking without my approval. "But that doesn't mean anything. I mean, I think lots of men are sexy as hell. I don't kiss them, though, or pretend to be their girlfriend to demons who can change their bodies at the drop of a hat. What happens to them when they disappear, by the way? Do they come back the way dragon hunters do? Helen said she will come back, although she didn't say how, or when, or in what form. Do you know? Am I talking too much? I am, aren't I? It's because I'm exhausted and my home has been broken into, and I feel betrayed and abused, and all my mental barriers are down."

He rolled over, looked hard at me, and then pulled me up against his chest. "If I were Sasha, I'd tell you that you need a hug, but I'm not, so I'll just give you one instead. Let me know when you are sufficiently hugged."

Despite all my anxieties, I found myself snuggling into him, breathing in his slightly lemony scent, relishing the warmth of his chest. "Oh, thank you. This is nice. And I don't like being touched a lot, but this is really enjoyable. Your chest is very—hoo!—and your tattoos are awesome."

Ian grimaced. "I appreciate the compliment, but their existence is not something to admire."

"Oh really?" I traced a finger over one of the symbols that was branded into his flesh. He stopped me by kissing my fingertip. "Why is that?"

"They are, for lack of a better explanation, a visual reminder of my bondage."

My eyes widened. "You're in bondage? What does that demon lord make you do? Horrible things to innocent people? Are you a hit man??"

"No, and before you ask if I torment mortals, the answer to that is also no. For the most part, Anzo uses me to eliminate her competition's demons, and recently I graduated to being her eyes in the mortal world. She expressed a desire for me to claim various items for her."

"Items like what?"

He gave a one-shouldered shrug. "Relics. Artifacts. Historical objects that for some reason she feels the need to possess."

"Ah." I had the sense of him withdrawing emotionally, and wracked my brain for something that would provide comfort. "Is there any way to get rid of your tie to the demon head honcho? I'd be happy to help if there is."

Surprise flitted through his eyes, followed by a warm glow of what might have been appreciation. "There is a way to break the bondage, but there is nothing you can do to aid me in that respect. Thank you for the offer."

"It's nothing, although I am very sincere in my offer to help." I was silent for a moment. "I'm being nosy, aren't I? I'm sorry about that. It's just that I always seem to have questions about people, and you're more interesting than most, so there are lots of things I'd like to know. Plus, it gives us a way to learn about each other. As a teacher, I know the importance of bonding with your student so as to make the learning more effective. Am I asking too many questions?"

"You are asking a good many, but you are overwrought. And now I'll answer one for you: demons do not come back once they are dispatched, if you are worried about that. If you break their form, they can return in another one, but dragon hunters are unique: our demon/dragon duality gives us the ability to destroy them permanently. It's our *raison d'être*, if you will, although I've never heard of one doing it with the demon's own sword..."

I sighed a happy sigh and relaxed against him, feeling a drowsy sort of contentment. "We come back, though, right? Dragon hunters?"

"We can, if the circumstances are right. Did your sister tell you she would return?"

"Yes."

"Ah."

"What does that 'Ah' mean?"

"It means that she would not tell you that if it wasn't the case."

I had a feeling he was keeping something from me, being selective with what he said, but I couldn't figure out a way to ask him without blurting out an accusation. "Oh. I don't want to have sex, Ian. Well, to be honest, I do, but I'm not going to. Do you want to hear my reasons why?"

"Of course. I wait with bated breath for your reasons."

I settled in against him, one distant part of my mind marveling that I felt so comfortable with him. Normally, it took me months to get to this point with a romantic partner, but Ian was different. He was...Ian. I took his hand and ticked off the reasons on his fingers. "First of all, I'm not the sort of woman who jumps into bed with the first handsome, tattooed dragon she meets. Second, I don't like to be touched."

"I can see that you don't," he said, grunting a little when I pushed him backward a smidgen and pulled his other arm out from underneath him so that it could go around me.

"Third, I don't play games, and you do."

"In what way?"

I tried unsuccessfully to stifle a yawn, and pressed myself tighter against his chest, tucking my head under his chin. "By telling the deceased Falafel that I was your girlfriend. You sure do know how to kiss, though."

"Thank you." Amusement filled his voice, something that made me feel wonderfully warm, almost as warm as the sensation of his arms around me.

"But mostly," I said in between a series of yawns, "I'm not going to have sex with you because if I do, you'll leave, and then I'll be heartbroken."

"You have a lovely opinion of me," he said drily. "Why do you think I'd leave?"

"Because other than one boyfriend who had a lot of psychological problems, all of my hookups have bailed after a night or two of rolling in the sheets. Either I'm really bad at sex, or I make men nervous." I pushed myself back from his chest and peered down at him. "I have issues, you know."

"I know," he said gravely. "But since I have my own issues, yours don't particularly horrify me. Do you want me to make love to you?"

"Yes," I said, wiggling my legs against his. "But I'm not going to."

"Because you don't like to be touched?" he asked.

"Because it would ruin us working together." I snuggled back into his chest, sighing in relief. "Maybe someday, but not now. I have far too much to learn from you."

He may have replied, but I didn't hear it. I drifted off to sleep happy and content that I had made a decision, a wise decision, one that my adult self approved of.

That contentment lasted all of three hours, until I woke up lying on top of Ian, my borrowed tank top having ridden up so that my bare stomach was plastered all over his. My legs were caught between his thighs, and worst of all, I could feel the heat of his groin against mine.

It made my intimate parts do wondrously tingly things, sensations I hadn't felt in a long time. I took a deep breath in preparation for peeling myself off Ian, but his low groan had me freezing. "Are you okay?" I asked in a whisper, not wanting to wake him up if he was dreaming.

"Not in the least bit. Stop wiggling against me in that seductive manner."

"I'm not wiggling anything."

His hands clamped down over my hips, making my little "trying to scoot off of him" movements obvious. "You're trying to drive me insane. Don't deny you are—for the last twenty minutes, you've tormented me every way possible, clearly trying to push me past what's bearable. Admit it, admit that you are trying to drive me mad with desire."

"I was asleep." I peeled myself off his stomach and sat up, pulling my legs out from between his and sitting astride his thighs. "I'm sorry if I was tormenting you in my sleep, but I didn't intend anything. Hoo boy. Sitting like this did *not* help things, huh?"

I looked down to where a very obvious bulge in his pants was pressed up against the thin material of my sleeping shorts.

He made a choked noise that didn't contain any actual words.

"You're really...wow. Do you mind if I touch?"

"Why not?" he managed to get out, a touch of hysteria about the words. "It seems entirely reasonable given that you've been sleeping on me for the last hour, torturing me with your soft belly, and your breasts, and the way you breathed on me. Why not touch my dick? Would you like me to get it out for you so that you can really torture me?"

"I have no intention of doing anything so heinous." I gently stroked the bulge. It grew bulgier. "It's just that...hoo...that's seriously impressive. I'd ask to see it, but that's probably going too far, huh?"

"Veronica."

I gave it a gentle squeeze and enjoyed the way he sucked in half the air in the room. "Hmm?"

"Do you want to have sex?"

"I don't want to ruin our relationship," I said, wishing I could just peel off his pants and have at it. I wondered if his offer to do just that was meant in earnest, or if he was being sarcastic. In my sleep-muddled state, I couldn't tell. "It means a lot to me that you're teaching me."

"It's your decision," he said, his voice as rough as rocks grinding together. "But I'm willing if you are."

I gave him another friendly squeeze. "Will you promise that it won't affect my training?"

"I promise." His hips twitched underneath me.

"Well...I shouldn't. The sensible me recognizes that. But the impulsive me that I've been trying to cultivate, because my therapist says it's good for me to be spontaneous, says what the hell, let's grab the bull by the balls and go for the gold. Or some such metaphor. So if you're sure you're good, then I am, too."

"I know you haven't had too much to drink, but are you always this uninhibited in the middle of the night?" he asked when I reached for the waistband of his pants, his hands on mine keeping me from yanking the pants right off of him.

For a moment, I thought he had changed his mind, but then realized he was making sure I was aware of the choice I was making. "I'm sleepy and my mouth says things before my brain approves, but I know what I'm doing, yes. Although I suppose I should be worried about my sword injury."

"What sword injury?"

"The one the demon— Oh. It's gone." I twisted around to see the spot where Falafel had stabbed me, but the injury had healed. *As if by magic!* the dramatic part of my mind said, all but adding a drum-roll after that sentence to emphasize it. I told my inner drama queen to chill, and since my side was no longer an issue, returned to what was important. "Do you happen to have any condoms? I don't, and I'm not really comfortable going at this without some form of protection for diseases. My IUD will take care of the rest."

"I do have some, but I mentioned that dragon hunters are immortal. We don't catch mortal diseases."

"Yeah, but..." I made a vague gesture, unable to put into words the discomforting thought of sex without a layer of latex between us.

He didn't answer, but rolled over to dig around in nightstand drawer, emerging with a strip of condoms.

"Oh, good," I said, relieved. "Now I can really go to town on you without worrying."

"I don't know whether to be offended that a condom would make such a difference, or intrigued by what your idea of going to town is. I think I'll go with the latter."

"Good choice."

I was at the waistband of his pants before the sane part of my mind could ask me what I thought I was doing. I ignored it when it pointed out all the reasons I'd given a few hours before, ignored common sense, ignored even the anxious animal who warned that I knew little about Ian, and that for all I knew, he could have bizarre sexual fetishes. None of that raised a concern in my sleep-muddled, lust-filled state. All that mattered was the man lying beneath me, and my own needs, which were fast overwhelming my mind.

With his help, we got him out of his pants, and me out of my shorts and tank top, leaving me just in my undies.

"So much to play with," I murmured, taking my spot back on his thighs, my hands immediately taking possession of his balls and penis. "It's amazing how soft and hard this can be at the same time. And you're uncircumcised."

"I am. Is that a problem?" His voice was very breathy, as if he was inhaling on every word.

"No. Luckily for us both, my somewhat sociopathic ex was also uncut, and he taught me what to do with the extra bit."

His hips bucked upward as I let my fingers run wild on the scenery, stroking the soft squishiness of his balls before moving up to slide skin around on his decidedly not-soft penis. "Veronica, would you mind if we didn't talk about your ex's dick right now?"

"Sure," I said, looking up with concern. His voice sounded tight and a bit higher than normal. "Is something wrong? You look like you're having another painful gas bubble."

"I didn't have one the first time you said that," he said, giving a little laugh before grabbing the sheets beneath him with both hands and moaning. "Christos, woman, if you keep doing that, you won't have to worry about a condom."

"Oh, should I stop?" I released his genitalia, giving

them a gentle pat of approval. "Sorry. I didn't mean to be grabby."

"I wouldn't mind taking my turn," he said, pulling me up along his body, so that my entire front side was pressed up against him. He nuzzled the tops of my breasts with cheeks that were stubbly enough to send shivers down my back. "Do I have your permission to explore your body as you've explored mine?"

"I didn't really explore. All I did was play with your naughty bits," I said, arching my back when he slid his hands between us and caressed my breasts, his thumbs rubbing on my nipples. Another shiver went down my back at the sensation, and I thought to myself how different touches could be. Where my former lover was prone to just grabbing my breasts and squeezing them (until the day I did the same with his testicles), Ian's touch was gentle, teasing me with heat that stirred up an inferno within me.

"I'd like equal time, if that wouldn't upset you," he said, rolling us over so that he was on top. His mouth followed his hands along my breasts, making me moan and writhe with delight.

"You can do anything you want," I said in between gasps. He moved his kisses to the valley between my breasts, his hands drawing intricate designs on my belly and hips as he shifted downward. "Except oral sex."

He looked up at that, his face level with my belly button. "You can't be serious."

"I'm very much so." I twined my fingers through his

hair, reveling in the smooth coolness of it. His hair felt like a cross between silk and water, sliding over my fingers in a way that made me restless.

"Why?"

I tightened my fingers on his hair, giving his head a little shake. "Are you kidding? There are so many reasons why it's just a no!"

"Name them," he said with an obnoxious amount of patience in his voice.

"Sure. One, it's just ew! I mean, ew! Two, I don't wax. I am *au naturel*, and as any fashion blog will tell you, men do not like women with the full complement of pubic hair."

He looked down at my pubic bone. "I don't mind it at all. To be honest, I think it looks silly when women carve little strips into it. Next objection?"

"It's ew!"

"That was number one, and I don't see anything ew about your vulva." He pulled back enough to prod around in the area in question. "Everything looks perfectly normal to me."

"Ack!" I said, letting go of his hair to flail my arms about. "Stop looking at it!"

"We're going to have difficulty engaging in sex if you don't want me to have anything to do with your vagina," he said, sliding a hand up my leg and kissing a path up the inner thigh. "I hope you don't prefer alternate entrances, because that doesn't interest me much."

"Oh, good goddess, no!" I shuddered at the very

idea. "And I don't mind sex, normal sex, it's just the idea of you putting your face in there...bleh!"

"Right," he said, kissing the other leg's inner thigh so it wouldn't be jealous. "Then we'll just do this the standard way, shall we?"

"Please. Also, do you mind if I don't oral you? Because that's..." I grimaced and indulged in some vague hand waving.

"Ew?" he asked.

"So very," I agreed.

"I will never ask you to do something you don't wish to do," he said, kissing a line across my belly and carefully nipping my hip. "Somehow, I am guessing you want to be on top."

"If you don't mind," I said. "Honestly, Ian, I feel like I should apologize to you for all my weird hang-ups. If you don't want to do this after all, I'll understand."

"Don't be silly. You aren't weird, just, I suspect, inexperienced. And perhaps the recipient of less than stellar lovemaking in the past. No, do not tell me what your almost-sociopath boyfriend used to do—this is our time. You do what makes you comfortable."

He rolled off me and spread his arms, inviting me to frolic on the playland that was his delicious body.

"Be sure to tell me if I do anything you don't like. Er...should we get you dressed up?" I hesitated when I sat back on his thighs, eyeing his crotch.

"You had your hands all over me before. Is something wrong now?" he asked, handing me the package of condoms.

"No, I don't mind touching you, but I don't want to get all caught up in the proceedings, and then, you know, one thing would lead to another, and boom, you'd be all up inside me without anything between our naughty parts."

"You keep saying that phrase," he mused, watching while I slid the condom down onto him, giving his penis another encouraging pat when I was finished. "Do you find genitals naughty?"

I fondled his balls again, gently, ever so gently scraping my fingernails up his inner thighs and across the balls themselves. "Do you really want to get into psychotherapy now? Because I was thinking about bone jumping."

He waved his hand toward his penis. "Be my guest. I am suitably clad, and awaiting your actions."

I shifted forward until my knees were around his hips, positioned him, and sank down. The sensation of him parting my heated (and very welcoming) inner parts was enough to make my breath hitch in my chest. "Hoo. You are really…there…aren't you?"

"Very much so," he agreed.

I enjoyed the sensation of him being so firmly inside me, when it struck me that something was missing. I stopped focusing on my inner self and looked up worriedly. He was lying passive, his hands resting on my thighs, but there were no flames in his eyes, no sense of the heat that I'd experienced a short while ago. "Hey," I said, moving upward to dislodge him. "The first time is supposed to be super-hot. Exciting. Breathless. Why are you none of those things?"

"I'm enjoying myself," he protested, and gestured toward his penis. "I wouldn't be hard if I wasn't."

"There's enjoying yourself, and then there's having flame eyes. You are allowed to help, you know. I say we start over." I crawled up his body, and decided that perhaps the reason he wasn't as hot and bothered as I wanted him to be was because I wasn't paying him enough attention. There was no reason why I shouldn't kiss his chest, why I shouldn't fondle and taste those parts of him that didn't trigger my anxieties. So I did so, kissing his belly, nibbling on the wonderful line of muscle that sat on his flanks, using my fingers and mouth to map out all the contours of his stomach and chest. By the time I reached his tattoos, his chest was heaving beneath me, a fact that pleased me greatly. I discovered that I liked him breathless. "Mmm. You taste...indescribably good. I like this a lot."

"I really am going to require equal time with chest torments," he said, taking my breasts in his hands. I leaned into them, which allowed me to kiss his nipples. After a moment's thought, I licked one, then gave it the gentlest of nips. He groaned. I repeated the action with the other one, then nipped his chin and scooted higher until I could kiss him properly. His hands were on my hips now, sliding back to my butt cheeks, caressing them while his mouth opened to welcome my tongue. For some reason I couldn't begin to explain, I found exploring his mouth a wonderful experience.

Maybe it was the slightly spicy taste to him, maybe it was the heat that seemed to be contained in him, or maybe it was just that the feeling of his tongue stroking mine fired up pools of heat deep inside me, but tasting him didn't set off one single "Danger! Contamination!" warning in my head.

"For someone who has an oral aversion," he said, in between kisses, "you certainly know how to use your tongue."

"I know." I grinned down at him, reveling at the flames that licked the outer edges of his irises. "It's the weirdo in me. Other OCD sufferers might freak out at it, but it's the one thing I'm okay with. Shall we give this another go?"

"I will be very unhappy if we don't," he said, and this time when I sank down on him, he helped by pushing his hips upward, until we worked out a rhythm that had my focus narrowing down to that moment in time and space, of Ian's body moving with mine, and of the fire that he stirred inside me, building in intensity alongside my orgasm until I felt myself going over the edge into the burning inferno of ecstasy.

Literally burning, as it turned out. I had collapsed down on his chest, his shout of completion still echoing in my ears when I realized that he was on fire.

"Eek!" I shrieked, and scrambled off him despite my body's desire to stay exactly where it was. Ian's tattoos were alight, fire merrily burning along the thick curves and swoops of the designs. "You're on fire! Should I get a towel? A blanket? Where's your fire extinguisher?"

He tried to look down at his chest, but the tattoos were too high up. "It's nothing," he said, patting at his upper chest and collarbone.

"Seriously, I know you're a dragon and all, but that's fire. Real fire. You, Ian, are on real, actual fire."

"Did I miss any?" he asked, trying again to look down at the tattoos.

"Yes, there's a bit under your chin."

"Take care of it for me, would you?" he asked, tipping his head back.

"Are you insane?" I gawked at him openmouthed. "I'll burn myself!"

"It's dragon fire, Veronica. You are a dragon hunter. It won't hurt you."

"You don't know that," I said, utterly irrationally; then with an annoyed *tsk* at myself because he did, in fact, know, I tentatively reached my hand toward the bit of flame burning in the center of his collarbone.

Oddly, it gave off no heat. I ran a finger quickly through it, but there was only the mildest of sensations. Taking a deep breath, I closed my eyes and quickly patted where the flames burned along a tattoo.

There was no sensation of fire, just a pleasant warming.

"Now, that is interesting," I said, sitting back on my heels to examine my fingers. "It didn't even feel like fire. I've run a finger through the flame of a candle, and this wasn't even as hot as that was."

"Dragon fire," he said, and padded into the bathroom, assumedly to remove the condom. When he came back, he stifled a big yawn and got back into bed. I was reminded it was the middle of the night, and I'd just had what was literally the best sex of my life, and by conventional standards, I should now be snuggled up next to him enjoying my endorphins, the sensation of bonding after sex, and some mild pillow talk.

"Sorry. I have to take a shower. It's nothing about you; it's just one of my weird quirks."

"By all means," he said, yawning again as he waved to the bathroom. "Help yourself. There are fresh towels on the rack."

He was asleep by the time I was clean and returned to bed, and as I carefully pressed myself against his back, relishing the heat and reassuringly solid feel of him, I allowed a cautiously hopeful thought to echo around in my head.

Maybe we were meant to be together. Maybe we were immortal soul mates, destined to live our lives intertwined. Maybe I would fall in love, and live happily ever after, even if that meant centuries rather than decades.

Maybe life was, just this once, giving me a break.

CHAPTER ELEVEN

"I DON'T FEEL RIGHT ABOUT THIS AT ALL," IAN SAID, shifting uncomfortably in the seat of his car.

"You're just being precious," Sasha said, making a face at herself in the mirror affixed to the pull-down visor. She had changed her hairstyle three times in as many minutes and was now trying a fourth.

"I am not precious," he said, irritated by her new latest favorite word. Last week it had been "dude." The week before, it was "douchecanoe." He supposed that given those last two choices, he really had nothing to complain about. "I simply do not like doing things in an underhanded manner. Where did you put it?"

"Pencil jar on her desk. How do you feel about hair coiled into circles over the ears? Is it too medieval?

Would mortals gawk at that look? Would it make me look too precious?"

"It would make the geek population happy," he said, wondering how to explain the phenomenon of *Star Wars* movies to someone who had never experienced them. There were so many ways Sasha was an innocent, and yet she knew more than he could even imagine. "How good is the range on that microphone? I don't hear anything."

Sasha dug through the enormous bag she'd taken to carrying and pulled out a pair of oversized sunglasses, slipping them on before judging her appearance in the mirror. "That's because no one is there yet. If you look closely, you'll see the lights are off in the chicky's office."

"Chicky?" Ian was aware that he was unusually prickly this morning. He very much wished he could spend the day with Veronica, but she had claimed a prior commitment and dashed off before he could persuade her that time with him was a better use of her day.

Then there was the fact that he needed to find the courier and rescue the esprits before Falafel found them.

"Chicky, yes. You know, the one who works there."

"The Witness, you mean?"

Sasha waved an airy hand. "Whatever she's called."

Ian wondered briefly how someone could be so old and yet have so little grasp of the beings of the Otherworld. "Witnesses are what we call those members of the Church of the Mortified Flesh of the Anguished Witness."

"Hmm." She studied her reflection. "The magazine you got me said I should add highlights to my hair for the summer in order to set off my healthy bronzed complexion. How do I get these highlights? Is there a pen or a wand or a glamour, or something?"

"You go to a store like a normal person, and shop in the hair care aisle. Beyond that, I don't know. I'm going to give it five more minutes, and then go. I can't wait here all morning."

"I think you should stay." Sasha's voice was muffled since she all but had her head in the bag while she dug out something else. It turned out to be a headband with two long springs that wobbled in all directions, topped with golf ball–sized blobs of red and yellow yarn.

"Why?"

She shrugged.

Ian had a feeling she was keeping something from him, and not being a man who suffered in silence, asked, "Do you want to tell me the real reason you want me here?"

She pursed her lips and played with one of her deely boppers. "You're so suspicious. Honestly, Ian, I don't know why you took me on as a partner if you don't want to listen to my advice."

The look he gave her was one of pure outrage. "I didn't take you on as a partner."

"Maybe not, but you didn't stop me when I showed

up on your doorstep, just like you didn't stop it when people dumped all those animals on you."

"The animals are yours," he said with stony indifference.

"You had all those animals except Chicken and Duck when I got there. Admit it," she said, nudging him with her elbow. "You're a big softy, and you just can't stand anyone knowing the truth."

"To what purpose is this conversation?" he asked, admitting no such thing. It would be a lighthearted day in Abaddon before he indulged in introspective contemplation.

She giggled. "I worry about you. What's going to happen when I'm done being your apprentice? Who's going to make sure you don't give in to your demon side then? You need someone to keep you from committing heinous and horrible acts should your boss lady decide to make you do that."

He ignored the familiar feeling of guilt and failure that plagued him whenever he thought of the past. "The fact that I haven't given in to my demon side in the last few years aside, of course?"

She waved that away. "There's more at stake now."

He thought about that. She was right; there *was* more at stake now that Veronica had entered the picture. She must be protected, kept from Anzo's knowledge. He was torn between wanting to do just that, and the knowledge that he had failed to keep his mother and Adam safe.

"You are seriously grumpy," Sasha said suddenly.

"And here I thought sex with Ronnie would have put you in a better mood. She sure was smiling when she left this morning."

He said nothing, relaxing back into his seat, his gaze firmly affixed to the rearview mirror where the offices of Fuller Realty were slowly coming to life. It was clearly time for another change of subject. "We're here, and that's what you wanted, although I wish you'd tell me why."

"You never know who might show up," she said, twanging one of her antennae.

"That tells me nothing." Ian wondered for the fifth time in an hour why he had let himself be talked into this plan when he could be teaching Veronica the joys of sexual playtime. Just the memory of her the night before had dragon fire burning hot within him.

Sasha twanged another antenna. "Sometimes nothing is everything. Ah, there she is."

"Veronica?" Ian sat up from where he'd slumped back in the seat, his mind filled with the warmth of the woman who was fast bewitching him, but the figure in a red power suit who crossed the street behind them was not familiar. "Oh. I assume that's the Witness?"

"That's the chicky, yes," Sasha agreed, and swapped out her sunglasses for a pair of zebra-striped ones.

Ian got out of the car, and froze for a moment as two women emerged from a VW Bug and hurried into the real estate office. "What is she...? Stay here," he ordered Sasha.

"Are you insane?" Sasha scrambled out of the car

and ran after him as he strode across the street to the office. "Wait up, your legs are longer than mine!"

He waved off the inquiry of a woman at a desk, and headed straight for the Witness's office, opening the door to hear her say, "Yes, of course we have the names of people who rent the properties we handle."

"Oh, good, then you can help us find Ronnie's friend. We need the names and addresses of whoever moved into town in the last few weeks."

"Oh, no, I couldn't do that," the Witness protested. "It's against any number of privacy laws—excuse me, sir, but I am busy at the moment." This last was addressed to him. Both of the women in front of her desk turned, identical expressions of surprise on their faces when they saw him.

"Hello," he said, trying to come up with a reason why he should be there. His gaze went to Veronica, and moved over to her side, putting a possessive hand on her shoulder before leaning down to kiss her. "Sorry I'm late . . . darling."

Her eyes widened a little as she stared first at him, then in amazement at Sasha. "Oh, we're doing that again, are we?" she finally asked in a whisper.

"Yes. Play along." He straightened up and gave the Witness a long, hard look. "I don't believe we've met. I'm Ian. Veronica and I are . . ." He let the sentence trail off suggestively.

"Shut the front door!" Teresita said, slapping her hand down on the arm of the chair. "I knew it! I just knew it! I could tell by the way Ronnie was all happy and giggly and so not like her normal self this morning that something between you two had gone down. I didn't know it was your respective pants, but I highly approve of this."

"Indeed." The Witness smiled a smile that seemed to Ian to involve an impossibly large number of teeth. She reminded him of a former beauty queen, with teased red hair, a flawless complexion that probably came from a bottle, perfect makeup and nails, all swathed in a heavy floral scent that made his nose itch. "Well, Mr.... er ... " She waited for a moment, clearly expecting him to offer his surname. He just raised an eyebrow slightly. "Well, as I told your partner, I'm unable to give her the information she seeks."

"We understand that you can't just give us the names of all the renters," Veronica said, glancing upward at him before turning back to the Witness. "But surely it doesn't violate any privacy policies to give us a list of what rental properties are available in the area? I believe that information is freely distributed to online real estate sites."

"That is true," the Witness allowed, dabbing her forehead with a tissue. She had a light sheen of sweat that struck Ian as being odd. Just at that moment, the woman gave him a curious look and leaned forward, giving an almost inaudible sniff.

Ian stepped back three paces, giving a little grunt when Sasha, who had been poking around a large potted plant, suddenly threw herself on Ian and hung off his front, her hands around his neck and her yarn bobble antennae bopping him gently on the chin. "Lumpypants! Hugsies! I need lots of hugs right now!"

Veronica turned a face upon him that expressed first surprise, then outrage. Ian gritted his teeth while Sasha rubbed the scent of a being from the Court of Divine Blood on him, wondering how it was that he ended up in these situations. On the whole, he was a good man, one who spent his time—when he wasn't under direct order by Anzo—doing good works by rescuing animals, and in general, contributing to the betterment of the world.

And now look where that got him.

"Er...I thought you were together with Ms. James," the Witness said, her eyes narrowing on them.

"We're a threesome," Sasha said happily, turning around and wiggling her back against Ian. He gently pushed her forward, feeling that she'd masked his demon-riddled scent enough. "Aren't we, Ronnie?"

Veronica stared first at Sasha, then at Ian, and blinked a couple of times before facing forward. "We sure are."

"You are?" Teresita asked, a hint of amazed awe in her voice.

"Sure thing. *Ménage a trois*, that's us all the way to the bank and back. So, how about those addresses, Ms. Fuller?"

"I'm sorry," the Witness said, shaking her head. "But it's still not something this office does. John, my husband, you know—John, I'm sure, would not like it."

"What John doesn't know won't hurt him," Teresita said persuasively, having managed to stop staring in stark surprise at Veronica.

"We could really use your help with this," Veronica told the Witness.

"Yes, but you don't say *why* you are trying to find whoever moved to town." The Witness dabbed at her upper lip. "I really can't...Oh, dear. I'm sorry, I'm just a bit queasy at the moment. I can't think why...It must be breakfast disagreeing with me."

"We can come back another time," Veronica said with obvious disappointment.

Ian watched the Witness with growing concern. She really did look sick to her stomach; the lines around her mouth were showing starkly despite the careful application of cosmetics. He wondered if her sudden illness was a coincidence or not, and glanced speculatively at Veronica.

"No, no, it'll pass, I'm sure." The Witness waved the tissue in her hand and straightened her shoulders as if she could will herself into feeling better. "Perhaps if you told me why you were attempting to find a new resident of our fair Daniston, I might be able to see my way into releasing the list of rental properties."

"Pull up a carpet square, because it's a killer story. There's this woman—" Teresita said, and settled back to relish the story she was clearly about to tell.

To Ian's surprise, Veronica reached in front of him and dug her fingernails into Teresita's arm, effectively interrupting her. "It's very simple, actually," Veronica said with a smile that was clearly as fake as the Witness. "This summer, I'm trying to be more mindful of those around me who could use a helping hand. I thought it would be nice to reach out to all those folks in my immediate vicinity in case they need assistance in getting settled."

"Commendable, I'm sure—urgh." The Witness stopped and fanned herself with a glossy brochure featuring pictures of a house. "I'm so sorry, I am never sick, absolutely never. You can ask anyone. I don't quite know—"

Without another word she leaped up and ran toward the back of the office. Teresita and Veronica exchanged glances. Sasha, who had been looking out of the window, did a little twirl that made her black-and-white-striped miniskirt spin out and plopped herself down in the Witness's chair.

"Food poisoning, do you think?" Veronica asked.

"Probably. But I like to call it opportunity! Hey, Sasha, take a look on Aspen Fuller's computer for us, would you?"

"Teresita!" Veronica looked nervously over her shoulder, obviously worried someone in the office would see Sasha at the desk. No one was paying them the slightest bit of attention. "Do not encourage her to snoop. There's probably all sorts of private info on there."

"Of course there is, but how else are we going to get the info we need? And speaking of which, why did you dig your claws into me? That hurt!"

"I'm sorry, but what Helen told me was secret. At

least I think it was. And I didn't want you telling Aspen about the abused woman."

"You told me," she pointed out. "And Ian."

"You caught me when I was weak," Veronica said, lifting her chin in that manner that so delighted him. "And Ian is a dragon hunter, and promised to help me find her."

"I did?" Ian raised both eyebrows. He had no recollection of doing any such thing.

"Yes, you did. Yesterday, when we were making the deal about you teaching me. I told you about this woman that my sister wanted me to help."

"Ah." He didn't remember agreeing to that, but decided that it may well fall under the umbrella of general dragon hunter education.

"What do you see?" Teresita asked Sasha, who had dutifully started tapping on the laptop keys.

"Hang on, I'm almost done."

"You are?" Veronica scooted forward on her chair, glancing again over her shoulder. "What did you find?"

Sasha looked up, the antennae bobbing gently with the movement of her head. "It's kind of confusing at first, but you know, I don't blame these birds for being angry. It's not right those green things trying to steal their eggs."

"You're playing Angry Birds?" Teresita made an exaggerated slap to her head before giving Veronica a shove. "Go look before Aspen gets done barfing."

"I am not going to do anything so morally disreputable," Veronica objected.

Teresita gave her another shove. "Come on. It's the perfect opportunity."

"Then you do it," Veronica said.

"This is your caper, babe. Ian and me, we're just the trusty sidekicks."

"I beg your pardon?" Ian gave Teresita his best "I am a dragon, you should really fear me" look, but it was apparently wasted on her.

She made shooing gestures toward the laptop again. "Just do it quickly, and no one will be the wiser."

"Done! Finished the level," Sasha said, rising and stretching. "Mama needs caffeine. There's a coffee place on the corner—let me know when you *get the info you want*."

The emphasis on her last few words was impossible to miss. So that's why Sasha insisted he spend his morning here—the Witness must have some information on the courier. Ian considered the laptop, then watched Sasha bounce out of the office before turning to examine the rest of the employees. No one was even glancing their way.

"Hmm." Ian headed for the laptop just as Veronica, evidently having had enough of Teresita, did the same.

"Oh…uh…" She hesitated. "I was going to look for the addresses. Did you want to do that?"

"No, by all means, feel free to go first," Ian said, gesturing at it. "I was simply going to look for a bit of information on my own project."

"Really?" Her head tipped to the side in a wholly adorable way that had him wanting to kiss her. "Is that why you're here? I was going to ask, because at first I thought you might be following me, but then I realized you wouldn't bring Sasha with you if that was the case—"

"People!" Teresita interrupted. "I hate to break this up, but Aspen could be back at any time. Get a move on and find those addresses, babe."

"She's right," Veronica said, taking a seat and flicking around on the laptop screen. "Although I want to point out that if we get caught, I'm totally blaming you, Teresita."

"That's the spirit. I'll stand guard to make sure she doesn't walk in just when you are copying all her private files," her friend said, rising and moving to the door. Ian watched closely when Veronica flipped through the windows that were open on the Witness's computer. One of the screens had the title Church of the Mortified Flesh of the Anguished Witness. He decided that was a likely spot to look, assuming the Witness did, in fact, have information about the courier, but before he could say anything, Veronica flipped past it to a screen full of property listings, highlighted for the area.

"I think we need a secret word in case Aspen comes back suddenly," Teresita said from where she was casually slouched against the door. "What about Albuquerque?"

"Too hard to say," Veronica murmured, her attention on the screen.

"Whip-poor-will, then. I like that word. Whiiiippoor-wiiill. It has meat, that word."

Ian wondered at what point his life had turned into a Hollywood spy farce, and decided he probably didn't want to know.

"Here we go." Veronica pulled a small notepad from her pocket. "There were six people who signed rental papers during the last six weeks, only one of which is a solo female. I'll just write down the info and we'll be—"

"Whip-poor-will! Whip-poor-will!"

Ian caught sight of Aspen crossing the room, a paper towel crumpled in one hand. Hurriedly, Veronica ran for her chair. Ian sat down and flipped back through the windows.

"What are you doing?" Veronica whispered, glancing over her shoulder again. "I wrote down the info already."

"I'm putting the screens back in the order you found them," he answered, doing that, but also taking the few seconds required to scan the document with the church's name on it. As he scrolled down it, he scanned the text, freezing at the list of three names, his own included. Following that were a list of half a dozen demons that had been seen in the area and the addresses of four "safe houses" for members of the church. He quickly memorized the addresses, then took his place by Veronica.

And just in time. Teresita stood in the doorway, clearly blocking view of the inside, and said loudly when the Witness approached, "You okay? I was just going to check on you. We were worried you were, you know, stuck on the toilet and might need some meds, or extra toilet paper, or something."

"No, no, I'm fine. I felt much better once I splashed a little water on my face." The Witness came back into the office and sat down, glancing first at the computer screen, then quickly over to Teresita and Ian.

He kept his expression neutral. Veronica patted her pockets and made a distressed sound. Without a word, he pulled out of his pocket a small bottle of hand sanitizer and handed it to her.

She sent him a look of surprised appreciation and blithely dabbed it on her hands.

"Since your motives are as pure as they can be, I'm sure," the Witness said, evidently deciding no funny business had gone on while she was away, "I have decided to give you the information you seek."

"Awesome," Veronica said. "We much appreciate it."

The Witness tapped on her keyboard before saying, "There are, in fact, two rentals that have been taken off the market in the last two months. Here are their addresses. Do you have paper?"

Veronica brought out her notepad and made a show of writing down the two addresses. She frowned at them for a moment before catching Ian's eye. Clearly, the information didn't match what she'd found herself.

"Thank you," Veronica said. "I will definitely do the welcome wagon thing with them."

The phone rang at that moment. The Witness glanced at it and tightened her lips before saying, "Excuse me a moment...Hello? I'm afraid I have some people with me right now. If you can leave a number— Oh, you're here at last. Good. No, we'll come out and meet you shortly." She hung up and tried to give them a smile, but it failed miserably. She was looking more than a little green under her makeup. She reached for a tissue and dabbed at her mouth. "Where were we?"

"We were thanking you for your help," Veronica said, rising. "We'll leave now since you look so under the weather."

"You are entirely welcome. Please don't hesitate to come to Fuller Realty if you have any questions about—urgh." While she was speaking, she had stuck her free hand out to shake hands with first Teresita, then Veronica, but the second the latter hesitantly shook her hand, the Witness doubled over, her hand over her mouth.

"Oh, dear, you really are sick. Sip a little club soda, if you can," Teresita advised. "Works wonders on my kids when they are ralphy."

The Witness glared at her for a moment, then straightened up, clearly trying to fight the nausea, her gaze raking Ian before turning to Veronica. Still clutching the tissue, she hissed through clenched teeth, "Just who the hell are you?"

Veronica took a step back, obviously surprised at the vehemence in her voice and raw fury that lit her eyes. Ian moved closer to Veronica, just in case the Witness might think of attacking. "Me? I told you my name—"

"Not your name. Who are you? Who sent you

here?" Her gaze scanned Veronica angrily, clearly trying to find some sign. "*What* are you?"

"I'm...I'm..." Unseen by the Witness, Veronica's hand found Ian's, her fingers tight with obvious distress. He gave them a reassuring squeeze.

"What exactly are you accusing my...girlfriend... of?" He moved slightly so that he partially blocked Veronica from the Witness's acid gaze. "She has done nothing but seek your assistance so that she might aid others."

"She's done something to me," the Witness hissed. "She's not human."

"Of course she's human," Teresita chimed in from where she was standing at the door. Ian sent her a quick glance that, thankfully, she rightly interpreted, for she took her friend's arm and all but tugged her out of the room. "She's as human as you or I. Well! This has been fun, but just look at the time. We have a yoga appointment, don't we, Ronnie? I'm sure we do. Nice seeing you again, Aspen. Hope you feel better. Love to John and the kiddies. Thanks for all the help. Later, tater!"

Teresita had backed up while she spoke, taking Veronica with her.

"A word to the wise," Ian said in a flat, unemotional voice that he had perfected when speaking to Anzo. "Do not harass my girlfriend. She has done nothing to earn your venom."

"Ian," the woman said, her nostrils flaring. She either did not notice, or didn't care that Veronica and

Teresita had hurried out of the realty office. "What did you say your surname was?"

"I didn't," he answered, and with a brief nod, he turned and strolled out to the street.

To his annoyance, Veronica was nowhere in sight. Part of him wanted to run after her and demand to know what she was doing having contact with a Witness, while the other part of him wanted to focus on his own jobs. The sooner he found the esprits, the sooner he could break ties with Anzo, and then he would, at last, be free. Free of his bondage, free of the burden set on him with Sasha, and free to do what he was born to do—roam the earth unimpeded, protecting the innocent and bringing justice where there was none.

He strode to the coffee shop to find Sasha, wondering why the idea of being free to do his job no longer seemed so attractive. He had a suspicion the reason was tied up with a dark-haired temptress whose quirky ways entranced him like no other.

Damn it all to Abaddon and back.

INSERT SOME PUBLIC DOMAIN POETRY QUOTE HERE THAT LETS THE READER KNOW JUST HOW UPSET I AM. UNLESS MR. MANNY SAYS THAT'S MORE FORESHADOWING.

SHE'S NOT HUMAN.

The words echoed in my head as Teresita pulled me out of the office, chatting with the other employees in that friendly way she had, but keeping us moving until we were clear of Aspen Fuller and her compatriots. My skin felt like it was crawling when we hurried out of the building, and the animal in my mind encouraged me to run away, to go immediately back to the sanctuary of my apartment, and hide from the hate and accusation that had been so visible in Aspen's eyes. But hiding simply was not possible, not least because my apartment was no longer a sanctuary.

"That was a close one," Teresita said, glancing back at the building. "Do you think we should rescue Ian?"

"I don't think he needs help, no," I said, fighting with my own fearful emotions. "He's pretty badass, and Aspen didn't look like she was going to attack him right then and there."

"You're right. He's a big boy, and he has a big sword. Hey, that's an innuendo." She dug an elbow into my side. I paid no attention and just kept walking, blind to everything but the struggle within me.

"I wonder what information he was trying to steal from Aspen. He didn't tell you anything about that, did he?" Teresita asked. "You know, in pillow talk and such?"

Just the thought of my apartment made my stomach ball up onto itself. I knew I should take charge of the mess, but it seemed too much right now.

She's not human.

I shook my head to try to get rid of that accusatory voice. Of course I was human. The idea of anything else was ludicrous ... Why would simply being near me make her sick? I shook my head again. No. I couldn't think about that, either.

"Maybe you could let Dan and me join your threesome next time. We'd love that. Or better yet, you and I and Sasha could get a three-way going."

I sighed at my desperate attempt of denial. I knew from long years of therapy that denial never worked. It only put off the problem, usually making it worse than ever. I needed to cope with my life, starting right that moment. I stopped in the middle of the sidewalk, making Teresita bump into me. "Where are we?"

"About two blocks away from Aspen's office. You with me again?"

"What do you mean?" I turned around to retrace our steps, since my car was parked in the opposite direction.

"Oh, nothing. Just that you didn't bat an eyelash at the idea of having a three-way with Sasha and me."

"What is wrong with you?" I asked her, giving her a long, stern look. "You know I would never do a threesome, despite what Ian claimed. That was just because... because..."

"Yes?" she asked with annoying curiosity.

"Well, I don't know why he said that, or why he let Sasha rub all over him, but he must have had a rea— Oh." A thought so profound struck me that I stopped where I was, right in the middle of a crosswalk, only continuing when a car honked at me. "That has to be it."

"What is?"

"Yesterday, Ian made a big song and dance about me being from the Court place that Sasha is from, and made sure I was sitting on the couch, where she had a sweater and pair of leggings, when that demon came to his apartment. I bet you he did that because Sasha smells different."

"She does?" Teresita wrinkled her forehead. "She smelled fine to me, not that I stuck my nose in her armpit or anything."

"Demons smell awful. It makes sense that people who come from not-heaven must smell, too. And that would explain why Sasha rubbed herself on Ian's chest in Aspen's office—she was covering him in Court smell. All of which means that Aspen...No, but how could she?"

"How could she what? And who are we talking about, Sasha or Aspen?"

I got into my car, checking the street, but there was no sign of either Ian or Sasha.

Teresita got in next to me, her voice plaintive. "I hate it when you are mysterious. Dish, sister."

"It means, my dear..." I slid her a fast look before starting up my car. "Aspen Fuller isn't what she seems. If she's the sort of person who can smell a demon, and who is obviously affected by being near demon hunters, then she's not at all normal. And she had the balls to ask me what *I* was. Ha!"

"Where are we going?" Teresita asked when I pulled out.

"Remember that package I gave you this morning?"

"When you borrowed my second best pair of yoga pants, and told me to hide the package somewhere that the kids couldn't find it? Of course I remember that. It was only two hours ago."

"Well, that package contains my replacement sword, and we're going to get it."

"Ooh," she said, looking impressed. "Are you going fighting?"

"In a manner of speaking. I've finally realized that Ian was right all along—a dragon hunter should never be without a sword. I'm going to take my replacement, find that woman Helen wanted me to help, and then go back to deal with my apartment. And I'm not going to let my anxiety beast get the better of me."

"Look at you, girl!" Teresita said, doing a supportive fist pump. "That's the badass superhero I know you are. Right, so as your trusty sidekick, I get to come with you to help the abused woman, right? Because I made up a care package for her, with a few things like some tampons, and socks and underwear, and a bunch of samples of shampoo and things. And chocolate, of course."

"Of course you can come. I'm sure she'll be very grateful for your kit of goodies." I felt moderately better about coming to a decision, although a niggling thought worried in the back of my mind.

Just what was Ian at Aspen Fuller's office to find? I knew he was trying to find someone for his demon lord boss, but how a Realtor was supposed to help was beyond my understanding.

"Unless she's not a real Realtor," I said aloud.

"Oh, she is—she sold my mom her condo, remember? But I just bet you that she's something else, too," Teresita said, her voice filled with satisfied suspicion. "That whole shtick with asking you what you were, when all along she was just as guilty of being woo-woo."

"I am a dragon hunter," I told her with great dignity. "We are not woo-woo."

"Of course you are. What I want to know," she said when I pulled into our apartment parking lot, "is whether I get related powers for being your sidekick.

We need to Google that. Also, should we have t-shirts, don't you think? Or costumes!"

A half hour later we were on the street again, having picked up my sword, and headed off to check out the address I'd copied down.

"I still think it's weird that you're carrying around a demon's sword."

"It's better than nothing," I told her, peering out the window as I crept down a small side road. "Besides, it doesn't feel bad. It feels pretty right, to be honest. Here we go, four-fourteen. Wow. Who knew people still painted their houses the color of Pepto-Bismol?"

"Bright," Teresita agreed as I pulled up in front of the house we sought. It was a small Craftsman-style house, painted a lurid pink with shiny white trim. "What are you going to say to the woman?"

"Assuming she's in, I'll tell her we're here to help her start a new life." I got out of the car and strapped the sword to my waist. "Aren't you coming?"

"Nope." She pulled out her phone. "I know the role of a good sidekick, and that is to let the hero do her thing when she needs to. Just yell if you want backup."

"You're one smart cookie," I told her, and proceeded up a tidy flagstone pathway to a glossy white door.

A girl of about eight opened it up after I knocked, holding a white plastic wand with long stiff filaments on the end, each of which was topped with a glittery silver star. Clearly, she had been playing a fairy or princess. "Hi," she said, after removing a candy sucker from her mouth.

"Hello. Is your mom at home? Wait, I suppose I should tell you my name, because there's nothing quite so annoying as someone asking for your mom without telling you who she is. Who I am. Oh, Lord, now I'm babbling. I'm Veronica James, and my sister Helen asked me to help your mother out with...er...a bad situation."

The girl scrutinized me for a few seconds, then popped the sucker back in her mouth, and standing on her tiptoes, bopped me on the head with the wand.

"Ack!" I said when a fine wash of silver glitter dribbled down my hair and onto my t-shirt. "What the...Man, that stuff gets everywhere."

"You need it," the little girl said, waving her wand at me so it doused the front of my legs with more of the fine silver.

"I'm going to have a thing or two to say to your mom about the toys she lets you play with," I muttered, brushing off the silver. "Is she here?"

"She's making Sparkle lunch. Sparkle always has to have a special lunch. She's a princess."

"Of course she is." I relaxed a little, telling my anxious beast (which was on high alert for some reason) that a little silver glitter wasn't going to hurt me and that there was nothing wrong with little girls with healthy imaginations. "Elsa? Cinderella? Sleeping Beauty?"

"I'll get Indigo," the girl said with the faintest hint of an eye roll. I decided that since she hadn't shut the door on me, I could step inside without being too forward, and pretended I didn't see the silver footprints I tracked into the hall after me.

After a few seconds, a woman dashed out from a back room, her red hair making a fuzzy halo around her head. "Helen? You are Helen Larson?"

"Hi," I said when she skidded to a stop in front of me. "I'm Ronnie James, Helen's sister. She...uh... she couldn't be here."

The woman had a slight accent, something Germanic. "I see. And you are here why?"

"Helen said you needed to be protected from your ex. I assume you need a bit of a hand getting started in a new life." I hesitated, not sure how to go on. I wasn't sure if she was hinting she didn't want my help or was just trying to adjust to a change in plans. "She asked me to help you, and I'll do everything I can, of course. If you need to find a new place to stay, I am more than happy to find you safe digs."

She stared at me for a few seconds, then brushed past me to the door and opened it, gesturing. "Thank you. Goodbye."

"What?" I took two steps to the doorway and stopped, confused. "I'm sorry, did I say something wrong? I'm new at this, so if there are rules that I violated—"

"We just got here; why would we want to leave?" Her face turned red with suppressed emotion. "Besides which, a local church said they would help us. You may leave. We have no use of your so-called protection."

"I'm sorry if I can't give you the help my sister was insistent that you receive," I said stiffly, noticing out of the corner of my eye that a couple was striding down the sidewalk toward us. "I guess the only thing I can say is that if you need anything, I'm happy to help— What is *he* doing here?"

I interrupted myself when I got a glimpse at who was approaching. Ian was marching determinedly toward us, a purposeful expression on his face.

"Who?" the woman asked, about to close the door on me.

"My...er...for lack of a better word, boyfriend. You don't have to worry that Ian's a threat or anything. He's a good guy, too." I mentally ran through the options open to me. There was no helping it—if I wanted to help this poor, scared woman, then I'd have to make a sacrifice or two. "You know, my sister said that Alexander might know we were coming here. Maybe you shouldn't stay at this house—after all, if I could find you, what's to stop a determined ex? You'll just have to come back to my place."

"Your place? Where is that?" the woman asked, suspicion plastered all over her face. "We only just arrived, so I don't see how anyone could find us."

I remembered the mysterious phone call of a few nights past. "My sister seemed to think he could. And if you're still packed, then you shouldn't have a problem moving quickly," I said cheerfully before turning to greet Ian. "I'd accuse you of following me, but this time, I'm so happy to see you I could kiss you all over."

Ian had looked like a black storm cloud when he approached, but at my words, he paused and gave me the oddest look. "Why would I follow you? More to the point, why are you here?"

"I'm here doing my job." I shot the woman at the door a bright, confident smile that didn't at all demonstrate just how unsure of myself I was at that moment. "But if you weren't following me, then what are you doing here? Did Helen ask you to help this woman, too?"

"I told you that I'd never met your sister." Ian eyed the woman. "I take it you're Indigo?"

"Yes," she answered, clearly nervous. She pulled the door closed a few more inches, as if it would protect her from us. "You're the dragon hunter's boyfriend?"

"For lack of better word," I said hurriedly, giving Ian a look that said he'd better play along with me since I'd obliged him in the past. "He's also a dragon hunter. See? That's his sword. Oh, wait, you probably can't see it."

"She can see it," Ian said.

"Oh, good. Well, then. Why don't you and your little girls grab what you need for a couple of days, and we'll get you to my apartment."

"What's going on? Are we having a meeting on the front porch?" Teresita pushed alongside Ian and smiled at the woman at the door, who had pulled it closed another inch or so. "Hi. Are you the woman on the run? Don't worry about anything. My friend here is a kick-ass superhero partial dragon woman, and she'll keep the big bad jerkshit away from you. I'm Teresita, by the way."

I thought the woman was going to slam the door in our faces, but after another suspicious look at us all, she gave sort of a defeated sigh, and said, "I suppose it doesn't really matter. I'll get our things together. It'll just take us a few minutes."

"Do you need a han—" The door shut firmly on my offer of help. I grimaced at it, then turned to the others. "I guess not. So, Mr. Mysterious, how do you know her name if Helen didn't ask you to help her, too?"

For a moment, Ian appeared to have been turned to stone; then he said in a voice that was rough around all the edges, "Indigo is the woman your sister asked you to help?"

"Yes. She's on the run from a bad ex-husband or partner."

"I should have known," he said, rubbing his forehead as if he had a headache. "I should have guessed nothing would be straightforward. It's not like I ask for an easy job. I wouldn't dare. But simple? How can that offend the Fates by asking for simplicity in my life?"

"Are you having some sort of an episode?" I asked him, wondering what the hell he was talking about. "And while we're on the subject, how do you know my battered woman?"

He closed his eyes for the count of three, then said, "She is part of a job I'm on. Anzo wished for me to locate her. I should have known this would happen, since life always seems to twist whatever I try to do into something impossible."

"Really?" I was getting all sorts of weird vibes from him, ranging from anger and sorrow all the way up to dread and repugnance. "Why does your boss want her, if you don't mind me asking?"

"It's not something I can discuss here." He turned to look back down the street, and raised his arm, waving it back and forth a couple of times. "I assume your intention is to take Indigo back to your apartment."

"That's what I was thinking, yes. I mean, it's still a mess, but if she helps, we can make it livable pretty quickly. And to be honest, I don't know if I can live there after what happened."

"Did you see her place?" Teresita asked, waving when Sasha appeared at a trot down the sidewalk toward us. "Some rat bastard shredded literally everything she had. I saw it this morning, and it's like a bomb exploded in there."

"We'll get it cleaned up," I promised. "You can help."

"Gee, thanks," she said, giving me a lopsided grin.

"I thought you couldn't face going into your apartment," Ian said softly when Teresita went to greet Sasha. "That's one of the reasons why I offered to help you clean it."

"And I appreciate that offer. I just…" I gave a little shiver. "I can't think of living there anymore. But if I'm just mucking it out for someone else to stay there? Yeah, that I can do. Um. That is, if you don't mind me staying with you for a few days until I can find some-where else? Somewhere that hasn't been...tainted."

"You are welcome to stay with me as long as you like," he said, rubbing the bridge of his nose. I had hoped for a little passion in his eyes, something that would tell me he was happy to have me share his bed, but he looked more distracted than aroused.

At that moment, the door opened behind me, and two little girls hopped down the stairs. They looked similar in age, although not identical twins. Each wore a back-pack while Indigo followed with two wheeled suitcases.

"This is a bit ridiculous, you making us move just after we arrived," she said when I went to help her. "Who's that?" She nodded toward Sasha.

"That's Sasha. She's an...uh..." I didn't know what to say about Sasha. Ian saying that Indigo could see his sword meant that she wasn't a normal mortal being, but then again, she didn't look like superhero material, either. She looked, to be honest, like a frazzled woman at the end of her patience.

"Apprentice," Ian finished for me, taking one of the suitcases from her.

"She's from the Court?" Indigo asked, narrowly watching Sasha and Teresita.

"She is." Ian eyed the little girls as they ran to the street, their suitcases bumping after them. "And speaking of that, I assume those are—"

"Yes," Indigo interrupted somewhat breathlessly, pushing past me. "If you insist we leave, then let's go. I have to alert the church of our new location."

"Sure. My car is the VW Bug across the street. Um. Ian, can you take their luggage? Indigo and her girls can ride with us."

His eyes flickered to mine, an oddly unreadable expression in them. I felt like he was trying to tell me something, but I couldn't decipher what it was. "My car is bigger. If Indigo and her charges would like to come with me, Sasha could ride with you. My car is just at the end of the block." He took her arm and started to escort her down the sidewalk.

I leaped out in front and grabbed Indigo's other arm. "Are you kidding? And have the ghost of my sister haunt me to the end of my days? No, thank you. We'll all fit in the Bug if you take the luggage. You can have Teresita, too, if you like."

"I can hear you, you know," Teresita said, interrupting a comment to Sasha.

I grinned at her and tugged Indigo toward the street where my car was parked.

"I think everyone will be more comfortable in my car," Ian insisted, and more or less stole Indigo from me and had her several feet down the street before I realized what happened.

I set down her suitcase and ran after them, blocking the sidewalk so Ian had to stop. "Look, my sister made me swear I'd help this poor lady—"

"And no one is saying you can't help," Ian said, talking right over the top of me. "But there's no reason we shouldn't travel in comfort, is there?"

"We will be fine in my car," I argued, my chest and

face flushing as anger rose within me. I didn't know why Ian was being so obstinate, but I wasn't going to stand for him stealing my abused woman! "Now kindly back the hell off."

"Look, I don't care whose car we ride in, so long as we don't stand out here where anyone can see us," Indigo said, looking by turns exasperated and annoyed.

"It would be safer for them to ride with me," Ian said, taking a step closer until we were toe-to-toe. I couldn't help but notice the flames in his eyes, indicating he was riled. Well, he could just join the club.

"Oh, you'd like that, wouldn't you? Really, Ian, I hadn't pegged you as the sort of man who grabs glory like that... What in the name of Simple Green is that?"

About twenty yards beyond Ian, smack dab in the middle of the (thankfully low traffic) street, a strange thing happened. Or appeared. Something about the air caught my eye, some...thickening...of the air. It was as if the space there gathered itself up into a long pucker that stretched from the street upward about eight feet.

Just as Ian turned to see what I was staring at, the air rippled and tore open to reveal blackness, through which emerged four people, one woman and three men. As soon as they stepped through, the torn blackness dissolved into nothing.

"Demons!" Sasha said brightly.

"Get in the car," Ian said, pulling out his sword and starting forward.

"What? No, I'll help you fight."

"Get the esprits to safety!"

"Hey, look, it's Aspen." Teresita, with her back to the odd scene, noticed something was up and turned to stare at the people coming toward us. "And there's John. Hello again, Aspen!"

"What?" Indigo asked, turning back to look at the demons.

"Get in the car!" I yelled, running toward Teresita, pulling my car keys out. "Here, take these. Get Indigo and her girls out of here. Sasha, you go with them. Take them to my apartment."

"What's going on? What is Aspen doing?" Teresita shaded her eyes, peering at the group of four. Aspen and a man I assumed was her husband knelt in the middle of the street, drawing something on the ground with cans of black spray paint. A car turned onto the street and stopped, tapping on its horn politely. The two other men strode over to it, ripped the car door off, and pulled the driver out, throwing him across the street. Ian, who had been walking toward the foursome, now broke into a run, and headed straight for the two men who I guessed were demons.

"GET IN THE CAR NOW!" I bellowed, shoving Indigo and her two girls into the backseat, their luggage abandoned on the sidewalk.

"What—" Teresita started to ask.

I grabbed her by both arms and gave her a little shake, my face in hers. "You are my trusty sidekick. Get Indigo and her girls to safety. Don't ask questions, just do your job."

"Aye aye," she said, saluting sharply, then without another quibble headed for the car. Indigo, in the backseat, managed to extricate herself from her daughters, and looked like she was going to crawl out when Teresita got into the car, blocking her exit. Sasha hesitated a second, watching me while I pulled out Falafel's sword, then to my surprise ran over to me and gave me a quick hug.

"Zizi's blessings upon you," she whispered, then was gone, leaping into the car just as Indigo started shouting something that I couldn't hear over Teresita gunning the motor. She sped off with a little spray of gravel, allowing me to face the four people in the road, my mind alternating between wonder that my anxious animal was nowhere to be found and the hot rage that suddenly filled me.

Ian had reached the two demons by this point and was fighting with them. Both had swords, short, ugly-looking weapons. I stalked toward Aspen and her husband, who now had drawn a complicated triangle symbol on the street, strange runes chasing each edge.

"What the hell do you think you're doing?" I asked as I got closer, my fingers tightening around my sword. "That's defacing public property, not to mention your friends assaulted that poor man. Sir, just stay there, don't try to get up. I'll call the police and an ambulance for you."

"Do you think the mortal police can do anything to help you?" Aspen looked up from where she was spray-painting a semicircle below the triangle. "You brought this upon yourself when you sought to steal the sacrifices from the church."

"What church? What sacrifices?"

"Kill her," the man next to her said, bringing a pocket knife out, flipping open a blade, and quickly slashing his forearm so that it bled onto the triangle.

"What?" I shrieked, bringing the sword up to protect myself. "Are you insane?"

Aspen rose, her face hot with emotion. I glanced beyond her. Ian had one demon down, crawling away from him, and was now battling the second. I saw him glance over my way. I lifted my sword to show him that I was all right and didn't need his help.

That's when Aspen launched herself at me like she was a bullet, her head hitting me in my gut, not only sending me stumbling backward, but also knocking my breath away.

I gasped, reeling for a moment, but when she started drawing runes in the air, the same sort of black symbols that the wrath demon had tried to use on Ian, I saw red.

Literally. A wave of crimson burning anger washed over me, sending my anxious beast running for cover. With a snarled curse that I'm not proud of, I swung my sword, intending to scare Aspen into stopping the casting of whatever spell or curse she was engaged with, but she thrust her arm forward at that moment, throwing the black runes toward me. One of them clipped my wrist before dissolving into nothing, sending a cold, searing pain up my arm. I had little time to wonder at that because suddenly, Aspen was down to possessing just one arm.

She shrieked, and we both stared with disbelief at the arm that lay in the road between us. Normally, I would have fainted dead away at that point, since I am averse to blood and gore of any type, but there was nothing gory about the scene. It was just an arm, a slightly bloodied arm that lay in the street, and above it, Aspen was dancing a little jig of pure anger. Her shoulder, I was amazed to note, was also not gory. I had no idea if it was because she was also some sort of supernatural being, but whatever the reason, it allowed me to regain my wits.

"How dare you! That was my arm!" she screeched, snatching up the limb in question and shaking it at me. "I *use* this arm! Now what am I going to do?"

"Uh…" I lifted the sword in order to examine the blade. The blood on it was red, which meant one thing.

"You're not a demon," I said, wondering if it was impolite to ask just what she was.

"Of course not!" she snapped, one lip curling in disgust. "We are priests of the Church of the Mortified Flesh of the Anguished Witness, and you will die for what you have just done to me!"

"Whoa, now, let's not have any more accidents. I can't stomach another— Ack!" She lunged while I was speaking, and before I could gather my wits, I had taken off her other arm.

"ARGH!" she screamed, her voice echoing off the row of houses.

I pursed my lips at the sight of the two arms in the street, and sent up a silent prayer to whatever deity wished to hear it that there was no gore. "Well, now we've gone into a Monty Python movie. I hope you're happy."

"I will kill you!" she screeched again, dancing an infuriated dance.

"Aspen, what are you doing?" her husband said, looking up. "What have you done to your arms, woman?"

"She took them! She cut them off, and now I'm going to kill her!"

I twirled my sword. "Really? You want to do the whole Monty Python skit? Because you'll just end up with no legs, too, and I can't think that's a good look for you."

"Kill her!" Aspen shrieked, realizing the truth of what I said, and unfortunately, her husband decided she had a point, because he rose, pulling a gun out of his pocket.

Before I could yell a warning to Ian, John shot. Instinctively, I jerked to the side, the sword held up in front of me like it was a shield. I felt the shock of the bullet hitting the sword and being deflected to the side.

"Holy shit," I said, staring at the sword. There was a long scrape on the blade where the bullet had slid off the metal. "I really *am* Wonder Woman."

"Kill her, kill her, kill her!" Aspen chanted, hopping up and down next to her arms.

John took aim again, but this time, I embraced the

heat of anger filling me, making me feel like my skin was alight. I charged him, my sword raised. To my surprise, he didn't fire—he simply turned, made an odd symbol on the air, and disappeared into the black rift that opened in response to his gesture.

As soon as he disappeared, the air smoothed over just as if nothing had happened.

"John!" Aspen shrieked, her face showing both disbelief and the realization that he had abandoned her. Ian handily beheaded his last demon and started for us, the two bodies behind him dissolving into wisps of black, oily smoke.

"You bastard!" Aspen's voice broke, her face bright red with emotion, her skin glistening with sweat. I didn't know if she was talking to me, Ian, or her husband, but Ian stopped in front of her, carefully avoiding her arms.

"Why do the Witnesses want the courier?" he asked her.

"Who cares about her?" she sneered, which isn't an easy look to pull off when you are spitting mad and your arms are on the street. She seemed to calm down then, because she continued on in a more reasonable tone. "You won't get them. We have plans for the sacrifices."

"Since when do Witnesses use esprits for their nefarious purposes?" Ian asked.

I raised my hand, having wiped the sword on some tissues from my pocket. "Can I ask what you guys are talking about? I don't see what that weirdo church—

sorry, Aspen—has to do with the sword spirits. And who's being sacrificed?"

"I know who you are now," Aspen said, her eyes narrowing on Ian. "You're the man that demon said was sent to find the courier and her sacrifices. You're Alexander."

"You know Falafel?" Ian asked quickly.

"She's been very helpful," Aspen answered. "She told us about the courier."

"Wait, wait, wait. What do you mean Ian is Alexander?" I asked, my skin going goose bumpy. "His name is Ian Iskandar. Alexander is the man who abused the woman I'm helping."

She smiled. It sent a cold, clammy shiver through me, making me feel like something was gripping my stomach. "Ask him what Iskandar means. Go on, ask him."

INSERT SOMETHING SMART HERE. SMARTER THAN ME, THAT IS.

I LOOKED AT IAN, THE GOOSE BUMPS GOING INTO FULL-fledged skin-creeping before I shook my head at Aspen. "No. He can't be Alexander. Indigo would have freaked out when she saw him. You're just trying to confuse me because you are pissed about your arms, which, I'd like to point out, was mostly your fault, what with all your threats and throwing yourself forward in the path of my sword. Ian." I turned back to him. "What does Iskandar mean?"

His jaw flexed a couple of times. "In itself, it means nothing."

"I sense a 'but' in there," I said, surprised at how calm both my mind and my voice were. My gut, however, was filled with dread. I clutched the hilt of the sword so tight, it left marks on my fingers. "You might as well tell me."

"Yes, you might as well. And then you can pick up my arms and get me to the nearest mage to see if they can be reattached," Aspen said with a sniff.

"Ian?" I kept my gaze on him, and saw the moment his anger flared.

"Iskandar is the Tajiki version of the name Alexander. Is that what you wanted to know?"

I took a step back from him, feeling as if I'd been hit by a wrecking ball. "You're the Alexander my sister warned me about? The one who abused Indigo?"

"I have no idea what your sister said, since I wasn't there. And I have abused no one, man or woman, let alone Indigo."

"Helen warned me to beware of you. If it's not Helen you were chasing, then why would she warn me about you?"

"I have no idea." His face was stony.

"But why—"

"Oh, for the love of the seventy legions of the dark earth master...he wants the sacrifices! Now can we get me and my arms to a mage before it's too late?" Aspen stamped her feet and glared at me in a manner that indicated she would be waving her arms around if she could.

"Sacrifices?" I asked, taking another step back from Ian. My heart felt leaden while my brain tried its best to justify how I could have become so smitten with the man whom Helen feared.

"The esprits!" Aspen all but shouted. "The two esprits who will become sacrifices to the glory of the dark earth lord and who will raise us all to an exalted state."

Horror crawled out of my mental beast's cave and filled my mind. I stared at Ian, unable to believe it. "You want the two little girls? What kind of monster are you?"

He had both my arms in his hands before I could even register that he moved. "I understand that you are distressed, but I would have thought you trusted me a little more than that."

"I did trust you," I said, scanning his face for any signs of depravity. My mind told me that something was very wrong with the situation, but my heart—oh, my heart believed him. Ian wasn't evil. He couldn't be evil. He was the most chivalrous man I'd known, and was definitely a protector, not an abuser. "Now I don't know what to think. Why did Helen tell me you were bad?"

"I don't know." He rubbed the bridge of his nose again, his slumped shoulders and lines around his mouth speaking volumes. "I didn't hear the call she made to you."

"She told me to beware of Alexander—" His words filtered through the confusion in my brain, and I stumbled backward, holding up the sword without being aware I was doing so. "You heard the call she made to me?"

"No." He frowned. "I don't know how many times I have to tell you that I've never met Helen Larson."

"But you knew she called me? You were there, weren't you? Helen talked to someone while she was on the phone to me...oh, my goddess, you *did* kill her!" Rage and sorrow and betrayal bit hard, sending my temperature soaring.

"I'll just go get in your car now, shall I?" Aspen kicked her arms in the direction of Ian's car. "If I get a road rash on my beautiful arms, I know who I'll be cursing."

We both ignored her.

"Why do you want me to answer when you already have decided my guilt?" Ian answered, his face a mask of pain, but I didn't let that soften my anger.

"Because you're lying! You have to be—Helen warned me about you!" I yelled, and attacked him. His sword was out and blocking my attack before I was within a foot of him, as I knew would happen. "And if you didn't, you know who did, and you are deliberately shielding that person."

He parried my thrusting stabs, easily turning them aside with a grace that I would have admired any other time. He said nothing while I yelled out all of my frustration and anger and fear.

"And that means it has to be Sasha, because there's no one else who you would protect, at least no one I know about. Why did Sasha kill her? Why did you let her kill her? She was my only sister, and she was a good person!"

I slashed, and stabbed, and hacked, and each attack was turned away easily.

"You used me!" A new thought popped into the misery that was my mind. "You used me to find Indigo and her little girls. You followed me to the real estate office just so you could find this address!"

I lunged forward, trying a spinning move meant to disembowel, but Ian was well out of the range of it, his sword always in place just before mine had a chance to strike a blow.

"You slept with me just so you could get information!"

That finally did it. One second I was swinging wildly, the next he had me in his arms, his body hard against my softer curves. I could feel the heat of him, the fiery inner dragon that called to the one that now resided within me. "Did you get it all out of your system?" he asked, his voice husky with desire. "Because any minute now, the glamour is going to wear off, and mortals will see us, and I'd like to be away before they notice a woman kicking her arms down the street, not to mention you trying to beat the shit out of me very ineffectively with a large black sword. We will have to work on your swordplay this afternoon."

I thought of struggling, of pushing out of his hold, of telling him he was a sister-murdering monster, but I didn't believe it. Not really. I felt in the deepest part of my psyche that Ian was not a man who killed the undeserving. I rested my forehead against his shoulder. "I'm done. What's a glamour?"

"A spell to alter perception. Sasha no doubt cast it on this block as soon as she saw the Witnesses, but it won't last for much longer."

I sighed, drained now that my fit of anger had passed. "Ian, why didn't you tell me?"

"That my surname had an Anglicized meaning?" He shrugged, his lips caressing my forehead in gentle little kisses. "I had no idea it mattered to you."

"But I told you about Helen, and how she asked me to look for the battered woman because there was a bad man named Alexander after her, and you didn't say a word, not one single word."

He frowned, his pretty green irises no longer licked by flames. "When did you tell me?"

"The other day. Yesterday?" I pulled back out of his embrace, and put my sword back into its scabbard before rubbing my forehead. "I've lost track of the days. I told you about the task Helen gave me after she turned me into... well... this."

Ian looked thoughtful for a moment while cleaning the demon blood off his sword and sheathing it. "Yes, I remember something about that, but I believe I was distracted at one point. I must have missed you telling me what your sister said."

"Gee, thanks. It's so nice to know you were blatantly ignoring me when I was standing right there in front of you baring my concerns and worries and tale of how I came to be there in the first place."

One side of his mouth quirked up. Desire licked my insides, making me restless and wanting. "I apologize for that, but in my defense, you'd just given me something precious, and it consumed my thoughts."

I frowned a little frown, searching my memory of

the last few days. "We hadn't had sex then, so if it wasn't my body, what precious gift had I given you?"

"Hope," he said, then took my arm and escorted me toward his car. I don't know how Aspen managed to get herself and her arms in the backseat, but she had. Around us, the street seemed to come to life again, with people popping out of their houses, cars traversing the street, and pedestrians taking to the sidewalks.

The ride home was spent listening to Aspen bitch about us taking our own sweet time to get her to a mage for arm reattachment and being abused by me lopping them off in the first place, not to mention her husband leaving her there to be further tormented by us, and finally, how she'd wreak revenge upon both her husband and us once the dark earth master was summoned.

"Okay, first of all, mages are a thing?" I asked Ian in an undertone while Aspen was ranting about how no one ever gave her credit for all of her many and varied talents.

"They are."

"And they can put arms back on people?"

"Only certain types of beings, and no, mortals are not included, if you were thinking of suggesting they become medics."

"Oh." I sat back and looked out the window for a few minutes, having been about to suggest just that. "What exactly is the relationship between this weirdo church and Indigo and her kids? Wait, they are kids, aren't they? With sword spirits in them?"

"No, they are esprits in human form. Why they

chose children as those forms, I have no idea. I assume it was whimsy, although it might have been at the courier's suggestion."

"You mean Indigo, their mom?"

"I doubt if she's related to them. Those esprits are probably hundreds if not thousands of years old."

My brain boggled enough that I kept silent the rest of the way back to the apartment house.

Until we got out of the car, and then I asked, nodding to the backseat where Aspen was struggling to open the door with her feet, "What are we going to do with her?"

"Take her to a mage. Eventually. Once we're sure the sacrifices are safe."

"Will you stop calling them that!" I glared at him when he opened the door, collected Aspen's arms, and wrapped them in his jacket. "They're little girls, whether or not they have sword soul inner centers or not. Aspen, will you kindly shut up. People in this apartment complex are very nice, and we have several veterans and others who are missing limbs, so no one will stare at you unless you continue to make threats and references to old gods cleansing the earth from the blight of the unworthy."

She narrowed her eyes on me. "You will be the first against the wall. The dark earth lord will hear of your acts this day!"

"Yeah, yeah, tell it to the hand," I said, holding open the door for her. My hope that she'd stay quiet was a vain one. She continued to bitch up the three flights of stairs until I realized where Ian was guiding us. "Wait, what are we doing at my apartment?"

"She has to stay somewhere," Ian said, holding out his hand for my key.

Slowly, I brought out my keychain. "Yes, but she's obnoxious. Sorry, Aspen, but you really are when you're in full rant mode."

"The dark earth master will smite you as you have never been smitten!" she said with a dramatic swing of her hair.

"Smote, I think, is the term you want," Ian said.

"Smitten," Aspen insisted.

"Smited?" I offered, rolling it around on my tongue. "No, I think Ian's right; it's smote. I smite, he is smiting, you smote."

"Although the past participle version would be 'he has smitten,'" Ian said thoughtfully.

"True, but I think smote works for that, too—"

Aspen's scream of frustration interrupted us. "I don't care what it is; he will do it. To you! Now, get me a mage!"

I gave Ian the keys. "Fine, she can stay in my apartment, but that means Indigo and her girls have to go to your apartment with me, because I'm not letting Her Craziness here hang out with a woman who may or may not have been abused by someone with your name. I'll go get them now."

I hurried down the hall, but not before I could hear Aspen exclaim, "What in the name of the dark master happened here? This place is a dump!"

Teresita opened the door before I'd landed more than two knocks. Her eyes were a bit wild around the edges, and she pulled me inside before looking up and down the hall and slamming shut her door. "Thank God the kids are going to my in-laws after camp today. Do you know what those two little girls are?"

"Soul spirits," I said, entering her sunny living room. Normally, much as I love Teresita, her apartment gives me the willies because her kids aren't the tidiest of beings. It took us a while to work out a policy whereby I had one wooden chair that I was allowed to clean before I sat on it without Teresita being offended, and I would ignore the rest of the apartment. Now, however, I marched over to where the girls were sitting on the floor playing with a game console and plopped myself down onto the couch without regard to the scattered miscellany of items found there. "Indigo, I need to ask you a couple of questions. They might not be the easiest to answer, but I need to know the truth. Did Ian assault you in any way, shape, or form?"

"Ian? No. I've never seen him before. Why?"

"Because he…" I glanced over to the girls. "Er…Aspen implied he did, and I didn't think he could have, since he's a nice guy, but I thought it was better to check. Are these girls your daughters?"

"No, of course not. I wasn't born until 1874, and they are far older than that. Not to mention that I don't have any children." She gave me an odd look. "Why are you asking these questions? Glitter said you were acting funny earlier. Are you sure you don't have designs on them yourself?"

"I'm just a helper monkey," I protested. "It's my newly inherited job to help, not hurt you. Er…did you say Glitter?"

"Glitter is the one on the left. That's Sparkle on the right," Teresita said in a loud whisper. "They're angels, Ronnie. Actual, living, breathing angels. Right here in my house! It's almost enough to make me forget I'm an atheist!"

"They aren't angels," Indigo said with a dismissive click of her tongue. "They're simply esprits."

"Esprit is French for spirit…Wait, my living room is full of ghosts?" Teresita's voice rose on the last word.

Quickly, I explained what esprits were in this brave new world in which we found ourselves. "And now, if you don't mind, I'd like to get you and the…er…I'm just going to call them girls, because that's what they look like."

"We are female," one of the girls said, glancing back at us. She had to be Sparkle, since it was Glitter I met at the door. "Glitter bears the soul of a stone-age warrior matriarch."

"And Sparkle's original body was that of a Mesopotamian princess," Glitter responded, setting down the game controller.

"Why did you choose the form of little girls, then?" Teresita asked, her expression doubtful.

They both shrugged. "Why not?"

"Right, let's go downstairs to Ian's house." I hesitated for a moment, wondering if I was sending my charges into the den of the lion, but I reminded myself that I trusted Ian. Since the day when I'd gone to fetch Helen's sword, he had protected us from demons, refused the aid of the powerful Falafel, and showed compassion toward Aspen despite the fact that he obviously would have preferred to leave her to her own misery. "Quarters will be a bit tight, but until we can figure out what we're going to do with you, we'll just have to tough it out."

We entered Ian's apartment to find his living room had undergone a change. No longer were there two couches, a couple of chairs, and a number of end tables holding various animal cages, crates, and houses... Now there was a huge construction in the center of the room that appeared to be made up of all the furniture and animal houses, as well as at least six different blankets draped over it all.

"You made a blanket fort?" I asked Ian, who had opened the door for us.

"It's mine, thank you very much. I made it because Indigo and the esprits are to have my room," Sasha said, popping her head out from underneath a blanket.

"Isn't that a bit..." I bit off the word *childish*, not wanting to insult her, and fished out another word instead. "...awkward?"

"Not really, no. It's quite comfortable in here, although Ian isn't allowed in. He's being punished because he said I have to rehome the two kittens I found when we drove back here. See?" She held out her hands, which held a little calico kitten about four weeks old and its white-and-black sibling. "You can come into the fort if you like, though. I know you won't be as heartless as Ian is."

"I am not heartless," Ian said, closing the door with a little glance skyward, as if he was seeking patience. "I simply pointed out that until you know if those kittens are healthy and free of disease, they shouldn't mingle with George, Paul, and Ringo."

"The three of them are visiting that nice old lady on the ground floor. Her cat just died, and she said she'd welcome the distraction of the fab three until we knew about the kittens."

I glanced at the clock. "You work fast. You've only been here twenty minutes or so, yes?"

She grinned and retreated back into her blanket domain. "Time for music therapy! I think the kittens would like Aerosmith."

The two little girls (as I would continue to think of them, no matter how old and how warrior-like they had been in the past) made noises of pure pleasure and crawled in to join Sasha. Immediately, the sound of seventies rock emerged, followed by three voices singing along in absolutely no harmony at all.

"I'm going to lie down," Indigo said, glancing at her watch. "I have a headache that could drop a horse. Which room...ah. Thank you." She disappeared into what had been Sasha's room, closing the door softly behind her.

I glanced first at the blanket fort, then at Ian. "Will they be okay with her?"

"With Sasha?" Ian looked startled. "Of course. Why wouldn't they be?"

"Well, I gather they're kind of special, and people mean them harm. I didn't know if Sasha..." Once again, I bit off what I was going to say, trying to find a more circumspect way of asking my question. I couldn't shake the feeling that something had gone on between Sasha and Helen, but I wasn't prepared absolutely to believe that she had killed my sister.

"If Sasha was what?" Ian asked.

"Prepared to monitor them," I finished with a lameness that made me particularly unsatisfied with the situation.

"She is a dragon hunter, even if I won't let her have her *élan vital* back for a bit," he pointed out, then turned and went into his bedroom.

I made a face at his back, but decided I needed to talk to him, so I followed, making sure the front door was locked before I retreated to his room.

CHAPTER FOURTEEN

"IAN, WE NEED TO HAVE A TALK— OOMPH!"

Ian waited until Veronica was in his room and the door was closed before he did what he'd been wanting to do all day—take her in his arms and kiss every last breath out of her lungs.

She resisted for about two seconds before she melted against him, her delicious body clearly trying to seduce his with her soft, curved bits pressed tight against his. He loved the feeling of her in his arms, the scent of her tantalizing him. She smelled like a complex mix of honey, growing things, and sunlight, a scent that seemed to sink into his bones, captivating and capturing him. He moaned deep in his throat when his mouth came down on hers, filling his senses with the essence of her being.

"Oh, boy, do you know how to kiss," she said, wriggling against him in the most tantalizing way. He wanted her right then, but knew she might have issues with them making love when others were in the apartment.

"I do, but you're helping. And I agree we need to talk, but not right now. I've been wanting to do this since I saw you at the Witness's office," he murmured as he plundered her mouth again. He gave himself up to the moment, her dragon fire running just as high as his. He was amazed for a moment that he could feel it in her, but he had no time to wonder at that because his body was demanding that he give in to its urges and kiss every square inch of her. But first, he had to make sure she wasn't uncomfortable. "Are you okay with this?"

"With you kissing me?" Her breath was ragged, which just made her breasts rub against his chest in a highly distracting way.

"With that, and whatever else happens."

"Oh." She glanced at the bed, then back at him, and with a slow smile, reached behind and twisted the lock on the doorknob. "So long as no one can come in, yes, I'm fine with wild, steamy dragon sex with you."

"Good, because I don't think I'd be able to last much longer without touching you. Tasting you. Doing all the numerous things to you that even now I'm adding to."

"Oooh," she said with a particularly tantalizing

shimmy against his penis. "How many things are on the list?"

"Fifty-seven," he answered promptly, then thought of her doing that same shimmy while they were in the shower, wet and slick with soap. "Fifty-eight. Fifty-nine if you count the one in the swimming pool, but I don't think that's likely to happen given the public nature of it."

"My boobs miss your hands." Veronica's back arched when he took her breasts in his hands.

"My hands missed them, too. So did my mouth. Are you going to let me try oral sex this time?"

"I don't... I think maybe... I'm not absolutely..." The idea of such intimacy clearly stirred up her anxiety, although he noted a bit of hesitancy that he hoped boded well for the future. "I have this weird desire to lick you, which is shocking because not only is it a scandalous thought, but it's also so unsanitary. And yet, I still kind of want to... only, I'm not sure I'm ready yet."

"There is time enough for that. At least, I hope there will be," he said, his hands caressing and stroking her breasts. He loved the weight of them, the way their curves fit into his hands. He wanted to feel them against him, to taste them, but he knew he had to give Veronica time to build her own passion. He would take things at her pace, even though it meant enduring a painfully hard erection.

She almost ripped the buttons off his shirt, her hands sliding up the planes of his chest, touching, teasing him with every stroke of her fingers.

They moved in synch toward the bed, Ian helping her peel off her t-shirt and bra. The scent of warm woman—his warm woman—was intoxicating, and all he wanted to do was to give in to the desires that were building impossibly hot fires within him.

It was at that moment that she pushed herself back from him, frowning a little. "What do you mean, you *hope* there will be time? Is that a reference to me taking forever to get over my phobia? Because if it is—"

"No." He stopped her objection by kissing her, her mouth sweet and hot and spicy all at the same time. "I am more than willing to give you whatever time you need to get comfortable with the idea."

"Oh," she said, clearly mollified. "Good. Because I'm not saying it won't ever happen, but I don't like to be forced."

"I told you that I would never ask you to do something you don't wish to do," he said, quickly ridding himself of the rest of his clothing.

Veronica used the moment to wiggle out of her jeans and espadrilles, moving over to slide her hands around him, beneath his underwear, taking both cheeks in her hands. "You have the nicest butt I've ever seen. Or, in this case, felt." She gave his ass a little squeeze. "I just want to bite it."

His eyebrows rose. "Literally or figuratively? Because if it's the former, then I would say that is a good step forward."

She squeezed a cheek again while she considered. "Figuratively right now, although I have to say the thought of biting your behind is definitely in my mind. Do you think anyone will know what we're doing in here?"

"I doubt they will, but would it bother you if I was wrong?" His hands slid down to her own ass, its delightful fullness driving his desire even higher.

"Noooo," she said on a half moan when his hands took possession of her bare breasts. Ian froze for a few seconds until Veronica realized what happened.

"Sorry, that wasn't a no to stop. It was an answer to your question. Ian, I don't want to do oral sex, but you can...you know...touch me downstairs if you like."

He waggled his eyebrows at her in a way that had her giggling, and scooped her up to carry her the three remaining steps to the bed. "I am more than happy to oblige, although you have to let me try out a theory of mine."

"What's that?"

He just smiled and peeled off his underwear. "Have you heard of aversion therapy?"

Veronica blatantly ogled him, moving quickly to strike a seductive pose on his bed. "Boy, you really are...I mean, I know size isn't the be-all and end-all, but you're just...girthy. Wait, what did you say? Aversion therapy?"

His smile turned wicked when he crawled up her legs, her delectable, luscious legs, pausing every few inches to drop a kiss along their silken lengths. "It's a method of making people more comfortable with things they don't think they'll like."

"Ian," Veronica said sternly, giving him a look that a mother gives an unruly child. "I was diagnosed with OCD at sixteen. When I say I'm very familiar with aversion therapy, you can believe it. But this is different than not being able to take the trash out without having to take three showers in a row. This is something wonderful between us, and I don't want to ruin it."

He returned the look with one of his own. He was utterly and wholly captivated by her, and for the life of him, he couldn't pinpoint anything extraordinary about her. She was quite lovely, but not the sort of beauty who made men stop on the street and stare. She had an imaginative mind with a quirky sense of humor that appealed greatly to him, but she clearly wasn't overly concerned what others thought about her. He liked the fact that despite the emotional challenges she'd had to face—not the least of which was unintentionally becoming a dragon hunter—she was down-to-earth, and without airs and the mantle of victimhood.

She was simply the most delightful woman he'd met in several hundred years. Possibly in his entire life. And despite knowing it was folly to even consider a future with anyone, he found himself doing just that.

But first, he had to show her she could trust him. "I will let slide the implication that I'd force you into something after reassuring you I wouldn't, and instead, show you what I mean." His head dipped down, and he gently bit the inside of her knees.

He felt her watching him while he moved from leg

to leg, slowly inching upward, kissing, licking, and nibbling along the way. He put aside his own needs and passion, determined to show her that she had nothing to fear from him, and everything to enjoy.

For a moment her legs were tense and unyielding, but she clearly forced herself to stop fighting him. "Okay, I'm going to relax now, because either I trust you or I don't, right?"

"Right," he said, eying her crotch. He badly wanted to show her what pleasures he could give her, but he knew that would violate the bond of trust they'd developed. He rubbed his cheek against her inner thigh instead.

"And I do trust you. Implicitly," she said with a sort of wonder in her voice. He glanced up to see her face slightly flushed, her eyes almost glowing with emotion, so pure and honest, it almost hurt to look. She was falling for him—he'd seen that look in other women's eyes over the ages, but it had never pleased him before. Whereas a love-struck sexual partner had hitherto been cause for separation in the past, that same look in Veronica's eyes made something deep inside his chest glow with warm satisfaction...that turned to dread. How could he think of a future with her? He couldn't even keep himself out of trouble, and now he wanted to expose her to potential danger.

It was folly, sheer folly, and he had to stop.

He dipped his head again, kissing her pubic mound before sliding his fingers past her underwear so as to gently tease her inner parts until they were as flushed as her cheeks. Folly it might be, but for the moment, he was unable to resist her siren lure.

It was a temptation to give her secret parts a little flick of his tongue, but he held his desire in check and kept to the bounds she had set. Even if it killed him— and it might well do just that, considering the amount of sexual frustration he was experiencing—he'd give her pleasure so great she would see stars.

"Oh, that is so . . . oooh, two fingers? Holy moly, that little curl you did . . . narng!"

"Are you speaking in tongues now?" he asked, amused, aroused, and damned near desperate to bury himself in her heat.

"Possibly. Wait, do you have fiery eyes?"

He looked up. He had no idea what his eyes looked like, but a ring of silver flames licked the edge of her irises.

She smiled. "Good. I just wanted to make sure, because I swear I can feel fire inside of you."

"That's my dragon blood calling to yours. Now. Let's see if I can do this right."

"Do what?" she asked, propping herself up on her elbows to watch him.

"You'll see." He considered removing her underwear but decided he'd let her choose when that moment was right. Instead, he spread her legs a bit wider, his fingers drawing intricate runes along her inner thighs. He frowned, concentrating, trying to master that which so often eluded him.

"Why are you staring at my crotch?" she asked, clearly worried. "Is something wrong? Is it my underwear? I can take them off if you like. In fact, they pretty much have to come off in order for us to go for the shiny brass ring, although you were doing just fine with them on a few minutes ago."

"Hush," he said. "I'm trying to concentrate."

"On my undies? I know they aren't fancy, but I've never found sexy lingerie particularly comfortable—"

"Hush," he repeated, lifting his head enough to cock an eyebrow at her. "You're making this harder than it should be."

"I thought that was the whole idea," she said with a saucy smirk that warmed him to his toes. He had a feeling that she didn't joke often with lovers, and the fact that she felt comfortable enough to do so with him was a sensation he cherished.

He returned to rallying his dragon half, summoning the fire that always seemed to simmer inside him, trying to shape and form it the way he had been told full-blooded dragons mastered at an early age.

"Okay, not to be critical, but I'm kind of losing the warm, tingly feelings all that touching, and beard on inside of thighs, and little love bites generated—"

The dragon in him gained the upper hand over the demon, allowing him to breathe fire all over her thighs and groin.

"Glarg!" Veronica grabbed the sheets with both hands, her back arching, her legs taut. Her body trembled, and for a moment, he thought he'd pushed her too far, but at that moment she grabbed his head and tried to pull him upward, over her body.

"Oh, my goddess, you have to finish!" she demanded, simultaneously wiggling out of her underwear and trying to wrap her legs around him, even as he rose up and positioned himself. "That was incredible, Ian. Why aren't you moving? Why aren't you inside of me, making me sing songs I didn't know that I knew?"

He wanted to laugh, but his body was wholly focused on only one thing—joining his body and soul with Veronica's. "A gentleman waits for a lady to finish talking before he dives in."

"Dive!" she commanded, slapping her hands along his arms before sliding them up to his shoulders. "I'll shut up."

"I don't want that. I like how you tell me what you're thinking. I've never had a sexual partner who did more than moan and issue instructions," he said, easing himself just inside of her. The heat seared through him, driving his own blaze even higher.

"Glorioski," she said on a gasp that took in a huge quantity of oxygen. She was panting, her fingernails digging into the muscles along his shoulder line.

Ian was unable to keep from asking, "Are you having a painful gas bubble? Should I stop?"

She pinched his shoulder, giggling and tightening her legs around his waist in an attempt to pull him in deeper. "Nice time to use my own words against me. Can you do the fire while you're doing this?"

"Yes, but it takes a while for me to summon it. Dragon fire does not come easily to me." He leaned forward, sliding a bit more into her, using the position to lave her breasts with his tongue. "Next time, I'll blow the fire inside of you."

Her eyes opened as wide as they'd go while she clearly considered such a thing. "That sounds… dangerous. Can I do it to you?"

"Breathe fire? You have to learn how first." His head dipped down to kiss her, the sweetest kiss he could offer, one that promised everything and demanded nothing in return.

"Teach me," she said, her eyes soft with passion and pleasure. He wondered if she knew she was falling in love with him, and wondered if he should caution her against a doomed future, but he was unable to make the words come.

He wanted her in love with him. He wanted her to reciprocate the feelings that he didn't want to admit were forming in the dark, neglected parts of his soul that were hidden from Anzo…He drove that thought from his mind, knowing the fear for her future would drive away all sexual pleasure if he allowed it to continue.

Since she had stopped talking—a coping mechanism, he suspected, for rationalizing what they were doing—he flexed his hips and slid even deeper, the sensation raising the need to claim her, to make her his. He fought the need, knowing the depths and strength of it might shock her, but at the same time, feeling the shreds of control slipping from his grasp. Desperately, he clawed it back, barely keeping the dragon within from manifesting its nature.

She rocked her hips, her legs pulling him in deeper, while at the same time, she bit the thick line of muscle along the top of his shoulder, and that was it for his control.

The dragon rose hot within him, and he made a noise deep in his chest that had her purring in response. Before he realized what he was doing, he pulled back enough to slide one hand under her and flip her over onto her stomach, pulling her hips up to meet his insistent thrusts.

"I'm sorry," he managed to get out, his heart pounding in his ears while he wrestled with the dragon need to shape-shift. It was rare for a dragon hunter to be able to do so, but for the first time in his life he felt like he might actually be able to manage it. He knew without a shred of doubt, however, that Veronica would not be receptive, and focused on the woman beneath him and making her as wild as he was. "I have to do this...the dragon...Christos, woman, don't wiggle that way..."

She moaned, and panted, and clutched his pillow, but didn't protest the new position, and in fact, seemed to be quite happy with it, especially when he did something he'd never done before during sex: he breathed fire. It swept along her back, signaling the start of his orgasm, and powerless to stop it, he was about to help Veronica to her own when her body shuddered around him. She moaned, collapsing down onto the bed, taking him with her. He lay insensate for a few seconds before realizing that he might be too heavy for her, and rolled off, his body both highly charged, fueled by dragon fire, and feeling as weak as a newborn kitten.

"Remember before when I said holy moly?" Veronica pushed herself back off her stomach and onto her side, her delightful chest heaving with the effort to breathe. "I want to say it again, but this time, let's put it in all caps, because Jehoshaphat, Ian, that was—hoochiwawa! That was the best thing that has ever happened to me, and that includes graduating cum laude, which, until this moment, was the high point of my life. That fire was...hoo."

Ian was amazed he had the power left to speak, let alone roll onto his side and pull her up against his chest. "It was good. Very good."

She pinched his nipple. "Understatement, sir. When can we do it again?"

He laughed. He couldn't help himself, she was so completely open, she charmed him like no other had ever managed, not in the length of his long, solitary life. And he knew then that he was in trouble, a very great amount of trouble, because he wasn't going to be able to walk away from her when the time came to do so.

But would she want him when she learned the truth about him? Would she still hoochiwawa him once she found out he'd failed to save not just her stepfather, but also his own mother? That he'd been driven by failure into turning his back on dragon hunters?

She was so brave, and fearless...and his soul was stained and dark with misery. She would have no trouble walking away from their blossoming romance. From him.

Something inside him died at the thought.

BADASSERY AND OTHER SHENANIGANS. ALSO, CHECK WITH MR. MANNY IF BADASSERY IS A LEGIT WORD.

"I SUPPOSE WE SHOULD CHECK ON ASPEN," I SAID, taking a towel that Ian had handed me.

"I will need to find a mage." He was dressing, having taken a quick shower after our connubial time, and I was about to do the same. My anxiety monster might have been mostly tamed by my metamorphosis into dragon hunter, but it couldn't stand the thought of spending the rest of the day among other people when I smelled like Ian. "Then yes, we should address the situation with your apartment. And find who stole your sword. By now, they've probably taken the esprit and used her for...who knows what."

"The esprit? She wasn't in there when Helen gave the sword to me."

Ian turned a look of astonishment on me. "What? Are you sure?"

"No, but she said..." I cast my mind back to that horrible night. "She said it was missing something, that it was empty. That means the esprit, right?"

"I assume so." He closed his eyes for a moment, my heart aching at the lines of pain and exhaustion etched on his face. "Why didn't you tell me this?"

I gave a little shrug. "I didn't realize what she meant at first. You couldn't tell?"

"No, it was in its scabbard." He took a deep breath. "At least we don't have to worry about the esprit being stolen, but now I very badly want to know what happened to it."

"I'd still like to know who took it." I hesitated before I stepped into the shower. "I would add 'finding out who killed my sister' to the list, but I suspect you wouldn't like that."

The look he gave me was steady and completely without emotion.

"I thought so. You're going to have to tell me someday, you know," I said, picking up a clean towel. "I trust you, and know you wouldn't intentionally hurt anyone who wasn't horrible or a demon, but that doesn't mean I'm happy about the fact that you haven't told me everything you know about the situation."

He blinked.

I sighed and left the subject to hurry through my shower. I had made my mind up that I would not push the point about Helen's death until I had to, but it still rankled a bit that Ian was unwilling to share with me. That annoyance aside, I was dressed and ready to go ten minutes later, but Ian was still sitting on the bed, his attention focused on his phone. "Any ideas on that subject?"

"Which one?" he asked absently, typing in a text quickly. "I found a mage an hour away. She says she's willing to come to us."

"Good. I was talking about my sword, by the way. Finding out whoever stole it, assuming it was the same person who broke into my apartment, and I don't see why that shouldn't be. Also, what are we going to do with Indigo and the little girls?"

"Ah." He looked up at that, but what I saw in his eyes sent a spike of fear through my gut. "About that."

"You're not going to turn them over to the demon lord who hired you," I stated, alternating between worry and disbelief. "You know I'm not going to let you do that."

"I know you would try to stop me should I wish to do so," he said with a smile that any other time I would consider adorable and sexy as hell. He laughed outright at my expression, pulling me onto his lap. I tried not to notice the scent of his body wash, or the heat of his chest against my side, or even the way his hair curled, but it was hopeless. "You don't have to look as if you wish to gut me, Veronica. I've done what I could to keep from Anzo the true nature of the esprits, and as luck would have it—and honestly, I don't think luck has anything to do with it, but we'll let that go for now—Falafel did likewise, evidently focusing Anzo on the courier instead."

"Why would Falafel do that?" I asked, puzzling over such behavior. "Hide the esprits, I mean? She was a servant of Anzo, too, wasn't she?"

"Yes." Ian's gaze darkened. "I believe she was working with the Witnesses to gather esprits to help her attempt to usurp Anzo, but since Falafel is gone, we can't pinpoint just what her plan was. The Witnesses, however, clearly have some interest in the esprits, as well, or else they wouldn't have shown up to meet Indigo."

"Then we'll just have to keep them safe from the Witnesses, and all will be well. I mean, they're totally safe with you since you won't let Anzo have them, right?" I asked, not liking the grimness of his expression.

He looked away, his jaw tightening. "You know I am bound to Anzo."

"Yes," I said slowly. "But you're not a monster. You wouldn't give two little girls to a demon lord. I know that about you, Ian. You're an honorable man. Sasha told me this morning that you're almost a hundred years old, which means you must have saved...oh, thousands of people being a dragon hunter, right?"

His expression froze. "Far from that."

"Okay, not thousands, but hundreds, right?"

His gaze flickered away, but not before I saw the pain in his eyes. "I suppose I should tell you now. You'll find out sooner or later, and it's just as well that you know the truth now."

"What?" I asked, my skin crawling. "Oh, goddess, you did kill Helen!"

"No," he said, his words grim and abrupt. "I didn't kill her, but I did kill her father."

I stared at him in horror. "That's not what you said earlier. You said that you thought Falafel killed him while you were being Anzo's slave."

"Yes, but Falafel should never have been given the chance to do that." His hands tightened into fists, his eyes staring straight ahead at the wall. "If I'd had my *élan vital* with me, I might have dispatched her when I first saw her, but I didn't."

I looked at the sword that sat across the foot of the bed. "You never go anywhere without it. I don't understand why—"

"That's not my sword," he interrupted, making an abrupt gesture before running a hand over his hair. He looked both anguished and angry, his dragon fire running hot within him. I wanted to help him in some way, but I had no idea how. "It's Adam Larson's. He gave it to me."

I sat silent while he explained what had happened with Adam.

When he was finished, I put my hand on one of his fists and gently stroked his knuckles. "I know you blame yourself for Adam's death, but really, you did everything you could to save him. You took his servitude upon yourself. You got Falafel out of the way for a couple of weeks. You gave Adam time to do the work he wanted to do. You aren't responsible for his death."

He took a deep breath. "If I'd had my *élan vital*, Falafel would have died that day, and Adam Larson would be alive now. I failed him just as I failed my mother almost a hundred years ago. She died by the hand of a wrath demon, too. I should have saved her, but her *élan* was destroyed, so I bequeathed mine to her. When the monsters who were trying to purge the world of demon hunters descended upon us, she was overwhelmed…and I had no way to help her. A dragon hunter without his *élan* is…nothing."

Silence filled the room, thick with sorrow and fury. I knew Ian well enough to know he was damning himself for not protecting someone he loved. "How did you escape being purged, too?"

He turned eyes filled with self-loathing upon me. "The cult—a predecessor of the Witnesses you met earlier—conducted a ritual using the esprit they'd stripped from her sword. She threw herself onto it as they were consuming it to purge us, breaking the bonds and causing everyone touching it to… implode." He sighed heavily. "I was being held prisoner in another room. I didn't know they'd all been destroyed for days, until I managed to break out of my shackles. Then I found their ashes, and I knew my mother had given her life because I had failed to do my job."

I wrapped my arm around him, leaning into him, trying to pour into him all the warmth of my inner fire. "Or maybe she simply wanted to make sure that you lived on so that you could save others."

He was silent, but I felt him withdraw from me emotionally.

"Ian, you're not a god. You are a badass dragon hunter, and you're sexy as hell, but you aren't omnipotent. Your mom did what she had to do to save you and probably a bunch of other dragon hunters, just as you bound yourself to Anzo in order to save Adam."

"If I'd had my *élan vital* with me," he said, making another of the abrupt gestures that expressed intense frustration. "If I hadn't turned my back on being a dragon hunter—"

My heart, already at the brink of falling for him, pushed itself over the edge at that moment. This lovely, tortured, warmhearted man who put the happiness of others ahead of his own desires had clearly sacrificed himself for another. "You don't know what would have happened. Maybe Falafel would have killed you right there, and then where would we have been? Adam would be the slave of Anzo, and you wouldn't have saved me from those demons in the parking lot. I'm not a believer in any organized religion, but this is truly one of those times when I believe that things happen for a purpose. Your mom sacrificed herself for you, and you sacrificed yourself for Adam."

"It wasn't enough," he insisted, somewhat obstinately, I thought to myself.

I looked at him, love filling me at the sight of his wonderful, tortured self. "That you put Adam before your own self says a lot about you."

He grimaced. "Some might say it says a lot about my stupidity."

"No," I said, leaning forward to kiss the corner of his mouth. "It says that even though you didn't want to be a dragon hunter anymore, you were chivalrous, and generous, and selfless, and you did what had to be done to save an innocent man. You truly are a badass hero."

I swear he blushed a little. He certainly looked very uncomfortable, and muttered something about simply doing what was right. I decided the moment was ripe for distracting him from his inner flagellation. "So the sword you have is Adam's? What happened to yours?"

"It was destroyed with my mother."

"Huh." I thought for a moment. "What happened to the esprit in it?"

"When it was destroyed in the explosion, you mean?" Ian asked.

"Yes. If they are spirits, can they be killed?"

"Not in the sense you mean." He looked thoughtful. "The demons we destroy are gone for good. I assume it's the same for the esprits when they give up themselves."

I rubbed my forehead, feeling a slight headache coming on. "Okay, so we have Adam working on a fix for dragon hunters and asking you to find his esprit, and Falafel ruining everything. But what happened to Helen's sword? Why did its soul spirit leave?"

"You will have to ask her that," he said after a few seconds of silence, one where he refused to meet my eyes.

"She's dead," I pointed out.

"She said she would be back. I assume she knew what she was talking about."

"That's true, but I don't know when she's coming back. Or even how. All that aside, do you know the reason why her sword spirit left?" I had the uncomfortable feeling I was balancing on the edge of a razor. There were so many secrets, so much I didn't know, so many ways for me to fall and lose myself, and yet in the midst of all the confusion and uncertainty, Ian was my safety net. He was the one person who, I realized with a start, didn't make me feel nervous at all. It was almost as if he was an extension of myself, one that my anxious animal had accepted fully.

"No," he admitted with obvious reluctance. "But an esprit does not leave an *élan vital* unless it has a good reason, or it is stolen. Adam said he let his esprit have a day off, which is unlikely, but knowing Adam, not unbelievable. I didn't know your sister, though, and it doesn't sound like she relinquished her esprit willingly."

I thought back to that horrible night. "I wish I'd thought to ask her, but I had no idea about all of this. And even if I did, I don't know that she *would* have told me that since she was rushed on explanations. But, Ian, if you are implying that she did something wrong, something heinous that would make the pure-as-driven-snow esprit bail on my sister, then you are wrong. Helen wasn't a bad person. Her only thought at the end was to protect Indigo and her girls from ... well, from you. She told me an informant had said you were after them."

"Informant," he said slowly.

"Falafel, do you think?" I asked, puzzling that out.

"I doubt it. Your sister was an experienced dragon hunter—she would be able to recognize a demon when she saw one. I think it's far more likely that one of the Witnesses told her about me, although how they knew I was in the area is beyond me. Unless Adam told someone what happened."

"That could be," I agreed. "She didn't say much about her dad, though. I think it's far more likely that the person who punched the hole in her middle took her soul thingie and told her that you were a baddy in an attempt to have her find the esprits before anyone else—namely you—could locate them."

"No," he said, and shook his head, just like that was that.

And with that one word, I knew my plan to let him tell me the truth in his own time had shriveled to dust. I could no longer pretend he might be hinting at something. I had to know the truth.

"Dammit, you *do* know who killed Helen, don't you?" I stood up to confront him, my emotions in such a turmoil, I couldn't begin to untangle them. Except one: sorrow. "Ian, I've tried to be patient, but I can't any longer. It's too much. You have to tell me."

"I don't have to, you know," he said pleasantly.

I slapped my hands on my legs. "You do!"

"Why?"

"Common decency?" I asked, grinding my teeth a little.

He considered this for a minute. "I agree that it would seem that way, but the reality is that you would be more distressed knowing the situation concerning your sister than you are being angry at me for not giving you that information."

"Oh, you arrogant bastard!" I said, frustrated. "How about this: you should tell me because I'm your girlfriend."

"Falafel is dead. There's no reason you need to maintain a pretense regarding that role any longer," he said with maddening calm.

A sharp stab of pain followed his words. Was that all I was to him, just a convenient excuse who was no longer needed? For a moment, tears pricked the backs of my eyes, but my anger quickly dried them up with what I was coming to realize was my own dragon fire.

"How's this for another reason, then," I snarled, marching over to the door in frustration before marching back to face him. "I'm in love with you, okay? So now I'm your *real* girlfriend, and Helen was *my* sister, and you *have* to tell me what you know about her death."

He froze for a moment, then smiled a long, slow smile. "I wondered if you'd realize that."

I fought the urge to deliberately misunderstand him, saying instead, "You don't have to look so damned happy about it. Since you just said I didn't need to bother to pretend we have a relationship, I assume that means you are completely indifferent to me, unable to trust, or love, or commit to me."

"I never said any of that—"

"Then who killed my sister?" I yelled the question at him, no longer concerned if the others heard me. "Tell me, please, Ian. I need to know this. It's important."

He was silent a moment, then stood, taking my upper arms in his hands. "I will tell you if you insist, and despite your belief that I'm a cold-hearted bastard who only values you for sexual favors, but I do so under protest. You will not like what you hear."

"I can take it," I said, mentally bracing myself. "I'd rather have the truth than be protected because you think it's best for my happiness."

"So be it." He was silent for a moment before he added, "Sasha blasted that hole through your sister's torso."

"What?" My shriek must have been heard a good five miles away. Rage filled me, rage and the red-hot burning desire for revenge. My skin prickled with heat that I was only now coming to understand was my dragon fire manifesting itself. "What the hell? Why would she do that? Why? Oh, when I think of her being all cute and quirky and anime adorable, and all the time she murdered my sister—"

I struggled to get out of his grip so that I could go confront her.

"Veronica, stop fighting me."

"I will if you let me go," I said, still struggling. "And don't you dare give me that look that says it's totally wrong to go out and demand Sasha tell me why she would do something so heinous, and then smite her on the spot."

"Now you are allowing your emotions to dominate your common sense," he said with that same maddening calmness. "You said you were a pacifist. Despite the beheading of Falafel, and the Witness's arm removal, I believe you truly do abhor violence."

"I do, but what's the good in being a dragon hunter if you can't cover people in dragon fire and roast them alive?"

"There is much wrong with that image, but that aside, you don't know the situation. It's certainly not what you are currently thinking it is," he said, trying to keep me still. I gritted my teeth and managed to drag us a few feet toward the door before he dug in his heels.

"Of course it's what I think," I said between gritted teeth. "Sasha killed Helen. There's no other way to look at that fact except facing the truth that your precious little apprentice killed my sister. Goddess, you were in on it, weren't you?"

"Yes," he said slowly. "But not in the way you think—stop fighting me, and let me explain."

"No," I yelled, and managed to wrest my arms from his grasp. Despite the need to go out and confront Sasha, I had to face the betrayal that Ian had just dealt me. "How could you? How could you do that to my sister and then kiss me? Make me believe in you? Make me fall in love with you and never say a word about the truth?"

"Helen asked Sasha to kill her!" Ian shouted over my rant.

"How could you—" I stopped and stared at him in utter disbelief. "She *what*?"

He took a deep breath, his eyes filled with a plea. "She begged Sasha to end her life. You have to understand the situation she was in…She was literally faced with the same dilemma as her father—end her life, or become the servant of a demon lord, with no will of her own, a puppet of pure evil unleashed upon the mortal world. Her esprit was gone. Her father was dead, most likely killed by Falafel. There was no protection for Helen with her own esprit missing, and no one to turn to. I took Adam Larson's bondage onto myself, but I couldn't save his daughter. Sasha did what I could not do."

I shook my head. I couldn't seem to wrap my brain around the idea. "But you didn't punch a hole in my stepdad."

"No, I did not." For a moment, his face was filled with regret, so deep it physically hurt. "Helen Larson hadn't yet been taken to Anzo by Falafel when Sasha found her."

I swallowed back a painful lump of tears, my throat aching with the effort. Part of me wanted to cry for my stepfather and Helen, the other for Ian's sacrifice. My voice was choked when I managed to ask, "Even if I believed that Helen wanted to kill herself, how was punching a hole through her middle saving her?"

"It gave her time to call you," he said calmly. I felt like

screaming at a world gone suddenly mad, and yet Ian stood there like nothing was wrong. "It gave her the time she needed. She could recruit you, talk to you one last time, and arrange for her charges to have the protector she wanted. Sasha didn't tell me any of this right away, of course—she waited until you had taken your sister's place, then told me simply that she had saved Helen from a fate that would have given her endless torment."

I closed my eyes for a few seconds, remembering that night, remembering Helen's strange calmness and acceptance of her imminent death. No wonder she wasn't at all distraught by the horrible situation—it was the end she had chosen for herself. And she had picked me to pass along her legacy to, one she knew I would have to honor. That didn't dispute a fact that hurt me almost as much as her death... "You were there when she died. You lied to me."

"I have never lied to you, and I have no desire to start now. I know what happened to Helen Larson, but I wasn't there," he said, taking my hand. I pulled it back. He took it again, his fingers tight around mine, but his thumb was making gentle little strokes across my knuckles. "Sasha was trying to help me locate the esprits and found Helen in a bad way."

"She couldn't have been that bad if her torso was whole," I said, suddenly feeling so weary I wanted nothing more than to curl up in Ian's bed and hide from the world. "Why didn't Sasha tell you where Indigo and her girls were if she was right there with my sister?"

"She didn't know their location. Helen didn't tell her. I gather they were en route at that time. That's one thing that's puzzled me, as well. I assumed she told you where to find them."

"She didn't, but things were...chaotic." I thought for another minute. "What did Helen do that allowed Falafel to grab her like that?"

"I don't know that, either. Sasha didn't say other than Helen was afraid of what would happen should she lose her will."

"That doesn't make sense." I rubbed my temples, trying to fit the puzzle pieces together. "You're bound to a demon lord, and you have all your abilities. You don't have to do what the demon lord says. You've already said that you aren't handing over Indigo or the little girls to her. What's the deal?"

Absently, Ian scratched at one of the tattoos on his arm. "I can resist the compulsions Anzo lays upon me because my *élan vital* is whole and intact. Adam Larson had none. Helen's was missing. It's only by the strength of the esprit in my sword that I have retained some autonomy."

"Helen was vulnerable without her esprit..." I had a vision in my mind of a superhero turned evil, and thought I could understand a little why Helen had made such a desperate choice. "Oh, Ian, why didn't she tell me?"

"I can't answer that. How long were you with her?"

"Not long enough," I admitted. "She said we had to hurry, so she probably left out all the explanations."

"It is quite a lot to take in, especially if you haven't

been born into this world," he agreed, then asked, when I started toward the door, "Where are you going?"

"To talk to Sasha. I have to find out what happened that made the esprit leave Helen, and I just bet you Miss Hole Puncher of the Year knows."

"I don't think you want to—"

Ian had followed me out into the living room, but he stopped when I did, staring at the deflated blanket fort, now nothing but a wad of blankets on the floor, with several cushions scattered about. All the animals had been released from their cages and were milling about in a confusion of mostly small furry things.

"Christos, what...Sasha!" He ran for the kitchen, then to the bathroom, calling for her.

I went to the other bedroom, but it was as empty as the living room. "Indigo is gone, too," I said, scooping up a couple of guinea pigs and hurriedly stuffing them in their home. Ian was doing the same with the hamsters, bunnies, birds, and kittens. "Do you think they went somewhere? To Teresita? I'll check."

He said something when I dashed out of the door, but I didn't wait to hear what, instead running upstairs to bang on Teresita's door, counting the seconds impatiently until she opened it up. "Dude, what is your— Oh, it's you."

"Are Sasha and the girls here?" I interrupted.

"No." She looked taken aback. "Why, did they do a runner?"

I swore to myself. "I don't know. They aren't at the apartment."

She frowned. "But you were there, right? Didn't you see them leave?"

"No, we were...busy."

"Doing what? Oh, man, really? In the middle of the day?" Teresita looked strangely pleased, but I didn't have time to discuss a burgeoning relationship—if Ian and I had such a thing—and instead ran back down the stairs.

"Should I come with?" Teresita called after me.

I paused long enough to say, "No, you stay here in case they come back. Call me if you hear anything," before continuing on. I caught sight of Ian on the stairs going to the parking lot and followed him down the second flight, catching up to him as he ran down the length of parked cars, clearly searching.

"Nothing?" I asked, panting slightly as I ran after him. I made a mental note that if my anxious animal would let me, a membership to a gym might not be out of place. "Is my car...Oh, it is here. I wondered if they might not have taken it for some reason."

"Sasha would never take the esprits away without telling me," Ian said, whirling around and glaring down the street as if he expected to see them. His eyes narrowed; then he spat out, "The Witness!"

I was really puffing by the time we ran back inside and up the three flights of stairs to my apartment. I got the door open and burst in, expecting to find the apartment devoid of life, but Aspen was still there.

Gagged and tied to a chair, her arms stacked tidily in front of her on a mound of clothing that she'd evidently kicked from my bedroom.

"What in the name of Mr. Clean is going on here?" I asked, looking around the room. Although Aspen had evidently spent her time in my apartment by kicking the detritus of the destruction into tidy stacks, my happy yellow-and-peach-colored walls were stained with strange black marks, spray-painted without the least bit of care or artistic skill. "Well, isn't this lovely. As if having all my possessions destroyed isn't enough, now someone came in and graffitied me."

"That isn't graffiti; it's a series of spells. That bit there is Latin and has to do with speaking the truth," Ian said, pulling Aspen's gag off so she could speak. The gag appeared to be a bit of torn bath towel. "What happened here, Witness?"

"I'll tell you what happened here, *dragon hunter*," she said, spitting at him, which shocked me until I realized she was doing so to get bits of towel fluff out of her mouth. "You left me alone without a mage, and that rat bastard of a husband tracked me down and forced me to tell him where the sacrifices were. Me! His own wife, a priestess of the dark earth lord! I will never forget what he did to me. *Never*!"

Ian cut her free of her bonds, and she stood up, stamping her feet, either from ire or to emphasize her point. I wasn't sure which.

"The Witnesses took them?" Ian's eyes flashed fire. "Where?"

Aspen sniffed and looked away. "I don't know that I should tell you. You said you'd get a mage to put my arms back on, and yet there they are. Unattached."

"I will get you a mage," Ian argued. "Just as soon as the esprits are safely away from your murderous crowd."

"Oh, no, I'm not falling for that. You'll just stuff me up here again in this disaster zone of an apartment," she said, giving me a disgusted glance. "I don't know how you could live like this. An animal is tidier than you."

I just glared at her while Ian said, "I will not bargain with you. Did they take them to the church head-quarters? Another location?"

"I know where the church is," I told him. "It's about twenty minutes from here. We can pop over and check."

"We don't have time to run all over town. We need to know *now* where they are." He turned back to Aspen. "Tell me what I want to know, and I will arrange for the mage to come sooner rather than later."

"What guarantee do I have that you won't just run off and leave me in this hell pit of filth?" she asked, suspicion written all over her face . . . which also bore a slight green tint and looked unpleasantly moist. I wondered if it was me personally that made her sick, or if it was something else.

"You have my word," Ian said, looking moderately affronted. I smiled at him, a sudden warmth in my belly warning that my desire for him hadn't been dimmed despite the realization that he had kept the truth about Sasha's involvement with Helen from me.

"Ha! Like that's worth anything."

The only excuses I can claim for my next actions are the fact that I was tired of her bitching, time was running out, and I very much wanted to get Ian back into bed where I could let him apologize properly for not telling me everything. Without a word to either of them, I walked into my kitchen, stepping over stacks of papers and books, taking one of Aspen's arms as I passed by. I stopped at the kitchen sink, turned on the water, and then put my hand on a wall switch, holding the arm just above the mouth of the drain. "Right. Do I turn on the garbage disposal, or do you tell Ian what he wants to know?"

Aspen's eyes opened so wide I thought her eyeballs might just roll out onto the floor, but she gave a horrified sort of gasping hiss and said through her teeth, "You wouldn't dare! You are a dragon hunter."

"So?"

"That means you cannot attack those who are unarmed or at a disadvantage!" She looked utterly outraged but kept sending little nervous glances over to her arm. "It's a rule. For all I know, it's an oath you take."

I tapped the switch with my fingernail. "I am not like most dragon hunters. Are you going to answer Ian's question, or should I see what this does to your manicure?"

"You unholy bit of cow dung!" she snarled, but when I raised one eyebrow and looked at the garbage disposal switch, she commenced speaking, her words running together. "Fine! All right! I'll tell you, but I am so going to tell whoever heads up you hunters just what you're doing, because it has to be against all sorts of laws and rules and codes of honor."

"One chewed up set of fingers it is," I said, plunging the hand into the mouth of the drain.

Aspen spat out a word that I won't use here, because Mr. Manny doesn't think profanity has a place in popular fiction, but before we could say anything, she added, "They are in the crypt."

"What crypt?" Ian asked just as I said, "You guys actually have a crypt?"

"In the basement of the church, yes. Now give me back my arm." She hovered protectively over her other arm, clearly intending on fighting me if I tried to take it from her.

"Here, I'll set it with the other one. And thanks. Ian, I know where the church is; you don't have to look it up on your phone." I pulled my car keys from my jeans and started for the door. "We'll take my car."

"Hey!" Aspen protested when Ian followed me out of the apartment. "What about me?"

"What about you?" Ian asked.

"I want to go with you." She narrowed her eyes in a glare so potent it was just about able to shoot laser beams. "I have a thing or two I want to say to my husband. You can have the mage meet me at the church. Bring my arms."

She sashayed out before me. I looked at Ian. "Do we have time to argue with her?"

"No," he said, and gathered up her arms before following me out.

CHAPTER SIXTEEN

"WHAT IS IT ABOUT ME THAT MAKES YOU SO SICK TO your stomach?"

Ian flicked a glance over at Veronica. She had turned around in the car to look back at the Witness, who sat with her head, dog style, hanging out of the window.

"I don't wear perfume because so many of those chemicals are bad for you, and I put deodorant on after my second shower, and this is Teresita's second-favorite pair of yoga pants, so I don't think they stink or anything."

The Witness pulled her head in and curled her lip. "It has to be the demon in you. No one else has made me feel the way you do."

"Gee, thanks." Veronica looked astonished and mildly offended at the same time. "Although I have to say that even though dragon hunters technically have a demon side to their psyche, Ian thinks I don't have much of one because my stepdad was changing my sister. Perhaps what's making you sick is Ian? He's got a huge demon side."

"Thank you," Ian said, once again amused by the way Veronica's mind worked. She left him feeling adrift on a sea of the unexpected, and oddly, he relished that sensation. He could easily see himself spending years with her at his side, in his bed, and tangling herself up in the deepest, darkest depths of his soul. What there was left of it.

Only there would be no future. It was simply too dangerous to risk Anzo finding out about her.

"That sounded rude, didn't it?" Veronica wrinkled her nose. "Sorry, Ian. I didn't mean that you're stinky or evil, but you *do* work for a demon lord, and you *do* have those tattoo brand things, and you said yourself that your demon bit tries to overtake the dragon side."

"It's not him," the Witness said. "It's you. By the dark earth master's blood, you're not a virgin, are you? Purity always makes me ill."

"Hardly," Veronica said with a conspiratorial glance at Ian that left him wishing they were back at his apartment. "I think maybe your nose is confused. Or whatever it is that makes you react to demons, because as I said, I don't feel demonic at all. My sister's demon side was in the process of going away, so it makes sense that I'm the same. It's just me inside, and sometimes a lot of fiery intensity, but nothing evil. I think Ian has to be the answer."

"It's not him," the Witness repeated. "I took a whiff of him when he left me in that hellhole you call an apartment, and he didn't do anything but make my nose itch. This is all you." She shot a grumpy look at Veronica and put her face back out into the air rushing past them as they drove to the church.

"How can my demon part be worse than yours?" Veronica asked him in a low voice, clearly affronted by the thought.

"It's not a matter of being better or worse—because your sister was changed, you are different from most dragon hunters. However, I'm beginning to wonder if she's not reacting to something that surely must reek of demon—your sword."

"Deathsong isn't bad," Veronica said, bristling a little as she patted the sword at her side. "The spirit inside is happy to be out and about doing good in the world, instead of being forced to do evil for Falafel."

"I have no doubt that's true, but the rest of the sword was forged by a demon, and it could be your proximity to that which is making the Witness ill. Regardless, you are going to need every last bit of your dragon abilities in the next hour, so don't worry about whether or not you smell demonic."

"You think there's going to be trouble at the church?" she asked, her knuckles whitening around the hilt of the sword.

"Of course there will be. Anything else would be far

too easy." He spoke with bleak humor but wasn't sure if she caught it until she flashed a concerned look his way.

"It does kind of seem like we're smack-dab in one of those weird indie movies where people walk around with a bowl of fruit salad in their arms while investigating the mysterious disappearance of an all-male glee club. Turn left at the light, then it's the fourth right."

"You watch vastly different indie movies than I do," he commented, following her instructions.

"Why are you stopping here?" she asked a minute later. He pulled to a stop three blocks away from the church and parked the car beneath a voluminous walnut tree. "The church is a couple of blocks to the right."

"It can't hurt to keep our presence here quiet as long as possible," he answered.

"Good point."

"Now, here's what we're going to do," the Witness announced. "You and the stinky evil one are going to provide a screen for me."

Veronica turned to glare at the backseat. "You can just knock off the insults, because if there's one thing almost twenty years of therapy has taught me, it's that I do not need to take crap from anyone, especially a woman who evidently belongs to a cult that plans on killing two little girls in order to raise some Lovecraftian old god."

"I don't think Lovecraft had a very solid grip on just how horrible the dark earth master is," Ian said, getting out of the car and opening the door for the Witness, who was trying to grip the door handle with her teeth.

"Really? That doesn't sound good." Veronica got out of the car looking a little worried, but stopped when Ian handed her the Witness's arms. "Aw. How come I have to be on arm-carrying duty?"

He gave the Witness a little shove forward, keeping a grip on the back of her shirt in case she had ideas of bolting. "I'd let you escort her, but I'd prefer to keep her from vomiting until we are done. Proceed, woman."

"Damn you!" the Witness snarled, but didn't make any other protests until they turned the corner onto the street where the church was located.

He felt the glamour even before the utter silence registered.

"Demons," the Witness said, peering down the street to where a line of seven people stretched across the width of the street, each one in possession of weapons ranging from axes, to war hammers, swords, and even what looked like a morning star. "Looks like a protective guard. I'll let you two handle this lot."

"How very gracious of you," Veronica said softly, but she pulled her sword and gave it a little twirl. "I'm ready for them."

It was on the tip of Ian's tongue to demand she go back to the car while he dealt with the demons, but while his need to keep her safe was almost overwhelming, he wouldn't for the world do anything to undermine her newfound faith in her abilities. He'd just have to make sure that her lack of experience didn't cause her harm.

"If you leave before we give you permission," he told the Witness, allowing her to scurry behind them, "I will see to it that you never get your arms back. Veronica, lock them in the car."

"Aye aye, Captain Hunkypants."

He waited until she had done as he asked, and gave her a look that let her know he was deadly serious. "There is no shame in retreating if you are overwhelmed. Stay close to me, and don't listen to anything the demons say to you."

"Kind of like an exorcism, then? They tell lies to make you weak and vulnerable?"

"More like they will attempt to cast a spell on you if you give heed to their words."

"Well, that's horrible. Although...can we do that, too?"

"With training, yes."

"Cool." Her eyes were alight with dragon fire as she shifted the sword from one hand to the other. He could feel his own blaze kindling at the sense of danger that permeated the street, the familiar thrill of a fight firing his blood and doing much to push down the doubt that had driven him from practicing his birthright.

"There's just something about the knowledge that you're ridding the mortal world of a few more demons," he murmured softly, but not softly enough.

Veronica nodded. "It's kind of an endorphin rush, isn't it? I feel like...rawr! All superhero and badass, and all those other things that Teresita said. It's a shame she can't be here to see it. Honestly, at this point

I feel like I could take on the world! I don't know when I've ever felt this powerful. Is that the dragon part kicking in, or am I suddenly a danger junky?"

"Most likely it is a manifestation of your dragon self." He was silent a moment, fighting to control the surge of dark power that threatened to engulf him in its warm, sticky embrace. "Just be aware that it can stir your demon half as well. Keep the dragon uppermost. Let its fire burn bright within you, and do not let anything that feels insidious grip your mind."

"Got it." She glanced around. "How come there are no sounds? A big truck went by on the street behind us, but I didn't hear it."

"It's a glamour. I hope whoever cast it knew what they were doing, otherwise the mortals in that block will be exposed to a show the likes of which would haunt their dreams. Are you ready?"

"Yup. No talking to demons. Keep balanced on the balls of my feet. Anticipate whenever possible. Heads are a priority, followed by arms."

The Witness snorted and said something rude under her breath.

"Stay close to me," he repeated, and with a little prayer to no specific deity, he charged forward into the line of demons.

It was a short battle, much shorter than Ian imagined it would be given that there were seven demons all bent on keeping them out of the church. Veronica and Ian slashed at the line of them, knocking weapons, arms, and heads aside with the vengeance of the righteous.

He was moderately distracted making sure Veronica didn't get overwhelmed, but to his surprise and pleasure, she held her own against them, evidently having learned quickly from the few points he'd taught her... that or her dragon side was starting to take hold, sharpening her instincts and reaction times.

"This is... ugh, demon blood everywhere!... actually a really good workout. Maybe I won't have to... watch out, that one you sent flying into the tree is crawling back... won't have to go to the gym after all," she said, panting a little while she twirled and neatly severed the head of a demon who was in the middle of bringing a morning star down on her head.

Ian dealt with two demons who decided that disarming him would be the best plan of action.

"That was the wrong choice," he snarled when together the pair jumped him, one of them bashing his sword hand with a battle hammer. His sword clattered along the pavement a good sixteen feet away, causing Ian to think briefly of making a dive for it. Instead, he allowed his dragon nature to have its head. Roaring, he punched one demon in the face with a fist covered in fire, sending the man flying backward into a picket fence, impaling him on the jagged shards of wood. The second demon slashed at Ian's head with a short sword. Ian doubled over to avoid being decapitated and kept moving, head-butting the demon in the midsection, causing the demon to stumble backward and fall. Ian was on him instantly, twisting the sword out of the demon's hand, stabbing downward into the demon's chest with his full strength, effectively pinning the man to the earth.

Ian straightened up, avoiding the demon's flailing legs while it desperately attempted to pull the sword out, and snatched up his *élan vital* before tackling the last two demons, both of whom were descending upon a panting but elated-looking Veronica. She roundhouse kicked at the nearest demon, following it up with an attack that left the demon without its head, shoulder, and an arm.

The last demon was dispatched while it ran toward Veronica, an axe held high over its head. Ian lopped off the head and gave Veronica a stern look. "What did I tell you about using martial arts during a fight with demons?"

She wiped her sword on the shirt of the demon at her feet before looking up, scowling. "Dude! I just killed three demons on my own!"

"Yes, and you could easily have lost a leg by roundhousing that demon." He sheathed his *élan vital* and glared down at her, his arms crossed and his heart beating madly at the idea that she had put herself at risk, even if it was a small risk. He nodded to the ground at a lifeless corpse just before it evaporated into a foul, oily, black smoke. "That demon had a sword. All she had to do was swing it down while you were kicking her, and you'd be without a leg right now."

"But she didn't, and I'm not," Veronica pointed out with blithe disregard for his concern. "Was that a roundhouse kick? I have to say, that's kind of cool I can do that now. I've never done any martial arts, but it just kind of felt natural at the time. So do I have like a black belt or something now? If so, that's pretty slick that being part dragon means you're a Jackie Chan or Michelle Yeoh. Teresita is going to be so impressed."

Ian took a breath and reminded himself that Veronica was new to her powers and still in that phase when everything seemed possible. He didn't want to ruin that for her with the realization that although she wasn't as demonically inclined as the rest of the dragon hunters, there was still a dark element to her psyche, and sooner or later it would manifest itself.

He hoped against all reason that, perhaps given Adam's research and her sister's transformation, Veronica wouldn't ever have to suffer from the demon inside. The thought of her trying to cope alone with that on top of her other emotional issues cut deep with the intensity of a laser.

For she would be alone. He couldn't risk her well-being just to keep her with him, and he couldn't break the tie to Anzo without sacrificing someone else for his own selfish purposes. Even if he found a willing victim, he couldn't live with such an act. Regret swamped him, making him want to rail against a world that would dangle happiness just out of his reach. It was a torment worthy of Anzo herself.

"Ian?" Veronica's voice was soft, filled with emotion that seemed to wrap itself around him. "Are you okay? Are you painful gas bubbling again, or is something wrong?"

"Well, that took forever. You, Stinky, get my arms and bring them with you. I will want them when the mage arrives." The Witness strolled past them, wrinkling her nose and stepping carefully over the black smears of the demons' remains. "I hope someone plans on cleaning up the street, because the smell here is absolutely vile. It's all I can do to keep from ralphing everywhere."

"Ian?" Veronica gently squeezed his arm.

"I'm fine. My painful gas bubble moment—which again, I'm happy to inform you I've never had—has passed."

"If you say so." She cast him a couple of doubtful looks but said nothing more and followed when he gestured for the Witness to proceed them.

Although the street was lined with leafy walnut trees that, for the most part, hid the church, a suitably gothic-looking spire loomed above. By the time they approached the church, Ian could see the building that hunkered in between the tidy houses was old, with the high arched windows common to late nineteenth-century buildings, crumbling moss-covered steps, and a yard overgrown with clover and tall weeds. The windows—once lovely—were now blackened and scribed with silver runes.

Closer inspection showed the steeple in the process of falling down and black doors covered in graffiti. Everything about the building gave off an air of decay and neglect.

"How do we get to the crypt?" Ian asked when the

Witness stopped at the crumbling stone stairs leading up into the church proper. "Is the access inside or out?"

"Inside," she answered, tossing her head. "But if John is expecting you, he'll have the entrance protected."

"By spells and things like that?" Veronica asked, looking with distaste at the untidy building. "This place could use a bucket of bleach and some really stiff scrub brushes."

"I'm sure John arranged for something more than just magic to guard the crypt," the Witness said, nodding toward the door. "Well, what are you waiting for? Go on in. I don't have all day to stand around here while you two debate unimportant things."

"We aren't debating anything, but if we were, that would be how easy it would be to eliminate you completely," Veronica said with a smile that would have done a shark proud.

Ian laughed to himself as she marched past him to the door, saying under his breath, "You're turning bloodthirsty, aren't you?"

She yanked open the door and flashed him a grin. "Being a dragon hunter is oddly freeing. I mean, look at me—I am holding a doorknob, Ian. An actual doorknob that other people have touched with their icky, sticky, germy hands, and I have not only *not* wiped it down before touching, but I also don't plan on using hand sanitizer as soon as I'm inside. I'm a wild, carefree sort of person now."

"You are daring personified," he agreed, his heart

warming at her joyous embrace of her new role, and at that moment, he knew he was in love with her. Wholly, irreparably in love. Until the time when he ceased to draw a breath, his heart would be hers.

He wanted to sob at the unfairness of it all.

DRAGON HUNTER 101 (CHANGE IF MR. MANNY THINKS THAT TITLE IS TOO FORESHADOWING. OR CONFUSING. OR BOTH)

"No pushing! If you make me fall and hurt myself, I'll sue!"

I ignored Aspen's threat when Ian gave her a shove into the building, and blinked a few times at the darkness of the church interior, my nose wrinkling at the musty smell of old building, rodents, and damp. A dim light filtered from around the imperfectly painted-over windows, as well as from a couple of nasty fluorescent bulbs that occasionally buzzed and flickered overhead. "And you thought my victimized apartment was a dump."

She glared at Ian before giving me a condescending sniff. "We don't spend much time upstairs. This is all for show, mostly to keep the neighbors off our back."

"Where is the entrance to the crypt?" Ian asked, peering around the big main room of the church. It was filled with dusty pews, a ratty altar, and a stack of water-damaged cardboard boxes lined against a far wall.

"I'm guessing right there. Oh, hello. Am I right in saying you don't look much like someone who has been kidnapped?" Movement to my right had caught my peripheral vision, revealing Indigo as she slowly emerged from an arched doorway.

"Who are you— Oh, it's her." Aspen gave another of her annoyed sniffs, then, with a foul look at me, moved a few feet away. "She's nothing but a courier. Don't waste your time on her—go after John, and do your dragon thing on him."

"*Just a courier*?" Indigo stopped in the doorway and leaned against it in studied nonchalance. "I assure you I'm very much more than *just a courier*. I'm the High Priestess of the Agonized Flesh."

"You can't be," Aspen said, sneering at her. Ian stood still, his hand on his sword and his gaze on Indigo with an intensity that surprised me. "There's only one High Priestess of the Agonized Flesh, and I'm it."

Then again, a lot of things surprised me, like why Indigo was evidently not in distress from her recent kidnapping.

Unless it wasn't a kidnapping at all.

"You *were* high priestess," Indigo said calmly. "But my darling John removed you from that position a little while ago and named me high priestess. You will get on your knees and honor me as the conduit to the dark earth master."

"Hoo," I said in an undertone to Ian, who had moved over to my side. "That's not going to go over well with Aspen."

"*Your* darling John?" The words shot out of Aspen with the velocity of bullets, and I was oddly thankful she had no arms at that moment, because I suspect she would have leaped on Indigo and throttled her. "That two-timing asshat! That lying, cheating rat bastard! Oh, he is so going to suffer for this! If he thinks he can raise a stink because last month I wanted a girls' night out, and all the time he had a little floozy on the side—"

"I am not a floozy," Indigo protested.

"You're a man-stealing bitch, that's what you are! You knew full well he was married, and yet you obviously didn't let that bother you one bit." Aspen stamped her feet and glanced over at me. "Stinky, arm me!"

"I'll make you sweaty and sick," I warned her, pulling forward the cloth cross-body bag we'd used to carry her arms.

"This is important," she said, glaring back at Indigo.

"Okay, but if you have to barf, aim it on her, please. These are borrowed clothes." I took out the arms, and bending both at the elbow, stood behind Aspen, holding them so it looked like she had her hands on her hips.

"If you think I'm going to take your perfidy as well as that of my cheating husband lying down, you have another think coming," Aspen said, stamping her foot again. I raised one arm, pointed a finger, and shook it at Indigo for good effect. "Just as soon as the mage comes and puts my arms back on, I am so going to hex you."

"I'm sooo scared," Indigo said with a sneer.

"You ought to be," Ian said in a low, cold voice. He marched over to Indigo, and before she could do more than back up two steps, he was on her, shoving her against the wall with an arm across her throat. "What is your role in this? Why have you delivered the esprits to the Witnesses?"

"Don't forget Helen. I bet she had something to do with Helen," I reminded him, tucking away Aspen's arms, since her moment of indignation seemed to be over.

Ian continued, "Where are the esprits? What are you doing here? Why did you contact Helen Larson for help?"

"All of that's none of your business." Indigo's voice was defiant, but wheezy.

Ian was silent for a moment, and I knew by how high his dragon fire was that he was considering what the best action would be. I half hoped he'd go dragon hunter crazy on her, but instead, he tipped his head toward me. "Veronica? Take off her arms."

"Oooh," I said, coming forward, taking the precaution of first draping the arm-bearing cloth bag across Aspen's torso. I pulled out the wrath demon's black sword and made a show of examining it. "Sure thing. Although maybe her legs would be more effective?"

"You wouldn't dare," Indigo said with a choking gasp.

I pointed to Aspen and raised one eyebrow.

"You bitch," Indigo snarled. "I'll tell you why I put up with that annoying dragon hunter, but only because there's no way it will do you any good. She heard there were esprits in California and hunted us down, and told me she'd help us get to safety. She wanted to take us to Canada, but I told her I knew of a small town where we'd be safe."

"So you arranged to come here?" Another piece of the puzzle slid into place. "Why?"

She smirked. "Why do you think? John, of course. I couldn't shake off the dragon hunter without her becoming suspicious, so I went along with it. Plus it kept the esprits quiet. They thought I was taking them to be dispensed to worthy recipients, and so I am...they'll go to a primal god instead of even more stupid dragon swords."

"You self-serving hussy! It was your plan all along to come here and steal my husband, wasn't it?"

"I wouldn't really use the word *steal*," Indigo said, looking like a cat who'd eaten a whole plate of goldfish. "More like allow him to sweep me off my feet."

"Oh, I'm not absolving that hussy-imbibing bastard I'm married to of any guilt—he gets the bulk of that. But it makes sense now why you contacted me." Aspen looked nobly martyred, saying to Ian and me, "She called me two months ago and said she was about to take possession of something that a wrath demon wanted, and would the church pay more for it. Naturally, I had John discuss it with her. It's clear that the two-timing rat's ass hooked up with her then."

"Why didn't she just hand over the little girls at that time?" I asked.

"I doubt if she had them then." Aspen pointed with her chin. "Go ahead and lop her legs off. She deserves it after what she did to me."

"Are the esprits downstairs?" Ian asked.

Indigo pursed her lips but said nothing.

I twirled my sword and moved closer, slashing open the shoulder of her jacket. She spat out a word I wouldn't repeat in mixed company, and snarled, "Yes, damn you. Now let me go."

"Oh, I don't think so." Ian spun her around, pulled her arms back, and before I could realize what he was doing, had a zip tie restraint around her wrists. "I leave you in charge of the courier, Indigo."

"Goody," Aspen said, her eyes narrowing. It was the accompanying small, cruel smile that had me biting back a question about whether she would be okay watching Indigo; instead I followed Ian when he headed to the stairs from which the latter had emerged.

"Restraining me won't do you any good," Indigo called after us. "Better you should just leave now, before you are destroyed by the power of the Anguished Witness."

Ian said nothing, just started down the stairs.

"Do you always carry zip ties with you?" I couldn't help but ask.

"Yes. They come in very handy in subduing mortals, demons, and immortals alike."

"I bet. I'll have to get some and add them to my dragon hunter kit."

"What kit?" he asked, feeling along a wall for a light switch.

"The one I'm going to make just as soon as I get my apartment mucked out and purchase all new things. It's clear that there's more to being a dragon hunter than just a sword, so I thought it would be good to make up a kit with first aid stuff, lots of moist towelettes for sword wiping and general demon blood removal, a disposable rain slicker, because honestly, I don't know if any detergent is up to washing out black bloodstains, and hand sanitizer. Oh, and I'm thinking a shower cap to keep the hair clean when blood is a-flying. You wouldn't believe what I washed out of my hair yesterday."

Ian shot me a look that was two-thirds amused and one-third appalled, but once he found the light for the stairwell, he started down for the basement crypt. After two steps, he stopped.

"What is it?" I asked, bumping into him.

"Look." He pointed ahead.

I peered over his shoulder but didn't see anything except dimly lit wooden stairs. "What am I missing? All I see are steps."

"Look closely at the middle of them. Do you see a pattern?"

He shifted to the side so I could lean forward and

study them. "Not really. I just see— Oh." For a second, I thought I saw movement on the step, like the wood grain had shifted.

"That's called a banehook. It's a form of spell cast intended on harming whoever steps on it."

"Like a magic land mine?"

"That's a good term for it. Brace yourself for a hard landing."

Ian turned on the step and put his hands around my waist to lift me up, and with strength that had my inner girl squealing in delight, literally tossed me past the be-spelled step and down onto the landing.

I was prepared for a hard fall but still cracked my head on the wall.

"My apologies," he said, leaping down the stairs and immediately pushing my fingers away from where I was rubbing the side of my head. "Let me see if you are bleeding."

"I don't think I am. But I bet I'll have a big lump there."

"And I'll bet you won't." Finished with examining my head, he smiled at me, an act that lit up all my insides with a happy glow of love. I wasn't ready to face the fact that I'd fallen so hard and fast for this strange, enigmatic, troubled man, and yet a simple thing like a smile could make me want to dance and sing with joy. "You are now immortal, remember. Along with being impervious to mortal diseases and aging, you heal all but the most grievous wounds."

"Except getting your middle punched out," I said, my happy glow fading away.

"Except that," he agreed, and with an odd look at me, started down the second set of stairs, taking each step slowly and scanning for any further magical land mines.

We made it to the bottom without incident, finding ourselves in a small antechamber. A couple of broken wooden chairs littered one side, while the other was full of old hymnbooks.

I was eyeing the latter while Ian studied the door. "And here we have a bane."

"Hmm?" I looked up from where I was nudging aside a stack of hymnbooks, wrinkling my nose as they toppled and released a small mushroom cloud of dust.

"The magic used on this door is called a bane. Like the banehook, it is intended to cause harm to someone who attempts to break it, in this case, by turning the doorknob to open the door."

Something pale white gleamed in the dust and grime, poking out from under the books. I used my shoe again to move the books, surprised to see a white plastic wand with silver stars bristling at the end of gold filaments. "Huh. What's Sparkle's wand doing here? Poor kid must have lost it during the kidnapping. Or maybe she tossed it to let us know she's down here. What?" The last was said in response to the look that Ian was giving me when I picked up the wand and dusted it against my pant leg.

"If you want to live long enough to be a renowned kickass superhero dragon hunter—"

"I thought I already was?" I asked, waving the wand at him with a half smile.

"—then you need to pay attention, because this is potentially deadly. Look at the doorknob and you will see a particularly powerful example of a bane. Do you see the pattern of it?"

I bopped him on the head with the wand, which must have released the glitter compartment, because a light shower of silver glitter coated Ian's dark curls. I averted my eyes quickly and decided I'd tell him about the glitter-bombing later. "Let's see...yes, I see what looks like a triple Celtic knot, the kind you see in old Irish books of hours. What would it do if I grabbed the doorknob and turned?"

"Probably take off your hand. Or the entire right side of your body. Or turn you to stone. Any number of unpleasant events, none of which I recommend, since..." His voice was filled with dry amusement, but his eyes— Oh, his eyes. They were warm with an emotion that answered the call my heart seemed to be sending out.

"Since what?"

He turned back to the door, a little frown drawing down his brows. It didn't take someone who'd spent years thumbing through psychology magazines in therapy waiting rooms to know his body language was expressing discomfort and a sudden emotional withdrawal. "Since it would likely mean we'd be down yet another dragon hunter, and the mortal world can ill afford that."

"You don't have to do that, you know," I said, wanting desperately to put my arms around him. I could feel the pain inside him, deep and dark and as cold as ice, sending little tendrils of frost spiraling around him, despair trailing in their wake. He was clearly over-whelmed with emotion.

"Do what, exactly?"

"Withdraw from me. Ian, I feel your sadness. I don't know how I'm doing that, but maybe it's be-cause we're both dragon hunters, or we slept together, or Mercury is in retrograde and therefore I'm sud-denly privy to your emotions, but I know that you're unhappy about something, and I have a horrible feel-ing it's me. Us. This thing that we have together."

"This thing called you being in love with me?" he asked with a little quirk to one corner of his mouth.

I'd take teasing by him over profound sorrow any day. "Sure, although it would be nicer if you would reciprocate. Is that what this is about? Are you feeling guilty that you don't feel the same way about me? Be-cause if it is, you can stop worrying that I'm going to manipulate you into saying you love me, too. I've been through far too much therapy covering everything from my emotionally stunted mother to my own quirks to do something like that."

He sighed.

"Tell me that sigh wasn't loaded with all sorts of emotions," I said, bopping him on the shoulder with the wand. It left a residue of silver that splashed down di-agonally across his chest. I hoped he didn't notice.

"No, it was a sigh loaded with the discovery that you pick the worst times to talk about complicated subjects such as emotions and relationships. Now put the wand down and focus on this bane. I will show you how to get around it."

"Oooh, goody, practical skills." I tucked the wand into my back pocket and leaned forward to study the pattern that appeared to be etched onto the doorknob and a circle about four inches wide surrounding it. "Proceed, maestro."

Ian took a step back and kicked the door right next to the doorknob. The wood cracked, and the door flew open in the very best Hollywood style. He grabbed a couple of dusty books and wedged the door open before preceding me into the room.

I'm not sure what I expected a church's crypt to look like, but I had vague images from an art history class I'd taken in college and assumed there would be vaulted stone archways, massive sarcophagi, and the odd weeping angel or two hovering over some effigy of a Victorian timber magnate or miner who hit it rich two centuries ago. What we found when we entered through a short hallway, however, was a large room, mostly empty except for a long, narrow table covered with a runner of purple velvet and what looked like an altar set up at the far end of the room. To our left was a row of chairs lined against the wall, three of which were occupied by the two little girls and Sasha.

"There you are!" My shoulders slumped a little at the sight of them. I had half expected to find them tied down to medieval torture devices, but although all three were tied to the chairs, they looked unharmed.

"We were so worried about you. Girls, are you all right? Those bad people didn't do anything to you, did they? Sasha, I've got a few things I want to say to you, but they're going to have to wait until a better time. I'm glad you're not hurt, though."

"I'm glad, too," she said, wrinkling her nose and looking thoughtful. "I don't think I'd like it at all."

"I tried it once," the girl named Glitter said, shifting in her chair. "I fell off a swing and made my knee bloody. I wouldn't recommend it."

"Interesting," Sasha said, considering her. "I didn't know you went in for that sort of thing."

Glitter shrugged one thin, girlish shoulder. "When amongst the mortals and all that."

"Good point," Sasha agreed.

"I have to visit Mrs. Nature," the other girl, Sparkle, said suddenly, addressing the three people in front of them.

I looked from the girls to where two men and a woman stood, all three armed with guns.

"That's far enough," one of the men said, ignoring Sparkle to focus on Ian and me.

I narrowed my eyes at him. He was the man whom I'd seen earlier in the road drawing symbols. That was clearly Aspen's husband, John Fuller, head of the church and consorter of Indigo.

"Put the weapons down, Witness," Ian ordered. "You know you can't kill a dragon hunter, not with bullets or magic."

The second man glanced at his compatriots, looking nervous. "Er…he has a point, John. Dragon hunters can't be harmed by mortal means. Everyone knows that."

"Don't be ridiculous. They aren't gods," John answered.

I had kept an eye on Ian, feeling that as the senior member of our team, it was up to me to follow his lead rather than just charge in and try to get the girls away from the crazy people, but Ian just stared down John, clearly unimpressed by the threat.

"How about this," I said after Ian remained silent. Maybe he was giving me the opportunity to take charge of a situation? Stranger things could happen. "You let the three girls go, and we don't go medieval on your ass. Er...asses. Respective asses. Boy, editing yourself while you're speaking is hard. I just hope Mr. Manny appreciates me trying to be grammatically correct all the time."

"Who is Mr. Manny?" John asked after a moment's silence. He waggled the gun toward Ian. "Is that the dragon hunter's name? If so, we will be sure to add it to the list of those we present to the dark earth master."

"It's my writing instructor," I said loftily, wondering if a surprise attack with the demon sword would end in triumph or failure. I considered just throwing caution to the wind to find out, but a glance at the two little girls and Sasha bound to the chairs had me reeling in my suddenly brave-as-all-get-out anxiety monster.

"She's writing a book," Sasha said. "Ian told me so. It's all about her life, and how she became a dragon hunter and took over after I killed her sister, and how she fell in love with Ian, and won't mind living with all his animals."

"They're your animals," Ian said at the same time I asked, "How do you know about Ian and me? And we really need to have a talk about my sister."

She grinned one of her adorable anime grins, full of dimples and mischief. She'd changed her clothes at some point, so now she was wearing black-and-white-striped stockings, a short hot pink tulle skirt that looked like she stole it from a ballerina, and a black hoodie. She rubbed her nose briefly and answered, "I know because we've waited so long."

The "for what" was on the tip of my tongue, but John reminded me this was not the moment to go into any of the mysteries surrounding Sasha.

"Can we get back to me?" John demanded. "You two are in our way. We have a ceremony to finish, and the second sacrifice must be conducted before any more time slips by. You will both turn around and face the wall."

"John," the gun-toting woman next to him said in a soft, breathy voice. She glanced nervously between Ian's sword (held easily in his hand), my sword (which was pointed at John), and her compatriot. "Perhaps we should rethink the plan. One dragon hunter we might just be able to handle. But two of them—"

"Three," I interrupted, nodding over at Sasha. "She's one, as well, although Ian took away her sword, but you probably don't need to know that. Oh! Helen! Is that why Ian took away your sword, because you killed my sister?"

One look at Ian's face confirmed that, as well as the fact that I might be blathering too much. He shot me a look that probably would have dropped someone who didn't have the blood of dragons and demons flowing through her veins. I blew him a little kiss.

The three members of the church turned to look at Sasha, who waved at them.

"It doesn't matter how many of them there are," John argued. "We are almost finished. Just one more sacrifice, and the dark earth master will be summoned."

I glanced back at Sasha, it having struck me that twice now I'd seen her hand. I mouthed, "Are your hands free?" to her, but she scrunched up her nose again and shook her head in incomprehension.

"They can't stop us now," John continued. "We are too close. Dragon hunters or no dragon hunters, I will not have this ceremony fail. We have waited too long for sufficient sacrifices to summon the dark master, and we are almost there. This is a minor hiccup, nothing more."

"Are your hands free?" I mouthed silently to Sasha.

She lifted her hands in obvious question, clearly not skilled in reading lips.

I ground back an oath at myself for not seeing the obvious and mouthed, "Get the girls!"

"What?" she mouthed back.

"The girls! Get them free!" I added a couple of subtle gestures to the silent speech, and realized at that point that no one else was speaking and glanced toward John and the others.

All three were watching me.

"Oh, hi," I said, and gestured toward them with the sword in as menacing a fashion as I knew how.

John looked like he wanted to roll his eyes, but instead he addressed us both. "I don't even know why you are butting in on our business. Dragon hunters are concerned solely with eliminating demons. You have nothing to do with our cause."

"We have been known to defend mortal beings who are threatened by anything of an Otherworld nature. That includes defying those who would sacrifice esprits to summon a god who I've been informed will rain destruction upon all," Ian said in a manner that left me in full appreciation of his newly reborn dedication.

He was protective, and selfless, and cared so much about those who were helpless…Could there be a more ideal man?

"What happens is on your head, then," John said with a shrug. "I know these bullets won't kill you outright, but unloading the clips into your head will leave your brain as dead as a doornail, so don't try anything funny."

"That's prime coming from a man who two-timed his wife."

"Two-timed…" His eyes opened wide for a moment; then a martyred look crossed his face so profound it had me snickering to myself. "You didn't bring Aspen here, did you? I thought you killed her! Why didn't you kill her? You were supposed to kill her!"

"We don't kill innocents," Ian said, moving to my

side in what I felt was a show of solidarity. I told my now-brave animal that it needed to stop urging me into rash actions, and managed in the meantime to get a grip on my dragon fiery self. "Despite your wife being annoying as hell, she isn't guilty of any crime other than bad judgment and a poor choice in men."

"Aren't you clever," John said with a disgusted look on his face, and then before I could blink, he lifted the gun and fired point-blank into Ian's face.

GLITTER SUCKS. NOT LITERALLY, BECAUSE GLITTER THE LITTLE GIRL WAS NICE . . . OH HELL, THAT'S FORESHADOWING. NOTE TO SELF: CHANGE THIS CHAPTER TITLE BEFORE MR. MANNY HAS KITTENS OVER IT

IAN HAD HIS SWORD UP TWO SECONDS AFTER JOHN started firing, but it wasn't enough to stop the first few bullets. He staggered backward, and my heart seemed to stop beating while I braced myself for the inevitable sight of the man I loved covered in blood and gore, but to my utter surprise (and profound relief) there was no blood, nothing gooey and gross. It was as if the bullets completely missed him.

"What the hell—" I started to say, preparing to tackle John.

"Veronica, no!" Ian commanded, but not fast enough. When John turned to fire at me, Ian threw himself in front of me, but by then I'd realized something very odd—the bullets weren't striking either of us.

"Hey. We're bulletproof," I said, moving to the side of Ian. And that's when I saw the blood cascading down his left arm. "Holy bucket and mop! Ian, sit down! No, don't move. Here, let me use a bit of my shirt and I'll tie up your owie till you can heal. WILL YOU STOP SHOOTING AT HIM!" The last was yelled at John, who continued to fire his gun at Ian and me. I managed to get my sleeve torn off of my shirt and bound it around Ian's arm.

"I will not! It's my job to stop you, and stop you I will," John said, and shot me a couple more times. Except the bullets didn't touch me. They just seemed to dissolve in the air about three inches away from me.

"Are you okay?" I asked Ian, whose face reflected pain, anger, and an oddly warming look of martyrdom.

"Would you believe me if I said yes?" he asked.

"I would, because I don't think you'd lie to me, although you might well play down how much pain you're in just because you don't want me to worry."

"I would, would I? Why should I do that?" Amusement touched his eyes now, eyes that flashed sparks of fire.

"Because you're falling in love with me, and you don't want me to suffer when you're in pain."

He sighed. "We really must have a discussion later about appropriate times to explore personal relationships."

"I know," I said, and kissed the tip of his nose. "We'll do that after we save the girls and Sasha and take down this douchecanoe."

"Douchecanoe," Sasha said from the sidelines,

rolling the word around on her tongue. "I so love that phrase. Canoe of douches. I really need to use it more."

"Asshat is good, too," Glitter said with a little nod. "I called someone an asshat the other day. It was very satisfying."

"I *still* have to visit Mrs. Nature," Sparkle complained, squirming on her chair.

"Hang in there, kiddo," I told her. "We have to deal with these guys first, okay?"

She shot me a glare, but said nothing more.

"What is wrong with this gun?" John scowled, looked at the gun, then looked back at Ian, and casually, as if he were experimenting with something unknown, shot him in the left arm again.

Ian roared. Not yelled, not screamed, the man outright roared, and for a moment, I beheld the true nature of the dragon that resided within him. John Fuller's two other companions must have seen what I did, for they froze for the count of four. Then both of them bolted, rushing past us and up the stairs without a single word.

John didn't have time to comment on his buddies bailing on him—Ian, moving so fast he was basically a blur, slammed the flat edge of his sword down on John's head, sending the latter reeling backward.

"Why are some of the bullets hitting you?" I asked, ripping off my other sleeve to bandage the second wound, located about four inches down his bicep from the first. "I don't get it."

"Didn't you tell her about the wand?" Sasha asked Sparkle.

"Why would I do that?" the little girl asked, still squirming.

"Because she has it in her back pocket."

"The wand?" I was distracted for a moment watching Ian spin the befuddled John around and whip out another pair of the zip ties to bind his hands. "Oh, nice going, Ian. I'm glad you had extras."

"This is ridiculous. I am going to see Mrs. Nature right now," Sparkle said, and with a few wiggles, she managed to extricate herself from her bonds and slid off the chair, marching determinedly to the stairs. "Don't lose my wand!"

"I don't…Oh, it's in my back pocket." I pulled it out, intending to give it back to the little girl.

"Veronica," Ian said, and nodded toward Sparkle.

"Sure, so long as you're okay," I said, tucking the wand under my arm so that I could hurriedly bind his second wound.

"I'm fine. Just don't let the esprit out of your sight. Keep your sword handy and your wits sharp. We don't know where the other two went."

"What's going on down there?" Aspen asked a half minute later when Sparkle and I emerged from the stairwell. "Oh, you have one of them. Where's the other? Did you destroy John?"

I glanced around. Aspen was alone, leaning against the end of a pew. "Where's Indigo?"

"Oh, that." Aspen pursed her lips, but before she could say more, the girl next to me made me jump.

"I said I have to visit Mrs. Nature!" she bellowed. "*Now!*"

"Scouring bubbles, that made me jump. Have you never heard of an inside voice?"

She glared back at me.

"Right," I said, resigned to the inevitable, and asked Aspen, "I'm going to want full details on what happened to Indigo, but first, where's the bathroom?"

"It's not nearly as exciting a story as you might think," Aspen said, jerking her head toward the far end of the church. "Bathroom is through the vestry." By the time we had found the bathroom, let Sparkle have her time in it, and returned to the main part of the church, the big room was empty.

"Well, this is just maddening," I told Sparkle. "It's like some horrible mystery book where people keep disappearing the minute your back is turned."

"I like weeping angels," Sparkle said apropos of who knew what, and held out her hand. "Can I have my wand?"

"Sure." I gave it to her, watching her wave it around for a few seconds. "I know you're not going to want to go back downstairs to the scene of your kidnapping, but we—"

She was halfway down the stairs before I realized she'd moved. I dashed after her, leaping over the stairs that still bore the banehook, and followed her down into the basement.

The scene that met my eyes was bizarre, to say the least. In the middle of the room, the two people who had originally been next to John were laid out on the floor, unconscious, each of them with one arm outstretched to touch the fingers of the other. Just past their heads, an intricate drawing had been made on the floor, runes entwined in symbols that I knew from the electrical feeling in the air must be magical. Looming above it, Indigo stood, freed from the zip ties and looking extremely angry.

Clearly, things had been happening while I'd been busy with Sparkle.

"John, you self-righteous bastard, I swear I'll mmm-rfm—"

John slapped duct tape over Aspen's mouth before quickly winding cord around her, binding her to the chair where Sparkle had been sitting.

"What in the name of Mr. Clean is going on here?" I demanded to know, stalking into the room, looking toward Ian.

He stood protectively next to Sasha, his body hiding Glitter from John. His sword was in hand and glinting in the blue-white overhead lights. "You are not going to have them," Ian said, ignoring me. His eyes almost glowed green, and palpable waves of fury rolled off him.

"There she is," Indigo said, turning her head to speak to John, who was now clad in a black velvet cloak, just as if he were a high school theater villain. He stood watching Ian for a moment, then skirted Indigo and returned to his magic circle. "I told you that he was lying. She's too stupid to leave him and the other sacrifice. Dragon hunters are so blind that way, never realizing when it's smarter to cut their losses and leave, always determined to do what they think is right, even when it means their own destruction."

"It's okay," Sasha said, smiling at us all. "No one is going to hurt the esprits. Not while Ian is he—"

Indigo's hands flashed while Sasha was speaking, the glint of metal catching the light before it embedded itself in Sasha's throat. Sasha gurgled, grabbed at her neck, and then toppled over.

"Ian!" I bellowed, and leaped forward, but before I was more than a few yards closer to them, Indigo used Ian's horrified distraction with the dying Sasha to wrench his sword from his hand.

He snarled something quite rude (but which was very fitting), and would have leaped on Indigo, but she backed up a few steps, turning so she held the sword in both hands, swinging it between Ian and me. When she spoke, though, she addressed him. "Don't think of it, dragon. I've met your kind before, and I know just how weak you are without your precious *élan vital*. One move toward me, and your bit of fluff over there will suffer."

I was confused for a moment whom she was talking about, part of me wanting to run to help Sasha, the other wanting to feel the demon sword go to work on Indigo. I was horrified to see a dull blackness creep out from the wound on Sasha's neck, her skin turning an ugly matte gray that reminded me of stone. Even the blood that had spilled crimson down her front was slowly taking on a dark gray hue.

Clearly, some horrible magic had been imbedded in whatever weapon Indigo had thrown.

Sasha twitched once, then went perfectly still, the horrid grayness claiming her.

Sparkle started forward to where her sister was sitting behind Ian, peeking around him at what was happening with a perfectly calm expression. I grabbed Sparkle's thin shoulder and pulled her back. "Stay here with me where it's safe, kiddo," I said, my gaze meeting Ian's. Pain filled his eyes when he picked up Sasha's limp body and gently placed her onto two of the wooden chairs.

"Is she dead?" I asked, my voice sounding thin and stretched.

"This body is damaged, but her being is not," Ian answered. He faced Indigo, seemed to have an inner struggle for a few seconds, and eventually said, "You are right about one thing—a dragon hunter without his *élan vital* is hampered, but you've overlooked the fact that I am not alone."

"That's right," I said, lifting up my sword, flexing my fingers on the hilt while I gave Indigo a long, hard look. "And I liked Sasha even if she did kill my sister, assuming the situation Ian said was true, and I have no reason to believe otherwise, so all in all, I'm about at the end of my patience. This sword is called Deathsong. You want to do this the nice way and just give Ian back his soul sword, or do you want Deathsong to open up a can of dragon hunter whoop-ass on you?"

Indigo rolled her eyes, and to my disbelief, tossed Ian's sword hilt first to John. "Here. You might as well use this one even if Miss High and Mighty wasn't smart enough to clear off when she could."

"No!" Ian started forward with a roar, but before he was halfway across the space to John, the latter held the sword aloft and spoke a series of words that I didn't understand. They sounded harsh against my ears, grating, and leaving me with a feeling of dread, a feeling that was increased when the sword suddenly changed... All the glossy, shiny beauty of it faded into the same dull gray that had crept over Sasha.

A small yellowish-white light the size of an orange fell out of it into John's waiting hand. He placed it carefully into one side of the circle of runes, directly above the unconscious man's head.

"Is that what you really look like?" I asked Sparkle in a whisper.

"Sometimes," she answered coolly, and tried to get out of my grip.

"You stay here. I'll protect you."

She turned enough to look up to me. "How?" she asked.

I waggled my sword. "I have a sword, too."

"It's a demon's sword," she said, touching it. The sword glowed warm under my hand for a second or two.

"I know, but it seems to work for me. Wait, you can touch it? I thought you guys were all goodness and stuff."

She nodded. "The sword is not evil, only its previous owner was. Dewberry, the esprit in this sword, is much happier with you allowing her to turn darkness to light."

I slid her a quick look, but couldn't take my focus off what was happening in the middle of the room. Ian stumbled and almost fell, his face ravaged by pure anguish, but I knew he was going to attack. Before he could, though, Indigo finished sketching in the air a spell, one lit with smoky black runes, and threw it over Ian. He fell to his knees, his snarl of rage cut off. Indigo smirked at him and, turning, strolled over to John.

I was torn—part of me wanted to run to Ian, to help him fight whatever horrible spell Indigo had used to bind him, but the other part of me knew he'd expect me to protect the girls. And with John having clearly taken the esprit out of Ian's sword, he was as unprotected as Helen and Adam had been. He would have no defense against Anzo's compulsions, no way to avoid doing anything she asked of him.

"Ian?" I asked, hoping he'd react to the love I poured into my words. "It's okay. We can fix this. Can't we?"

His shoulders tensed as he fought the spell, but he remained silent. The fire in him that I'd felt the second I entered the room ebbed, leaving me feeling bereft and hopeless.

"Fetch the other one," John ordered.

Indigo glanced over to where Glitter sat with the gray, lifeless Sasha.

"I know it's cliché to say 'over my dead body,' but really, over my dead body," I said, pulling Sparkle to the side so I could move into a position to defend both her and her sister.

"If you like," Indigo said with an indifferent shrug, but this time I was ready. I had the sword up, blocking the small, deadly blade she'd whipped out and sent spinning my way, at the same time shoving Sparkle over to where Glitter sat.

"Just get rid of her," John spat, kneeling inside the circle. "I will begin the summoning. Kill the woman and bring me the other sacrifice."

"Gladly," Indigo said, her eyes suddenly bright as she started sketching symbols in the air at the same time she moved away from Ian, toward the door. I backed up a few steps until I felt a chair bumping the back of my legs, and I realized then she had cornered me.

Ian still knelt, his hands hanging down impotently, his head bowed, and every line of his body expressing an impotent struggle. I glanced at him, wanting to take the pain from him and in return fill him with the love that burned so bright inside of me. Mostly, I wanted to strip the spell from him so that he could fight alongside me, where he belonged. Together, my anxiety animal declared, we could conquer anything. But with him bound as he was...I knew he would interpret this as yet another failure on his part.

But Ian would be the first one to say my duty was to protect the innocents.

Indigo continued to draw symbols on that air while I gathered the two little girls, keeping myself between them and the threats posed by Witnesses. With my heart singing a dirge to Ian, I lifted my sword again and said, "Look, I know you intend to pull your Cthulu-esque old god into this world—"

"Dark earth master," John snapped, and knelt be-tween the two prone members of his church so that he could touch both of their free hands with one of his own, while the other he used to connect to the circle. The air within it started the shimmer and shake, like it was made of translucent gelatin.

"But I am not going to let you hurt anyone else. Nor is Ian. Because we're dragon hunters, even if we don't have the proper swords. Or even a whole sword. And protecting people is what we do. Right? Ian? Right?"

My words were brave, but the worried thread in them was audible even to my own ears. And Ian con-tinued to kneel, head bowed, his shoulders twitching with the strain of trying to break his bonds, making my soul cry out to him.

Just as I thought he had completely retreated into his own personal hell, I felt a little spark of fire flare to life within him, one that burned with anger and fury, and grew with every second until his determination gave me strength. It called out to the blaze that raged in me, leaving me almost giddy with the realization that he must be winning against Indigo's spell, but since he re-mained in that submissive position, I knew he must be planning a surprise attack.

"You are too late," Indigo said, laughing a little as she nodded toward the circle. "The master is coming now."

"We need the second sacrifice to bind the master to the mortal world," John said, his words as sharp as a razor. "Stop stalling and get one of them, so that I can complete this."

A dark, vaguely human-shaped spirit started to form in the shimmering air, elongating until it was about my height.

I lifted my sword, my eyes narrowed on Indigo, praying to as many gods as I could think of that Ian had triumphed over the spell enough that he could take care of whatever emerged from that portal to who knew where. "Bring it, sister."

"I am *so* not your sister," she said with another one of her smirks, and then she cast her hands wide, as if she was throwing something on top of us. I braced myself, half expecting to be struck, but nothing happened.

"Well, now, isn't this a pleasant surprise."

A woman's voice spoke from the direction of the circle, but I didn't take my eyes off of Indigo to look at who was speaking. Neither did Indigo—in fact, she looked downright stunned for a moment, first examining her hand, then narrowing her eyes at the girls and me.

"Anzo?" Ian spoke at last, the one word riddled with utter disbelief.

"Darling! How handsome you are in black. I always did favor that color. But what is this? You look so surprised. Oh, did I not tell you about my origins?"

I took the moment of Indigo's distraction with the arrival of her old god to shoot a quick look down the room. A woman stood in the middle of the circle, of average height, with waist-length blond hair, a tight-fitting zebra-striped dress, and a big, toothy smile.

I stared openmouthed for a second before the word Ian uttered registered in my brain.

This was his boss, the demon lord who inspired such loathing that my sister and stepfather had preferred to die rather than serve her.

And Ian no longer had the protection of his sword to keep him safe.

CHAPTER NINETEEN

"Darling, you don't look at all happy to see me. Surely that is just the surprise of me finally being able to access your world, and not because you are displeased by my presence," Anzo almost purred, her voice flowing like silk and as sharp as a well-honed blade.

Ian heard Veronica gasp and knew from the pain burning across his chest and arms that his brands were bleeding again. Anzo was never subtle in methods of expressing her power over him, and now that he had no protection against her, he knew he was in a world of hurt. Literally.

"I am surprised you are here, yes. I wasn't aware that you could access the mortal world," he said, slowly getting to his feet and throwing aside his plan to lull the Witnesses into a false sense of security with his apparent defeat before attacking them. Not that he could do much without his *élan vital*, but still, he could take down at least the ringleader. "Nor did I think you had any desire to be here."

"And miss the chance to watch you in action, working away on my behalf? How you underestimate my interest in every little thing you do," she said, her voice seeming to tighten itself painfully around him, reminding him yet again of the bond between them.

He gritted his teeth, being careful not to glance at Veronica. If Anzo thought for one moment that Veronica held any sort of spot in his heart, they would both suffer untold torments. "You have demons to verify that I am acceding to your wishes."

Anzo waved his comments aside. "I have many demons, yes, although one has gone missing of late. You wouldn't know anything about that, would you?"

Ian raised his eyebrows but said nothing. Evidently, Anzo was too busy pursuing her own line of thoughts to notice his non-answer.

"Regardless of how many servants I send to attend to you, it's not the same as seeing you in person. Not that I wished to come here. Mortals! What do they have to offer me? Nothing but their insignificant lives, and I can get those anytime." She glanced around. "So long as I am here, though, I might as well see the courier you were to bring me. Where is she?"

"Your Grace," the male Witness said, shuffling forward and bowing so low his head almost touched his knees. "May I first welcome you to this, the domain of mortals, and that which I know you, in your infinite wisdom of ages long past, will make your own."

"Who are you?" Anzo asked, looking faintly annoyed.

"I am John Fuller, Your Grace. I am the anointed priest of the Church of the Mortified Flesh of the Anguished Witness, devoted solely to you and your determination to make the mortal world a bastion of death and destruction of the impure." The Witness bowed again. "It is my utmost pleasure to have summoned you to the mortal plane, an act which was in no way easy given the nature of those who have also devoted themselves to your cause."

The Witness shot a look of pure venom across to where his wife sat bound and gagged.

"Are the words that are spewing from your mouth like so much infected phlegm supposed to interest me in some manner?" Anzo asked in her most velvety voice, which instantly raised the fine hairs on the back of Ian's neck. He knew that tone, and knew well that it boded ill for whoever heard it. "I do not recall giving you leave to address me directly. Unless you have something that would be of vital importance to me, remain silent."

A snorting sound came from Aspen. Her husband sent her a look of loathing, then bowed again. Ian could have told him he was taking his life in his hands to continue to speak to Anzo after she ordered him to silence, but who was he to forestall the destruction of a man who so clearly wished evil upon the mortal world? He focused part of his attention on formulating a plan to get Veronica and the esprits out of there.

"Your most powerful and primal grace," the Witness said, bowing a third time, this one almost a grovel before Anzo. "I would not for the world do anything to cause you distress, but we've gone to a great deal of trouble to gather appropriate sacrifices for you, and thus, I seek to present them to you. They are over there, with the brave woman who brought them to us."

Anzo flicked a glance over to Veronica. Ian was delighted to see that Veronica was keeping Indigo at bay. The latter was, in fact, clearly casting spells upon Veronica and the two sacrifices, but he suspected it was the esprits' inherent magic that protected them. "Next to the dragon hunter? She looks ineffective at best. Speaking of dragon hunters, is that the one you collected for me, Ian? She doesn't strike me as being particularly impressive. I don't know that she will be nearly as delightful as you."

Ian was ready, knowing he had little ability to lie without the protection of his sword. "That is the courier, yes. The dragon hunter is newly made, not one who has mastered much yet."

"Disappointing," Anzo said, looking somewhat disgruntled. "I suppose I should take her and have you teach her how to best serve me, but that would distract you far too much from attending to me. And I will be busy with the courier, breaking Asmodeus and the other demon lords, at which point I shall rule Abaddon, as is right and proper."

Ian felt a swell of relief, but was careful to mask it. He didn't have Veronica safe, yet.

"But, Your Grace—" the Witness said, frowning.

Ian stiffened, glancing quickly at the man, worried that he might tell Anzo the truth about the esprits. If he did, then she'd likely destroy them on the spot lest they be turned against her. It was far, far better that she remain in ignorance about their ability to destroy dark power.

"Again you speak?" Anzo snapped her head around to glare at the Witness. "You dare much, priest."

"Yes, Your Grace. That is, no, but this is important."

"Would you like me to remove him from your presence?" Ian asked, feeling a bit of desperation to get the man out of the room before he could ruin everything. "It is of a moment's work to clear the room for you."

The second he said the words, he felt Anzo's consideration and knew he'd taken a misstep.

"No," she drawled. "He may speak so long as he has something worthy of my ears."

"It's the esprits, Your Grace," the Witness said, and gestured toward the two little girls.

Anzo frowned. "What about them?"

The Witness started to visibly sweat. "Surely you will want them, not Indigo, er...the courier who brought them."

"And why should I want beings from the Court? They have no power in Abaddon, whereas the courier, I'm told, can help me greatly."

Beads of sweat dotted the man's forehead. If Ian hadn't been so worried he'd blurt out the truth about the esprits, he might have enjoyed the moment. As it was...he looked toward Veronica. Indigo now lay facedown on the ground, both esprits sitting on her while Veronica bound her hands with a bit of torn shirt. "I...I thought you would want them. We took great pains to acquire them via your faithful servant Indigo, who brought them to us in her role as our high priestess. She is most valuable to us, and we would not have been able to summon you without her aid and devotion to your presence."

Anzo's eyes flashed with a deep red light that caused Ian to back up two steps. "Repeat that."

The Witness licked his lips. "I...we knew that the dragon hunter had two esprits that we needed to give power to our summoning, so we took them."

"I see." Anzo was unusually still. "It would appear they have some use after all. I did not know they could be used to give power to those wielding them."

Ian took another step back, his gut sick with dread. A warm presence on his left side caught his awareness. From the corner of his eye, he saw Veronica. To his utter relief, she didn't attempt to touch him or in any way indicate that they had anything in common but a similar occupation. He was in hell, mental hell, wanting her out of the room, safe somewhere that Anzo couldn't touch her, and aware that with his *élan vital* broken, he was severely limited in his abilities. The truth was he needed

Veronica's strength, needed her help to overcome the situation before them.

He just needed her, something he never thought would happen. Fate was especially cruel to deliver that realization when he was a hairsbreadth away from complete destruction.

"Ian." Pain lashed through him at the word, and he felt Veronica start in reaction to it. He willed her to express disinterest as he bowed his head to his master.

"Yes?"

"Collect the esprits for me. They may not be of use to me in Abaddon, but perhaps I can use them here, to destroy those who would oppose me."

The dread grew until Ian thought he might be sick. He knew without a shred of doubt that Anzo intended to use the esprits against Veronica, something he would die before he allowed to happen.

But before he could summon up an excuse for not heeding a direct command, the male Witness drew Anzo's attention.

"Your unholy grace," the Witness said quickly, gesturing to the small glowing ball of light at his feet. "Much though I would give the esprits to you in the knowledge you would use them to purge the unworthy, we've only acquired three, and one of them is spent giving strength to our summons. The other two are earmarked for other things."

"You defy me?" Anzo asked, her eyes flashing.

Ian felt Veronica start and move back a few feet. He didn't blame her one bit. He prayed she was well out of the way when Anzo took out her wrath upon him when he refused to hand over the esprits.

"You dare to defy me? I will not have this!" Anzo's voice sliced like a knife, a fact that evidently the Witness felt, since he all but cowered before her, whimpering pitifully.

"We needed the power to summon you," the Witness pleaded. "We need to use the other two in order to ensure you can leave the circle and rule the mortal world as you were meant to do."

"I don't give two snaps for the mortal world, you fool!" she snarled, and Ian flinched with the wave of pain that blasted him with the impact of a bulldozer.

The Witness fell to the floor, cowering in a fetal ball.

"Mortals have nothing to offer me, nothing at all. I've let you prattle on about summoning me here because it was a change, and I wanted to see for myself how my servant was conducting himself, but you...you have nothing I want. You are nothing to me. You cannot aid me in my battle as the courier can. You are worthless! Less than worthless! In the end, you have achieved nothing but summoning me into this world!"

The Witness was babbling now, his words tumbling over themselves as he curled up before Anzo, his hands protectively over his head.

"You are not worthy of existence," Anzo said, then shouted out a name. "Quen!"

A small, dark woman tore open the fabric of space and stood obediently before her master. Veronica stifled a surprised intake of breath, and Ian risked a quick glance back at her, trying to tell her with his eyes to do nothing that would bring Anzo's attention down upon her. To his immense relief, she gave a little half nod of understanding.

"My lord?" the demon asked, waiting patiently for an order.

"Take this...thing...with you. He needs a lesson in the proper way to speak to me."

The demon gave a curt bow and dragged the babbling—and now pleading—Witness through the tear back into the depths of Abaddon. For a moment, Ian felt sorry for the man, but realized quickly enough that he had brought about the deaths of many and would have caused many more in the future had his plan come to fruition.

"He is not at all like you," Anzo said to Ian, dusting off her hands as if she had gotten them dirty. "You do not waste my time with trivialities. How the people in the mortal world plague me. Ian, my darling, I believe you have spent enough time in the mortal world. Retrieve those esprits and use them to destroy the dragon hunter. I know, I know, I told you I wanted you to bring her to me, but if she is as new as you say, she's worthless. Destroy her and return with me to Abaddon."

"There is much to do here yet," Ian said, trying to come up with a viable reason for him not to do as ordered. His mind was blank, the demon within him struggling to be released. For a moment, he despaired that it would gain the upper hand, but his dragon self managed to wrest temporary control, allowing him to add, "Despite what the Witness said, I do not know that an esprit can destroy anything."

"He said they give power to your desires. Therefore"—she waved a hand at Veronica—"you shall use them to give power to my desire."

"What? Oh, I don't think so!" Veronica snorted with anger and hefted the demon sword. "With all due respect, not that I have a lot for a demon lord, you're nutso, lady!"

He needed her out of there, now, before he lost control of his demon. It was responding to Anzo, forcing him to her will since he had no esprit to help him fight the compulsion. He had to do something, had to take action in the next few seconds.

"Do you disobey me?" Pain lashed at him with Anzo's words, causing him to stagger backward a step, his demon self seeping dark power throughout his body. He felt the dragon control slipping and knew it would be consumed in the thick blackness of Anzo's command. "I will not have it! Not even from you!"

"Look, lady—" Veronica started to say.

Ian shut her out of his mind, focusing every atom of strength he possessed to keep his inner demon leashed, pulling hard on the dragon fire even as it started to fade. He eyed the frail esprit, knowing he couldn't enter the circle to retrieve it. There was only one way he could ensure Veronica survived this encounter, one slim chance that he knew he had to take. If Anzo could be forced out of the circle, if he could reclaim the weakened esprit and restore his *élan vital*, he could send the demon lord back to Abaddon, and Veronica would be safely out of her reach.

He lunged forward at Anzo, intending to physically knock her out of the circle, but at the same moment, Indigo rolled toward the esprits, kicking at them. Veronica ran to protect them just as Ian's body crossed the boundary of the circle containing Anzo.

For the time it took for one second to melt into another, time seemed to stop, hold its breath, and wait to see what happened. Ian knew he couldn't fail in removing Anzo from the circle, for he would destroy himself willingly before he did as Anzo demanded. He might not have been able to save his mother or Adam Larson, but he would not be responsible for the death of the woman who made his soul sing.

He crossed the lines of the circle, intent on thrusting Anzo out of it. When he lifted his arms to shove her out of the circle, she flicked a finger at him and he froze, unable to control his body. Without an esprit to give his dragon side strength, his heart stopped beating, his blood slowed to a sluggish drift in his veins, and his lungs refused to draw in and exhale air.

He knew true panic then, the kind of panic that turns the world red with fear, a mind-consuming horror that he would not be able to save Veronica, and that yet again, one whom he should have protected would now suffer. Had he not taken Adam Larson's judgment upon himself, he would never have been bound to Anzo. If he hadn't gotten involved with Veronica, she wouldn't be here now. And if he had stopped the courier from delivering the esprits, Anzo would never have been summoned.

It was all his fault. His recklessness just sealed their fates. He wanted to apologize to Veronica, to tell her what she meant to him, to plead for her forgiveness, but his body had ceased to respond to his wishes.

"Darling! How impetuous you are. You should have told me you wished to join me here in the circle, and I would have had that priest set you up here. But what is this? Your eyes, darling, your eyes! They are all but spewing hate at me. Could it be that you wished to do me harm, your very own Anzo? *Tsk.*" The demon lord smiled at him, all too aware that his body, no longer able to carry out its functions, was beginning to die. "I don't know how I feel about that. Wait, yes, I do."

Black spots began to form in the air in front of his eyes, while in his brain, synapses weakened and began to fail.

"I feel hurt. Betrayed. *Angry.*" Anzo bent and plucked the esprit from where it was bound into the summoning circle. "I think you need to be punished, my darling. I think you need to be brought fully into the darkness, and while I may not have the ability to destroy your dragon half on my own, this should have enough power left to give me the *oomph* I need to do just that."

Ian couldn't turn his head to see what Veronica was doing, but he heard a noise that sounded suspiciously like a woman dragging a bound courier over to a chair and gagging her, and rejoiced with what few bits of brain were able to conceive that emotion.

"To be honest, I've never liked the dragon part of you. It gets in the way, doesn't it?" Anzo, the esprit in her hand, slammed it into his chest, grinding it painfully into him. "This thing may be weak, but it should have enough power to cleanse you of the annoying dragon blood. You will like letting your demon self have free rein, Ian. It's so invigorating! You won't have any of those pesky obligations to the dragon hunters, and just think, you'll be able to spend so much more time with me. Doing everything I bid you to do. We won't have any more of those horrible times where you try to fight the compulsions I lay upon you. Won't that be lovely?"

"No, it won't be lovely. It won't be lovely at all." That was Veronica's voice, and Ian's soul wept with the knowledge that he had just damned them both.

Anzo ignored her, standing with her arms crossed over her chest, her eyes closed as she began a chant, every word of which struck Ian's body like daggers.

The esprit burned deeply into his chest, filling him with a heat that went far beyond dragon fire, bringing with it bone-deep, piercing pain. Fear came close to consuming him, but at that moment, a miracle happened—with a swish of air that he recognized, a sword dug deep into the ground in front of him, the blade quivering with the impact.

"I bequeath to you this sword," Veronica's voice

called out to him. "Temporarily. You know, until you get your own back. But for now it's yours."

The heat from Anzo's esprit raged in him, scorching away everything he was, but as the esprit in Veronica's sword glowed with a brilliant golden brightness, the heat and pain eased somewhat, and he managed to reach out and grasp it.

Beyond the circle, Veronica was strapping the struggling Witness to a chair. Behind her, the two esprits hopped excitedly up and down, the one with the wand waving it wildly.

He gripped the sword with both hands, drawing from it the strength he needed. Anzo was still reciting, posed dramatically above him.

She finished her chant, opened her eyes, and flung wide her arms, saying, "That's it, my precious one. Give yourself over to it. You can't fight me any longer, so you might as well embrace the darkness." Anzo practically cooed the words at him.

"Ian!" Veronica's call, the fear in her voice, was barely audible. "Why aren't you doing anything? You're supposed to be doing something."

"At last. Now you are mine, darling. Truly, forever—" Anzo frowned at the sword Ian gripped with every ounce of strength. "Where did you get that?"

"Ian?" Veronica's nearness forced Ian to his feet. He would not let Anzo get hold of her. Not while there was breath left in his body.

He wanted to tell Veronica just how much she meant

to him, that he knew now he couldn't live any form of a happy life without her, and that despite the fact that things were about to be fundamentally changed for him, he wanted her. In every way. From now until the end of their time together.

"I love you," he said, getting to his feet.

Veronica's jaw dropped as she gaped at him. "Huh?"

"I said I love you. You were right." The pain inside him continued to ease, but his heart was leaden with the knowledge that he had only a few minutes before the demon took over. "I do love you. With every breath of my body, every beat of my heart, and lots of other poetic things that men say to women in romantic movies, but which I can't think of right now because everything you've known about me is about to be replaced with evil."

"You are deranged is what you are. As if I'd let you turn bad guy," Veronica said, flashing him a smile that he felt down to his toes. "But I love you, too. Can you please take care of her now?"

"Yes," he said, and turning to Anzo, he put both hands on her shoulders and shoved her outside of the circle.

"Aww. You're not going to cut off her head?" Veronica sounded disappointed.

Anzo fell forward onto her knees, her eyes wide with panic. Ian left the circle, for a moment jubilant, knowing he'd done it, he'd saved Veronica from Anzo. He hoped he'd have enough time to tell her how to protect herself before he was called back to Abaddon to pay for his betrayal.

He swung the sword at Anzo, a massive, percussive blast following when it touched her neck. Anzo twisted and compressed, her sibilant scream echoing in his ears as she disappeared into nothing.

"Woot!" Veronica yelled, and she threw herself onto him, kissing every part of his face she could reach. He allowed her to do so, his heart sick, for he knew any second he would pay the price of his actions.

"Wait, why aren't you kissing me back?" she demanded to know, pushing back enough to glare up at him. "Why do you have your martyred look on? Why aren't you happy?"

He closed his eyes for a minute, hoping he had enough time to say everything he needed to say before the inner demon filled him. "Anzo is gone, but only from this world."

"So? Why don't you look happy about that?"

He sighed, sorrow gripping him like a smothering cloth. "Would you be happy if you'd had all the dragon burned out of you, leaving nothing but a demon inside?"

She smiled a long, slow smile. "Ian, you are handsome, and brave, and normally so smart, but now you're being an idiot."

"What are you talking about?" Ian felt the urgent need to get out everything he wanted to say to her before he turned wholly evil and was summoned back to Anzo, but damn the woman, she insisted on distracting him with compliments and silly chatter. "Anzo burned the dragon out of me."

"Uh-huh." She put a hand on his cheek. "Do you feel demony?"

He thought for a few seconds. "No . . . not really. But it hasn't taken charge of me yet, that's all."

"Do you really think an esprit would do that to you?"

"Yes," he said, inwardly poking around the dark corners of his soul. Odd, there didn't seem to be the hot, stifling, insidious warmth that the demon side always embraced. "She was using it to give added power to her spell. I told you that esprits were sometimes used that way."

"Right, but that was before I gave you my sword. Once you got that, once its esprit kicked in, you could resist her. Resist the spell, right?"

He looked downward at his chest, pulling from it a feebly blinking ball of light. "Did I?"

"I think so. You don't feel dark and icky to me; you feel warm. Golden. Filled with steamy dragon goodness."

For a moment, hope filled him. The darkness that fought him, always threatening to consume him, did indeed seem to be gone. "I rather think it did a lot more than that. I think by giving me your sword, you gave me the ability to resist the esprit Anzo set to burn out my dragon, so it did the only thing left to it . . . It turned the demon side to light."

Veronica grinned and kissed his chin. "I hoped my sword would give you the strength to resist, but that's even better." Her smile faded, a puzzled look pulling her brows together. "Or I thought it was. Why are you looking like someone ran over your best friend?"

He took her arms in his hands, aware of the two esprits standing behind her, but he had no time to be worried about baring his soul in front of them. "I'm still bound to Anzo, whether or not I have a demon half. She will summon me to Abaddon and punish me for what I've done. I want you to be aware that she might send some demons to confront you. I won't be able to help you, but there are others who can. Other dragon hunters. You must contact them, my love. You *must* be safe. I couldn't live with the idea that my actions caused you harm. Promise me that you will protect yourself."

"What?" She looked confused, then angry. "You talk like you aren't going to be here. We can fight this demon lord, Ian. I love you! You love me! I'm not going to let you go now, not when we finally are in a good spot. Not when I have you. No! Stop looking so obstinate and self-sacrificing, because I won't let you go!"

"My loveliest, my most enticing fake girlfriend," he said, bequeathing her the sword before kissing her hands, and wishing with all of his heart that his sacrifice would be the safety net she needed. "There's a reason people avoid being bound to a demon lord—there is no way to break the bond once it has been made except death or replacement. And before you offer yourself, no. I would sooner die."

The little esprit light buzzed in his hand. He set it down outside of the circle.

"That's not true," one of the little girls said, the one with the wand.

"What isn't?" he asked, frowning at the interruption. There was so much he had yet to say to Veronica.

"Your bond is made up of dark power," the other said, scratching her ear. "We can break it."

"What? Hoo! That's awesome!" Veronica dashed back a few fat tears that had rolled down her cheeks at Ian's words and swept the girls before her. "Go ahead. Do it now, before that she-devil—wow, literally, too—tries to suck Ian back to make mincemeat out of him along with John Fuller."

"No," Ian said, stepping back when the two girls lifted their hands toward him. "You don't know what that means, Veronica. They will destroy themselves doing it. Before I met you, I thought about nothing but breaking the bond to free myself. But now, after seeing you protect them, after watching your love blossom for them, for me, for...hell, everything—I can't destroy them for my own salvation. You might be new to the art of being a dragon hunter, my love, but you are the epitome of what they stand for. You are everything that I wish I had been, and I will go to Anzo knowing that your light will make the world a better place."

"That is the loveliest thing anyone has ever said to me," she said, sniffing and wiping back another tear. "Also, the stupidest. But still, lovely. There has to be another way—"

"There isn't," he insisted, his heart breaking. Veronica was so lovely, so perfectly unpredictable, so filled with warmth that had nothing to do with dragon fire and everything to do with the perfectly imperfect woman. His woman. He couldn't stop himself from stepping forward and taking her head in his hands, giving her one goodbye kiss that he hoped would say everything he couldn't.

"We aren't destroyed," one of the esprits said, causing Ian to look down at her.

"You aren't?" he asked. "But that one is used up."

The other esprit shrugged. "She's tired, that's all. She'll go back to the Sovereign when she's spent, the same as us."

"Who's the Sovereign?" Veronica asked.

"It's the name of the being that heads the Court of Divine Blood," Ian answered, hope blooming despite the dire situation facing him.

Veronica gasped. "You mean God?"

"That's a mortal idea," one of the girls told her. "The Sovereign is more a manager of the Court."

"That's still pretty impressive. Wait, so this means that you won't die if you break Ian free from that hussy who hurt him?" Joy shone in her eyes.

He knew just how she felt. He'd never once stopped to think what happened to the esprits once their work was done. He had assumed they were like the demons he destroyed, but if they weren't…if there was a chance…

"It's the same as what happens to the dark power. It goes back to its source—the demon lord to whom it was bound—and we go back to our source."

"The Sovereign," the second esprit said, nodding.

"Well, holy extra strength Toilet Duck! Then let's do it!"

Ian didn't have time to say anything before the girls laid their hands on him, and a brilliant light, white and yellow and seemingly made up of all the colors he could imagine, wrenched him away from Veronica, away from the basement of the disused church, and away from everything he'd ever known.

The last thing he heard before it was all taken from him was Sasha's voice saying, "Wow, did I have a weird dream, or what?"

SOME SORT OF WRAPPY-UPPY TITLE HERE. EPILOGUE? SOUNDS KIND OF MEH. FIND SOMETHING BETTER.

"You know, you could have told me the truth about Sasha." I stopped talking for a few seconds while I waited to see if Ian was going to be able to stand on his own. He looked a bit wobbly, but after a few seconds of holding on to one of the chairs that had lined the wall of the church crypt, he managed to take a few steps. "I wouldn't have freaked out or anything."

"Really?" He cocked an adorable eyebrow at me, and I was possessed with the deep and desperate need to kiss him. And touch him. And goddess help me, lick him.

"Well, maybe there would be a little freaking out going on. The anxious animal in my head would have had a hard time wrapping itself around the idea that Sasha is God."

"The Sovereign is not a god, let alone the Judeo-Christian idea of a deity." He bent and picked up the still faintly blinking blob of light that had come from his sword. "She is in charge of the Court of Divine Blood, that's all."

"And she can come back from the dead!" I pointed out, handing him the gray, lifeless sword that I assumed he was going to want.

"I told you that only her form was destroyed. And as it turns out, that was incorrect, although I assume the two esprits who used themselves up to break my bond to Anzo gave her the ability to mend herself. Why are you giving me that?"

I laid the sword down on the table in front of him. "Because it's yours. Aren't you going to put the little soul thingie into it, so it fixes it and makes it yours again?"

"I couldn't if I wanted to," he said, setting the ball of light carefully onto the table next to the sword. It bobbed its way over to it, settling on a spot just below the hilt. A pale gold light seemed to shimmer over the sword, making it almost glow with life again. "That *élan vital* belongs to a dragon hunter."

"Yes," I said, wondering if the act of ripping him away from the demon lord Anzo had taken more of a toll on him than just knocking him out for almost half an hour. "It's your sword. Don't you remember? That bastard John broke it right in front of you. What's wrong? Why do you look like you're having another painful gas bubble that you swear you aren't prone to?"

He gave a little laugh and pulled me ever so gently into his arms. I leaned against him, breathing in the scent of him, drinking in the wonderful warmth of his body pressed against mine, and glorying in the knowledge that he loved me. Me, the most neurotic person in the world! I was still a bit overwhelmed by the idea, but it was one that filled me with the most exquisite joy.

"My love, a dragon hunter is a unique being."

"I know. You said there are only a handful of us."

"And there's one less, now that the esprit Anzo used burned the demon out of me."

"That's good, isn't it? Less demon, I mean?"

"It would be in most circumstances," he said slowly.

"So what's the problem?" I licked his chin, and froze for a second, shocked at what I'd done. But the animal in my brain decided that Ian tasted nice, and even though he'd collapsed to the floor when the little girls freed him from Anzo in a huge blast of light that left spots in front of my eyes for a good ten minutes, he didn't taste in the least bit like he'd picked up any dirt or germs. He tasted...nice. Golden and warm. Sexy.

"The problem is that all that's left in me is dragon. Well, a form of dragon. I think a new sort of dragon, one that has been tempered by my demon half. And a dragon cannot be a hunter. I did not relish my demon side, but it served its purpose, and the dragon in me was always strong enough to win out over it in the end. If I could set back time and keep Anzo from stripping it from me, I would, but other than you having a handy time machine, such thoughts are useless. I am no longer a dragon hunter. I am now...well, I am a dragon, nothing more."

"How do you know you aren't a dragon hunter?" I asked, a horrible vision rising in front of my eyes of a future where Ian was not at my side, fighting to save the innocent. "Maybe you are, and the demon bit was just there as kind of a useless appendage."

He shook his head. "The duality is what defines dragon hunters. The demon part has to be in there, just as the dragon does. The dragon part may always be uppermost, but light without some shade of darkness is less effective."

"I'm not demony," I pointed out. "I don't struggle with it like you say you do."

"But you are evidently the new breed of dragon hunter that Adam Larson envisioned, one where the demon element is wholly subservient to the dragon, there to give us power over other demons without attempting to gain control."

I blinked a couple of times, processing this. "So... because Adam was experimenting on Helen, and her demon must have been changed to demon lite, you think I have that, too?"

"It's the only thing that explains why you do not have to battle your dual nature." He looked at me with approval. "If this is what dragon hunters will be in the future, there is hope for them. Adam Larson will rest easy knowing that."

"So, why can't you be a dragon badass instead of a dragon hunter?"

"I told you, my love—dragons, even badass ones, can't destroy demons. Only hunters can."

"So much death," I mused, sad at the thought of Helen and Adam being made pawns at the hands of such evil beings. "I don't know that I can do this by myself."

"Glamour's gone!" Sasha announced from the entrance to the basement crypt, forestalling Ian's answer to my lament. "The street's back to normal. And there's a mage upstairs who says you owe her a metric shit-ton of money."

"Sasha!" I said, scandalized and amused at the same time. "Language! You're the head of heaven! You can't be saying things like 'shit-ton'!"

She pulled a face and then twirled on her heel and ran up the stairs, making the amount of noise that only a teenager could produce, calling over her shoulder, "I'll go upstairs and tell the mage to calm her tits while you and Ian make out. Oh, and the esprits want to know if you want a new sword, because otherwise, they want to go to Australia and see the quokkas before they find new dragon hunters to serve."

"You know," I said, looking at Ian's former sword that sat now shiny and gorgeous on the table in front of us, "it seems a shame to let that sword go to waste."

"You can have it if you want. Assuming the esprit agrees to the change."

I made a face at him. "That's not what I meant, and you know it. Besides, I like Deathsong. Sparkle says the esprit is happy with me, and the irony of using a demon's sword to kill other demons is just too sweet to let go. So you can have your old sword back."

He hugged me to his side and kissed my forehead. "I love the fact that you want me to be a dragon hunter again almost as much as I love you, but nothing can change what has happened. I can't be what I once was. I will aid you and support you, and do all of the many and varied sexual things to you that occupy my list, but I can't be what I was. The sword doesn't belong to me anymore."

"Just look at it," I said, picking it up and balancing it on the palm of my hand. "It misses you, Ian. It wants you to hold it. It wants to be your righteous right hand of Sasha. Speaking of which—why was she pretending to be a dragon hunter?"

"She wasn't pretending; it was part of her training. She just took over the position of Sovereign and is learning the jobs of all the beings in the Court. She more or less foisted herself on me with the promise that she would be needed at some point, and I would unleash an evil on the mortal world if I didn't allow her to be an apprentice. And she was right. She was needed."

"To save Helen by killing her, you mean?" I asked, amazed once again at the depths of Ian's devotion to protecting the people.

"Yes."

I set the thought of my sister's actions aside. I was still coming to terms with what Sasha had done, and Helen's own sacrifice. "Back to the sword. Just give it a little cuddle."

He looked at me as if I was suddenly made of mashed potatoes. "Touching it won't change anything, love. It will give me no strength, no special abilities. Most *élan vital* don't wish to be touched by anyone who isn't connected to it."

"Ow!" I said, deliberately sliding my thumb along the sharp edge of it. The sword trembled a little in my hand. I liked to think the esprit in it was laughing. "Damn, I cut myself."

"Let me see," Ian said, and reached for my hand.

The sword jumped, and he cursed, jerking back his hand. Across his palm, a line of red welled. "What the—"

I leaned in to him, my lips teasing him as I pressed my thumb onto his palm. "You're going to marry me, right? Because otherwise, it's going to make '*with this blood, I thee make my dragon hunter*' sound lame."

He shouted a laugh up to the sky, picked me up and spun me around, and kissed the ever-living life out of me.

"We're going to have such a lovely future together," I said a few minutes later, kneeling next to where he was crouched over, barfing as my blood changed him to the new and improved version of dragon hunter. "It's going to be utterly splendid."

And it was!

DON'T MISS KATIE'S NEXT
DRAGON HUNTER BOOK:

DAY OF THE DRAGON

Coming in Spring 2019

ONE

Two years ago

Arvidsjaur Center for the Bewildered
Entrance interview conducted by Dr. Kara Barlind
English translation

Dr. Barlind's note: The following is the interview held at the admission of Patient A upon the demand of her family members. Clear signs of schizophrenia were demonstrated, and a reluctance by Patient A to admit that her story more resembled a fantastical movie than real life. She expressed a great desire to tell her story, however, which was encouraged and which we hope will facilitate recovery.

INTERVIEW BEGINS:

Dr. Barlind: Good afternoon, Miss A. How are you feeling?

Patient A: I've been better, and my name is Aoife, not Miss A. It's Irish, and pronounced EE-fuh.

Dr. Barlind: My apologies. Aoife. Some patients choose to be anonymous in our reports, but I will make a note of your preference. Would you like to tell us what happened that made your brother and sister decide you needed our care?

Patient A (shuddering): I'd rather not think about it, but I suppose if anyone is going to do anything about it, then I'll have to tell you what happened last night. It was last night, wasn't it?

Patient exhibited signs of distress and was reassured that the triggering event had occurred the past evening.

Patient A: Okay, good. I thought I'd lost some time there, too, which, let me tell you, isn't as freaky as it sounds. Where should I start?

Dr. Barlind: Wherever you are comfortable beginning.

Patient A: I guess it all started with the date. I had no idea that anything...weird...was going to happen. I mean, Terrin looked perfectly normal. He certainly didn't seem like the type of man who could die and resurrect himself at will.

Patient A shuddered again and rubbed her eyes as if wishing to remove mental images, but ceased before self-harming.

Dr. Barlind: Why don't you start with your date with this man, then.

Patient A: Yeah. The date. It started all right. Nothing fantastic, but pleasant enough…

* * *

"Isn't the band great?"

A dense wall of throbbing bass surrounded us, thickening the night air and making me feel unusually…needy. In a sexual way.

"What?" My date shouted the word at me. He had to in order to be heard over the noise of the Swedish band that was playing.

I eyed him. I'd only known Terrin for a few days, having bumped into him while attending the traveling circus known as GothFaire. We'd both been in line to have our palms read and had struck up a conversation, ending up with me meeting him for the concert that was now under way.

"I said the band was great. You like it, don't you?" I yelled, almost into his ear. We were bobbing along with the dense crowd of people, not exactly dancing but moving in time with the music, as if the steady, pounding drumbeat triggered a primal need to move. I was a bit worried about whether Terrin was enjoying himself, not because he looked old—he appeared to be around my age, in his midthirties—but because he gave off a vibe that I couldn't help but classify as "accountant." He was the personification of the word *nice*—everything about him was mildly pleasant: his brown eyes were innocuous, his voice had absolutely no accent, his brown hair was cut short but not super short, and his face was indistinguishable from a thousand other men. He looked like a perfectly respectable, ordinary, white-bread kind of guy.

Whereas I was anything *but* white-bread. At least, ethnically speaking.

"It's quite effective, isn't it?" he answered at the same volume as my question.

"Effective?" I bellowed back.

"The glamour, I mean. Even back here, at the fringe of the crowd, it's very potent."

I stared at him. What the hell was he talking about? Maybe I'd made a mistake agreeing to a date, but I had figured that a public location like the GothFaire was safe enough. I must have misheard. "I've never heard the band before, and my family has lived in this area since I was a little kid, but they're good. Different. The music makes me feel..." I stopped, not only because my throat was starting to hurt from shouting everything, but also because I hesitated to admit the odd feeling that had come over me.

Terrin might be giving off the vibe of being just an ordinary guy, but I wasn't about to risk saying something that could have very bad consequences.

"Horny?" he asked, still bopping along to the music.

My eyes widened. Could he tell that I was suddenly possessed with a desire to kiss him? To touch him? To feel his skin on mine...Desperately, I shoved down those thoughts. Terrin may very well be a nice guy, but that didn't mean I should be thinking about him touching me, and vice versa. "Er..."

"That's all right," he yelled, putting an arm around me and pulling me against his body. He smiled, his eyes not expressing anything but friendly interest. *Trust me*, they seemed to say. *I'm a clean accountant.* "There's no reason to be embarrassed. It's not as if you could resist the urge."

I leaned into him for a moment, breathing in the smell of soap, shampoo, and nice man. My inner hussy swooned at the feel of him and the clean smell that surrounded him, but my brain pointed out that there was nothing so special about him that warranted his last comment.

"Um...yeah." With more strength than I thought possible, I pushed away from him. He didn't look offended, thankfully. He just gave me a bland smile and took my hand.

We listened to the band until the song ended, at which point he suggested that we see the rest of the Faire.

"I've seen most of it already," I told him when we left the big tent. It was located at one end of the U-shaped arrangement of vendor and attraction booths that constituted GothFaire proper. I pointed to the sign that hung off the entrance of the tent. "I saw the main magic act earlier today, and *herregud* was it amazing. Have you seen the magician? It's a father-and-son act, and they do this trick with eggs that gave me goose bumps."

"*Herregud?*" Terrin's brows pulled together in a little puzzled frown.

"Sorry, it's a Swedish colloquialism. It's kind of on par with *holy cats*, or *oh my God*, or something like that."

"I thought you were American?" Terrin asked, his hand still holding mine as we strolled down the main aisle of the Faire. There were a few people out still, visiting the various booths to have their fortunes told, palms read, or any of the other fun faux-creepy things that the Faire people offered up.

"I am. Mom is from Ireland, and my dad is from Senegal. He met my mom while he was in New York City studying to be an architect. She was playing the harp in Central Park; he stopped to watch her and said he fell in love with her right on the spot." I stopped talking, wondering why on earth I was telling him so much about my family.

"How did you end up here?" he asked, waving a hand around that I took to mean Sweden, rather than the GothFaire itself.

"Dad got a job with Ikea. And, no, I don't know how to put furniture together. I'm all thumbs when it comes to things like that."

He held up my hand and pretended to admire it.

"Your fingers look perfectly fine to me. So, what would you like to do? We've already had our palms read. Have you been to the personal time-travel advisor? I'm told she's very good."

I looked at the booth he pointed to. "Not really my thing. I'm perfectly content with the here and now."

"Ah. A traditionalist? Let's see . . . piercings?"

We both looked at the body-piercing booth, then looked at each other.

"No piercings," Terrin said with a pinched look about his mouth.

I laughed. "Yeah, I'm not into pain or stabbing bits of things through body parts. It was all I could do to get my ears pierced when I was sixteen."

Terrin stopped in front of a red-and-black-painted booth. "Hmm. There's to be a demonology demonstration in half an hour. That might be interesting."

"Eh, demons," I said, making a little face at the booth and moving forward. "I can take 'em or leave 'em."

"Really?" He looked mildly surprised. "You have depths, my dear, positively unplumbed depths."

"Yeah, we Irish-Senegalese Americans living in Sweden are often deep. What's that?" I pointed to a sign with a camera. We stopped in front of the booth in question so I could read the text. "What's a soul photograph?"

"I assume it's a euphemism for an aura photo, but I could be mistaken."

"Oh, I think I read about those somewhere. A picture together might be fun, don't you think?" I swung our hands and gave him a winning smile, then suddenly worried that he might think I believed in auras. "Not that they're real."

"The photographs?"

"No, auras."

He handed over some money to the bored teenager who was manning the front of the booth and held up two fingers to indicate we wanted a photo together. "I'm a bit surprised that you want a photo, then."

"Oh boy, did I just put my foot in my mouth?" I gazed at him in consternation. He didn't look offended or angry, but then, I wasn't sure someone with his calm, unemotional personality type got upset about things. "You believe auras are real, don't you?"

"It's difficult to dismiss something that you've seen, yes." He held aside a long black curtain so I could enter the tent. Ahead of us stood an old-fashioned camera on a tripod, the kind with huge bellows and large square glass plates, just like something out of a silent movie. A woman was seated on a low bench having her photo taken. The photographer, a bald little man with a fringe of carroty red hair and an elaborately curled mustache, was behind the camera, telling her to think happy thoughts.

We moved to a couple of chairs that had been placed to form a makeshift waiting area.

"You've really seen an aura?" I asked Terrin in a low voice.

He nodded. "In photographs, yes. I don't have the ability to see them with the naked eye, unfortunately."

"Oh." I relaxed, feeling much better. I tried to pick out judicious words. "I read an article on a skeptical website that talked about how people make those, you know. Evidently there are some things you can do before the film is developed to make pretty halo effects appear around people's heads and whatnot, and of course, digital images are super easy to mess with."

His eyebrows lifted slightly, just enough that told me he was disconcerted by the fact that I was dissing his aura photos. I hurried to try to smooth things over—there was no need to ruin the evening by being a big ole party-pooping skeptic. "Lots of people are taken in by them. Even experts! And I suppose they don't really do any harm, do they? It's just a picture, after all."

"It is that." He was silent for a moment, still watching me with those eyes that expressed mild interest. "I find it curious that you desired to visit the GothFaire since you don't particularly believe in things like auras."

"Are you kidding?" I gave a jaded laugh that I tried to nip in the bud before it got away from me. "We're not exactly in the hotbed of fascinating life here in northern Sweden. The nearest big city is hours away by train, and there isn't a whole lot that's interesting to do or see except rivers and snow and fishing and that sort of thing, and most of the year it's too freaking cold to do anything but huddle around the fireplace with a stack of books and a bottle of brandy. When Rowan— he's my brother—told me that a fair was coming this far north, I leaped at the chance to see it. I've been here every one of their three days."

"Ah. I see the attraction of the fair, then."

The photographer waved us forward, took the slip that Terrin had been given, and told us to arrange ourselves on the bench in whatever manner we liked.

We sat somewhat stiffly side by side while the photographer fussed with extracting a plate and inserting another.

"It's not that I don't appreciate other people's beliefs and such," I told Terrin. "It takes all kinds to make the world go, and I'm certainly not going to bash someone if they really believe that such things as demons existed, or time travel, or auras. I mean, it's really kind of a suspension of disbelief, isn't it? Like when you're watching a movie, and people suddenly burst into song with a full orchestra that isn't there. You just go with the flow and believe it in order to have fun."

The photographer told us to angle ourselves slightly toward each other, then to turn and look at the camera.

"That seems to be a sensible attitude to have," Terrin agreed.

"Hold that for seven seconds," the photographer said, and disappeared under the black cape that hung off the camera.

"But you think I'm wrong?" I asked without moving my lips from the smile I'd presented to the camera.

"Not so much wrong as perhaps imperceptive."

There was a click from the camera, and the photographer emerged. He got out another large, glass square plate and swapped it into the camera. I turned my head to look at Terrin. "Imperceptive? So you believe that all the stuff here, at the GothFaire, is real?"

"Yes." He didn't look at all disconcerted by admitting that. His face held the same placid, pleasant expression as it had all evening.

"Hold the pose, please."

We held our pose. I waited until the photographer emerged a second time from the depths of the camera cape and rose when he told us that the photos would be ready in fifteen minutes. We exited the booth just as an older couple entered.

"So, you believe in that?" I asked, pointing at the booth next to us.

"Scrying? Of course. Have you ever had someone scry for you? It's fascinating, truly fascinating."

"I didn't even know what it was until the first day here, and then I had to ask the lady who does it."

"It's a shame the booth is closed, or I'd treat you to a session." We strolled along the one long arm of the Faire. I noticed that Terrin didn't take my hand again and damned myself for questioning him about his beliefs.

And yet…dammit, I was trying to decide if I wanted to pursue a relationship with him, and in order to do that, I had to know if we were going to be compatible. Which is why I nodded to the booth across the broad center aisle and asked, "That doesn't strike you as just a wee bit too Harry Potter?"

"The spells and charms booth, you mean?" He gave it due consideration. "I see where you might think so, but I blame popular culture for that more than the woman who runs that stall selling tangible forms of magic."

"Uh...yeah." I had many other things to say but kept them behind my teeth.

"The proof is all around you, my dear, if only you choose to see it. For instance..." He gestured toward something behind me. I turned to see a tall man with shoulder-length black hair striding across the open space of the center aisle, obviously heading for the parking area. Next to him was another man, also dark-haired, who kept glancing around as if he was looking for someone. "Dragons."

I stopped admiring the way the first man filled out his black jeans and turned back to Terrin with an obvious gawk plastered all over my face. "What about them?"

"Those two men," Terrin said, gesturing again toward the two men in black. "They are dragons. Black dragons, I'd say, although they could be ouroboros. I'm afraid I'm not terribly up-to-date on the happenings within the weyr since it was destroyed."

"And a weyr is...?"

"The collective group of dragon septs."

"Of course it is. So, you're saying—" I stopped, shook my head, then pointed at the two men in question as they disappeared behind the booths. "You're saying those two guys—those two perfectly normal-looking guys—are dragons? The big-scaly-wings-and-tail-and-eats-medieval-virgins dragons?"

"I'm sure the virgin sacrifices stopped a long time ago," he said gently. "But to answer your question, yes, they are dragons."

"They looked like men," I couldn't help but point out.

"If you had the choice of appearing in dragon form or that of a human, which would you choose?"

He had me there. "Point taken."

"So you see? There is more to be seen than what's on the surface. The same can be said for auras."

"Oh, come on," I said, unable to keep the words from escaping my mouth. It was pretty clear to me that he wasn't going to be boyfriend material. He had the right to believe what he wanted, of course, but I could see that there would be countless arguments and debates about the differences in our respective points of view. Opposites may attract, but that didn't mean they could live together in harmony.

His eyes twinkled at me, positively twinkled at me when he dug into his jeans' pocket before holding out his hand, palm up. Lying on it was a gold and beigey-white object. "Still don't believe me, hmm? Perhaps I can change that. Would you like to see some magic, Aoife? *Real* magic?"

I looked from the ring that lay on his hand and back to his eyes. The latter were still full of amusement. "You have a *magic ring.*"

Disbelief fairly dripped off the words.

"I do. In fact, I have no doubt that it is this very ring that has drawn the pair of dragons to the area. You may touch it if you like. It won't harm you—since it was remade, it has developed what, for lack of better words, might be described as a mind of its own. It cannot be used if it does not wish the user to do so and thus far has shown affinity with very few people. Its original creator was one, and the woman who re-formed it is another, but she has no wish to use it and turned it over to me for safekeeping. I've been trying to find out if it is simply inactive or choosy about who it reacts to."

I took the ring, of course. I like jewelry, and it looked old and worn, and I wanted to get a good close look at it, but I really didn't expect anything magical to happen the second I touched it.

And nothing did.

"I guess I won't be joining those two special people," I said, running my fingers around the outside of the ring. It appeared to be made of ivory, or something like that, with the outer edges bound in gold. There was nothing inscribed on it, and no design scratched into the ivory, but it still felt nice in my hand. "Wouldn't the person who created it want it back?"

"The originator?" A fleeting expression of amusement passed over Terrin's face. "I'm quite sure he would give much to have it in his possession again, but that would not be at all wise."

"Oh?" I slid the ring onto my finger and admired it. "He's not a giant orange eyeball, is he?"

"Nothing so dramatic to look at," Terrin said with a little laugh, glancing over my shoulder when, behind me, someone gave a little screech. It was impossible to tell if it was just some kids being kids or someone who just discovered what a Prince Albert was. Given that the piercing tent was down that way, I thought nothing of it. "But nonetheless, extremely dangerous."

"So why do those two men who you think are dragons want it if it's so bad?"

"The ring is not bad in itself; it's the user who dictates whether it is used for good or evil. And all the dragons, not just those of the black sept, have sought the ring since the weyr was destroyed. But that is a long story, too long to tell you now."

"Uh-huh." I held out my hand and looked at it. "Since I didn't disappear when I put the ring on, I don't quite see what's magical about it."

He chuckled. "It's not a Tolkien sort of ring. Its magic is...unique. That is, it's unique to whoever wields it and whatever the ring wishes to be used for."

I looked at the ring, half expecting a wee pair of eyes to look back at me. "Wow, that's...weird."

"As I said, it is unique."

"It's pretty, though. I just hope," I said, starting to pull the ring off, "this isn't one of those bad kinds of ivory, like from an elephant or something. I'm a firm believer in karma, and I don't want to think what sort of horrible thing will happen to me because I admired a dead elephant ring."

"Ivory? Oh no, it's horn." That twinkle was back for

a moment. "Unicorn horn, as a matter of fact, and I can assure you that the unicorn in question donated her horn for the purpose of reinforcing it."

"Riiight," I drawled, and removed the ring. I was just about to hand it back to him when a blood-chilling scream ripped high into the night air, so loud we could hear it clearly over the throb of music.

ABOUT THE AUTHOR

For as long as she can remember, KATIE MACALISTER has loved reading, and grew up with her nose buried in a book. It wasn't until many years later that she thought about writing her own books, but once she had a taste of the fun to be had building worlds, tormenting characters, and falling madly in love with all her heroes, she was hooked.

With more than fifty books under her belt, Katie's novels have been translated into numerous languages, been recorded as audiobooks, received several awards, and are regulars on the *New York Times*, *USA Today*, and *Publishers Weekly* bestseller lists. A self-proclaimed gamer girl, she lives in the Pacific Northwest with her dogs and frequently can be found hanging around online.

Fall in Love with Forever Romance

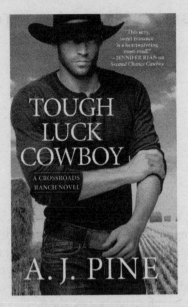

TOUGH LUCK COWBOY
By A.J. Pine

Rugged and reckless, Luke Everett has always lived life on the dangerous side—until a rodeo accident leaves his career in shambles. But Luke's injury means he now gets a chance to spend time with the woman he always wanted but could never have. Don't miss the next book in A.J. Pine's bestselling Crossroads Ranch series!

Fall in Love with Forever Romance

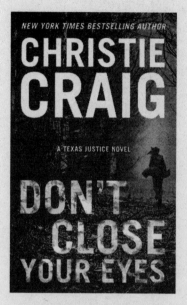

DON'T CLOSE YOUR EYES
By Christie Craig

Annie Lakes is starting to remember things about the night her cousin Jenny disappeared. Things that make her believe her family was involved—and what they're hiding is much worse than she ever imagined. She needs someone she can trust to help her unravel the truth, someone like sexy Detective Mark Sutton. But when Annie becomes a target herself, will he be able to protect the woman he's starting to fall for?

Fall in Love with Forever Romance

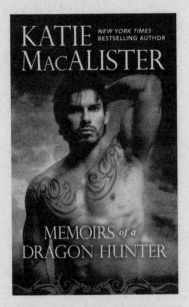

MEMOIRS OF A DRAGON HUNTER
By Katie MacAlister

Veronica James leads a seemingly normal life—that is until her sister dies and leaves her with a sword and a destiny as a dragon hunter. Now it's Veronica's turn to protect humans from the demons she never even knew existed. Fellow hunter Ian Iskander is the only person who can help Veronica figure out who—and what—she is. But trusting him is dangerous...because when you play with dragon fire, someone always gets burned.